THE SCORING SECRET

A HOCKEY ROMANCE

AINSLEY BOOTH

For the girls who are bossy in the streets and bratty in the sheets

GLOSSARY

aka WTF does the r *come before the* e *in theatre?*

The Scoring Secret takes place in Canada, and is written in Canadian English, which looks and sounds a lot like American English, except for when it sometimes looks and sounds a little bit like British English! One example of this is that we often spell words with an -re instead of an -er, like **theatre**.

I've also highlighted two hockey terms you may not have heard of before. For more Canadianisms, check out the first book in this series, *The Playing Game*, which also has a brief glossary.

Theatre - Canadian spelling for theater (as well as other Commonwealth countries)

Victoria Day long weekend - the first long weekend of the summer in Canada, which includes Victoria Day on the second last Monday in May (the weekend before American Memorial Day); in some parts of the country, it's nicknamed "May Two Four" because it falls close to the 24th of the month, and is also often celebrated with a 24 pack of beer brought to a cottage opening or a backyard BBQ party; it's also sometimes called the "May Long" (*In this book, it is referred to as May 2-4, which should be pronounced as May Two Four*)

Barn - a hockey rink or arena

Hatty - a hat trick, when a player scores three goals in a single hockey game

CHAPTER 1
TY

Miami Beach

February

It sounds obnoxious, but I really do have the best fucking life. I don't remember the last time I needed an alarm to wake me up for my early morning run, for example. The South Florida sun calls to me—a hockey kid from upstate New York—like nothing else I've ever experienced.

I roll out of bed whistling and pull on shorts and athletic socks, then stride to the kitchen. We have a game tonight, but the morning skate is optional, and I'd rather take mine outside under the sun. I drink a supplement mix while I warm up, already imagining the waffles I'm going to devour after my skate down the South Beach strip.

Visualization is one of the most important sports psychology tricks I've learned. Picture the steps it takes to achieve the success you want, and for me, that's strapping on my rollerblades, finding someone hot to treat to a nice brunch, and then bringing them back here for a hard and fast tumble across my sheets.

Step one: grab the skates from their spot by my front door.

Step two: head downstairs, no music today. Keeping myself wide open to the possibility of a warm, tight body stumbling across my path, and being able to give them my full and undivided attention.

Step three: look fucking good as I step outside and gaze down Ocean Drive. My playground, where I am king.

It's a warm one today, and the bright morning rays feel good on my bare chest. I take the first lap down the strip easy, warming up, then pick up my pace. Sweat pricks my skin in that lazy, good workout kind of way.

Ahead of me, a beautiful Black woman bounds into view, her long legs stretching in an eye-catching way that drags my gaze to her high, tight ass, just in time to realize she's not alone, and the lighter brown-skinned man she's running toward doesn't appreciate this white boy ogling her.

I give him a shameless grin and glide past them. No harm, no foul.

And just ahead of them is a curvy redhead with a jiggly tummy that would look real good beneath me on a bed. Back arched, pale tits turning pink as she gets closer to a release… all the creamy white skin painted with my own release, after she has another.

It's not hard to imagine how we could spend the next few hours, if she's single and willing.

And if she's not, then there are plenty of fish in the sea. Or in the sea-adjacent park, as it were.

Best. Fucking. Life.

I'm about to pull alongside her and introduce myself when my phone vibrates.

Slowing down, I answer it, not bothering to look at the screen. Nobody calls me at seven in the morning unless it's important. "Yello."

"Ty, I'm sorry to call so early. Do you have a minute?" It's the general manager of the NHL team that drafted me twelve years ago, the only pro team I've ever played for.

I hear myself reply as if from a distance. My rollerblades feel like lead on my feet, and the redhead bounds ahead, suddenly out of reach.

Waffles aren't going to happen, either.

The conversation is brief. I'm being traded to the newest team in the league, the Hamilton Highlanders.

Hamilton, Ontario, Canada, on the shores of Lake Ontario. Not that far from where I grew up outside Buffalo, New York.

I tip my head up to the sun, as if I'm a photovoltaic battery and I might be able to store just a little bit more of this best fucking life before I need to put on a fucking parka.

I'm being traded to the fucking *Highlanders*?

Their mascot is a bagpipe playing wild boar, for God's sake.

My next call is to my agent. "Hamilton?" I ask incredulously. "We didn't put them on my no trade list? You know I don't do snow, Nina."

She makes a soothing sound in my ear, as if she were my grandmother, and not an ambitious baby shark who graduated from law school like ten minutes ago. "Hamilton is great. You're going to love the owner, Jack Benton. He's going to arrange for a private plane to take you to meet the team later today. They're playing in Montreal tomorrow."

"Sounds fucking cold."

"He likes players who are from the area," she says, continuing as if I hadn't made it clear that while I might be *from* the area, I do not *like* the area. "You're going to fit in great. They're still working on some of the details, so the trade won't hit the wire for another hour or so. Go home, pack up. Do you want to go to the arena there and pick up any of your custom gear?"

Of course I do. That barn is my home. I want to go there, pick up my gear, and put it on, because I have a game tonight. Here.

But I don't anymore.

Fuck. Well, yeah, I still want my shit. And I need to say a quick goodbye to some of the staff. "How much time do I have?"

"The plane will wait for you. You're the only passenger."

I make it back to my apartment, reeling from the news. It's a shock, but maybe it shouldn't be. The writing has been on the wall for a hard rebuild for more than a year now. I was on borrowed time, and ignoring the signs because I like having morning skates outside a little too fucking much. *You got too comfortable. Too happy. Too big for your britches.* Whatever the fuck britches are.

Hockey is a brutal business, and now it's serving me humble pie.

Inside, I toss my rollerblades into a closet because I'm sure as shit not going to need those in Hamilton, Ontario, in fucking February. Pack a bag. Do an aimless circuit, trying to figure out what needs to be done. Someone needs to make a *so you've been traded* checklist of tasks for stunned hockey players. I empty out the fridge, shoving everything perishable into my freezer. Text my cleaning lady to let her know the apartment needs to be closed up for the next few months. I might not be back until May, I tell her. I don't want to say June. That might be hoping for too much. That would mean we've made it into the final rounds of the playoffs, and I don't think Hamilton is good enough yet.

That has to be my last critical thought about the team, I tell myself. *My new team has all the raw talent it needs to go all the way.*

I've seen guys make the shift, coming to Miami from other places. Now it's my turn.

By the time I land in Montreal, I'll be one of them.

I leave the keys to my car on the counter, in case I decide to have it transported north, but more likely, I'll buy something up there. Something appropriate for the Snow Belt. *And now I'm having flashbacks to early morning practice at rinks with unheated dressing rooms.*

Whatever I get up there—some kind of truck with monster wheels, maybe—has to have heated seats. And a remote start.

I need to distract myself from the thought of blizzards. Once I'm settled in the backseat of the car that will take me to the rink—and then on to the airfield where Benton's plane will meet me—I do the next thing that comes naturally to me. I open the Lusty and Tinder apps on my phone and change my location from South Beach, Miami, Florida, to Hamilton, Ontario, Canada.

Lusty first. It's not technically a hook up app. The tag line is *Live the Wanderlusty Life*, and it started as an anonymous travel and food reviewing blog for Millennials. But the message boards can be pretty horny, and they've recently added a profile browsing feature that feels a lot like a dating app, and their latest ad campaign specifically says, *For*

Singles Who Wander. Smart decision, because the user base is mostly single and we already have a lot in common. I'm incognito on Lusty because nobody needs to know what restaurants in Miami Ty Connor goes to—but a guy who writes reviews as BeastMode doesn't get a second glance.

I can't imagine I'll find a lot of must-eats in Hamilton, but you never know.

Once that profile is updated, I go to Tinder. The familiar scroll, scroll, swipe is soothing, I guess. Nice to get a heads up about who I might get a chance to meet in a few days.

Lots of nice smiles. Big tits, small tits. Scroll, scroll.

And then I stop, captivated by a sweep of dark, wavy hair over half a face, partially obscuring a luscious mouth and a darkly lined eye, the lashes sweeping low. The next picture is a proud display of tall curves poured into blue jeans and a black tank top, the type of banging body that screams *I used to be on the volleyball team and now my preferred cardio routine is riding hockey players' faces.*

Her name is Ki. And her bio is perfect.

Here for a good time, not a long time, because I'm working on my boundaries. Likes: Road trips. Dislikes: Clingy liars.

I check out her other pictures. Thick thighs at the gym. A glimpse at a pale belly in a selfie taken from above, on a bed, as she unbuttons a baseball jersey. An angle that promises, *this could be your view after a softball game, jiggle jiggle.*

And the last one makes me laugh. It's just of her legs— with a closeup on those calves that look like they could lock around a man and hold him in tight—but she's tangled up in a dog leash. The pup in question is offscreen, but I don't care. All I can see is the way the leash presses into her soft flesh.

Didn't see myself being jealous of a strip of nylon cord

today, but whatever. It's a weird day, bring on the unexpected cock twitches.

I swipe right. And I save her profile to come back to later.

Then I keep scrolling, but no one else grabs my attention. Just as I arrive at the rink, I get a text message from Nina. The trade is finalized and will be announced in moments, which means I need to text the team. My old team, now.

TY

Heads up, fellows. I've been traded. I love you all, and I still expect wedding invites this summer.

But once I grab my shit from the arena, it's on until the end of the season. Nothing personal.

And then I leave the group chat before anyone can reply.

At the arena, the security guard is surprised to see me. I break the news. Inside the team space, though, word has already started to spread among the trainers and the coaches, so I'm spared needing to say the words again.

I grab a bundle of my sticks, my skates, and a box of extra blades from the equipment guys, and the custom base layers I love with the special pads built in over my collarbones. The new team will have them made for me in their colours, too, but in the meantime, I'll wear what I have.

I leave the rink carrying a Miami equipment bag for the very last time.

It's a short drive to the private airfield, and I spend it staring out the window.

I don't check my phone again until my gear has been stowed safely and I'm sprawled in one of the four oversized leather seats on the plane.

No match from the hot girl on Tinder. And that's still the case when we land in Montreal, where there isn't a jiggly belly in sight, because it's February and Montreal is 1500 miles due north of the south Florida sun I already miss more than I should.

This is professional hockey.

Trades happen.

Ty Connor, say goodbye to the sun, say hello to a series of hotel rooms as you learn the systems and structures of a whole new organization.

Because the team that drafted you, where you once won the Cup and got close two other times, no longer has need of your very specific, spectacular talents.

Time for a rebuild in Miami, and rebuilds don't happen around thirty-year-olds who eat up too much cap space.

But Hamilton?

It's not that I'm unfamiliar. I'm fucking familiar. Hamilton is only an hour and a half from where I grew up outside Buffalo. It's what you drive past—gritty steel plants and all—on your way to the hockey centre of the world, Toronto.

I mean, it could be worse. I could have been traded to Toronto.

But.

But.

Fucking hell, I miss my apartment with a clear view of the Atlantic Ocean already.

And when I'm peering out the car window at the restaurant where I'm about to meet most of my new teammates for the first time off the ice, all I can think is, *I wish I'd packed a warmer coat.*

CHAPTER 2
KILEY

Hamilton, Ontario

"Have you seen it, Kiley?"

I've been trying to ignore the conversation about a breakout TV comedy show, but now one of the two nurses having the convo turns to me and directly pulls me into it.

No, I haven't seen *Good Morning Kitsilano*. I am painfully aware of the quirky hit about a group of misfits who take a yoga class in the Vancouver neighbourhood of Kits, though.

Crys Graham, the creator and co-star, wrote the pilot two years ago, just before I met him.

It was almost his complete focus in the year that we lived together.

I was so proud of him for having an artistic vision, and so in love with him, that I didn't realize he wasn't in love with me. Not until I was forced to hear him fucking someone else in our bathroom.

That's why I'm here now, getting ready for an evening shift as a ward clerk at a hospital in my hometown, and not working in Vancouver or Nashville or Houston as a stage manager, the career I built over the last eight years.

Because theatre work is precarious at best, and supporting Crys Graham for a year and then leaving him before he hit it big destroyed me financially.

"Oh my *Gawd*, he's so hot," one nurse says.

It's a testament to how far I've come this year that I can calmly think, *Yeah, I understand that reaction*. That was me, once upon a time.

I shake my head. "Haven't seen it. Is it good?"

"So good." She flutters her hands in front of her face. "He's geeky, but endearing, you know?"

I don't tell her that Crys doesn't have a geeky bone in his body. And his endearing traits are best observed from across the country, where he can't gaslight you into paying his bills.

There's a knock at the break room door, and the clerk from the day shift pops her head in. "Sorry, Kiley, I know you're still getting ready, but could you keep an ear out for the phone? I need to run down to the pharmacy."

I jump up. "I'll go."

"You don't mind?" She gives me a grateful smile. "I've still got a few things to finish up before we switch."

"Yeah for sure." It's a good escape from this conversation.

I have worked hard to not dwell on the past, or what might have been if I were a different kind of girl.

―――――

Vancouver

Ten months earlier

Crys's apartment is above a shop on Commercial Drive, in the middle of a vibrant arts community, and conveniently located to get to auditions, film sets, and theatres.

Hopping off the bus, I walk briskly to the end of the block, then turn the corner. A glow from upstairs catches my eye. Crap, Crys didn't turn off the lights before he left for his audition. And he'll give me attitude if I mention it, but he's not the one paying the electricity bill. I am, now, after he forgot for the third time in five months, and it got shut off.

Thinking calm thoughts, I let myself in the side door and climb the stairs.

When I push the door open, though, my threatening grumpiness fades. He didn't leave the lights on when he left, because I can hear the shower running. And it sounds like he's running lines.

I make a rueful face. His audition must have been cancelled, but at least he bounced back and is moving on to the next thing.

"Hey, baby," I call out. "I'm home early."

There isn't really room for both of us to stand in the tub —Crys thinks it isn't sexy when the plastic shower curtain touches him—but maybe if I give him a blow job he won't complain about sharing the hot water.

I pull off my sweater and walk through the apartment to tell him I'm joining him, but I halt abruptly a few feet away from the bathroom.

"Fuck, you're so hot," he groans.

And then a woman giggles.

Giggles.

That's not running lines.

My heart plummets as my brain spins, trying to make sense of a giggle coming out of my bathroom where my boyfriend is having a shower when I'm supposed to be at work, and he never likes it when I laugh during sex…

Then there's a moan. And then—

"Yeah, lift me up," she pants. "Uhhh, Crys!"

No.

No.

He's fucking someone he can lift in our tiny shower that we both don't fit in?

Hot tears spring to my eyes and I back up, bumping into the wall.

My hands shake as I fumble for my phone, where I always keep it in the back pocket of my jeans. I can't see the screen, I realize, as I stab at it angrily.

Stop fucking crying, Kiley, I command myself.

It doesn't work.

Wet, betrayed tears streak down my face as I search for a room at the nicest hotel I can think of downtown, on the waterfront.

Then I race to the bedroom and shove a few pieces of clothing in a backpack. I'm tempted to drag a bag of his clothing out to the fire escape and toss it into the dumpster, but I don't have that kind of time.

He doesn't have the sexual stamina I need for proper revenge here.

Instead, I stalk back to the kitchen and snatch the expensive bottle of red he's been holding on to for a celebration when he gets a big part.

And that's when my gaze falls on his bullet journal.

Crys hates technology. Where I do everything on my phone, he's a notebook kind of guy. That black leather book contains his entire life, including a year of notes about the stupid TV show he thinks he's going to sell to a network one day.

The notebook goes in the bag, too.

Finally, I grab my laptop, every single charging cable in the entire apartment, and my favourite photo of me and my best friends: my twin brother Grant and our childhood bestie, Harper.

The next thing I will be forced to do is ask them for help, and that's going to take everything I have.

How. Fucking. Mortifying.

My heart races as I stare at the bathroom door. The shower turns off, and I have a moment of considering whether to confront them.

But I can't do it. I can't see who she is, how pretty and little and sexy she is, wrapped in my towel and nothing else.

Or God forbid they come out naked.

My stomach heaves, and I twist around, getting to the door without really seeing it.

Back on the small landing at the top of the stairs, I pause and think about what they might do next. Curl up in my bed for a bit of Netflix and chill?

I don't fucking think so.

I yank my laptop out of the bag and quickly, fingers feeling numb, log in to the remote access for our WiFi router. I change the password to AntiCrys666.

Then, for good measure, I delete him from the Netflix account I pay for before heading for the street, tears streaming down my face again.

———

I have to hold my breath as the hotel runs my credit card for a hold when I check in. It clears, thank God, but that's all my available credit right now, and my car is at the garage for the third time in six months.

Call Grant.

I really don't want to. My twin brother never liked Crys, or understood my zigzag career from journalism school to being a theatre stage manager/temp worker.

Call Harper.

That feels easier, but she'll just call Grant. Or worse, if I beg her not to, she'll loan me the money I need herself, and she doesn't really have it. Not the way Grant does. She's a nurse who had to pay a lot of her own way through school. He's a doctor, and my parents paid for everything.

They probably still pay for things for him even though he just got a second job as assistant medical director for the NHL's latest expansion team, coming to Hamilton this year, for goodness sake.

And if I ask for money, they'll need to know what specifically I need to spend it on. Calling my parents is a nonstarter. I don't want their money, because there are strings attached. Strings like getting a real job and not living on the other side of the country.

"Here is your room key," the clerk says. "Enjoy your stay."

It's a good room. Nice view. Giant jetted tub. I start the water running, then plug in my laptop.

Revenge ideas have been spinning through my head since I left the apartment. Maybe it's scary how quickly my brain has pivoted to hurting him, but after the crush he had on his co-star last summer, and the "speed wobble" that caused in our relationship, I'm beyond giving him a second chance.

With his co-star, he tried to gaslight me into thinking it was nothing, but I knew otherwise. Then in the fall, there was that house party we went to, and the way he slung his arm around our friend Greer's shoulders.

I should have trusted that gross feeling in the pit of my stomach then. I won't ignore it now.

No, this isn't the first time he's cheated on me. I know that now. I know it with a vengeful clarity.

It's the first time I had to hear it, and it's the first time I know for a fact sex happened.

With a sinking feeling in my gut, I pull up a video clip of the show he plays a recurring character on. There's a series regular, who is my complete opposite. Blonde, petite, bubbly.

Giggles on command. That's her fucking thing on the show.

And in my shower.

I hit play, but I don't need to confirm that I recognize the voice.

Damn him.

But also, damn me. What's the saying? Fool me once, shame on you. Fool me three times in a row, and it's time to burn this bridge and leave town.

My phone vibrates.

CRYS

When are you home? The WiFi is down and I can't find my phone charger.

I snarl. My fingers shake, desperate to reply, but I need more time first. I force myself to put it down.

I strip off my clothes and slide into the tub instead.

When was the last time I could stretch out fully in a bath? I'm tall, two inches shy of six feet, and the only bath I've had in our stupid apartment in the last year has been with my knees bent up and out of the water.

Gross.

Never again.

I think of my brother's apartment in Hamilton. It's another old and worn place, "full of character", too, but at least the bath tub is deep enough for tall people.

An intense, surprising wave of homesickness rolls over me, and I close my eyes. I left home at eighteen for college, and I haven't looked back. Grant and Harper stayed close to home for school and training, and now they work in the hospital where we were all born.

Not me.

I sob as I let myself sink under the pulsing water, and when I drift back up to the air, I know what I need to do.

Harper answers on the first ring. "Hey, babe, what's up?"

I don't say anything. I can't.

"Kiley?" Her voice softens. "What's wrong?"

"I need a thousand dollars to get my car repaired tomorrow." The words wobble out of me.

"Okay." No questions asked. That's my bestie.

"I'm coming home. I'm gonna…drive." A sob threatens to burst out, and I swallow it back.

"What happened?"

Nope. That's all the words I have tonight, apparently.

"Babe," she whispers. "How about I fly out there and we drive home together?"

I nod silently, tears falling.

And that night, after she transfers money to my account,

promising me she borrowed it from Grant for reasons she will refuse to divulge, I finally tell her what happened. On opposite sides of the country, her in a break room in the hospital where she works and me in a hotel room I can't really afford, we do all the petty revenge ideas we can think of.

I change the name on the utilities to Crys Cantkeepitinhispants.

I post an online ad under his name and phone number, offering acting lessons for $20/hour, with unlimited online mentoring. I word it carefully so anyone who knows what they're looking for will think it sounds too good to be true, and steer clear, but anyone horrible and selfish will hound him until he has to change his number.

And I torture myself by flipping through his bullet journal, looking for any small piece of evidence of his infidelity.

I find them over and over again, and I die a dozen tiny deaths.

What a fool I was.

What a stupid fool.

But he was worse.

Once I'm ready for him to know that I know what a fucking snake he is, Harper steps in. She texts him a heads up that I won't be home tonight, or ever again.

I block his number before he can blow up my phone after she hits send.

Crys isn't the first shallow but charming manwhore I've ever fallen for, but he will be the last.

I'm going home for a while to lick my wounds and figure out how I can come out the other side of this a smarter, wiser Kiley Forge.

And then I'm going to live the absolute best life I can,

because the ultimate revenge will be forgetting this man ever had any kind of hold on me.

CHAPTER 3
TY

Montreal

February, again

The guy I know the best on the Highlanders is Kieran Marsh, who I've clashed with on the ice many, many times, and partied with on All-Star breaks more than once.

He's the first to shake my hand when I stride into the restaurant where the team is having a group dinner. "Nobody told you to pack a warmer coat?"

I shake my head because it was the exact same thought I had. "Fuck off, Marsh. I was rollerblading in a pair of shorts this morning, okay? And then I get a phone call and told to get on a plane to the middle of Siberia." I clap him on the shoulder. "Introduce me to everyone? And let's leave out the colourful bits."

He makes the introductions, and I start making the mental shift from these guys being my opponents to my teammates who now have endearing nicknames to learn.

There's a slew of young players, because that's who other teams generally expose in an expansion draft. Forwards Jenson "Haler" Hale (aka Mom), Hiro Watanabe, and Hayden "Hooner" Calhoun, and defensemen Mohammed "Mo" Ahmadi, and Roan "Smash" Dodaj all look like a fresh NCAA team.

Only Rusty and Gusty, veterans Russ Armstrong and Magnus Gustafsson, are in their thirties, like Marshie and me.

And those two are the assholes who really rub in the fact that I left my rollerblades in Miami, because I won't need them for months to come.

Rusty tries to hold a straight face as he promises that Hamilton Bay is *really* nice...for the first two weeks of September.

I give him the middle finger. "I'm not giving up my Miami Beach apartment."

Kieran tips his glass at me. "That's goals."

I cheers my glass against his. "Right? How about you? How do you feel about the transition to Steel Town?"

On the flight, I read a packet from the team PR's department, familiarizing myself with my new city. It's an industrial town proud of its blue collar roots.

He claims he doesn't miss the more cosmopolitan life he lived in other cities.

Armstrong laughs. "He's in love."

Wait, for real? Kieran Marsh, famously Not a Relationship Guy, is in love? "No shit. Really?"

His whole face transforms. "Yeah. Met someone. She's the real deal."

He raves about her work as a nurse at the children's

hospital, and how watching her work with kids shifted everything for him.

His head-over-tits-in-love vibe is sweet, and I'm in the business of making friends tonight, so I lean into it.

"Yeah? Does she know any other nurses who might want to welcome me to the city? A pretty best friend?"

Across the table, Rusty chokes on his beer. "Yeah, Marsh," he strains out after he recovers. "Should we introduce Ty to Kiley?"

Kieran scowls at him. "No."

But now I'm intrigued. "Who's Kiley?"

"Off-limits, that's who," Marsh says dryly.

Roan "Smash" Dodaj swings into the conversation, leaning over Armstrong. "Who wants another drink?"

Marsh glances at his watch. "One more."

"Dad says it's okay!" Smash pumps his arms in the air. "Yeah, baby."

The last player to introduce himself to me isn't at dinner that night.

Instead, when we get back to the hotel, and Haler and Marshie are making sure everyone gets tucked into their beds before curfew, I get a video call from the team captain.

Max Tilman is back in Hamilton on the injured reserve list—and since I know he's a bit of a prima donna, I know that's gotta burn. Dude hates being sidelined.

I would, too.

He says nice things, though, and introduces me to his wife Shannon, who immediately promises to get on a text chat with me and set me up with whatever I need at home— meaning Hamilton—while I'm getting up to speed with the team on the road.

She immediately gives me a good vibe, and her shark of a husband is going to be fun to play with.

This is all good.

Less good is that the next night, I don't get to play against Montreal.

Because moving from an American team to a Canadian team comes with some immigration logistics that we can't just magic away on a Saturday afternoon, I have to watch from the press box up top as my new team loses.

The team itself is fine. Good, even. Different vibe than the team I spent a decade with in Miami, though. The Highlanders are still figuring out their systems. Not so entrenched in what structures work that they aren't open to new ideas, and as a former captain...I have ideas. A lot of them.

So then I think, all right, this ain't all bad.

We get on the team plane, which is nicer than Miami's plane, and after my visa is approved, I'm added to the roster and we win in Minnesota.

Four days after I'm traded, I finally land in Hamilton. It's not quite a blizzard, but it's definitely not running shirtless weather, either. I settle into a long-term suite hotel Shannon Tilman recommends, and she hooks me up with a real estate agent, too, in case I want to buy a house.

My house is a condo in Miami, I think.

I say I'll look for a place in the summer.

I buy a truck. The Lambo shouldn't be exposed to the salt and sand they have to put on the streets here to combat snow and ice. It can stay at home for when I visit.

And then I get serious about finding some recreational activity.

There's an art to being on apps as a professional athlete.

My profiles are pretty anonymous, even with photos that show enough to not be a creep. My standards are reasonably high. She has to be roughly the same age as me or older. I want our early conversations to cover the basics in a straightforward way, like protection and no strings, and this is probably just once. If all of that turns us both on, we're good to go.

I know I shouldn't rush into finding a warm bed just because I miss the fucking sun, but I was horny as fuck back in Miami, and now that I've got a (temporary) bed in Hamilton, I'm still fucking horny.

So when I match with a woman named Anna on a night off, and she brings up all of my basic requirements within a few minutes of chatting, I figure it's meant to be.

She introduces herself as Ava when she opens the door, which makes me pause. But when I repeat it, with a question mark, she looks at me like I definitely misheard.

"Anna," she says with a pretty enough smile that it's fine. It's not as if I'm using my real name either. "And this is Daffodil."

A warm panting body nudges against my calf, and I nearly jump out of my skin. At my side is a dog that looks like her name should be Inky or Brownie. *Does Anna/Ava know that Daffodils are yellow, not black?*

"You said you like dogs." She says it smoothly, like we talked about dogs for longer than a nanosecond before pivoting to *do you use toys* and *do you like to watch*, because yes and yes. That's why I'm here.

No offense to Daffodil.

"Sure," I say smoothly. "But I like making women moan even more."

Her smile gets even brighter. "Then let's have some fun."

CHAPTER 4
KILEY

"Are you sure you can't stay for breakfast?" The question is mumbled from deep inside a pillow so nice it probably cost more than my phone.

I haven't stayed for breakfast in any of my hook-ups over the last year, and I'm not about to start now.

My one-night stand from the night before isn't making any moves to get up and make me coffee, of course. He's just being polite, and that's not necessary. We both know this was a simple itch scratching.

I don't usually swipe right on people who work at the hospital. That's a little close to home, and I've devoted the last year to putting myself first, prioritizing having fun with a singular focus.

A year of being slutty. A year of positive vibes only.

Having at least one date a week, encouraging no-strings-attached physical connections.

That's all I want from men now.

But when I swiped right on him last night after my shift was over, and he turned out to be a surgical resident leaving for the day at the exact same time—on a day I didn't have a drive home—the convenience of sharing a shower after our shifts yesterday couldn't be denied.

A nice shower, too, in a luxury townhouse on the edge of the city.

Then he was pretty good at sex, too, considering how sleep deprived he was.

Him falling asleep with his arm wrapped tight around my tummy...could have done without that, but the nice pillows made up for the cuddling.

Shame I won't experience them again.

"Nope," I say, pulling on my jeans. "Gotta go pick up my brother's dog."

He rolls over, gives a lazy grin, and flexes his arms as he crosses them behind his head. "See you around at work, then?"

"Sure." We don't work in the same department, and it's a big hospital. Probably not.

I order a ride share to meet me at the coffee shop on the edge of his complex, and walk there as I check my messages.

A text from my brother, confirming that he needs me to pick up Puck.

An email from the staffing department at the hospital, offering half-shifts for clerks willing to cover in other departments. Time and a half if we've worked over full-time hours already this week, which I haven't yet, but if I took two of those shifts, I might.

I think about asking my parents to take Puck overnight, then shake my head.

I can't take the extra shifts while Grant is busy this week. Which is fine. My bank account is relatively healthy, and if I'm not going to buy a car...

I still might.

I should.

But there are three other emails, too. Notifications from a theatre jobs message board I signed up for a few weeks ago on a whim.

Not a whim.

No, I signed up because of a calendar reminder. The one-year lease I signed last May, taking over my brother's apartment when he moved into a condo, will be up soon. And if I want to give my two months' notice that I'm going to move, I could do so as early as March 1.

Which I'm not going to do.

Not March 1.

But soon, maybe.

I grab a coffee, then meet my driver outside.

"You're going to the arena?" he says, checking his phone for the route.

"Yep."

"Cold morning."

I barely noticed.

"Apparently we're going to get freezing rain soon."

I frown and glance out the window. "Yeah?"

"Should start in the next hour."

Crap. There goes my plan to exhaust Puck on a long walk.

"You work at the arena?"

"No."

"I met some of the players last week. Super nice."

"Yeah?" I mean, I know most of them are. I've met them, too. I helped one of them win my best friend's reluctant heart before Christmas.

But I don't offer that information to random Uber drivers.

He drops me at the Bay Street entrance as the first angry drops of rain lash down from the suddenly stormy sky. Great.

Puck doesn't actually mind the cold and wet, but at this point in the season, I'm over it. Bring on spring, any time now. The good news is that the Highlanders have an indoor dog park area for the team and team-adjacent puppers, and when I make a face at my brother about the weather, he tells me to go and tire our beautiful but energetic chocolate lab out up there.

I bump into Harper's boyfriend, Kieran, on my way out of the medical bay. He drops to a squat and offers his palm to Puck. "Hey there," he croons softly. Then he stands and gives me a friendly smile. "You heading upstairs?"

He knows that Puck and I use the indoor dog play area more than any of the players' dogs do—and he doesn't mind at all. Harper and Kieran are basically Puck's godparents, anyway. "Why, do you want to panic grill me on what kind of engagement rings Harper might like best?"

He arches an eyebrow. "Is that the attitude you want to take when I might actually have photos of the top contenders on my phone?"

My mouth drops open. "Are you serious?"

He looks pretty damn proud of himself. "I have a favourite, but I thought I should run my gut check past you."

"When are you going to ask her?"

"I don't know. The right moment, whenever it happens. I just want to be prepared." He holds the stairwell door open for Puck, and she pulls a little at her lead, eager now to get upstairs.

I remind her that we're walking at my speed, and she settles down.

As long as I can remember, Forge dogs have been been well trained, and Puck is no exception. If anything, I think Grant went above and beyond with her training, because he lives in a high-rise condominium apartment. We exercise her a lot, because there's no backyard to go out to when she's squirrelly. We need to anticipate her energy needs and meet them in advance.

Upstairs, I check to make sure we're alone in the space, then let her off leash and she runs to her favourite part of the doggy climbing structure.

Kieran immediately pulls out his phone and shows me the rings he's considering. They're all stunning, and each of them would be a good pick for Harper, matching her personality and style in different ways.

"Which one do you get the most excited about when you think about asking her?"

He bites the side of his lower lip in concentration and flips back and forth before a funny look settles on his face. A little soft, a little nervous. "The solitaire," he says, and I swear his voice shakes.

Kieran Marsh, who is nothing but confident, even when he's going all in on my bestie, is overcome by the possibility of proposing to her.

I love it.

I'm about to give him a hug when there's barking in the hall.

I call for Puck, who comes to me even though she's wondering who this new dog arriving is.

A sleek black lab races through the door, tugging along the newest player on the team, Ty Connor.

This is the first time I've seen him in person, and he's taller than I expected. Bigger, too, especially across the shoulders. Golden brown hair frames a strong, angular face. Cheekbones for days. A jaw made of steel, apparently.

Even in a building filled with men at their athletic prime, he stands out, and I force myself to focus on clipping Puck's lead onto her collar. Even while I'm looking down, I can feel his presence.

He's got one of those faces, like any average person would immediately know that he's a celebrity, even out of context.

Whatever my previous impressions of him were—elite goal scorer, league hot shot, maybe—they're now replaced with something else, something overwhelming that I don't even have a chance to accurately define for myself because his dog is going nuts.

The lab yanks away from him and starts nosing at my pocket.

"Sit," I immediately snap, firmly.

The dog sits. For a split second. But then it surges forward to nose again at the treats I use to reward Puck for being good.

"Sorry," Ty says, swearing under his breath. Up close, he smells like clean laundry and sporty deodorant, like he just rolled out of bed and pulled on team-branded clothes and a very expensive looking puffy jacket. "Got distracted. Daffy, don't do that. Sorry, she's...I don't know."

Daffy? Like the duck?

Like his face, his voice is different in person. It registers in my brain immediately as dangerous to my people-pleasing self.

You know fight or flight responses that most people have? I fawn.

And people like Ty Connor are very easy to fawn over. It would be just like me to get a crush on a guy like him, and that is not what my life is about right now.

So I notice the red flag, and I promise myself to abide by it.

Of course, that doesn't stop me from imagining him naked for a split second. Naked, rambling out of bed. Stretching those long arms out as wide as he can, then up high, before sliding on the team t-shirt and promising his dog they'd go to the rink.

My brain tries to remind me that I left a man—a doctor—in a bed not that long ago. I had sex last night, I'm pretty sure, not that I can remember it right now.

Don't compare your hookup to a professional hockey player who is a walking, talking thirst trap. You know better than that, Kiley Forge.

His dog—Daffy, apparently—helps me out by jumping for my pocket again. Again, I tell her to sit, and this time, I hold eye contact until she stays. Finally, when I think she's got it, I flick a very quick glance at her owner, who looks shell-shocked now. "Can I give a treat?"

Ty doesn't answer. He's staring at me with startling green eyes. A lock of his golden brown hair flops forward, high-lighting again his classically handsome features. The kind of face that belongs in a museum, not chasing after ill-behaved animals. The kind of face that in another time would belong to a duke or something.

Do they make plaster busts of hockey players' faces?

They should with this one, I think. He's far too pretty to only be photographed.

But as handsome as he is, he's not really great with the listening. He has that in common with his dog.

Kieran, who looks like he's trying not to laugh, says his name.

Ty starts. "Yeah?"

I sigh. "Your dog? Can I give her a treat for sitting?" I smile down at the lab. "You're a good dog."

Good is a stretch here, but…she's trying.

"It's not my dog," Ty says. "Just, uh, dog-sitting for the morning, I guess. But she didn't leave any rules about food."

I decide a basic treat is probably fine. I fish it out of my pocket and reward the dog. Then I pick up her lead, straighten up to my full five-foot-ten inches of height, so we're almost eye-to-eye since he's slouching, and hand the leash over. "First rule of dog-sitting is know what they can and can't eat. Second rule is, don't let go of this."

He blinks.

Listen, Ty Connor, I say in my head. *It's either snap at you or develop a crush on you, and the former is definitely better for both of us.*

"So many rules, so early in the day," he says, suddenly smiling in a way that lights up his whole face. I'm sure that's devastatingly effective with women who don't care about dog safety.

Does he think those rules shouldn't apply to him?

I frown. "Our dogs need to share this space, so, yeah. Rules."

I glance at Kieran, hoping he'll back me up. I don't want to be rude to his new teammate, but this guy literally just moved here. Why is he dog-sitting, anyway?

Kieran is clearly on the same wavelength. "I need to head downstairs for practice. And so does he, soon, so you'll have the space to yourself shortly." He gives Ty an exasperated look. "Do you have a plan for the dog during practice?"

"Her owner is..." Ty looks at his smart watch. "Ten minutes away, she swears."

There's a thread of uncertainty, even as he tries to make it sound like no big deal. My eyebrow shoots up, I can't help it. *Dog-sitting,* my ass. He's been here for a hot second and he's already found an unreliable puck bunny with a badly behaved—or at least under trained—dog. Of course he has. He makes sweatpants look like they belong on a fashion catwalk. Of course he's tumbled into bed with someone who probably spends more time on her hair than on keeping her dog properly exercised.

Ty Connor is officially ridiculous. Remembering that will help when I inevitably get distracted by how perfect his profile is.

Kieran clearly wants to remove himself from this entire situation. He takes a step towards the exit. "I'll see you later, Kiley."

"Oh, this is Kiley!" Ty grins again. "The famous Kiley."

If literally anyone else on the team said that to me, I'd probably reply with charm. My brother is one of the team's doctors, my best friend is about to be engaged to one of their stars. My dog reigns supreme over the arena. Plus, I follow most of the team on Instagram, and half of them follow me back. I genuinely love everything the Highlanders are doing for my city, and I do my part in hyping them up. In some ways, I've made being a fan of the team central to my reinvention of self. Of course I'm famous here.

But there's something about the way *this* man says it.

Like…he expects me to be impressed that he's heard of me. While he's holding the lead of some random puck bunny's poorly behaved pup. As if women everywhere always fall for his charm, and that gets him out of trouble.

Annoyed tension twists up my spine. I want to snap back something like, *and you are?* But I'm not sure I have it in me to lie like that, and I don't know how it would go over with Kieran. So instead I simply I tug on Puck's leash. "Come on, Puckster. Let's go explore down the other end of the hall."

And I leave him staring at my back.

Ty Connor isn't going to ruin my positive vibes. The day is still young, and good things can still happen. Just maybe not while I'm in the same building as the cocky hockey superstar.

The good news is, the chances of me developing a crush on him are now infinitesimally small. Impossible, even.

CHAPTER 5
TY

When I woke up this morning in a stranger's apartment, alone with her dog, I seriously thought today was going to be a disaster—and the first two hours were definitely not great, what with Daffodil being my unexpected companion.

But as I watch a very grown-up, very curvy Wednesday Addams clone stalk away, all I can think is, *Hamilton might be fun after all.*

As soon as Kiley's out of hearing range, Kieran points at me. "Don't."

Oh, I definitely will. I drag my memory for every fragmented reference I'd heard about her since the trade. "This is Harper's best friend?"

"She's really sweet."

"Seems like it," I drawl.

She almost ripped my face off for daring to smile at her.

I want her to do it again.

Marsh clearly does not share the same interest in a repeat clash. "I don't think you've made a great first impression, and the whole…dog-sitting…thing is coming off in a weird way. Take your furry friend and head downstairs. Leave her alone."

"But she's..." My gaze tracks across the space. "Interesting."

"Not for you. Not today."

"Sure. No worries. Not today. We'll head down with you."

At the elevator, he sighs. "Okay, I'll bite. What's the deal with the dog?"

I wince. "Well...I swiped right on someone who, in hindsight, was really looking for someone to watch her dog for a few hours this morning."

He barks out a surprised laugh. "Excuse me?"

I shrug. "Ever been invited to a one-night stand that it turns out wouldn't really include you?"

He pauses and tilts his head to the side. He's still frozen like that when we get to the training room level. Stepping off the elevator restarts his brain. "I— How— Do I want to know?"

"Want to know what?" Russ Armstrong, the Scottish-Canadian enforcer and one of Marsh's closest friends on the team, nods in my direction. "You got dirt on the new guy?"

Kieran scrubs his hand over his face and groans. "I'm really not sure."

I give them both a not-at-all-embarrassed grin. "We all make Tinder mistakes."

"He showed up to a hookup that didn't happen."

Russ crossed his arms over his chest. "And?"

"And he stayed. Now he's dog sitting."

Russ barks a laugh. "Was it a breakfast booty call dupe?"

I wince. "Last night, actually."

"You stayed over just to watch her dog?"

"It was late, and she put on a bit of a show. I thought it was leading somewhere, and then I got tired."

"She let you sleep in her bed?"

"Twin beds."

They're both laughing at me now.

"She has twin beds?" Kieran shakes his head. "Man, she does this a lot. That's wild."

Well, when he says it like that, it makes a lot of sense. I sigh and glance down at Daffodil. "You knew from the second I walked through that door that I was going to be your pupsitter this morning, didn't you?"

Daffy darts around Kieran and picks up a sock in her mouth, making my teammate yell.

She doesn't put it down.

"Keep it," he sighs. "When is she leaving?"

Right on cue, I get a text message that her owner is here. Chances that she's sheepish? Probably zero. "Now. I'll be right back. Tell Coach I'm in the building."

After that, I decide to ignore Tinder for a while. I focus on Lusty instead. Nobody is using Lusty to find a temporary dog sitter.

My hotel is walkable to a bunch of different areas that the demographic that uses Lusty really likes. I check out coffee shops and lunch takeout options, snapping pictures to build my local review reputation. On a night off, I drive out to Westdale, the area around the university, for a well-reviewed open mic music night.

I don't take anyone home, but I have fun.

I'm figuring out whose recommendations are solid,

which is key for getting the most out of Lusty, and why it's turned into a cult-fave hookup app, too—because the people who like the same kind of food, entertainment, and travel that you like are a high likelihood to be a good time in bed, too.

The first few follows I make are guys just like me. Athletic, hungry for good food and warm bodies, but not super artsy. I'm into their recs, but they aren't the type I want to get naked with.

Then I see a top reviewer, TheatreGirl, who has rated every single hiking trail in the area with hilarious captions, and has a similar post for the burgers of Hamilton.

I smash the follow button, because what's not to like about a girl who's into diner food and long walks up and down an escarpment?

Then I check out her bio.

Right at the top is a Hamilton Highlanders hashtag. All right, she's a fan. Not a deal breaker. Some people don't like puck bunnies, but me? I like enthusiasm in all its permutations.

And then she lists a few things she's into. *Breakfast for dinner. Hot springs. Reylo fan fiction.*

What the hell is a Reylo? My curiosity gets the better of me. I Google, and immediately put my phone down.

Oh. Rey. Of course. It's Star Wars fan fiction.

Jesus Christ.

I mean, I have my own horny reactions to Leia in a gold bikini, so I can't judge, but Kylo Ren? If she likes them dark and emo, I'm not going to be her type.

And already, I'm giving this way too much thought.

It doesn't matter who she pictures when I'm bouncing her on my dick. I leave an appreciative comment on her hiking list, thanking her for the recs, from a new-to-Hamilton outdoor enthusiast.

I leave off the minor detail that I prefer it when the weather is closer to a hundred degrees, not hovering around zero.

That night, she replies.

And then she sends me a DM. It appears while I'm online, so I can reply immediately, too.

THEATREGIRL

Welcome to the Hammer.

BEASTMODE

Thanks. Appreciate the personalized recommendations.

Yeah I wrote those just for you to find.

I grin and get more comfortable, liking her slightly snarky vibe.

BEASTMODE

Have you checked out the open mic music night on King Street?

THEATREGIRL

A few times. It's pretty good, but it conflicts with my work schedule most of the time.

Ah. I travel for work, so it's hit or miss for me, too. Anything similar that takes place during the day? I work evenings a lot.

Are you looking for music-type things specifically?

Anything with a bit of funky culture to it.

She recommends a couple of art installations, and the student art gallery on campus.

BEASTMODE

Amazing, thank you. I'll check them out.

THEATREGIRL

Based on your profile, I'm surprised that's
what you're looking for.

Most of my public reviews are for hikes in various cities I've played in and had an extra day in, long enough to get my sweat on. And they are all appreciative of the people who have shown me a bit of their city and a lot of themselves.

BEASTMODE

Do you have me pegged as a dumb jock?

THEATREGIRL

Some of my favourite people are jocks. But
they don't generally go to art shows unless
they're there to hit on pretty girls.

Not gonna lie, that is part of the appeal

I'll be on guard at the next art show, then

Don't worry, I'm never pushy about my
relentless pursuit of some mutually
beneficial vigorous exercise.

LOL

You're definitely not a dumb jock. That's
clever. Mutually beneficial vigorous
exercise.

> Do you ever use this site to find workout partners?

> Actually, I'm halfway through a year of working out with a different person every time...

Damn. The girl knows what she likes. Good. My cock thickens.

BEASTMODE

> A whole year, huh? That's quite the project. And what happens in six months?

THEATREGIRL

> Not sure. Hopefully I'll know myself better, and have a lot more experience and understanding of the Modern Man so I can find a boyfriend who won't cheat on me.

> Ah

> Shit, ignore that I just said that

> Can't do that

> Anyway, one-night stands can't break my heart, you know?

> I sure do

> And I'm really enjoying my Year of Being Slutty

> lol as you should

So is it too crass for me to pivot to saying, I'm heading out of town tomorrow for work, but I'm free tonight if you want to show me anything. Something…downtown, maybe?

That sounds…so tempting. But I work overnight tonight. Leaving in ten minutes.

Ah crap. Maybe when I get back? You can pick the activity.

When you say I can show you downtown…

I mean I'd like my shoulders between your thighs

Definitely tempting

Good. I want you to be tempted. And in the meantime, good luck finding one timer exercise pals. I mean that sincerely.

Thanks?

What? Can't a guy wish a gal good luck out there?

It's a first for me

That's a shame

You, too. Good luck out there.

———

I expected a bit of hazing when I got traded to a new team. I wasn't expecting it to come from my former teammates, though.

When we get back from games out in western Canada, there's a pallet of boxes waiting for me at the arena.

"We signed for them," the PR intern said. "Wasn't sure where you wanted them."

Marsh strides in with his girlfriend, Harper, as I'm cutting away the plastic wrap protecting the boxes. "What's all that?"

"No clue." I frown as I recognize the small logo on the cardboard. "Oh, for fuck's sake."

He leans in. "Bud, did you order a shit ton of merch and forget what team you play for now?"

"I didn't order this."

He yanks the top box off the stack and flips up the flap. "You didn't order hats that say *Connor Loves Miami*?"

"Jesus Christ." I slap the flap down. "These have to go."

"You can't throw them out," Harper says. "If that gets leaked, then it's wasteful. And whoever sent it to you will know they got to you. You need to save these for some kind of revenge plot."

Kieran looks delighted. "That's my girl. Revenge plot, eh?"

She grins at him. "Too evil?"

"Just evil enough." He kisses her nose, then turns back to me. "Want a hand loading these into your truck?"

"I can't..." I laugh and shake my head. "I'm living in a hotel room, man. Where am I going to put these?"

"You can stash them at my place," Harper says. "Since the revenge plot was my idea. And my apartment isn't being used much right now."

"She's basically moved into my house," Marsh adds. "And she knows I'm not about to offer my garage."

"I was going to offer it for you," she says sweetly. "But I like parking in it more."

"You don't mind?"

"It's either my living room or a cold storage unit." She shrugs. "Be my guest."

Then she elbows Marsh, and he hands over her spare key while she types her address into my phone.

Our third line centre, Hiro Watanabe, strides up as she hands it back. "What's all this?"

"Nothing," I say at the same time Marsh tosses him one of the hats.

Hiro frowns at me. "What the fuck, man?"

"Shut up, they're not mine."

"His team misses him," Kieran teases.

"This is my team, you jerk."

"Hey, I'm the jerk who brought the brains who solved your problem." He winks at me. "Hiro, we need your help loading these into Ty's truck. He wants to take them all home so he can be alone with them."

I want to be alone, all right. I want to be alone so I can find someone hot to chat with while I stroke one out and try not to think about how long it's going to take to feel fully at home here. Or how much fucking work it's going to be to unload all these boxes into Harper's apartment.

I'm definitely going to wait to stash them there.

Jerk off first.

Pay the penance for having been traded later.

CHAPTER 6
KILEY

The only downside of catching a ride to the hospital with my brother is that he needs to be there for rounds that start earlier than my shift. The upside is that we both like to grab a good coffee on the way in, and I've been curating a good list of early morning brews on Lusty.

Today we drive a little out of our way to check out a pop-up espresso trailer parked in a commuter parking lot just off the highway. It's worth the extra ten minutes, and the toque-wearing barista has a beaming smile when I snap her photo.

I wait until we've arrived at the hospital, and I've consumed half of the delicious macchiato, before I write my review, then add that to my Early Morning Brews list.

The rest of my coffee is sipped slowly as I scroll through the app, looking for someplace interesting to take the hockey WAGs for our next girls' night.

Most of the Highlanders are single. Besides Harper, there are three other women attached to players. The captain, Max Tilman, has a gorgeous blonde wife, Shannon, who used to be a model in New York City before they met. The young alternate captain, Jenson Hale, married his high school sweetheart, a stunning Indigenous woman named Ani. And the youngest player on the team, Hayden Calhoun, is engaged to *his* high school sweetheart, Becca Kincaid, with whom he has a little boy named Charlie.

The four of them are the WAGs. The wives and girl-friends.

And I'm the…SOTD. Sister of the doctor.

But they've embraced me as Harper's bestie, and since I'm the more social, outgoing of the two, I try to meet their graciousness in kind with finding the best of my home-town's offerings to entertain them.

I star a couple of promising options, including a wreck bar that looks amazing and a new restaurant out in Stoney Creek connected to a popular winery, but when I scroll past a profile photo that is quickly becoming familiar, I get distracted.

The last time I looked at BeastMode's profile, it wasn't very detailed. The way Lusty works is that you have a different profile page for every city you visit or live in. The bio is the same, but photos, reviews, and status updates are localized.

When I moved back to Hamilton, I liked the app more than any other because it felt cathartic, like the app was a part of me starting over with a clean slate. All the reviews I'd made in Vancouver, when I thought I was falling in love with a handsome actor? Those don't exist here.

My mistakes don't exist here.

Here, I'm just a confident girl who likes coffee and fun nights out with friends.

And it looks like BeastMode is the same. His bio is now more specific to Hamilton, with a #hamont at the top, a mashup of Hamilton and Ontario—an early Twitter tag that proved convenient to differentiate the city from the historical figure when the musical became a worldwide sensation.

After that, is his Lusty List of favourites, which I saw the first time I messaged him. *Love a good workout. Like a good recommendation. Constant cravings: Italian food, endorphins, and sunshine.*

I scroll down, being nosy. He's only posted one new set of photos since last week, from a recently renovated bar at one of the downtown hotels. It looks great inside, and the view of the city and bay at night is amazing. I drop a comment on it that I think I've found the perfect location for the next girls' night, then I head upstairs to get ready for work.

It's funny, because BeastMode doesn't have any photos of himself on the app, but I'm finding myself quickly putting together a clear image of him in my mind. He likes food and fitness in equal measure, and he's got a job that is his whole life. Dating—and sex—are important to him, but not more important than his career.

That's what I want for myself. That's what I need.

In almost a year of fooling around with slutty abandon, I haven't found anyone else who is as much like me as this man seems to be.

And even without knowing what he looks like, I know I'm going to be attracted to him. I already am.

I tap on the message button on his profile.

THEATREGIRL

Good morning. Long day of work ahead of me, just wanted to say hi because I was thinking about you.

I head upstairs, brain shifting to the long day ahead. So it takes me a minute to recognize the man in green scrubs leaning against the desk, my desk, in the centre of the paediatric ward where I'm a clerk.

It's my hook-up from a few weeks ago.

"Hey, you," he says with an easy smile. "You didn't tell me that you're friends with Harper Roberts."

I pull up short. "Excuse me?"

"Do you ever go on double dates with her and the hockey player?"

"This really isn't the time or place for this," I say carefully. "I have to log in to my computer."

He shifts over, making room for me. Not enough room, though.

I pointedly look at the exit. "Don't you have surgery this morning?"

"It was cancelled, and I'm waiting to be paged for the next one. Thought I'd come and catch up."

Now that he knows my best friend is dating a famous athlete. Great.

For the most part, people we work with don't care about her relationship. If anything, our actual colleagues would be protective of it, and her. We saw it unfold, after all, as Kieran found her (again) through a team visit to the children's hospital where we work.

Not this guy, though.

It's not the first time someone has asked me about Kieran, or Harper in relation to Kieran, and it probably won't be the last, especially as the hockey season is coming to a close, and the Highlanders are looking like they might just make the playoffs in their inaugural year.

The entire city is on tenterhooks, and the players are under a microscope. And their girlfriends.

I quickly type in my password, then pull up the patient census and the staff list. Memorizing the names a patient/nurse pair at a time, I update the white board with neat black marker notes about who is working, who their patients are, and anything else the team needs to know at a glance.

The surgical resident watches me work until I'm halfway through the list. Then he says, "Rumour has it she's asked to be taken off the schedule for the summer. What's the deal with that?"

Rumour has it? Oh, hell no. Nobody talks about my bestie behind her back.

But that includes me.

This guy doesn't deserve to know anything about her life, or schedule, and any effort he's making to goad me into spilling some deets will not be rewarded.

"Jeez, you're not talkative this morning, are you?"

I cap the marker with a loud click and slowly turn to give him my full attention. He's tall and fit, and he knows he's attractive. It's a shame he doesn't seem to have any clue that he's also inappropriately nosy as fuck. "Do you have any patient-specific reason to be on this floor right now? Is there something work-related I can help you with?"

He rolls his eyes. "I was just making conversation. I thought we had a good time together."

"I'm going to be honest with you. It's a weird conversation. You seem to want to talk more about my best friend than me, or that good time we had. And—"

I'm interrupted by his pager going off.

Saved by the operating room.

He snaps into work mode and uses my phone to let them know he's on his way. As he shifts gears, I remind myself he was a one-night stand I will leave in my past. He means nothing, it means nothing.

But I can't shake the tender feeling of a rejection I didn't ask for, didn't put myself on the line for.

He's not Crys, and you're not the same Kiley. He's nothing and you're a goddess. Move on.

After he leaves, I complete my review of the staff and patient counts for the day. We have a couple of empty patient beds, and since we often run close to or at capacity, that likely means we'll get new kids on our floor within the next few hours.

I better use this quiet time wisely, because we're about to be slammed.

Over the last year, I've gotten used to the rhythm of working in the hospital, and I've come to love the pace of it. Originally, I applied for this job because it sounded convenient. Harper and Grant both work here, and my car died immediately after the road trip across the country that brought me home, tail between my legs. I was living on my brother's couch, and I had no money.

Any job was better than none, and a job where I could carpool with two other people most of the time was a winner. And it's a direct bus route on the few days a month when I can't mooch a ride.

I didn't expect to love working as a ward clerk. But in a lot of ways, it's similar to being a theatre stage manager, keeping track of who needs to go where, and when. Knowing what everyone needs to do their job, anticipating changes, and keeping track of everything in a giant binder.

It's not what I want to do forever, but I've finally saved

up enough money to consider replacing the car that brought me home, and then promptly died. Which is excellent timing, since I won't be carpooling with Harper anymore.

For the umpteenth time since Kieran showed me the pictures of the rings he was considering for Harper, I wonder when he will propose.

They're inseparable when he's home now.

It's both gross and wonderful. I'm happy for her, but I miss my best friend sometimes.

Today, though, I have a lot of work to keep me company. While the floor seems quiet, I check the patient nutrition room and the staff room, noting what might need to be restocked before the end of my shift. The clerk from the night shift put coffee on a timer—bless him—so I don't have to make a new pot for an hour at least.

My personal phone vibrates with a new message just as I return to my desk.

BEASTMODE

Good morning to you, too, TheatreGirl. And now I'm going to be thinking about you all day.

My fingers itch to type something back, but I can't be flirting on my phone at work.

That's for later.

But as the day spins faster and faster, I carry the warmth of his words in my chest.

The phone rings nonstop for an hour, doctors calling in for updates, other departments replying to appointment requests made overnight, and then Emerg, asking if we have room to admit a new patient.

My job is to keep track of the decisions made by other

people, and then make the basic shit happen. Have the patient file ready to go by the time they get up to us. Run and get a telemetry device when the nurse needs one swapped out. Update the patient census so there's an accurate report of how many beds are in use.

And on and on.

My fifteen minute morning break is eleven minutes long, which isn't the worst. There's an encouraging message from BeastMode that I should definitely check out that bar he went to, and seeing it fills my chest with a warm, fluttery feeling I'd like a lot more if I weren't still smarting from the morning's weirdness.

My afternoon break never happens.

By the end of my shift, my stomach is growling.

There's a text on my phone from my brother, saying he's still in the hospital if I want a drive home.

We meet in the parking lot, part of the stream of departing health care workers. The sun is low on the horizon, lighting up the sky in bright orange.

"Hope you didn't want to hang out," he says after unlocking his car. "I have a date at nine-thirty."

I laugh. "Amazing."

"Don't be jealous."

My laugh turns to a shudder. "Definitely not."

He frowns. "Why? What happened?"

"Nothing."

He gives me a skeptical look, then slides behind the driver's seat. I sink into the passenger seat, exhaling a little too vigorously.

"Out with it," he demands.

I groan. Then I tell him about the resident, and the questions about Harper and Kieran.

"Want me to talk to him?"

"Send my baby brother to fix my problems?"

"You're like, two minutes older than me, and I've been taller than you since the sixth grade. Let me pound someone into the ground for you for once."

"Eh, he's not the one who really hurt me."

Grant narrows his eyes. I've never told him the whole story about Crys. It hurts too much.

But he knows enough to know what I need: to feel like a queen.

He gestures impatiently. "Give me your phone. Let's swipe on a few new guys. Have you switched up your bio this month?"

"Yes, Grindr Master," I say teasingly.

Last year when I moved home, I was convinced I needed to swear off men. Three bad relationships in a row, all of them with men who felt more like projects than partners. And I am a sucker for a good project, but where does that get me? Cheated on, taken advantage of, disrespected.

Grant took me in, letting me sleep on his couch and lick my wounds. But once he moved out, and I got the bedroom —the whole apartment, beautiful in its imperfections—he also told me I should get back on the dating horse.

It was hard. But how I was doing it made it harder.

Grant taught me how to date like him. Which is to say, "date" in the loosest of terms. To use apps fearlessly and confidently.

"I don't think there's anything wrong with my profile," I insist. "I'm getting the same number of messages as usual."

He winces. "You're getting pickier."

"I'm trying not to!"

He ignores me and takes my phone. "You deleted the picture of your tits in the baseball jersey."

"Hey!" I blush. "Don't call them that."

He rolls his eyes. "Okay, you deleted the photo of your breasts—"

"Ew. Boundaries."

"I'm a doctor."

"And my tits aren't hockey players." I grab the phone back. "Never mind."

"All right, but any time you want a consult with the Master, you just let me know." He starts the car, and we join the line of vehicles leaving the lot.

He drops me off in front of the three-storey walk-up apartment building where I live. Where he once lived, upstairs from Harper. And now they've both moved on. Well, Harper hasn't moved out yet, not technically, but she's staying at Kieran's house almost exclusively now.

The front door can be opened by either a buzzer code or with a key, but I don't need to do either of those things, because it's slightly ajar—a piece of cardboard holding it open.

I yank it out, letting the door shut with a loud thumping click, then wedge the cardboard behind the hard plastic sign on the wall that says *Keep door closed at all times. Do not prop open.*

Someone in my building decided that particular rule didn't apply to them today, I guess.

There's a box on the second floor landing, but no culprit in sight. I pause just long enough to take a picture of it and text Harper.

There's a muffled grunt at the front door. I scoot up to the next landing, halfway between Harper's floor and my apartment on the upper level. Whoever the new neighbour is, I don't want to meet them right after inconveniencing their move in.

The door scrapes open, then heavy footsteps climb the stairs.

Curiosity gets the better of me, and I wait, expecting them to appear at the door I can see below me.

Instead, two more boxes get shoved onto the one that is in the middle of the hallway.

Then I hear muttering.

Quietly, I take two steps back down the stairs.

There's a large man wearing a fancy-looking puffy winter coat in front of Harper's door, fumbling with the handle.

"Hey!" I snap, hoping I can use the benefit of surprise and scare him down the stairs.

He twists around, moving faster than I expect—and not in the direction I want him to go. He puts himself firmly in front of Harper's door, a confident claim like he's in the right place and I'm the foolish woman who just accosted a stranger.

A stranger who's grinning at me now, because we've met before.

"It's the best friend," Ty Connor says with a cocky swagger. His golden brown hair glints in the light from the bare bulb above us, and he looks out of place. Because he is.

I sigh and take the final few steps down to be on the

same level as him, and parrot back, "It's the hockey player. What are you doing here?"

He slides a glance over my scrubs. "You work at the hospital, too?"

I cross my arms over my chest. "Not the topic of our current conversation."

"Conversations work best when they go in both directions. Something about you, something about me. I'm a hockey player, and you're a…nurse?"

"Ward clerk."

"Never heard of that job before."

"You're American?"

He nods.

"Unit secretary, then."

He shrugs. "Still no clue."

"Okay, I think we're done with my part of the conversation. Why are you breaking into Harper's apartment?"

He holds up a key. "Because I have permission. It's a long story."

I glance around. "No dog today?"

"I take it you don't want the long story. And no, no dog today. Daffodil was a one-time thing. Where's your pup?"

"With her grandparents."

He looks confused.

"Also a long story." My stomach growls, reminding me I haven't eaten since my salad at lunch. I point to the door behind him. "Were you trying to put the key in the dead-bolt? It just goes in the handle instead."

He ducks down. "Ah. I see. Sorry, I'm tall."

Three inches taller than me, it feels like, with both of us in sneakers. Just the right height to firmly look him in the eye and say, "Just because Harper is letting you use her apartment doesn't mean you can take advantage. And this building has a firm *never prop the door open* rule, okay? This isn't the best part of town."

"Got it." He nods. "Nice to see you again, Kiley."

There's something in the way he says my name. The way his voice dips. Like he's using it to make a point, like he wants me to be more familiar with him.

That's not happening.

I turn and hurry up the stairs.

Nice to see you again, I mouth as I shove open my own door.

As if.

CHAPTER 7
TY

BEASTMODE

Hey stranger

THEATREGIRL

Do I know you?

LOL I deserve that, I went radio silent for
another week

It's all good. I like seeing messages from
you. How have you been?

Swamped. My new job is kicking my ass.
Traveling again.

No time for extracurricular fun?

None. You?

Not recently.

Damn. Sorry to hear that.

It's okay. Maybe I'm entering a picky phase.

Good to have standards.

LOL in my experience, standards make for
lonely nights

Awww sounds like someone's a horny girl.

I am! How long are you away for?

Our next road trip is down to Florida. My first game back in my old barn, and I need to focus, no matter how fucking tempting that exclamation mark after *I am* is. The pure joy that zings off this woman's DMs is amazing.

When we finally land in the same bed at the same time, it's going to be very, very good.

The team has a morning skate at the arena in Hamilton before we board the bus to the airport. Some people drive themselves, so they can head straight home when we get back. A bunch of the guys live in a new community not far from the airport. Sprawling homes, big yards. The kind of domestic perfection that makes me feel a little hollow inside.

So I'm going to catch the bus with the staff and the players who live downtown.

Grant Forge is one of the doctors on this trip. I wonder if his sister will tell him about our run in outside Harper's apartment.

As we're waiting, Mabel from PR slides up beside me with a sympathetic smile. An *I know you might want to say no, but please don't* smile. "Would you have a minute to meet the new reporter from the Observer? And answer a few questions about heading back to Miami for a game?"

She's right. I want to say no, but I won't. The media is a part of the job, and it's not this guy's fault his first day covering me just happens to be the day we're heading back to the team that gave me away. "Sure."

The reporter is a young Black guy with glasses and natural curls. "Aaron Green from the Obs. Good to meet you."

"Yeah, same."

"How is getting ready for a road trip different with this team than it was with Miami?"

"Some of it is universal. Hamilton has more video coaching staff, so my homework load is a little heavier."

He smiles. Good. I can crack jokes with him, that'll make our relationship easier.

"And I like doing tape review, so that's fine. I've got more time for it now."

"Yeah?"

"No hot girls in bikinis on my runs in the morning, that's for sure."

He coughs. "Right. And on a personal note, Sunday is your first game back in Miami, this time on the visitor's bench."

"Yep."

"How do you prepare for a return to an arena you called home for a decade?"

We all know I wanted to call that arena home for my entire career. But that's not how this game is played. I'm not going to say that, not while I'm on *this* team. "I got some good advice from Marshie. He's done it a bunch of times now. I'll just focus on the game. This team is exceptionally good, and I know we have everyone in Hamilton rooting for us. Happy to be wearing Highlander red and white on Sunday. Every day."

"Thanks, Ty."

"Yep."

————

It's good that people in Hamilton are cheering for me, because people in Miami are *not*. Maybe they would have liked the little video montage the PR team put together if the score was reversed, but when it's four-zip for the visitors, the guy on hatty watch isn't getting cheers. It doesn't matter that I used to be the captain here.

Now I'm the first line centre on a divisional rival team that has Kieran Fucking Marsh on the second line. And tonight we are simply dominant.

Anton Petrov, who replaced me as the captain in Miami, is losing his shit.

Top of the third, my line jumps over the boards and into the action forty-five seconds in, and I intercept a pass Petrov definitely didn't see me inserting myself in the middle of.

Hayden reads the play perfectly, speeding up to create some stretch in our line, and suddenly he's in the clear. I snap the puck ahead to him and he's off, on a breakaway. His stick handling is tight, and I can see the goalie falling for the *left, right, tap* set up, but Calhoun doesn't shoot right away. It's a nice little move, faking the goalie out, taking an extra second before snapping the puck blocker side. Goal, and it's a sweet one.

Five-zip.

I'm grinning as we toss ourselves back on the bench. "Nice short shift," I pant.

Hooner fist-bumps me. "Next one's yours. Hat trick, motherfucker."

But it doesn't come in the shifts that follow, despite

having some sweet chances. I clip the posts twice, and the tension ratchets up in the arena—on and off the ice.

With four minutes left—not really enough time for Miami to score five and tie it up, but not past the point of no return where they stop being fucking mad about how the game has gone—we line up for a faceoff. I guess the aggression between me and Petrov is a little much, and the ref waves me out to the circle, wanting someone else in for the puck battle.

Calhoun takes it, so I cozy up to another of my former Miami teammates, Craig Roslin. Funny guy. Great hockey player, and underrated by almost everyone because he's a bit of a throwback. Likes his hot dogs and chocolate milk. Once upon a time—a month ago—he was my favourite teammate. Now he's the guy I need to beat to the puck once Hooner snaps it back.

He shoves against me, our sticks clattering. "Is freezing your nuts off up there in Hamilton turning you into a showoff?"

"Miss you too, bud." I jam my shoulder over, making hard contact. "Now get out of my fucking way."

———

It's on the short flight from Miami to Tampa Bay that I hear the first rumbles that actually, people in Hamilton aren't cheering for me as much as expected tonight.

"Hey, bud," Kieran says, sliding into the seat beside me. "So..."

"What?"

He winces. "Twitter thinks you're fat-shaming our fans."

I laugh. "Excuse me?"

"Something about bikinis."

"Is this belated hazing? Pranking the new guy?"

He hands over his phone.

@yourpucksucks

What? No. I'm pretty sure this quote is being taken out of context #HighlanderNation #dontoverreact #reading-comprehensionfail

@bagpipesbetweenthepipes

Or that he thinks the women of Hamilton are fatties

@yourpucksucks

Probably that it's parka season

@bagpipesbetweenthepipes

WTF does Connor mean by this? #hamont #HighlanderNation

I shove the phone back. "This is gibberish. And I don't care what keyboard warriors think about me."

"You have to tap in to see the quoted tweet. Then you read the tweets backwards." He shoves it back. "Don't you know how Twitter works?"

"No," I retort. "I have a life."

"Not anymore, you don't. *No hot girls in bikinis on my runs in the morning, that's for sure.* The Observer ran that quote in a story about the win tonight, and how you prep for games now that you're on our team."

Jesus Christ. "That's out of context."

"That's what Harper guessed, but she's fighting an uphill battle."

I scroll back up to the first account he showed me, the most recent comment, the only rational voice on a whole thread wanting to burn me at the stake for missing the sun— and the delicious, jiggly flesh that comes with it. "That's Harper?"

"Don't tell anyone. She likes to fight with people on the internet about hockey."

"That's hot."

He scowls. "Focus."

"I'm focused!"

"Is it an accurate quote?"

"I like bikinis and I hate winter. I didn't realize I needed to be explicit about the second point. And it was a joke in a conversation about having time to watch game tape."

"Who was it? MacLeod? He's an asshole."

I shake my head. No, I know MacLeod, and I agree, he is an asshole. A veteran reporter who has learned what gets clicks, and he doesn't care who gets bruised as he stomps his way to getting those clicks. "It was a new reporter. Aaron Green."

Kieran frowns. "His name wasn't on the article."

I sigh, then push out of my seat, towering over my team-mate. "All right. Excuse me, I need to find Mabel's minion on this trip."

By the next morning, Aaron Green has a thread on Twitter identifying himself as the reporter who got the quote in question from me. He explains in both an updated article and social media posts that the quote was dropped into the original article out of context.

Privately, Mabel texts me that he's livid that his notes were misused like that, and so is she.

But when I ask Marsh at morning skate if the correction stopped the Twitter storm, he grimaces.

"I'll take that as a no." I sigh and glance at Mo Ahmadi, the defenceman who sits in the stall across from me. "Mo, you know I'm not fat shaming anyone when I say I miss bikinis, right?"

He rolls his eyes. "Just winter shaming the Canadians?"

"Fuck!" I throw my hands in the air. "I like thick chicks in parkas, too!"

Which is the moment our alternate captain Jenson Hale walks into the visitors dressing room, a camera crew following him.

He turns around, makes a *cut this* gesture, then turns back and gives me the finger.

"Honestly, it might help the situation if we let them leak that clip," I point out.

Nobody agrees.

But I'm not wrong. We lose the game that night in Tampa, and the first question I get asked in media availability is why I haven't dated anyone in Hamilton.

Mabel's minion gives me a panicked look.

Am I the only one who saw this coming?

"My priority right now is figuring out my place on this team. You saw how good we can be in Miami, and I'm disappointed we didn't find that same level of success tonight. This is the best hockey league in the world. Every team is capable of dismantling us, and we need to rise to that challenge."

"Did you have time to hit the beach this morning?" That's a Tampa reporter. For years, she reported on me as a player on the *other* Florida team, so she's always been a little critical. I bet she's loving this gaffe.

Which means the only option I have is to lean into it and love it, too. I turn on the charm and give her a slow, *you just walked into it but that's okay, I'll soften your landing* kind of smile. "You know the Gulf coast doesn't usually do it for me, Meegan. But I did hear that the only bikinis on the beach this morning were Canadian snowbirds, excited for the game tonight, so of course I appreciated that."

The press corps laugh.

Mabel's minion gives me a thumbs up.

We fly home that night, landing in Hamilton at half-past one in the morning.

As I stride through the lobby of the hotel, my phone vibrates. I glance at the screen and my pulse skitters in a good way.

It pays to turn on notifications for Lusty when I get a middle of the night message from TheatreGirl. It's a meme that makes me laugh, a cartoon of two people texting. A human man on the left, his message reading, "You're a horny girl, aren't you?" And on the right, a pretty narwhal typing back, "I sure am!"

THEATREGIRL

Saw this and thought of you.

BEASTMODE

Is this your way of telling me that you're actually a sea animal?

Oh, hello there. I didn't think you'd be awake. Can't sleep?

Just winding down. You?

Working overnight. But it's quiet right now.

I groan quietly. Of course she's working. I won't send her anything too inappropriate. I'm keyed up, though, and messaging with her sounds like a better way to unwind than obsessively watching game tape.

BEASTMODE

Quiet enough for me to distract you a little?

THEATREGIRL

Yep.

Mmm good.

I type and delete a bunch of inane shit. *How are you doing? Been keeping busy?*

Then I cut straight to the chase.

BEASTMODE

Do you know how much I'd like to talk my way between your thighs tonight?

THEATREGIRL

Lol when you say it like that, it's pretty clear

Would you let me have a taste of you?

Maybe more than a taste

Fuck. Yes. A full on midnight feast.

And what about me? Do I get a taste of you, too?

The thought of her tongue swiping up a drop of my precome sends a shiver slamming up my spine.

BEASTMODE

You first, though. You always cum first. I'll spread you out on your desk and make you shake.

THEATREGIRL

My desk isn't private

I don't care … let people see what a hungry man I am

And me? They'll see me, too…

Legs spread, head thrown back… You'd be beautiful like that. But they won't get to see your wet, warm pussy. That's for me alone. That's my feast. All they'd see is my head between your thighs.

She doesn't reply to that immediately. As the minutes tick by, I wonder if I've overstepped. Did I read her wrong?

Just as I'm about to type *hey, never mind all that,* she pops up again.

THEATREGIRL

Work got busy, but that's…dangerously hot. Your head between my thighs…I want that.

BEASTMODE

If you weren't at work right now, do you think you could get off like this?

Texting?

Yeah.

Probably. You ever done that before?

Not like this.

Not with a stranger. Although TheatreGirl doesn't really feel like a stranger anymore. Not exactly.

THEATREGIRL

Same. But I'd like to try.

BEASTMODE

It's a date. The next time we're both free. Middle of the night or a quiet afternoon, maybe...

Any time.

I grin to myself. At least there's one person in this world who doesn't know or care that I've made a gaff about bikinis —and if she did, she'd probably understand.

CHAPTER 8
KILEY

After that middle of the night message exchange, BeastMode starts sending me a daily good morning text. We seem to have very different schedules, so we aren't online at the same time that often, but that makes it all the more sweeter.

I still haven't told Grant—or Harper—about this flirtation.

I'm afraid the second I do, the second I try to make it real, it'll dissolve into nothing.

It's sort of ironic that the hotter our connection gets, the slower I want to go.

So it's good that we're both busy with work.

It's fine that my only free night this week is taken up with a girls' night. I'm barely thinking about BeastMode at all, I tell myself. A lie, of course.

The hotel bar is even nicer in person, all deep blue velvet and gleaming copper details. Harper treated me to a blowout before we got dressed, so we look super hot as a group.

It's still a wintery mid-week girls' night in Hamilton, so we didn't go overboard on the outfits. I'm wearing a black turtleneck and dark jeans, and Harper, Ani Hale, and Becca Kincaid are all wearing variations on a creamy white top and light jeans.

"I didn't get the outfit memo," I deadpan to Shannon Tilman when she arrives, wearing an oatmeal sweater that slides off one shoulder, over pale denim jeggings that hug her model-perfect form.

She laughs and hugs me. "How have you been? How's the year of one-night stands going?"

"Well…"

From across the table, Harper's head swivels in my direction. More than twenty years of friendship have honed our bestie radar pretty sharply. Her eyebrows shoot up at the look on my face.

I take a deep breath. In some ways, it's easier to share this now. The other girls don't know about all of my history. As far as this group of WAGs is concerned, I'm just living my best single girl life. "I might be revising the plan for the last stretch."

Harper's gaze sharpens. *What happened?* she asks silently.

"It turns out," I say brightly, choosing a half-truth, "that the dating pool in Hamilton can't sustain a girl for having an entire year of top-tier hook-ups. So I'm getting picky, and revising the plan a little. Slutty is a state of mind that puts me first."

"Oooh, I like that a lot," Shannon breathes. "Good for you. Yes. That's hot."

"I saw it online," I say, fudging the truth a little.

Slutty is a state of mind.

Where I actually saw it was in a Lusty post BeastMode shared a few days ago, along with the comment, *Inspired by my favorite person on this app.* And then he sent it to me in a DM, with an apology that he was heading into his busiest season at work, but we'd connect again soon.

The over/under odds on him also sending it to a bunch of other girls keeps me from disclosing the BeastMode part of the evolution of my slutty era to my friends.

As long as he's just an online flirtation—or a one-night stand, if our schedules line up—nobody needs to know about him. He's just another guy in my year of doing things differently.

The conversation rolls on. Becca shares that she and Hayden have finally picked a wedding date for the summer after this one coming. "I want Charlie to be a little older, so we can leave him with my dad and Kerry and go on a proper honeymoon."

That spills us into a travel conversation, which leads to a comparison discussion of the best meals we've ever had.

And then Ani pulls out her phone to show everyone the Lusty app.

Heat crawls up the back of my neck, like my dirty secret has been revealed, even though it's one of the top five apps in the world right now. It's not as if they're going to discover my flirtation with BeastMode. Or how it feels like we might be close to tipping into something else. Something more like sex itself.

Do you think you could get off like this?
You ever done that before?
Not like this.

This thing we're doing feels different and raw. On top of

my fear that it might evaporate if I talk about it too much, I don't want to share it because I don't want anyone to know about it, to tell me I shouldn't sext with a hot stranger online.

I don't want to be judged for whatever this is, because it's hands down better than anything I've done in person all year.

And we've barely gotten started.

"Right now, all we can see is stuff here in Hamilton," Ani is explaining. "But if you go to Paris, for example, everything shifts. It's like a fun discovery game. And the recommendations are always on point."

"You can use a VPN to trick it into showing you a different city," I say, trying to look cool and unaffected and only knowledgeable for non-perverted reasons. "I used to do that when I lived in Vancouver, but I wanted to keep up with the Hamilton chat boards."

Becca, who is super outgoing and friendly, perks up. "There are chat boards, too?"

"Oh, yeah." I pull out my own phone, making sure Beast-Mode's profile isn't open before I show them my version of the app. "There's even one dedicated to the team. It's hopping. I'm more about the arts and food experiences, but I'm in there, too."

I noticed BeastMode isn't in that forum. He's not in any of the chat spaces. Only reviews, and my DMs. *And maybe other DMs, don't forget.*

I can't forget that annoying thought, now that it's in my head. Gah.

"Are the fans on Lusty mad about BikiniGate, too, or is that isolated to Twitter?" Shannon asks.

I swallow a laugh. I hadn't realized Ty Connor's bikini

quote had elevated to the level of a Gate drama. "Ummm… There's been some chatter. There was talk of a bikini flash mob to show him just how hot Hamilton bodies can be, but that seems to have died down."

"Max says that Ty smoothed it over as best he could." Shannon shrugs. "But it's a good reminder that every quote they give can be chopped up into partial pieces."

"*Will be* chopped up," Ani adds.

Becca chews on her bottom lip. "Hayden isn't the greatest with the press stuff yet," she says in a rush. "I worry about that sometimes."

"It comes with practice. And we can help, too. That's one of many reasons why we have these little get togethers." Shannon twirls her empty wineglass in the air. "We need more wine."

Happy to get myself out of a conversation I don't want to be a part of—because I have my own opinions about Ty's comments, and I think they're the opposite of the WAGs, who of course are going to be the most sympathetic to him—I jump up. "I'll get another bottle from the bar."

The bartenders are in the middle of the room at heavy white marble counters, and behind them are glittering glass and copper shelves. Through the glass, I can just make out the patrons on the other side of the bar.

As I wait behind a big, tall guy in a suit who is giving one of the bartenders detailed instructions on how to make a smoky old fashioned to his specifications, my attention is snagged by something at the hostess stand at the entrance. Someone, I realize. It's Ty Connor, with a sleek-looking woman wrapped in a trench coat. Her long honey brown hair is pulled up in a glossy ponytail and she's wearing giant hoop earrings that swing as she animatedly describes something to him.

He's gazing down at her with a fond smile on his face, although he's underdressed for a date, wearing black track pants and a white tank top that clings to his chest. A buttoned down shirt is tossed over his arm, but I guess he couldn't be bothered to actually put it on.

Or maybe he's still overheated from whatever they were doing before coming in here. *Ugh, brain, I do not need that mental picture.*

Ty Connor, naked with Little Miss High Maintenance.

Except I can't actually picture it, thank God. They don't look like they go together at all. He's all max relax, and she looks...bossy.

I don't think Ty is the kind of guy to want to be bossed around. If anything, he'd probably be a casually dominant lover. *Take it or leave it.*

As I fight with my overactive imagination to try not to go down that path, his shoulders stiffen and his head lifts, looking right in my direction.

I scoot forward and hide behind Mr. Smoky Old Fashioned. Now this guy seems like a good match for Little Miss High Maintenance.

Around the curve of his shoulder, I watch them be shown to a high top table on the far side of the bar. The woman in the trench coat is more visible than Ty, so I step to the side again to get a better view of the date—just in time to see her slide the trench coat open and flash him a lot of skin, barely contained by a top that is suspiciously bikini shaped, although I bet it's just club wear. Since it's winter, she's sensibly wearing a hip-hugging pair of black pants on the bottom.

But still.

A bikini top? Really?

I can't make out what he says over the tinkling bar sounds, but she throws her head back and laughs before winking and seems to say, "I know you've been homesick for something you can only get in Miami, big guy."

CHAPTER 9
TY

"Jesus, Nina, put those things away." I swipe my hand over my face.

"Too much?" My agent snaps her trench coat shut again, covering up a glittery gold top that might be illegal here. Or at the very least, ill-advised due to the risk of frostbite.

"You're always too much." It's why I hired her.

We matched on Tinder five years ago when she was a law student. We didn't click, because I'm not generally attracted to sharks, and she pegged me as an athlete right out of the gate. I still bought her a drink. She told me that my agent was lazy, which wasn't wrong. Instead of having sex, we spent the evening talking about all the ways hockey players get screwed over compared to our basketball and baseball contemporaries.

We kept in touch, and once she graduated, she did her impressive baby shark thing and scored a junior agent position with the biggest agency on the continent. I signed with her the same day.

Four years later, my endorsement income is now greater than what I make from my hockey contract.

Putting up with the occasional teasing from her is a small price to pay for that.

"I have a date tonight in Toronto," she says. "Getting to make light of BikiniGate was just the icing on the moment."

"I wouldn't expect anything less."

She leans back in her chair and taps her nails on the tabletop. "Did you know that your Miami jersey sold out online yesterday?"

"Did you know that I don't play for Miami anymore?"

She rolls her eyes. To Nina, I play for Team Ty first, Team NHL second, and Team Whoever Pays Us third. She wants my name to be synonymous with the game, not limited to any single market. "It didn't occur to anyone in the Highlanders organization to lean into the bikini thing instead of running scared from it?"

"We're not—I'm not running scared. I addressed it head on, and it went away." For the most part.

Her eyes glint with that deeply motivated gleam she gets sometimes, that turns that hard work I do on the ice into a very nice payday off the ice. "I was talking to Dorian and—"

"I didn't ask you to do—"

She continues like I didn't interject. "He agrees that there's more the team could have done."

Of course the General Manager is going to say that to her. Anything to get an agent off the phone.

"It's different here, Nina. Hockey is different here. The culture is more…game-oriented."

She waves her hand. "Nobody thinks that you aren't a hockey player first and foremost. That's ridiculous."

"There are four other superstars on this team already. I'm not King Shit. And I don't really want to make waves."

"Is this about your family? Have they asked you for money?"

I shake my head. Sometimes I think it might have been better if I just fucked her that night we met. Then she wouldn't know my secrets, and we wouldn't have inside jokes, and my agent wouldn't call my GM and suggest that they put my teammates in bikinis, or whatever she said to Dorian.

I don't want to know.

"You want a drink? They have some good non-alcoholic cocktails here. There's one with mango vinegar that might be right up your alley." I twist around, flagging down a waiter who recognizes me and hurries over.

When she nods, I order that for her and a beer for myself.

"I'm guessing you're feeling sensitive to being seen as The Guy Who Misses Miami, so let's talk local endorsements," she says once we have our drinks.

"If you suggest a bikini shop…"

She snickers. "You know I have higher standards than that. But I do like the idea of a swimwear brand."

"No."

"Okay, moving on." She taps on her phone screen. "I'm sending you a hot list to consider. Give me your honest yes/no opinions."

I tug my phone out of my side pocket and open the list she's just texted me.

This is something we could do remotely, but Nina is big on vibes. And she promises she didn't just make the trip to Canada for me. She has other clients to see in Toronto and Montreal.

Despite her razzing me, it's a good list. She did her research on the area and has highlighted the biggest companies that align with things I love: hockey, pizza, and being outside.

"Also, what would you think about playing up the Boy From Buffalo angle?"

I make a face.

"Maybe next season," she says smoothly. "But the cross-border ticket sales are significant. Something for you to keep in mind."

We run through everything she wanted to talk about, then she puts her phone away and gives me a scrutinizing look. "Why are you still staying here at the hotel?"

I roll my shoulders. "There's no time to go house hunting."

"Do you want help?"

"Nah. The captain's wife got me the name of a few real estate agents. I just need to use them."

"You might feel more grounded in the community if you actually, you know, lived in it."

"I go out!" As if to punctuate my social life, such as it is, my phone's screen lights up with a notification from the Lusty app.

I was tagged in a comment by TheatreGirl.

Tapping into the app, I think maybe I'll show Nina the reviews I left. But when I read what TheatreGirl wrote on my review of this very bar, my pulse jacks up, skittering under my skin like wild horses are suddenly handed the reins.

Thanks for the reminder about this place. It was great tonight for my girls' night out.

I'm out of my seat before Nina can ask me where I'm going. I stride through the dark, lush space, searching each velvet nook for…what, I'm not sure. A gaggle of women?

On the far side of the bar, I find a small group of my teammates' wives and girlfriends, which is the right idea, but the wrong women. Shannon Tilman, Ani Hale, Harper Roberts, and Becca Kincaid all give me a friendly wave as one, and I acknowledge them, too, in a distracted way.

There's no other girls' night type of group, and I realize TheatreGirl's party is gone.

She told me as much.

Thanks for the reminder about this place, it was *great tonight.*

Was.

She was here, close enough to meet face to face, with the safety of her friends around her…and I fucking missed it.

By the time I return to the table we were using, Nina is on her feet.

"I won't take the abandonment personally," she says dryly. "But I need to get to Toronto, anyway."

"Good to see you." I sound distracted. I am distracted.

"Same. And Ty, a word of advice?" She doesn't wait for me to say if I want it or not. "Don't be afraid of unexpected bikinis."

As soon as she's gone I settle up for our drinks, then practically sprint for my room.

BEASTMODE

Next time you go to the hotel bar, let me know. I'll meet you there.

THEATREGIRL

Mmm. Hey. It was really nice! But I don't
know if I'll want to go back again soon. My
nemesis showed up.

You have a nemesis?

It's a one-sided thing. Reminds me of my ex
in annoying ways.

I convince her to tell me about the asshole who cheated on her—repeatedly, it turns out—and we don't circle back to how close we were to meeting tonight. The conversation doesn't turn sexy, either, but we still chat for an hour before saying goodnight. Three times.

THEATREGIRL

I mean it. I really do need to go to bed.

BEASTMODE

You and me both. Let's be responsible
together.

But comparing completely unhinged stories
about the nemeses who don't even know
they're the problem is more fun than
sleeping.

I can't argue with that. Let's stay up all night
and rehash who hurt us in grade five.

Stacey Farrell. She was the first person to
call me a giant. You?

That would be my father, who spent our
grocery money at the track.

Oh. Shit. I'm sorry.

I'm over it. It's been a long time since I worried about the price of groceries.

Wasn't that long ago for me. I'd hate that for a kid.

You can distract me by joining me in my dreams tonight.

Right! Bed. We're going to bed.

For real this time.

Definitely.

I grin.

THEATREGIRL

Good night.

BEASTMODE

Good night, my sexy girl.

CHAPTER 10
KILEY

Last night was the first time I ever verbalized out loud that Ty is a nemesis of sorts. Of course I didn't tell BeastMode who exactly I was talking about. For all I know, he could be a fan, and that would be awkward.

But I got to vent to someone who doesn't work for him, and isn't in love with someone who works with him.

That helped me sleep like a baby.

So, too, did BeastMode calling me his sexy girl. It's just spicy talk, of course, but I liked it. A *lot*.

The girls are all going to morning skate today, and after the cowardly way I left early last night, begging off just because I couldn't stop thinking about Ty and his bikini-clad fly-in girl, I feel like I need to go to the arena, too.

Face my nemesis head on, so to speak.

Because it's not Ty himself. It's the idea of him, all that smooth charm and confidence—plus the complete disregard for everyone else.

So I don't need to confront *the man*. Just the space where his casually perfect face decorates billowing banners.

I text the group chat and ask what they're wearing, so we can coordinate better than we did last night. Apparently it's oversized blazer and wide-legged jeans day. Conveniently, I have exactly that outfit hanging in my closet. I pair them with my favourite silky black blouse and chunky black boots, and I load Aaron Green's latest podcast onto my phone for the walk over to the arena.

It's a good, careful exploration of working in a newsroom where quoted material gets shared and used by different reporters. He navigates the line between honesty and diplomacy well, better than most would, and I'm impressed on the deep dive.

I'm not sure if he'll remember me from school, but as Puck and I stride through the side access door at the arena, I'm thinking about sending Green an email saying that I like this episode.

So it takes me a second to realize that we aren't alone as we wait for the elevator.

Ty Connor is leaning against the far wall, and he's smirking at me.

"Hey, best friend," he says.

I wonder if he's forgotten my name. I put my headphones in my pocket. "Hey, hockey player."

"What were you listening to that made you smile like that?"

Was I smiling? I am now. "A podcast."

"What about?"

I almost don't tell him. But then his gaze dips, dragging down my body, and I don't like it. It's slow and indulgent, like he didn't just have Little Miss High Maintenance on his arm and in his bed last night.

So when that gaze that knows no bounds finally makes its way back to my face, I tell him the truth. "You."

"Me?"

"And your tragic plight of not having enough hot girls in bikinis to perv on during your morning run."

Ty's eyes narrow. That worked to pop his balloon. "That wasn't the quote."

I shrug and push the elevator call button again. "Close enough."

"It was a joke about how I have to focus on work because it's *winter here*. It wasn't a dig at anything but Mother Nature. If you want to wear a bikini, I'd be happy to run laps—"

"But it's not really about the literal meaning of a quote, you know?" Why is the elevator still up on the fifth floor? "It's the figurative bruise being pushed."

He stares at me.

I sigh. "Literal means exactly what the words say, and figurative means a hyperbolic symbolism that—"

"I know the difference between literal and figurative," he snaps, cutting me off. "What do you mean, a bruise being pushed?"

The elevator arrives, and the doors slide open.

Neither of us move.

"It's not exactly a state secret that you didn't like being traded here," I finally say.

His jaw rocks back and forth, but he doesn't say anything before the elevator doors start to close. He lunges forward, thrusting his hand out to get them to re-open.

Then he presses his palm over the sensor, holding the elevator for me. Expecting me to join him.

"I won't bite," he growls under his breath when I don't step on.

I choke on a startled laugh. "Okay. But I might, so… watch out."

"I'll take my chances."

I murmur a command to Puck, and we move past Ty into the car. He takes up enough space that my arm has to brush his, and I'm grateful for the oversized blazer and its protective shoulder pads, because without it I'm sure the awkward tension might singe me.

As it is, the air in the elevator feels thick, and I swear I hold my breath the entire way up.

We make it up to the fifth floor without another word—or anyone biting anyone else. Once we're up there, he heads off in the direction of the press box, and Puck and I head the other way, to Harper's favourite place to watch the start of morning skate, way up in the rafters.

And she's not alone.

Puck dashes to Grant.

"There's my girl," he says fondly as she gives him kisses.

I scoot past him, ruffling his hair, and plunk down in the seat between him and Harper.

"You look nice," she says when we find her. Then her attention fixes on my face. "Are you okay?"

"Just had a little run-in with someone," I mutter, throwing myself into the seat next to hers.

Grant snaps his attention to me, frowning. "Who?"

I make a face. "Ty Connor."

"What's wrong with Ty?" he asks.

Everything. But nothing that I can explicitly name, so I shrug.

Harper's mouth falls open, and she takes another look at me. "Wait, what is going on? Did he say something inappropriate to you?"

"No!" Not inappropriate. "Not like that. It's just a vibe."

They exchange a look across me.

"He's kind of intense," Grant says.

"Right? You feel it, too?"

He shrugs noncommittally.

Harper shakes her head. "I feel nothing other than confusion right now." Her brows knit together. "You think he's intense?"

"I—" I frown. And stop. That's not the word I'd use.

My brother goes back to loving on his dog. "Some people are just oil and water. Kiley doesn't have to like everyone on the team."

"Except that is famously her thing, liking everyone on the team," Harper snaps back. Then she looks at me. "You don't like him?"

"It's not that I don't like him. It's that I don't trust him."

Her eyebrows shoot up. "You don't *trust* him?"

"Like I said, it's a vibe. He's a weird mix of not giving a fuck and being too charming at the same time."

She presses her lips together.

"What?"

"Well…that sounds like the job description of a professional hockey player. Off the ice, I mean. That's literally the assignment—charm people, without getting invested in what people think about them. Grant, back me up here."

Grant has gotten a text message, and is distracted by his phone. "What?"

"Never mind," I say to him. "Harper, a year ago, you

were highly suspicious of all of them." I wave down at the players spilling onto the ice now.

She smiles, a warm, secret grin that reveals just how far she's come in her impression of at least one of those players.

The thing is, I see some of those same attributes in her boyfriend. But where Kieran exudes confidence in a clearly hands-off way, Ty is more…inviting.

Like, *come touch me and get burned.*

Ugh.

"I'd probably like him more if he was like…" I deepen my voice. *"We always try to bring our A-game, and tonight we fell short of that mark. But we never lose sight of what our fans expect, I promise you that."*

"Is that…" Harper's eyes widen. "Was that a Kieran impression?"

I grin. "Good?"

"Very," she breathes, laughter. "But what would your Ty impression be?"

It's harder to summon one, because I avoid his media availability clips now. They push on some raw nerve I have. But I think about the brief conversation we had at the elevator, and then I look down at the ice. He's not down there right now. He's in an office suite around the curve of the upper mezzanine, maybe talking about it's not fair that his morning skate needs to be on ice, because we don't have palm trees and warm salt air here.

"I guess he's more like, *we have to do the work, but it might be easier if we had cheerleaders."*

Harper laughs. Then cuts herself off. "Oh. You're serious."

Grant shakes his head. "That's a terrible Ty Connor impression. Truly bad."

I don't agree. "I'd pay money to see one of the local reporters ask him about cheerleaders."

"Oh-kay." Grant pushes himself out of his seat. "I gotta go downstairs. Puck, you stay here with Kiley."

She puts her chin on my knee, and I rub her head. He rubs my head, and then he's gone.

Harper is leaning forward, engrossed in what is happening on the ice now, so I pull out my phone.

THEATREGIRL

How do you feel about cheerleaders?

He responds almost immediately.

BEASTMODE

It depends. Are you the cheerleader in question?

THEATREGIRL

I'm too tall to be a cheerleader.

There is no max height requirement in my fantasies.

But IRL... are you yay or nay on cheerleaders for pro sports teams?

This feels like a trap. I'll go with nay, because I grew up watching baseball, but if you're team yay, I can switch sides.

Sorry. Not meant to be a trap.

Would it help if I grabbed a pair of pompoms and shook my ass like I just don't care?

It would!

I gotta run. Will your lust for my pompoms wait until later?

I'll manage. Have a good day.

You too, sexy thing. You, too.

CHAPTER 11
TY

The last big splashy part of our regular season is an outdoor game against Buffalo. It's just a day trip on a bus, an hour away from Hamilton, but there's a lot of media around it, especially because it's my hometown, and it's a critical game if we want to make the playoffs.

And for the couple of days around that event, it seems like my boneheaded bikini comment and the reaction to it stays online, just weird static that doesn't really matter.

I even make a date with TheatreGirl for a few days later, once her work schedule and mine lines up with a shared day off.

The outdoor match is a snowy, magical game that we win, and by winning it, we secure our spot in the playoffs, too. Then Marsh makes it extra magical by getting down on one knee after the game, in the middle of the outdoor rink, and asking his girlfriend to marry him.

She says yes, which makes sense—I'd marry the dude, too.

They're stupid happy. The Observer sports page does a

story on them, and one could be forgiven for thinking that the discourse had moved on.

But then, two days later, I come back from practice to the hotel I'm still staying at—because it's connected to the arena by a tunnel, and I'd like to avoid winter as much as humanly possible—to find a girl in a bikini trying nervously to talk her way into my suite.

A young, nearly naked teenager.

Fuck. Me.

I back pedal so fast I probably leave smoke in my wake, and I hightail it back downstairs to find the concierge. Or security. Maybe both.

"We're very sorry, Mr. Connor," the concierge says.

"It's freezing outside," I say dumbly.

"I'm sure security will help the young lady find a coat."

"I need to make some calls. Is there a place where I could…?"

"Of course."

"And I don't want her to get in any trouble."

"Of course not, sir."

I scrub my hand over my face, then nod my thanks.

"This way, if you will. I can put you in the—" He stops as he goes to lead me toward the ballrooms and meeting rooms, which are just off the glittering foyer.

Because there are four girls, in different locations around the foyer, all wearing bikinis.

And then three more girls rise, wearing parkas that they quickly throw off.

Oh-kay.

From somewhere, there's a loud sound of a PA system being turned on, and then the opening strains of The Weeknd's "Can't Feel My Face" ring through the lobby.

I dart my eyes left and right, looking for whoever is holding the camera, because of course someone is filming this for a viral moment. There's a smirking guy near the elevators, and a girl leaning against the wall behind a potted palm, both holding cameras at suspiciously-in-my-direction angles.

Great. Fuck.

I flip the hood on my puffy jacket up over my head and duck my face. I do not want to star in a bikini studded flash mob today. Not when I'm the supposed villain.

"New plan, sir," the concierge says crisply.

He herds me into a back office behind the front desk. There's a door off the back of that room that leads into a hallway that sounds like it connects to the kitchen. Pots clatter and dishes clink, a surreal backdrop.

I push my hand into my jacket pocket to find my phone, because I'm going to need a rescue here. My fingers brush against a cool, metal keyring.

Harper's spare key.

"Can I get to the parking garage from here?" I ask suddenly.

"This way." The brisk efficiency with which he guides me there makes me think the concierge is thrilled at the idea of me removing myself from the premises, and that makes two of us.

Once I'm in my truck, I fire a quick text to Kieran.

TY

Long story, but I need to get away from the hotel sort of urgently. Would Harper mind if I lay low at her apartment?

Nobody will think of looking for me there.

KIERAN

Yeah, she says that's fine, but the rental price is you coming over for dinner and explaining why in person.

TY

Deal

Keeping a cautious eye out for bikini people, I drive into the street, then navigate my way away from downtown, into the older residential neighbourhood lined with low-lying apartment buildings and cozy homes from the turn of the last century.

I park in a now familiar spot on the street, then jog up the stairs. I take care to make sure the door locks behind me—wouldn't want to piss off the best friend again—and then let myself into Harper's apartment.

It's pretty much as I left it the last time I was in here. My pile of Miami-themed merch is stacked below the front window. Jesus Christ, if people found out about that shit, it would make BikiniGate so much worse.

I can hear Kiley Forge tsk-tsking in my ear about proverbial bruises.

After I flop out on the couch, I call one of the team's AGMs and fill them in. "I need to do something positive with the community, ASAP."

"You just keep creating goals and winning games. The rest will sort itself out."

It sounds cocky to point out that I'm not familiar with not being immediately loved by a fanbase, so I swallow that protest back. "Yeah. Right."

"Do you need us to find you a new place to stay?"

I glance around Harper's apartment, a kernel of an idea forming. "Nah, I'm good."

Maybe what I need is a bit of humble hiding.

And, as much as it pains me, I have to put off meeting up with TheatreGirl. The last thing I need is to go viral for picking up strangers on Lusty.

BEASTMODE

I hate to do this, but I can't meet up, sorry … rain check?

THEATREGIRL

Sure. Everything okay?

I might be peopled out.

Alone time is important. Sometimes I come home from work and just need quiet.

One day, we should compare stories.

She doesn't reply immediately, and when she does, I can practically hear her drawing new boundaries. Can't begrudge her that when I'm the one who just bailed.

THEATREGIRL

There's some freedom in being totally anonymous.

BEASTMODE

Sure is.

That goes both ways. I won't be nosy.

Which means we could talk about anything here…

Anything at all

> You're a very good girl, aren't you?

> I'm whatever kind of girl you want

What the fuck are you doing, Ty? I don't know. I meant to message her and explain that I was going offline for a while. *Just until I get my new team through the playoffs.*

Instead, I'm two horny messages away from sexting with a stranger.

There's some freedom in being totally anonymous, she said.

This is safer than meeting her in person. And I've wanted her for weeks now. Maybe I'm lying to myself. Maybe this is just as gluttonous as any other choice I would make. Because the truth is, I'm not good at saying no to myself or my libido.

And I want TheatreGirl.

Footsteps above me remind me I'm not in a hotel with concrete walls anymore. Quietly, I lift my head and make sure nobody can see in the window, then I release my cock and give it a rough squeeze.

BEASTMODE

> Are you alone right now?

THEATREGIRL

Yes

> Do you want to have an orgasm?

Yes

Her straightforward want is so refreshing. Yes, this is what I need right now.

How do you like to get yourself off? With
your fingers? Toys?

My fingers, usually

A mental picture of long fingers dipping between swollen pussy lips, coming up glistening before disappearing again, makes me groan and throb.

That would be a beautiful sight…where are
your fingers now?

rubbing on the outside

warming yourself up?

mmhmm

What I would do to hear that sexy sound murmured in my ear. Would she sound pleased with herself? Would there be a hitch in her voice already?

I close my eyes and stroke again, imagining that the firm cushion of the couch is TheatreGirl pressed up against my side. Both of us touching our bodies. Getting off together.

Then I blink my eyes open again and type back roughly.

BEASTMODE

Can you type and rub at the same time?

THEATREGIRL

We're going to find out… I tend to type with
two thumbs, it's faster that way. I'm taking
turns touching and typing right now.

That's hot

If I go quiet, it might be because I'm close and can't stop touching.

That's even hotter

How do you do it?

One hand on my cock. And my other hand has the phone…My thumb's long enough for one-handed typing. And I want to get you off first, so I'm not trying to get there myself, you know? That'll get me close, knowing I'm turning you on. Figuring out what you like…

I like knowing you're stroking

Picturing your fingers between your thighs makes me hard, makes me need to jack it a little

Yeah?

You're driving me crazy in a good way.

I tell her how I wish it were my fingers stroking her pussy lips, how I want to feel how soft she is there, how wet she is inside, what a wonderful secret that would be.

The private, filthy messages fly back and forth, and then her responses slow down and get shorter.

Are you getting close?

mmm yes

Fuck. Yes.

BEASTMODE

You're so sexy.

Keep going. Rub harder. Rub faster. Are you all swollen now? Do you know what I'd give to feel your slippery perfection right now?

I want to hear your whimpers. Your sweet little pants. Tell me when you're close, gorgeous. I know it's hard to text right now, but give me a sign.

nnnggg

Fuck. Thank you for that sweet little noise. You're so good.

Go on, then. Cum for me. Cover your fingers in slick.

Soak your hand and imagine me shoving your thighs open and using all of that to follow you over the edge.

Make that soft, perfect pussy fly.

I'm...

I hold my breath, my heart pounding.

THEATREGIRL

omg

I press my fist to my mouth and groan. Fuck, yeah.

BEASTMODE

good one?

Great one

Are you all messy now?

My cock throbs as I picture her glistening, all sweet and swollen for me. My words did that.

I stroke faster and harder, staring at the screen, clutching it so tight it might break, and I don't fucking care, it'll be worth it when she replies, if she replies…

Need tightens inside me, a hot, pulsing ache, so desperate for release that I could beg her, I could fall to my knees and press my face into her wet, slippery cunt and spill at her feet and it would feel like the best sex I've ever had.

But she's not here, and all I have is a screen that hasn't moved, so I can't come yet. My body climbs right to the edge and my brain starts to go fuzzy at the edges, but I can't, I can't…

THEATREGIRL

So, so messy

A low, unholy groan tears out of me, and my whole body jerks with the force of my climax. A toe-curling, spine-snapping orgasm I'm rather unprepared for, now that jizz is pooling on my belly.

Worth it, though. I manage to tug my shirt off and flop it over my still-twitching, still-hard cock. So fucking worth it.

CHAPTER 12
KILEY

Harper and Kieran have decided to get married in four months, and everything is suddenly happening all at once.

Maid of honour duties.

The team is hurtling towards the playoffs.

And I have Puck full time for the next few weeks. While she's being a very good dog indeed, she misses Grant, and we try to FaceTime as much as possible.

"You need a stay-at-home boyfriend who can dedicate himself to your dog," I tell my brother when he calls from the arena after morning skate to check in.

Puck licks my phone in agreement. A second later, it vibrates.

BEASTMODE

Having fun? Getting into trouble?

I clear my throat. "Okay, Puck, you saw your dad. Grant, I gotta go!"

"Wait...I have tickets to the home game next Saturday night. Do you want to come with me?"

"Yeah, sure, whatever." I mean, I do, but I also want him to get off the phone. "Thank you. Love you. Bye."

I tap the end call button, then make myself check my email and close out of the theatre job search page I was looking at before Grant called. *Do not rush for any man,* I remind myself. *Be cool.*

But this is a man who made me orgasm without even being in the same room as me. He deserves a little rushing.

THEATREGIRL

Sadly not on either count. I was having a pretty boring day until you messaged me, just looking at job postings.

BEASTMODE

Job postings?

I haven't found anything good yet. Probably won't.

Can I make your morning more interesting? In a PG way, I'm at work.

Absolutely.

He sends me a preview of a review he just wrote for an Italian place that has been getting mixed reception. His review is funny, kind, and just scathing enough in places to be trusted as honest.

THEATREGIRL

That's an A+ review. I'm upvoting it as soon as it's live.

BEASTMODE

I wasn't too harsh? Because I eat pasta
every single day. I'm not sure if my standard
is the same as other people's.

I giggle at the image of him bellying up to an over-flowing plate of spaghetti, packing on weight so he can go to the gym and hulk out. Or whatever people who call themselves *BeastMode* do.

We talk about everything and nothing for more than an hour. When he says he has to go, I get a weird, warm ache in my chest that feels a lot like a crush.

Stop that, Kiley. Stop that right now.

I go back to the job board, and there's a new posting. A reward for me being a responsible grown up. It's for a Production Manager full-time position for an arts centre in Utah. I could just imagine Grant and Harper's reactions if I applied for a job in Salt Lake City.

That doesn't stop me from clicking in to the details, though. I'm not exactly qualified for it, I don't have all the experience they are asking for, but it's not that far out in left field.

And most importantly, my heart beats faster when I read it. There. That's the kind of warm ache I want to have. Crushes on job postings are allowed.

I send the posting to my laptop, then glance at the clock. If we go for a long walk now, maybe I'll shake off the nervous energy and write a perfect cover letter when we get back.

I probably won't. I'll probably spend the afternoon writing horny Reylo fairy smut instead. But either way, it'll be a well earned secret indulgence.

"All right, Puckster, let's go for a walk, shall we?"

She leaps off her bed under the window and hustles to the door. I put her harness on, then attach the lead. Sunglasses for me and some baggies for picking up after Puck complete our necessary supplies. She waits patiently as I lock up the apartment, then we take the stairs, her full of enthusiastic energy, me full of nerves.

Crushes are strictly not allowed in my Slutty Year. Crushes lead to feelings, and feelings hurt.

But to be developing a crush on a guy I've never even met? Extra not cool.

At the front door, Puck barks.

"Quiet," I remind her sharply.

She looks at me as if to say, *but I see someone I know.*

I glance out the glass door just in time to see Ty staring back at me. Bright green eyes flare in surprise.

"It's the best friend again," he says, hooking his hand around the edge of the door as soon as I push it open.

To my credit, I don't say *it's the bikini-obsessed hockey player who didn't want to be traded here,* but that's mostly because that doesn't roll off the tongue the same way as best friend, and I already called him *the hockey player* once. I don't feel like playing the *Ty doesn't remember my name* game without layering on an extra burn.

I give him a cool, detached nod. "Harper says you're using her apartment as a storage locker."

"Sure, that's one way to describe it."

"What, are you moving in?" I joke.

He doesn't laugh. "Something like that."

I blink.

He shrugs. "I like her couch."

I blink again.

He shifts, bracing the door open with his thigh, making me notice how thick it is.

For a second, I think about asking him if he likes pasta. Warning him off the restaurant that BeastMode reviewed, as a kind of peace offering.

But I can't imagine Ty Connor appreciating a hilarious take down of a pretentious Italian restaurant. If he's anything like Kieran, he's got his nutritionist on speed dial and wouldn't order takeout in a million years because it's too hard to track those macros.

When I don't reply to the couch comment, he grins at my dog. "So I guess I'll see you around more often, Puck. And you, too, best—"

"My name is Kiley," I say, my voice mostly waver-free.

He frowns. "I know."

"Which is exactly what someone who forgot my name would say." I make it sound breezy. Or I hope I do. Right now I'm reeling because of course my best friend isn't going to live in her apartment ever again, and someone else does need to move in at some point, but I didn't think that point would be today, and the someone would be Ty Fucking Connor. "What happened? Was there another bikini flash mob in your hotel?"

His gaze goes steely. "Sorry to disappoint you, Kiley Forge, but this really is just about liking that couch."

After him calling me *the best friend* so many times, hearing my full name drip off his lips is an electric jolt. I don't like it.

"She'll take the couch with her when she moves," I warn.

"Then I'll buy one of my own."

If conversations on our front step could have a soundtrack, this moment would sound like a high noon shoot out in an old Western movie. Both of us sizing up the other.

And then Ty shifts and clears his throat, a hint of colour popping in his cheeks. "But, uh…if anyone asks, I'm not here."

So the bikini flash mob threat is still hanging over his head. Great.

"Sure thing." I resist rolling my eyes as I tug on Puck's lead. "Puckster, come."

The second I'm around the corner, I'm calling Harper.

"Ty Connor is moving into your apartment?"

I can practically hear her squirming as she thinks about how best to answer. "You saw him today?"

"Yes, I saw him today! With a duffle bag slung over his obnoxious shoulder."

"Oh, Kiley."

"Oh, Harper," I snap back.

She laughs. "It's just until the playoffs. Then the whole team will be moving into a hotel for the duration."

I knew that. Grant said something about that. The coach is old school and since this is their first ever playoffs together as a team, they want to do everything they can to ensure success. But there's something hilarious about Ty moving out of a hotel, into our rundown walk-up apartment for a few weeks, only to go back to a hotel again. I bet the puck bunnies will find him there, too. "They better have security for his floor."

"This will have blown over by then," she says. "Hey, listen. I'm going to my mom's to talk about wedding stuff. Do you want to come?"

I glance up at the sky, which looks clear, then down at Puck. "We just headed out for a walk. Want to meet there?

Or you can pick us up on the way, if there's a time crunch."

"No time crunch. I was planning to spend the afternoon with her. Walk up the Mountain, and I'll drive you both home when you're ready to leave."

I head for the stairs that zigzag up the front of the escarpment. We take them slowly, Puck sniffing every corner on each landing. It takes another half hour to get to the neighbourhood where Harper and I grew up. My parents have recently moved out of the city, to a small winery town on Lake Erie with a robust retirement community, but Angela Roberts still lives in her small bungalow.

The little house is a familiar space for me. I spent my teen years feeling all my feels at her kitchen table. And later, when I decided to study creative writing and journalism at university, two career paths known mostly for instability and a deep lack of real job prospects out of the gate, she was the only person who encouraged me to follow my heart.

And then I added a minor in drama, instead of business, and again she cheered me on.

I've had so many cups of tea here, when I just needed to get away from my well-meaning family.

Maybe you should go back to school for something useful.

It's a shame you didn't have a calling like your brother did.

As if wanting to create things isn't a calling.

Angela understands. She worked as a bookkeeper for years until Harper was established in her own career as a nurse. Now she's a fine arts student at the university, and she's converted Harper's old room to a sun-filled studio.

That's where she leads me after she answers the door. "Harper's in my studio. We're talking design options for the wedding invitations."

I clap my hands, excited.

Harper's face lights up when I step through the door. "Look what my mom painted!" She lifts a protective cover sheet off a hard artboard, revealing an abstract lake landscape. Blue paint streaks around the bottom of the board, blending into a yellow glow that looks like sunshine. Dark edges could be Kieran's cabin, or a forest, or both. "Imagine white calligraphy here and here…something that says *We'd be honoured to have you join us*, but is also subtle enough that someone might keep it as a piece of art."

I tip my head to the side. "I love it. Are you thinking of sending it as an art print?"

Angela waves her hand. "Oh, no—" at the same time as Harper gasps and says, "yes! Oh, Mom, *yes*, we have to do that."

I purse my lips together, thinking. "What if the invitation details are printed on a vellum overlay on top of the print?"

"That's perfect." Harper throws her arms around me. "You're so freaking smart."

I'm really not. That's her territory. Hers and Grant's. I'm so different from both of them. Harper is sweet and earnest, a serious-minded nurse who has known what she wanted to do since grade nine, when she "hired" Grant to be her science tutor. They finished first and second in the class and never looked back.

Meanwhile, I still have zero idea of what I want to do when I grow up, ignoring the fact that I'm four months away from my thirtieth birthday.

Age is just a number, and I'm still figuring out…everything. Career, life. Men. It wasn't until six months ago that it finally clicked that some guys *really* like a tall, solid girl, for example. *Will fall on their knees and be very good boys* kind of like.

I wish I'd known that before wasting a year on the wrong jerk in Vancouver. Or eight months with the loser in Calgary before that. Or—

For the umpteenth time, I stop myself from running through the complete list of failed relationships where I thought I was proving my love by sacrificing my dignity.

Never. Again.

But also, no more dwelling.

"I guess that means the next thing on our to-do list is the guest list." Harper winces. "Kieran tried to narrow down the team invite list, but we got halfway through it and he can't bring himself to cut anyone. So that's twenty-two guys, some with plus ones. And he has some friends from previous teams, guys whose weddings he attended. In total, estimating that ten percent won't be able to attend, I think there will be about forty or fifty hockey players and their dates. At the moment, we think we can find rooms for about a hundred people, split between the inn at the golf course, and setting up an RV caravan park on the edge of the cabin property. So that leaves fifty people for both sides of the family, and his family is…big."

"Wait, RV caravan park?" I cycle my hands in the air. "Walk me back through that."

"Glamping," Angela says cheerfully, producing a wedding magazine out of thin air. "Martha Stewart did a spread on it for country weddings."

"Gotcha. Cool. I'm caught up now. The plans are all happening."

Angela winked at me. "Because we have a narrow window, you see."

"Mom!" Harper protests, but then she bashfully nods. "I want to take a break from wedding planning during the playoffs. If I'm distracted, it might rub off on Kieran…we need to be fully focused."

I don't miss the way she says *we*. Before Kieran, my best friend would never have adopted a boyfriend's job as her own identity.

But it's not forever. It's just a play-off series. Two weeks at most. And then another two weeks, if they win again. Over and over again, four times at most, to get to the Stanley Cup finals.

As a Hamilton Highlanders fan, I get it.

As Harper Roberts' oldest friend, my eyebrows hit the roof. I can't help it.

She notices and gives me a *look*.

Sorry, I mouth back, then brightly say, "So, guest list?"

Angela nods. "Let's go make some tea and look at the list."

As she fusses with the kettle in the kitchen, her daughter dives into a binder of papers at the table in the narrow dining room space between the kitchen and the dining room.

The last time we sat here, Harper's relationship with Kieran was new and fragile, and we were keeping it a secret from her mom.

And now she's planning a whirlwind wedding.

She glances up and catches my eye. "What?"

"Nothing."

She pushes the binder across to me. "I don't want to ask you for too much help, but I want you involved, you know?"

"I—" I cut myself off as Angela brings mugs of tea and sets them in front of us.

She raises her eyebrows. "Everything okay?"

"I'm not rushing into this," Harper blurts out.

In unison, Angela and I go, "Ooooh."

And then we all laugh.

"Okay," I say, flipping to the guest list section of a remarkably thick binder. "So you're a little overwhelmed?"

"Shut up," she mutters warmly. "And yes. I really didn't anticipate the play-offs being so…stressful. Which is silly, in hindsight. But now we're both really attached to a wedding this summer."

"Well, it just so happens, I'm a whiz with a binder. So let's break this down into tasks that need to be done before play-offs start, and those that can be delegated to your mom and me while you're focusing on cheering Kieran on. We'll need a decision-making matrix to use until they win the Cup, and—"

Harper jumps up and circles around to hug me. "You're the best," she whispers. "Thank you."

"I'm going to make you do all the work this afternoon," I whisper back. "And then it's just going through the checklists while you wear Kieran's jersey and cheer them on to victory."

"Matching jackets, actually." She lets out a watery laugh. "With the other wives and girlfriends."

I pull back enough to give her a look.

"I know, I *know*. We'd have laughed at that a year ago."

Before everything changed.

"Shannon says it's the done thing." She sucks a big breath. "Ani's going to design them."

I like her a lot, but Shannon is a force of nature. She's been in the hockey world for a decade, and before that she was a model in New York City. So if it was just her pushing matching outfits, I'd encourage Harper to push back if she wasn't comfortable—because we've all seen those photos go semi-viral in the hockey world. The kind of spotlight Harper still isn't comfortable with.

But if Ani is designing them, that makes it harder for Harper to be a naysayer. As an Indigenous artist married to a Black hockey player, Ani gets a lot of visibility—and it's not all positive, because some people are assholes. Harper loves her, and would want to wear her design proudly.

"I bet they'll be stunning, then," I say confidently. "Speaking of the WAGs, and over-the-top Shannon plans, I don't see a bachelorette party in the binder."

Harper squeaks and buries her face in her hands.

I grin at Angela. "Is that a yes to planning a girls' trip to Vegas?"

"Not Vegas," Harper groans. "Too hot in the summer."

"But something?"

She nods.

I grab a pen and make my first note in the binder. Now I'm having fun, and depending on if BeastMode is around later, I might just get into some trouble, too. The day is looking up despite the news about my new neighbour.

CHAPTER 13

TY

It makes zero sense, and I wouldn't admit this to our medical team. They hammer us with sleep science facts on the regular, but I'm sleeping like a baby on Harper Roberts' couch.

And I'm playing better than I have all season. In the week that I've unofficially lived at her place, we've played three games and I've notched up eight points, vaulting back up the league leaderboard.

"You're having a great end to the season," Aaron Green asks me after an evening home game that we win.

I grin. "Or an excellent start to the playoffs. It's all credit to the amazing fans in this barn every night. It's really special to play here."

Every single game, I give an appreciative nod to the fans. I am going to make the people of Hamilton forget the bruise of BikiniGate and remember how good PointsFest feels instead.

When I get back to the apartment, though, my usual spot on the street in front is taken.

As magical as the couch is, the street parking situation sucks balls.

I circle the block twice, finally settling for a spot near the corner.

Is two months of accidental celibacy the point at which a man loses his mind? Surely not.

But here I am, living in a shitty second floor walk-up apartment with mediocre street parking, putting myself in close proximity with a woman who has nothing but disdain for me.

Maybe I'm developing a previously unexplored masochistic streak.

After I wedge my truck into the spot, I pull out my phone and text TheatreGirl.

BEASTMODE

Is it possible to turn into a masochist in your 30s?

I hop out, ready to relax on the couch and maybe have a late night texting sesh with TheatreGirl, when the front door on the apartment building swings open and Kiley Forge jogs down the steps with Puck in tow.

Even from a block away, I'd recognize her sharply enthusiastic bounce. Her thick, wavy brown hair is twisted up in a haphazard bun, and she's got a pair of fluffy black earmuffs on.

That's her only nod to the fact that it's fucking cold tonight. She's wearing a sweatshirt and leggings, and as much as I appreciate that kind of outfit in a selfish way, it's not warm enough for a late night in March.

I step back to my truck and grab my parka out of the back. I wasn't going to wear it to just go inside, but if I'm going to have to offer her my polar fleece team jacket in a second—

Puck barks at me.

"Shhh," Kiley says. Then her gaze follows the direction of the doggie greeting, and her expression shutters. "Oh."

"Forge," I say.

Her eyebrows raise. "Last name, eh? That's an upgrade from best friend, I suppose."

"Or a downgrade from the full name. Which I remember, by the way."

I swear she rolls her eyes in the shadows cast by the streetlights.

Leaning in, I lower my voice. "Kiley Forge."

"Do you want a gold star?"

"Tough audience," I murmur. Then I fall into step beside her.

She glances at the parka folded over my arm. "Where are you going?"

"Where are *you* going?"

Instead of an eye roll this time, I get that same look she gave me when she thought I didn't know the difference between literal and figurative. I get it; she thinks I'm a dummy.

But I'm a dummy holding a coat, and she just shivered.

She hunches her shoulders up. "Puck had to wait until I got home to go poop. She was very patient, so we're just going to take a quick walk and she'll do her business."

"Hot date?" We're at Locke Street, and I still haven't said where I'm going. Maybe she won't ask again.

She chokes on a laugh. "Not tonight." Then there's a pregnant pause. "I was at the game."

"My game?" I grin. I can't help it.

"My brother had tickets. I went for him."

"And you watched me play hockey."

"I guess." She steps forward, as if to cross the street, then stops when I follow. "Where are you going?"

"Same way you're going."

"The park?"

I hook my hand lightly behind her elbow and tug her across the street. "Yeah, it's on the way to the…grocery store."

There's that *Ty Connor is a dummy* look again. "Food emergency?"

"I could have a food emergency."

She nods like she doesn't believe. "Sure."

"What?"

"You just got out of the truck that can carry you to the grocery store pretty quickly at this time of night." She shivers again.

"Nothing gets past you." I hold out my jacket.

"I—" She cuts herself off, then sighs and reluctantly takes it. "Thanks."

I hold out my hand. "Want me to hold her leash while you put it on?"

Her gaze drops to my outstretched fingers.

"No biting," I warn.

She shoves the handle at me, barely touching my skin—but I still feel it, her warm, brisk touch. Under her sharp bristles, Kiley Forge is a hot-blooded woman. Maybe that's what makes her so snarly.

But it's harder to believe her bite—literal and figurative—is any kind of actual threat when she's taking her dog out for a late night business break, wearing nothing but soft, touchable athletic wear. And now my coat.

I hand her the leash back as soon as she settles the jacket on her shoulders. Unlike her, I don't rush the handover. However we got off on this wrong foot, it won't be corrected by matching her tone for tone.

After she yanks the leash back, I shove my hands in my pockets. "It's colder than it seemed tonight."

"If you weren't tagging along, we'd already be there." She rolls her head, and a few strands of hair fall out of her bun. "Puck is a picky pooper. She's not a fan of sidewalks."

"Makes sense."

When we get to the end of the block, I wait for her to pick a direction.

She looks at me.

I look right back.

"Did you change your mind on the groceries?"

"I guess so."

She laughs. "Okay."

"Nice night for a walk, though."

"It's really not. And I'm wearing your coat." She shoves her free hand in a pocket, as if to make a point about the parka, but then she gets a funny look on her face.

"What?"

She pulls her hand out, holding up a condom. "Always prepared?"

Only one option here, and that's to brass it out. "I never, ever skip protection."

She purses her lips and nods. "Good to know. I'll recommend you to all my less picky friends."

"Less picky!"

"The picky ones aren't likely to forgive the bikini line," she says regretfully. And she pours so much warm empathy into it, I almost forget that she's roasting me.

"The way you keep bringing it up, it almost makes me think you were in on the flash mob, Forge."

"I wouldn't wear a bikini within a hundred yards of you, Connor." She stops on the edge of a park, and Puck wriggles her hips in relief.

Great. This weird walk from hell is halfway over.

"Besides, Gen Z organizers who do stuff like that don't like to take guidance from their Millennial elders." She pulls a plastic baggie from a secret pocket on that touchable sweatshirt, ready to clean up after Puck.

"Is that just a guess?" She said it with a lot of confidence.

"What?" She rustles the plastic bag.

"Gen Z organizers."

"I saw the video. They were kids."

"But how do you know they don't take guidance from people our age?"

Everything in the park goes still.

Kiley's attention is now laser-locked on her dog.

"Did you know about it?" My voice comes out cold and hard. Good. "I know you don't like me, but at the very least, it was a distraction for the team your brother works for. Did you think about that?"

"It was discussed on an open message board." She twists around and looks at me, really looks at me, maybe for the first time on this walk. Her gaze is challenging, not cowed. "What exactly would you have me do? Tell one of the team physicians that teenagers were planning a disorganized, half-assed attempt at a flash mob with not enough people and no clear point? In your fantasy, what would Grant then do?"

Nothing. We both know it. Her brother would tell her that the team's media personnel keep an eye on that, and if there was public discussion, my beef should be with Mabel in PR for not catching it, not Kiley-who-doesn't-work-for-the-team.

But that doesn't mean I need to go out of my way to make sure that she's warm and safe while walking her dog, given that she's the type to chuckle and watch as I'm embarrassed on a national stage.

Fuck.

She leans over and scoops up Puck's deposit, neatly and efficiently tying off the bag, then taking it to a nearby garbage bin. Hand sanitizer appears from the same place the plastic bag did, and then she briskly tells Puck it's time to go home for bed.

Silence stretches between us the whole way back.

Fuck.

At the apartment building, I unlock the door and hold it for her. She stops inside just long enough to yank off my parka.

"You tried to warn me?" I ask. "The figurative bruise?"

She shrugs and shoves the coat at me. "You didn't want to be warned. And it wasn't even up to the level of a warning at that point."

I tighten my fist around the puffy down. "But at some point it got real, and you said nothing."

Exasperated, she throws her hands wide. Puck whines and circles around her, wrapping the leash around her legs— which I notice, vaguely, but I don't look down, because I can't snap my attention away from the way her breasts jiggle freely under the sweatshirt. Spectacular jiggle, in fact. More than a handful, for sure.

All my lizard brain can think is, *good access*, even though the chance of me ever getting to slide my hands under Kiley

Forge's sweatshirt to cup her sweet flesh is somewhere south of never gonna happen.

Which is exactly the wrong thing to be considering when she's snapping, "Pretty sure by that point you'd already put Little Miss High Maintenance on a plane."

"Little Who?" I jerk my head up, but not before she notices where my eyes had gotten stuck. Damn it. I swipe my free hand over my mouth, trying to reset myself. Reset the conversation. "Back up."

Her eyes blaze. "No, I don't think I will."

She twists around, in the correct direction to untangle her from the protective loop Puck had dragged around her legs, and stomps up the stairs.

God, her ass is perfection, too. Firm and round, with a promising bounce.

Why does she have all these misconceptions about my dating life?

Put someone on a *plane*?

Jesus Christ.

I sigh. "Kiley…"

She doesn't stop. She reaches my landing and keeps going, climbing the next set of stairs and then disappearing.

And for a second, I think about chasing after her and demanding a do-over on the conversation, but that would only make the situation worse.

So instead, I let myself in to the quiet, dark apartment, and stretch out on the couch. Upstairs, I can hear Puck moving around, then settling down.

Have I ever noticed Kiley and Puck above me this specifically before? Kiley heads into a room above Harper's bedroom, where I haven't gone yet. It's not really my apartment, not my place to get too comfortable.

I'm moving out in a week. Then we'll have the playoffs, and the Highlanders are taking the extreme measure of housing the entire team at hotels for the duration.

Sometimes teams do that before a make or break game. But for the entire run?

It's gotten a lot of buzz, inside and out of the team.

I'm indifferent.

Or I was, before this week. Now I'm loathe to give up this couch, and the good luck that has come from me sleeping on it.

Besides, if I have to move into a hotel again in a few days, I might not get to the bottom of the mystery puzzle that is Kiley Forge.

The fiery way she glares at me should be a warning. Instead, it feels like an invitation.

As I listen to her turn on the shower above me, I'm haunted by the look of her hair, falling out of its bun, looking like someone had given it a hard yank. And I'm bizarrely wishing that was me who had tangled my fingers into her hair and tugged her to where I need her sassy, sharp mouth.

My phone buzzes. I don't look at it right away, though. I listen to Kiley's shower. She's efficient there, too. Ten minutes later, the water turns off, and then she quietly moves around for a few moments longer before going quiet.

When I finally check the message, it's a link from TheatreGirl to a BDSM kink profile test.

THEATREGIRL

Only one way to find out, champ

I begin typing back a response telling her that it was a rhetorical question, and I am definitely not a masochist. But then I would have to explain the earlier thought that I felt like I was punishing myself by moving into Kiley's building, and that feels like a private matter between me and the smart-mouthed brat upstairs.

Besides, I don't need a test to tell me that I'm a pleasure-seeking manwhore with a penchant for morning sex and wringing endless orgasms out of women.

BEASTMODE

Have you ever taken that test?

She doesn't reply. It's late now. I've missed my window to chat with her.

Lazily, I click on it.

It starts with questions I expect. Do I like making decisions for my sexual partners? Sure, sometimes. Would I be aroused by calling a partner names? I mean…it really depends. Each question has a scale from very red for disagree to very green for a strong agree.

I tap the middle neutral yellow button for degradation.

Other than maybe pinning Kiley down and asking her if she gets off on being a harridan, I haven't ever fantasized about name calling that I can recall.

There are questions about tying up my partners, which sure, yeah, I like. But I'm surprised how very green I am about the image of completely immobilizing someone up during sex.

Again, I picture Kiley and her stern Wednesday Addams glare.

My cock twitches.

Not Kiley, dude. Literally anyone else.

I speed through a bunch of questions about watching people have sex (obviously green, that's fucking hot), being fluid depending on the relationship (just makes sense), how many fantasies I have (a lot).

Do you need to growl and howl during sex (animalistic impulses)?

"Who doesn't?" I ask myself out loud. Very green, location permitting.

Do you like to chase your partner as if they are your prey?

That gets another cock twitch. Not gonna say no to that idea at all. Green green green.

Do you recognize that disobedience can be a part of a sub's pleasure?

I have to think about that one. I'm not sure if it's how the question is worded or what, but it rankles at me that it would be up to me at all to decide what pleasure is. If a sub is bratty, and they like it, then that's part of their pleasure. End of story. At least until they meet the consequences for that disobedience, but that, too, should be a part of it.

And now I'm officially overthinking a free quiz on the internet.

Green. Be as disobedient as you want, Imaginary Partner. Get the consequence you so desire.

I finish up the last page of questions and hit the submit button.

My results load on the next page, and I frown. The top result doesn't surprise me at all—I'm 98% a voyeur, and since I've never seen a naked body I haven't wanted to watch experience pleasure, that tracks.

But the next one on the list is a Rigger, which means I'd like bondage, and…I've never done that. Not really. I have used a tie to lash someone to a bed before. And I like to pin partners down with my own hands all the time.

But rope?

The third and fourth results are Dominant and Primal - Hunter, followed by "Brat Tamer", which makes me laugh out loud.

I glance at the ceiling and smirk. Yeah, that's why Kiley and I are like oil and water.

In the middle of the list are things that I would have expected to rank higher, like Experimentalist and Exhibitionist. And all the way near the bottom, at only 9%, is Masochist.

BEASTMODE

I took it. Definitely not a masochist. Some surprising results, maybe. Let me know if you want to discuss. Until then... Sweet dreams, sexy girl.

CHAPTER 14
KILEY

All night, I dream about various clashes with Ty. In all of them, I'm wearing my shabbiest leggings and my oldest sweatshirt, and he can't stop looking at them as he lectures me about increasingly egregious wrongs.

In the last dream, the one I remember the clearest when I wake up, I lead a group of protesting teenagers into the dressing room and march around in a circle as he sneers at the fact I forgot to wear a bra.

I wake up with a jolt, my hands grabbing at my chest.

The night before comes back to me in a rush.

I did not go for a walk with Ty—and get into a fight with him, sort of? —looking like a deranged schlub.

Except I did. That's exactly what happened. He invited himself along for what was supposed to be a six minute super quick park visit under the cover of darkness.

He made me put on his coat!

And when I pulled it off, shoving it back at him, he got a good look at me at my absolute worst. Torn leggings, a faded sweatshirt...and nothing else, because as soon as I got home from the game, I yanked off my bra and pitched it across my room just as Puck reminded me she'd been very patient but she really did need to go outside.

Ty Connor doesn't notice your tits, you idiot. That's just bad dream shit.

And I wouldn't want him to, anyway.

But if he were to notice them, I'd want them to look their best, lifted and round and presented—no, not *presented*—but on display—*not on display*—but looking good. Casually so.

Do I need to wear a bra every time I leave the apartment now that he's my neighbour?

Right on cue, Puck senses that I'm awake and comes into my room. Grant doesn't let her sleep on his bed, so I maintain that same rule at my apartment.

"You're such a good girl," I murmur to her as she sets her cute little face on the edge of my mattress. "Let me put on a bra and then we'll go for a walk so you can do your business."

She cocks her head to the side.

"I know, right? I shouldn't have to put one on." I head to my dresser. "But it's sort of like armour, you know?"

Puck doesn't care.

I stop for a second when I notice the condom I set there last night.

Ty's condom.

Who keeps bonus condoms in their outerwear? Is he having a hook-up emergency that often while in the middle of a blizzard?

I pick it up.

Put it down again immediately, as if it might burn me.

The label taunts me.

Extra large
Extra feeling
Extra protection

I bet he needs extra protection. I shove it into my top drawer and grab the clothes I need for a walk.

There's no sign of life from Harper's apartment as we head outside. *Ty's apartment.*

Puck does her business, then I hurry her back upstairs.

My phone alarm is going off when we come back into the apartment. I grab it, turn the alarm off, then notice the messages from BeastMode last night about taking the kink test.

THEATREGIRL

I don't know if I'm kinky at all. What if it tells you that I'm deeply boring?

Which isn't true, of course. I'm fascinating.

Good morning, by the way.

He doesn't reply. I find a Reylo fic to read and curl up in a tight ball, hugging my pillow as I slowly scroll, soaking up the push-pull between the characters. I love fictional tension. Much more preferable to in real life tension.

I try to think of how last night would have gone differently if I were Rey and Ty was Ben, fighting his inner Kylo, and I can't put the pieces together.

Because the in real life push-pull just feels raw.

Guilt jolts my stomach.

I should have apologized. For what, I'm not entirely sure. I didn't do anything wrong. But maybe I haven't done anything right, either.

I glance at the time. Is it late enough in the morning to go downstairs? Politely knock on Ty's door and say that I'm sorry I didn't find a way to warn him, or the team's PR people, maybe.

Even if a warning wouldn't have helped, it's the right sentiment now. One can wish for a different result, even when everything that happened was out of one's control.

I wish Crys had never cheated on me, for example. Because then I wouldn't look at Ty Connor and immediately distrust a man who would later give me his coat for a dog walk.

I play back the first moments of the walk last night. Puck and I turning onto the sidewalk. Seeing Ty close the passenger door on his truck. Him falling into step beside me.

Where are you going?

Same way you're going.

Guilt prickles inside me again. But as I stand, a notification appears on my screen.

BEASTMODE

You are deeply fascinating. (Good morning)

I look at the door, then back to the phone. My heart skips a beat, and I push the guilt away.

An apology can wait until the next time I see Ty.

I give Puck a new chew toy to distract her for a while, strip off my clothes, and crawl into bed naked, just in case he's up for something hot.

THEATREGIRL

Hey! Look at us being online at the same time.

BEASTMODE

Sorry I missed you last night.

It's okay. I wasn't really in a sexy mood.

We don't always need to talk about sex. I
like to think we're becoming friends.

Yeah, same. Although if you're alone
right now…

I am. Are you?

My cheeks get hot.

Very, very alone.

Do you want to cum, sexy girl?

The inferno that suddenly combusts in my body makes
my hot cheeks look positively Arctic in comparison.

THEATREGIRL

Yes, please.

BEASTMODE

So polite. Can you say it? Say yes please,
mister. Make me cum.

Yes please, mister. Can you make me
come?

Fuck

Is that a good fuck?

Oh yes. You're so good to me. It's fucking
sweet that you write it as come. Like you're
a nice girl who would blush too much
saying cum.

I like to think of myself as a reformed nice girl, trying my
best to be wickedly selfish these days, but there's something
about BeastMode that strips the act away.

THEATREGIRL

I am blushing right now

BEASTMODE

I want to taste your blush…how far down
does it go?

I press my hand to my chest, then slowly drag it lower,
where the overheated skin turns soft and swollen.

Almost to my nipples.

Should I "come" on your nipples, sexy girl?

You can say cum. I like it…it's hot.

Good. Because you make me want to cum
so hard. My balls are full for you.

I want to make you explode this time. You
did all the typing last time.

Make me explode, huh? Your sweet little
sounds do that, don't you worry.

Mmmm.

That's it. Fuck, I wish…

Dots appear, then stop.

BEASTMODE

You can say no if you want, but I think we
can send audio messages here. You just tap
on the microphone and hold it.

I suck in a breath. And then a new message appears, this one with italicized text. *Tap to allow audio messages from this Lusty user.*

Blood roars in my ears, and my fingers shake as I accept the message.

There's a quiet click as the message starts, then silence for a beat before a warm, low, growly voice says, "Like this, sexy girl."

Hot relief zaps through me like an electric current at how nice his voice is. It's just as nice as his texting "voice". It's almost familiar, like we've talked before, but it's also shockingly, perfectly new.

Like I've uncovered a wonderful new secret.

Like I'm meeting him on a new level.

Heart in my throat, I press and hold on the microphone. "Hi," I say, then immediately swipe that off the screen.

That sounds so weak compared to his growl.

"Mmmm," I say breathily, practicing. He said he wanted to hear my sounds.

Can I just make sex noises and send that back?

Probably not yet.

I take a deep breath and hold the mic down again. "That's me," I whisper. "Your sexy girl."

His text back is instantaneous.

BEASTMODE

Fuck. Your voice is so perfect.

Same. I slide my hand down my body, to where my legs have fallen open, and my pussy is hot and wet, slick for a man I've never met.

I hit play on his recording again.

Sexy girl.

Sexy girl.

I choke on a desperate sob and tap the microphone again. "I'm…rubbing," I whisper. "Listening to…your voice."

Time slows as it sends. My fingers work their familiar magic, sliding around my clit the way I always do, automatically doing what feels good. I'm not rushing, but an orgasm builds quickly anyway, the wild heat of the moment the only spark that is needed for a blaze to catch and tear through my body.

He sends a message back. It's just breathing sounds at first, followed by a low groan. And then, in the background, I hear a rhythmic slap.

Holy shit.

He said he was stroking, but to actually hear it is next-level hot, and my blood starts to sizzle.

I smash the microphone button again and close my eyes.

"Unnnnggg." I can't think too much about how that sounds or I'll lose the edge he's pushed me to, the delicious, knife-sharp point upon which my body is teetering. "Ahhhh, gonna…" I swallow hard as my clit pulses against my fingertips. Press, press, there, oh, there… my breath catches, holding, then exhaling in a rush before gulping in air again. "Please…" I let out a sob, wishing he was here between my thighs, that it was his thumb rolling over my clit instead of my two fingers, but then I'm there, and it feels like it is him, like he's making me come, and a low keen slides out of my mouth and into my phone. It ends in a muffled moan as I press my face sideways into my pillow.

When my heart stops pounding, I look at the phone. At some point, my finger slipped off the microphone, but I recorded almost two minutes of myself. I hit send, then record another brief message.

"You made me cum," I whisper, my face so hot it hurts.

He drops a heart response on that, then two long minutes go by.

When he messages again, it's a text.

BEASTMODE

Holy Shit.

And I heard you say the u in cum.

You sexy, sexy girl. Wow.

THEATREGIRL

My heart is pounding. And I'm giggling.

I want to hear that.

Oh no.

Why not?

Let's move on.

Nope, not moving past that. What's the story there? You're so bold about...all the rest. Which I love, by the way.

Ouch. No, you're right. It's, uh...a hangup from my last relationship. My boyfriend didn't like how I always laugh after sex. I guess I'm still working on not being self-conscious about that specific piece.

The asshole who cheated on you? His judgement cannot be trusted.

I know.

Do you always laugh? Every time?

Yeah.

Even when you're alone? Rub one out and then...?

Roll over and giggle into my pillow.

FUCK.

You like?

So much. What a loser your ex was. Seriously, his loss. I bet your laugh is fucking hot.

It really is. One of my best qualities.

That's more like it. I love your confidence. Feel free to surprise me with a giggle anytime.

Okay.

hey, want to know one of my best qualities?

what?

my ability to give orgasms.

Maybe it's time to rewrite your Lusty bio,
because that's a real selling point.

There's a pause before he replies, and I wonder if that's a misstep. But then he adds a thumbs up reaction.

BEASTMODE

How often do you switch up your profile?

I tell him about how my brother is the Grindr expert, and his advice is to write a new bio and update his photos every month to keep it fresh.

THEATREGIRL

He reminds me at the start of every month. I
can poke you to do the same, if you want.

BEASTMODE

Sure. Bonus points if it's a verbal reminder
complete with a post-orgasm giggle.

CHAPTER 15
TY

"What do you mean, there's no bachelor party?" Our team captain has picked the most important topic to focus on for the eve before our first playoff game.

We're in Toronto. Of course we're playing Toronto. Fate would have it no other way for our first playoff bracket.

Their fans are going to turn out in the tens of thousands, inside and outside the arena. There's an unverified rumour going around that some Hamilton superfans had their tickets refunded by the host team, refusing them purchased seats based on postal code. Other rumours are boiling over about local Toronto haters buying tickets and selling them at seriously inflated prices to Highlanders fans. And given that the two cities are just an hour apart, it's being called the Lake Ontario Series, and the QEW Series, and the Battle of Ontario—which pulls in all Ottawa fans who are outraged they've been supplanted.

In short, the energy is good.

Very good.

The only thing better would be having home ice advantage for game one, but beggars can't be choosers, and we didn't beat Toronto in the regular season standings, so here we are.

Team dinner. Family style, in a hotel banquet hall. Early to bed tonight, easy skate in the morning, and then it's go time.

Kieran leans back in his chair with the confidence of a man who knows himself. "I said, no bachelor *trip*. We should definitely go golfing the day before the wedding."

Max is undeterred. "Do they even have strippers in northern Manitoba?"

Kieran's jovial smile doesn't shift, but his gaze turns steely. "They have golf, which is more appropriate."

The *for married men in the public eye* part is left unsaid, but still pretty loud.

Given how quickly people jumped on me for a harmless bikini joke, I can't blame him for underlining that point for his teammates.

"Becca just warned me I'll have Charlie to myself for the last weekend in June," Calhoun says. "Are you sure the girls aren't doing a bachelorette trip?"

Kieran shrugs. "Maybe I trust your fiancée more than I do my teammates."

Hooner cracks up. "Yeah, fair."

"Where are they going?" It's my first contribution to the conversation, and everyone's heads swivel in my direction.

"A spa," Max growls.

"Ah. So not raunchy, then." I shrug. "We could meet that same kind of energy. Take over Marshie's house while his wife-to-be is away being pampered, and do a poker tournament over the weekend. Hooner, you can bring your son and we could arrange a babysitter? Or will he go to sleep there?"

"Now that…" Kieran gives me a relieved look and nods. "Yeah. I'm game for that."

Everyone pulls out their phones and puts the weekend on the calendar.

As we leave the banquet hall, Kieran's closest friend on the team, Russ Armstrong, slings his arm around my shoulders. "Good redirection."

I grunt.

"Does this mean you're coming to the wedding?"

I frown. "Did you think I wouldn't?"

"You've talked a few times about going back to Miami for the whole summer."

I mean, yes, I can't fucking wait. But there are multiple direct flights between Miami and Toronto every day. "I'll be here. This is my team. We're a team."

"Fuck yeah." He squeezes me tight. "Good."

I'm still thinking about that conversation when I let myself into my room for the next three nights, but as soon as I open the Lusty app and see a green dot next to Theatre-Girl's name, it fades in importance.

BEASTMODE

What are you doing online? I thought you had a date.

THEATREGIRL

It was a dud. But now I get to spend a few minutes with you, so…the night is looking up.

You always find a way to entertain yourself, though. What were you just about to do?

LOL! You think you know me, huh?

I'm not sure I do, but I like this game, and she's given me some clues over the last few weeks. But I still make sure my guess has a touch of humour in case I'm wildly off base.

> Dill pickle popcorn and…something voyeuristic on TV. Real estate reality show.

Oooh, very close. A glass of red wine and a Dramione fan fic while I watch hockey on TV.

That gives me a jolt. I'm going to watch tonight's games, too, but I've never told her I like hockey, so… I focus on the part that won't lead to me telling her I'll be on TV tomorrow doing the same thing.

I Google Dramione, the same way I had to Google Reylo. This time it's Draco and Hermione.

BEASTMODE

> How is that close?

THEATREGIRL

Same vibes. Like an extra big cup of tea and a stack of scripts. Big flavour, big story.

> You fascinate me. Is it too pervy to ask what the fan fic is about?

Mmm, no, but if I tell you, you can't make fun of it.

> Why would I do that?

Some guys say it's too weird.

What did I tell you about the giggles? Some guys are idiots. Weird is good. Weird leads to hot sex.

Seriously, are you perfect? There's no way you're this hot in real life.

I almost tell her I'm an NHL player, and she can see for herself what I look like tomorrow if she's going to watch all the games.

Not this hot. What actual fucking nonsense.

I'm even hotter in person. Way weirder, too.

LOL

tell me about the story. Let's be weird together.

———

One week later, I wish I could go back to that night and recapture the confidence that guy had.

I was so sure I was going to jerk off twice while talking to the hottest girl I've ever met, then go to sleep, wake up, and beat an objectively better team, simply on the strength of Highlanders hope and enthusiasm.

It turns out, hope and enthusiasm are no match for a team who have perfected getting shots on goal faster than anyone else in the league. One-timers? They all have them. Systems that somehow put a screen in front of our goalie at the same time as their top scorers get the puck on the tape.

We score, too, but it's not enough.

After game one, our goalie smashed his mask into a dozen pieces.

After the next game, our second loss in Toronto, we were sent home to crawl out of a two game deficit.

We managed to win game three in overtime, by the skin of our teeth, but it's hard. We're all in our heads and it fucking sucks.

It feels like everything is on the line for tonight's game, game four. If we lose at home here, we'll be heading back up the highway to Toronto for a game where we could be eliminated.

The coaching staff rides us hard at practice.

We ride ourselves even harder, until they kick us off the ice and tell us to get some sleep.

I'm tempted to head to Harper's apartment. I've taken some good naps on her couch. And there's always the off chance I might run into Kiley, which would be the kind of fun, zingy charge I could use today.

I miss the couch.

I miss the bossy neighbour upstairs, too, in a weird way.

Instead of indulging in those selfish instincts, I swing by the room where the team lunch is set up. All season, my game day lunch has been identical. Beans and rice with grilled chicken thighs, and a green salad. It's something our chefs in Miami perfected, and the Hamilton nutrition team does their best to match.

Each bite is familiar, in the same way the pasta I'll eat before the game will be familiar. Each bite is helpful. *This is what you eat when you win*, I tell myself. *This is peak nutrition for your optimized body. Use it to fucking win.*

Then I go to my room and slide into a newer but just as familiar routine—texting with TheatreGirl.

She's not actually online right now. She's at work, so it's just me and my right hand and our most recent messages.

My cock throbs against my palm as I replay our conversation from last night.

BEASTMODE

Do you know how hard I am?

THEATREGIRL

Tell me.

Very, very hard. You do that to me.

It's the story.

It's the girl telling me the story. It's the way you know just which parts to highlight.

You're good for my ego.

I wish I had told her who I was, so she could be good for my ego, too. Now it's too late. Now I'll sound desperate.

BEASTMODE

I want to be good for every inch of you.

THEATREGIRL

I'm tall. There's a lot of inches here.

Good. More to claim. More to make mine.

I think about kissing her, sinking into her body, taking her rough and hard, so I forget that my season is on the line. I imagine that sassy mouth whispering in my ear that I'm amazing, and meaning it in every way. And I come, my phone clenched in one hand as my other milks my release from my cock.

Then I bury my head under a pillow and take the same pre-game nap I've taken a thousand times before, hoping like hell tonight will be one of those nights where everything comes together the way it's supposed to.

CHAPTER 16
KILEY

The last ten minutes of the third period, the whole arena is deadly quiet. There were boos earlier, at the end of the second period, but now the fans are just watching gravely as the team they cheered for all season falls apart in front of their eyes.

The Highlanders are going to lose. Three minutes left in the game, and they're down by three. The seconds tick away, mocking their efforts to get something going. The goalie's been pulled, and it doesn't matter that they're six on five, because Hayden immediately misses an easy pass from Jenson, turning over the puck.

And then he throws a high shoulder at the next player to zip past him, impotent rage making him foolish, drawing a penalty just as Mo Ahmadi gets them the puck back.

Fuck.

On one side of me, Becca whimpers, her hands clutching at her knees.

On the other, Harper's wool Highlanders toque is pulled

down so low her eyes are barely visible. Beside her, Ani has gone still, a frozen statue of concern.

Their matching WAG jackets are beautiful, which makes the whole tableau all the more devastating.

I was originally sitting at the end of the row, with my brother, but Max Tilman took a skate to the forearm, so Grant headed downstairs to lend a hand to the doctor on call tonight, and Shannon left her seat here to be with her husband.

I don't know what to say to my friends. The team isn't out of the series yet, but the next game will be in Toronto, and there's a strong possibility this is the last home appearance of the year.

What a horrible night.

And for the first time this season, the worst player on the ice tonight was Hayden Calhoun. Maybe the pressure got to him, or he got inside his own head. It's awful to see his girlfriend beside herself, wanting to do something, anything.

Ninety seconds now.

They put the goalie back in, no point to try to play even strength with an empty net, so now they're a man down and it's one final penalty kill to end the game with an L.

Fans are streaming out of the stands already, but we wait until the buzzer goes off.

That's it. Game over, and they're down three games to one. Back to Toronto in two more days for a make-or-break game.

Harper glances across me to Becca, then meets my own worried gaze. "We need to go check on Shannon," Harper says quietly. "Can you…"

I nod, then turn to Hayden's fiancée. "Come on." I take

her hand. "Let's go downstairs. You can be waiting for him when he needs a hug."

She nods numbly.

This is my first time joining the crush of reporters and VIPs in the wide hallway outside the dressing room after a game. Someone wearing a team lanyard recognizes Becca and directs us into a small room adjacent to the press room. It's dark, and I realize once we're inside, we can see through one-way mirrors to both the press room and the hallway outside, so we can see the players come out of the dressing room.

Jenson Hale is the first Highlander to stride out of the dressing room and cross to the podium, his dark skin still sweat-slicked, his expression somber as he takes questions like a pro. His answers are clear and sharp and honest.

"This isn't the game we wanted to play. We fell short of what we know we're capable of, and we hate that we let our fans down. It's hard to lose at home. Hard to lose any game, but this one was especially tough."

The first question was tough. "In the first two games, it seemed like defence was the bigger issue. Tonight, though, your line didn't create a single high-danger chance for a goal."

Jenson didn't blink. "Yeah, we weren't good enough. We know the math. We need to create scoring opportunities, and if we don't do that, it lets the team and fans down. We hate that. We're going to take this feeling and convert it to a win in the next game."

There are a few more questions before he's ushered back to the dressing room, and then Hayden comes out next. He looks hollowed out, and my heart squeezes for him. He's a couple years younger than Jenson, and the age gap shows in the difference in their press confidence. Jenson listened to each question, no matter how hard, and lifted his head to make eye contact with the reporters and cameras on each answer. Hayden, on the other hand, keeps his head bowed, and he needs the first question repeated.

"Sorry, can you—"

It's the same question Jenson got, which feels kind of gross to see as an observer, especially when it's twisted to be more pointed about Hayden himself. "Your line didn't create a single high-danger chance for a goal. What do you see as your role in that failure?"

Becca gasps.

Hayden shrugs. "Probably all of it. I don't know what happened out there."

I wince.

Across the wide hallway, the dressing room door opens. As if by magnetic pull, my attention is yanked in that direction as Ty steps out. He's not wearing a shirt, just a pair of low-riding team sweatpants, and damp droplets cling to his bare chest.

My whole body goes tight, even though I don't think he can see me through the one-way glass on the window.

It's been two weeks since I saw him that night and we fought. I didn't see him again before he moved out again, and now it's basically a moot point. By the time he returns next season, fans will have another player on the team to hate.

Maybe Hayden, who doesn't deserve it.

As far as bad boys of hockey go, Ty Connor fits. He's clearly not used to it, because he was beloved in Miami, but looking at him tonight through this secret portal, it's easy to see him staying in his villain era.

He jerks his chin at the press room, talking to someone I don't recognize, and the feral violence in that small, tight action takes my breath away.

He's spoiling for a fight, it looks like, and I'm shocked and spellbound, but it's also hard to look at. He's all coiled muscle and dangerous prowl. Like he's a caged cat intent on being freed, and after being on the receiving end of his disappointment that had nothing to do with losing a playoff game, I feel sorry for the press corps he's about to tear limb from limb.

As he moves to lean in the doorway of the press room, I move, too, from watching him out the side window to standing right up against the front window. He's just a few feet away from me now, a pane of glass between us.

I'm close enough to see one of the droplets of water slides into the cut groove alongside his lower abs…clinging to that taut muscle for a second before being absorbed by the waistband of his sweats.

There's a faint buzzing in my ears, and it takes me a minute to refocus on the questions being lobbed at Hayden.

The next one is a doozie. "How do you feel staying together as a team impacted on tonight's game? Did you struggle with the change?"

"I…That's hard to… We stay in hotels all the time. Maybe… I mean…" He clears his throat and shrugs, stumbling over his words. "I guess it's good to have team time. But—"

"I want to get out of here," Ty says loudly. He lifts his chin arrogantly at the team PR person. "Can I go now?"

Hayden flushes.

"No, let him finish," Becca whispers.

But there's clearly some signal from the handlers,

because he leaves the room. In the hallway, Lanyard Boy stops him and points to the room we're in.

As soon as Hayden steps inside, Becca flies over to him, wrapping her arms around his neck. He scoops his arms around her waist and picks her up, burying his face in her hair.

"I'm sorry, Bec," he whispers.

Giving them some space is a good excuse to stop looking at Ty Connor's annoyingly compelling waistband. I immediately look for the nearest exit, which is not the door he just came through. I go out the back instead, finding myself in a quiet hallway.

Closing my eyes, I draw a breath deep into my oxygen-starved lungs, then slowly let it out.

I don't really need to wait for Becca now. I think about going to find Harper, but she'll probably wait for Kieran, and then they'll go home. My brother is probably busy for a while.

I should just go home.

I turn around and take my bearings. The team medical bay is in one direction, so equipment storage is the other way.

After the brutal game they just had, I imagine the therapy rooms are jammed, and my brother will just yell at me for being underfoot, so I head for equipment. I can go out the loading dock exit.

A door crashes open in front of me, and I stop, holding my breath again. It's Ty, still shirtless and visibly irritated. He drops his head back, looking up at the ceiling for a second, then he swears under his breath and explodes forward, kicking an equipment bag off a cart, sending it smashing into the wall.

I've just turned to head the other way when he snarls, "What are you doing here?"

Maybe he's talking to someone else.

I yank open the nearest door—which is a storage room full of hockey sticks. No exit.

"Did you get lost, best friend?"

The question is a command to stop, each word a barbed lasso that freezes me in place.

I snap my head around and glare at him. "I thought you were in a rush to get home?"

He advances on me.

I back into the small storage space.

Which is the stupidest move ever, because he follows me inside, the door clicking shut behind him.

He leans back against it, his gaze hooding as he fixes his green, glittering eyes on me. "That was your big takeaway from my press conference?"

I'm not about to tell him I didn't actually watch him take questions, because my friend needed alone time to comfort her fiancé, *his* teammate. Of all the potential self-centred, egotistical takes from tonight, this has to be the worst possible one.

I flip my hair over my shoulder and square myself to him. Not backing down. Not being awed by the mighty hockey star. "My big takeaway was that you didn't let Hayden find his feet. You cut him off. You embarrassed him. The headline tomorrow will be that he doesn't have the confidence of his teammates to even answer questions."

His mouth falls open.

I prop my hands on my hips. "You didn't expect me to point that out? Thought you could follow me in here and… what?"

Slowly, he brings one hand up to push his fingers through the four games worth of playoff stubble on his usually smooth-shaven jaw. His gaze darkens. A long, glinting examination.

That's all I get. A glare, but no answer.

Not that I have any right to demand he explain himself. I've slipped into a team-only space here.

Apologize, push past him, and go home.

I don't do any of those things. The longer he stares at me, the firmer my feet plant on the floor.

When he finally speaks, it's just to ask the same question as before. He jerks his head behind him. "What were you doing out there?"

"I came down with Becca. And then I ducked out when Hayden found her. I was giving them some privacy. I just went out the wrong door, I guess." To anyone else, it might feel like a reasonable explanation, but I can feel my words bouncing off him like he's not even hearing them.

As if anything I might say will be wrong.

I know he thinks I shouldn't be here in the first place. It's all fun and games for me to hang around the team on regular season practice days. But tonight? Now that they're down three games to one in their first ever playoff series together?

This moment should be private, and I'm not a part of this closed circle.

I know that. I was respecting that.

I don't need Ty Connor's look of censure.

I twist around, wanting to break free of his fierce gaze, and I bump into a rack of hockey sticks, sending some of them tumbling to the ground. I catch two that fall against me.

"Fuck." He huffs something else that I don't catch, then he's snatching the sticks from me.

I lean over to get the ones on the floor, and he squats faster than I can. His hands bump mine, the rough, unexpected contact scalding my skin.

Jumping up, I back away and slam into the wall.

He shoves the sticks back into the stand they tumbled out of, then turns to go to the door. But he stops, his big shoulders hitching up for a beat before he whirls around and stalks back to me.

"Nobody was supposed to be here." His bare chest is heaving, his eyes wild. He's close enough for me to notice that he smells like the churning ocean, like sunshine being drowned by salty chaos. It's probably the world's most expensive body wash, and it's fucking with my head. And then on top of that is an unexpected splash of something minty, like he brushed his teeth after the game. "Nobody was supposed to see me lose my cool."

"I won't tell anyone." My voice wavers.

"Yeah?" His gaze drops to my mouth. "You're going to start keeping my secrets now, Kiley?"

I'm filled with a wild, desperate need to prove his doubt wrong. I don't like that energy, that eager desire to please him.

Ty Connor isn't a project for me to pick up. I swore up and down a year ago that I wouldn't confuse dating and helping hopeless but handsome men ever again.

If he's a hot mess who doesn't like playing here and is annoyed with his teammates, it'll come out, eventually. I don't need to do anything to help that along, but I also shouldn't cover it up.

Doing nothing is a safe middle ground.

"You having a temper tantrum isn't interesting enough to tell anyone about, I promise." I wish that came out tougher than it sounds whispered between our bodies.

His mouth twists in a faint, humourless smile. "You'd be the only person on the planet to think that."

I lift one shoulder. "It's not interesting to me."

His gaze tracks my little shrug, then drags down over my Highlanders jersey. I'm wearing Jenson's number. I bought it the day the expansion draft was announced, and he was the first player to walk onto the stage. Our hometown hero.

When he lifts his head, his eyes have taken on a new, hard gleam. "Is this a thrill for you?"

"Uh…" My mouth drops open. "No."

I go to push past him, and he catches me by the elbow. A firm, hot grip that steals my breath.

"What were you looking for back here?" His thumb strokes a circle on the inside of my upper arm, and even through my jersey, it's hot and distracting.

"Nothing."

"Are you sure? I'm in the mood to give a girl whatever she's looking for." His voice drops, turning silky. Cajoling. Seductive.

Like he's seen inside me and figured out that despite not liking him, I'm not immune to how hot he is. Probably nobody is, and I've had such a dry spell since February, if you don't count BeastMode.

My pulse skitters. I can't deny there is a part of me that wants to take Ty's anger and turn it into something productive. How can he see that in me? When we've been nothing but adversaries so far?

But I can't forget how he intruded on Hayden's stumbling interview. My slutty instincts don't trump my loyalty.

Or my newly acquired, finely honed *wrong guy* radar that Ty Connor sets off in a big way.

He's a walking, talking, why-is-he-still-touching-me red flag. The type of man I regret kissing ten out of ten times.

Which is why I'm looking at his mouth, I'm sure. Inspecting it for landmines. I shouldn't be wondering if he'd taste like toothpaste or mouthwash, when I know—*I know*—he'd taste like a mistake.

I'm in the mood to give a girl whatever she's looking for.

And tomorrow he'll be in the mood to pretend it never happened.

I wrench my arm out of his grip and plant my hand against his granite chest. Ignoring the thump of his heart against my fingertips, I push him back. "You will never have what I'm looking for," I say as firmly and clearly as I can. "I think you're despicable."

Then I shove past him, hating the vulnerable pulse in the middle of my chest.

In the hallway, the equipment bag he smashed into the wall is still lying there.

My gaze locks on the name and number stencilled on the side. *Connor 70.*

He took his frustration out on his own gear.

I hate the hot, achy confusion that spirals through my core. It reminds me of mistakes of the past, of wanting more than I ever got in return.

He reminds me of mistakes of the past.

But that's good.

That will keep me focused on not making that same kind of mistake ever again in the future.

CHAPTER 17
TY

The door slams shut in my face, and I stare at it in disbelief.

Of all the fucked-up ways I could have dealt with tonight's loss, propositioning a woman who doesn't have a very high regard for me is definitely on the list. Doing it while angry, after stalking her into a storage closet…right at the top.

Where the fuck did that come from?

Thinking with my dick, that's where.

Jesus Christ, Kiley is a smoke show when she's mad. It would be a hell of a lot of fun to carry that energy to a king-sized bed nearby. That would be a guaranteed way to forget the pain of falling to three-and-one in the series. If she didn't think I was despicable, of course.

Despicable.

Fuck. Me.

That's a problem I will have to deal with, but not tonight.

Tonight, I need to get myself under control and figure out what my teammates need.

By the time I get back to the dressing room, the press conference is over.

Tilman's been stitched up by the medical team. His arm is bandaged and in a sling, and once he makes sure that all our teammates are present, he kicks out the equipment guys. "Give us some privacy, fellas."

I'm too amped up to sit, and it feels like a lot of the guys feel the same way. As we wait for our captain to say something, we're pacing in front of our stalls. The only ones sitting are the ones who have ice on their knees and ankles.

"From here on out, it's all or nothing for every game," Max finally says. "We had a fucking fantastic season. Better than anyone expected from us. Let's live up to that in the playoffs."

Calhoun swears under his breath.

Jenson Hale, who's closest to him, mutters something about everyone having an off-game.

Hooner shakes his head. "I fucked up. Don't try to make me feel better."

I get it. There will be time for that in the summer. Right now, he feels like shit, and he needs to let that fuel him. There's no pretending you don't feel one way and just acting like you feel another. Not in sports. You have to be honest with yourself—at the very least—about what you're bringing to the ice, and find a way to use it.

"Just don't do it in the next game," I growl.

He glares at me.

I glare back.

"I fucking won't," he snaps.

"Good."

Others have things to say, and everyone listens. Some of it is harsh, too harsh, but nobody overreacts.

And all I can think as we go around the room is, *this can't be the end for us.*

A familiar sentiment I've had at various penultimate games in playoffs of the past. But *us* always meant Miami, and tonight, maybe for the first time, I really and truly feel a part of Hamilton's team.

A weird, raw guilt twists inside me for finding that deeper sense of belonging, finally, in such a crushing defeat.

Maybe Kiley Forge has my number exactly. Maybe I am despicable. Which is what I should have said to her. I should have caught her by the wrist and told her she was right.

———

BEASTMODE

How's my favourite troublemaker?

THEATREGIRL

Ugh. Weird day.

Me, too.

What do you need?

I should ask you that.

Oh, my thing isn't actually important.

Mine is...but I'm up for a distraction.

What do you want?

I can't tell her exactly.

A re-do on my trade and the choices I made in the aftermath.

Is it too much to ask for the undying adoration of a fandom? Probably.

And I definitely can't tell her I need to find a way to fix things with another woman. Someone with whom I have a totally different relationship than I have with TheatreGirl.

THEATREGIRL
You still there?

BEASTMODE
Yeah.

You want to talk about it?

No. I want to fuck and forget. This time it's me who takes a few minutes to reply.

Maybe.

Agonizing decision, huh?

Brutal day at work. I'd rather purge it from my mind.

Ah. Fair.

Do you like your job?

I love it. It's my entire life. So when I fuck up, it feels awful.

I'm sure your boss and co-workers know that, then.

How about you? It's in your name, right? Do you love working in the theatre?

I don't actually, right now. Long story.

I'm all ears.

I traded it for a healthier savings account.
Now that I'm back on my feet, I'm thinking
about leaving on another adventure.

Oh yeah?

That's complicated, though. I have a track
record of falling in love with the wrong guys,
in the wrong places, and giving up my
dreams to stay with them.

Ouch. That's not great.

Right? I know that now. Only smart
decisions from here on out.

Attagirl

And if I get homesick again, I can always
come back.

For what it's worth, I've never regretted
following my dream.

You promise to keep telling me that when I
have to do the hard thing and leave my
family behind?

Absolutely. You want to tell me more about
that dream? Or your family?

nooooo this is all about you tonight… I have
to get to bed soon, no time to unpack my
trauma

we could talk about your bed, instead

we can...

After we unpack whatever you're
dwelling on

A trap!

But a sexy one

One I will fall for every time

You show me yours and I'll show you mine

Which is a deal too tempting to pass up. I take a deep
breath and ignore the anxiety warning bells in my head that
have kept me from sharing anything like this with anyone
else. Not that I'm going to share too much. I think about how
to frame it in a universal, generic kind of way.

BEASTMODE

I feel out of control. Like work is just
happening to me, and I can't get ahead of
it. I moved from another company where I
wasn't just good at this job, but everything
worked with me, around me... Fuck, that
sounds self-centred.

THEATREGIRL

It's okay. It's just you and me. And I don't
know you, so you can say anything you
want.

I took it out on the wrong person tonight.

Oh.

Yeah, I fucked up. Said and did some things
I regret. Now my head is spinning.

Stuck on the better things you could have
said in that moment?

Exactly

That's normal

Not for me

Would tits make you feel better?

I laugh out loud. And then I'm not laughing, because another message comes through, this time with a photo attached. A long, soft looking neck. Pillowy tits, and in the corner of the carefully cropped image, the hint of one tight, tiny nipple. A pale pink tip that looks hard and pointy and perfect.

A very deliberate stealth reveal of an intimate part of her body.

I'm instantly aroused. Painfully so.

BEASTMODE

Holy fuck

THEATREGIRL

I'm sorry you had a bad day at work. It'll
probably be better after some sleep, and in
my experience, sleep comes easier after a
nice orgasm.

And then she sends me a voice memo that is sultry and sexy, a whispered fantasy that drives all thoughts out of my head and makes me come so fast it might be embarrassing if it weren't so fucking hot.

———

The next three days feel like a few hours, and a lifetime.

The series swings back to Toronto. Different hotel, same routine.

I have an emergency call with a sports psychologist I've used before. We talk about what I know to be true. My pregame routine works. My body is healthy. My skill is elite. My team is good.

I don't tell him about my storage closet encounter with Harper's best friend.

I take extra naps and fit in an extra workout.

I look at the picture of TheatreGirl's tits as often as I need to in order to stay loose. I ask her if she wants me to reciprocate, and with what.

THEATREGIRL

Are you asking me if I want a dick pic?

BEASTMODE

After that beautiful gift, you can have any photo you want. Are you an ass girl?

LOL

I want to see your hands. You can wrap one of them around whatever you want.

So she gets a dick pic after all, but you can't see my cock very well in it, because I put the hard grip of my fist front and centre.

That gets me a string of heart emojis back, which makes me leak seed all over the hand she wanted to see so badly.

I get slick at the tip all over again each time I remember how hot it was.

And at nap time before game five, I take myself in hand. She's right. I do sleep better after an orgasm.

———

But when I wake up, I'm filled with the same feeling of dread I had before game four.

I'm painfully aware of the potential to lose tonight, which is the wrong fucking focus, but I can't stop thinking about numbers I usually never give a care about.

Eighty-two games a season for ten seasons, when I've spent half of those years aiming to just stay above a .500 record and not always managing that…I know what it's like to lose.

But it was never this confusing.

When Miami lost a game, it was because someone was injured or because the other team was better.

The other team is just better here.

Fuck, that makes me roar with anger, because no, they aren't. Well, yes, they are, maybe. If you squint. If you're selective about which stats you look at.

But Toronto's defensive systems crumble if you look at them funny. Why aren't we creating more scoring chances?

The coaches drilled us hard on that yesterday.

It's not like we aren't *thinking* about it.

Something isn't clicking, though. I know it in my gut, and I hate that I can't dredge up the necessary confidence to burn that traitorous thought to ash.

At the arena, I head to the visitors' locker room first and find Calhoun, Ahmadi and Watanabe with their heads pressed together.

"What's up?"

They jump apart. Calhoun looks flustered. "Nothing."

Ahmadi rolls his eyes. "Not nothing. The kid wants to try smelling salts."

"No," I snap. "Don't change your routine today. You ever done them before?"

Hayden makes a face. "No."

"Don't start today. You'll puke all over the boards."

"That's what I'm telling him," Mo says.

I throw a pointed glare at Hiro. "And you?"

He shamelessly shrugs. "Can't fucking hurt."

"Pretty sure gagging hurts," I say. "And it's not like Hooner is short on energy."

"But I fucked the bed last game and—" Calhoun cuts himself off, but the desperate look in his eyes finishes the plea, anyway. He'd do anything to avoid facing the press again, feeling humiliated.

Like I'd let him be dragged out there.

If we lose tonight, I'll make sure I'm the next one to the podium after Jenson.

The captain is out for the series now, so that leaves the alternate captains to carry the responsibility of talking to the press every single game. The way Hale and Marsh have it worked out is that Jenson starts the press conferences and Kieran wraps them up, bookending the media availability with the right messages. The rest of us, it's sort of optional. At my pay grade, it's not really optional at all, and I accept that.

Calhoun, though? On an entry level contract?

This team needs to train him better at that stuff, and protect him until he gets it. I had to distract the press with a show after the last game. I'd rather not do that again. There's only so much cocky that can be forgiven before one gets a locked-in reputation as an actual prick.

Marsh finds us next, and backs me up.

We're not changing anything. We're doubling down on what we know works.

And then it's game time.

We play better than we have yet in the playoffs. Our systems are tight, our chances are good, and we get a lot of great looks on Toronto's net. We even turn two of them into goals.

It's not enough.

We push it to a desperate double overtime, but the Hamilton Highlanders are eliminated in the first round of playoffs in five games.

We only managed one solitary win in a series we should have at least been able to push to the full seven. We should have been able to win it.

But we don't win.

The only silver lining on the night is that Calhoun scored the tying goal that got us into overtime. The final goal for our team is his, and that will be the story of how his first full season in the big show went down.

It's a better ending for him than it could have been.

For me…it might be the worst playoffs I've ever seen.

Fuck.

CHAPTER 18
KILEY

Fuck no. Do you put ketchup on your Mac
and cheese?

Are we no longer friends?

Nothing will ever come between us. Not
even that. But no, I'm a black pepper and
tuna girl.

Excuse me. Tuna?

Tuna.

You judge me for ketchup while you put
tuna in your Mac and cheese?

People put lobster in it and sell it for $30
a pop!

And now you're comparing lobster to tuna.

They both come from the sea

Are we no longer friends?

Does it make it better or worse that I add
peas to it?

You turn Mac and cheese into tuna
casserole

What can I say, I grew up poor. That was
fancy food.

Fair enough! I think I made a list of comfort
food last year after I moved back…you can
find it under lists on my profile.

Or you could tag me in the comments.

Oooh, taking our situationship to the next level, a public tag.

Is that what we have? A "situationship"?

I'm not sure what we have. But whatever it is, I think we just survived our first fight.

And we're stronger for it, KetchupGirl.

The day after the team is eliminated from the playoffs, Ty moves back into Harper's apartment. I see him from a distance, shoulders hunched up to his ears, and I give him a wide berth.

When Grant picks up Puck, he tells me the players have a day off, then tomorrow they'll do end-of-season inter-views and final press availability before they get the summer off.

In the late afternoon, Harper texts me to say that Kieran is getting together with his teammates for the evening.

KILEY

Excellent. I've got the wedding binder to hand back to you.

HARPER

Wine at my place?

By your place, do you mean the apartment that a grumpy hockey player is squatting in, or...

Or the very comfortable house with a fully stocked wine fridge?

I'm not over the fact that you've moved in
with a boy yet

I know

Are you going to invite the other girls?

If you don't mind?

Not at all...we can plan the bachelorette
weekend in more detail!

———

It turns out that Shannon is on some kind of detox cleanse and Ani, blushing, tells us they've started to try to get pregnant, so she doesn't want any wine either.

So instead of opening a bottle of red and a bottle of white, Harper digs out some fancy tea options, and we put on the kettle.

"You know what this reminds me of?" I say after the whistle goes, as I'm still trying to decide between the English breakfast and the Queen Anne afternoon blend. I wiggle both packets at her. "That first tea you made me when we finally arrived back in Hamilton."

"I bought the fanciest tea," she told me. "Come home and we'll have a tea party."

The promise of that tea party sustained me through the two days it took Harper to get a flight.

In that time, Crys tried pleading and threatening, as well as the old classic, gaslighting. I wasn't swayed, but I felt bruised and broken by the time she arrived.

Of course, when we picked my car up from the mechanic and drove it to Commercial Drive to load up, my slimy ex was nowhere to be seen. For all his bluster, he didn't try to fight for me at all.

"*Think of the tea party,*" Harper had said.

When my check engine light came on in Saskatchewan, we just started chanting, "*Think of the tea party.*"

"It's hard to believe that was only a year ago. So much has happened since then. And look at us now," I murmur as the other girls busy themselves making tea. "We won't have to lift a finger when you move the rest of your stuff from your apartment to here."

Definitely a lifestyle glow up power move.

Harper gives me a soft, happy smile. "We can do a load for old times' sake if you want."

I crack up. "I'm good."

We're still snickering when my phone lights up. It's a Lusty notification. The second she gets pulled away to find some non-dairy milk, I swipe in to the app, and sure enough, it's a DM from BeastMode.

BEASTMODE

What are you wearing?

THEATREGIRL

Why do guys always ask that?

I haven't asked you before

Fair point

He sends an evil-looking devil emoji next.

BEASTMODE

But I'm asking now

THEATREGIRL

We're never wearing anything sexy

Everything is sexy. Are you in a penguin
onesie?

I'm out with a friend

Is that code for a date?

Not tonight

Good. Save the penguin onesie for our first
date, I'd love that.

No you wouldn't!

What's not to like? Soft, warm, and a single
long zipper? Easy access to your boobs.

Sorry to disappoint, but I don't have a
boob-access zipper on

Are you in a three-piece suit? Something
formal?

Totally. A sequin-covered ball gown.

Panties?

Before I answer…what are you doing
right now?

Waiting for a meeting to start.

Two can play the evil game. I send him back an angel
emoji.

"I know that face." Harper, suddenly in front of me, twirls her finger in an assessing circle. I flip to a random anything-other-than-Lusty app as she continues, "That is your *I got a match on Tinder* face."

Impossible. I haven't had a good match on Tinder in months. And it's not like I'm not trying. It's just that Beast-Mode puts everyone else to shame.

Which is why I should never meet him in person. There is no way that's going to end well, and my tender soul has had enough heartbreak from pretty boys for a lifetime.

Not that I know for a fact he's pretty. I haven't seen his face—I don't want to. His body is more than pretty enough to obliterate my boundaries.

And I am nine months into a year-long plan to reclaim my body, reclaim my sexuality, reclaim my sense of self-worth. That plan is more important than any man, no matter how funny he might be or how many carefully defined ridges there might be on his six-pack.

Eight-pack, probably.

Well, I wouldn't know, because in the only photo he shared (of his hand wrapped around his impressive-looking cock) his mid-section was partially obscured, and I'm never going to ask for another one.

He works out a lot, though, as his name would suggest.

Harper's gaze narrows in on my phone. "Yeah, I need to see whoever put that look on your face."

"There's no look." I turn my phone over and show her the screen. It's an astrology app. "See?"

"Today is a day for massive change," she reads out. "Well, that's true."

I'm saved from further explanation by Harper getting a text message from Kieran. She smiles to herself, and that's a good excuse to get out the binder.

Planning wedding-related events is a lot of fun when money is no object, and before I know it, a whole bachelorette weekend is organized—even with semi-frequent interruptions as Kieran texts Harper a blow-by-blow of the team meeting he's having.

"Perfect timing," Harper murmurs, glancing at her phone for the tenth time (at least). "We might need to go rescue our husbands, friends. They've worked their way through a thousand-dollar bottle of scotch that Max brought, and have headed downtown."

CHAPTER 19
TY

We spill out of a few Uber XLs in front of a bar that Kieran likes. It promises arcade games and pizza.

"Guys, I cannot stress enough that we cannot look like we don't care about having lost the series," he reminds us.

That's an important message for the young guys, who have bounced back faster than those of us who only have a few more years to win a Cup.

Me?

I'm going to be a miserable ass all night. Zero chance of anyone recording me whooping it up tonight.

The only mistake I'm going to make is drinking so much I regret waking up tomorrow. And I might not yet be an expert on what makes Hamilton hockey fans tick yet, but I'm willing to bet another bottle of Max's best Macallan that the average bud would commiserate with my need to get blurry.

Inside, Kieran greets a bartender. We both hand over our credit cards at the same time.

"A round for the house," I say.

Kieran nods. "I'll get a second one in an hour."

"Sorry about the way the season ended," the bartender says.

"Thanks." It's a word that will grind out of me a dozen times over the next two hours.

———

I'm playing Pac-Man with Jenson when he twists his head to the side, game forgotten, and fixes his attention at the door.

"The girls are here," he says, his dark face lighting up in a way that I can't relate to at all. "I'm gonna get dragged home in a minute."

"Dragged?" I snort. "You look pretty willing."

"Damn straight." His grin turns wicked. "Ani's finally ready to try for a baby."

This kid is six years younger than me.

Sure, he just signed a ten-million-dollar-a-year contract for the next five seasons, so he's more than capable of providing for a family financially.

But emotionally?

I'm not saying Jenson can't do it. He seems like a fucking good husband. I'm sure he'll be a stellar dad.

I just can't imagine making that kind of decision, when I can't even win a fucking championship for my team.

He hooks his arm around Calhoun's shoulders, giving him a bear hug before squishing Watanabe next. "I'll see you guys tomorrow. We're a united front, remember?"

They tackle him again, then get back to their game. Since my own game has now been abandoned, I might as well take a piss.

A cute waitress who already brought me a drink—or two?—appears next to me. "Need anything?"

It's a clear offer.

And why the fuck shouldn't I take her up on it?

Except I won't. I haven't, for months, not since the Daffodil incident.

"Little boys' rooms back there?" I ask instead, gesturing in the direction of a hallway.

She blushes. "You got it. All the way to the back and on the right."

As I amble away from the crowd, from my teammates and their loving wives, all coming to collect them, I think about texting TheatreGirl.

But she told me she was busy tonight.

She didn't want to tell me what she was wearing.

Why was that too far?

She's sent me a photo of her nipple, for Christ's sake.

Perfect little peak it was, too.

"I don't understand women," I say out loud as I sway to a stop in front of the urinals.

"Same, buddy," some random guy says back. I don't even see him, but I'm glad I'm not alone.

I take my time washing my hands, studying the asshole in the mirror who could have done something really fucking amazing this season, but didn't because he was too caught up in his own fucking head.

"You're a fucking idiot," I tell him.

He's not impressed with me, either.

Back in the hallway, I take a slow breath. No more drinks. Tomorrow is exit interviews. The day after that, I need to find a place to live for real. A place I can bring women back to for the night and not worry about being caught on camera.

Or even worse, running into—

Suddenly Kiley Forge is in front of me, all flashing eyes. Her hair is up in a ponytail today, with dark bangs carefully set in place.

"Oh hello, Wednesday Addams," I slur.

"You're drunk," she says.

"You're pretty," I say.

And then I remember that the last time we were alone together, it was Not Good. She called me despicable.

So I make an exaggerated play of getting out of her way, and I bump into the wall. "I'm sorry."

Her eyebrow curves up. "To the wall?"

"To you."

"For what?"

"Many, many things." I exhale roughly.

Her eyes narrow. "How drunk are you?"

"Why?"

"I'm slightly sorry, too," she mutters.

I hear her, but I'm not a hundred percent sure I heard right. Also, I want to hear it again. "Pardon?"

She rolls her eyes. "I only want to say it if you'll remember."

"I'll definitely remember this," I promise her.

She holds her breath for a second, then brings her gaze back down to meet mine. "I'm sorry for some things."

"That makes two of us." I hold up a couple fingers. Maybe two. I hope it's two.

Her lips plump up, pursing. Pretty mouth. "Can you itemize them? The things you're sorry for?"

"Not at this precise moment." The words drawl out of me, slow like molasses. "But that doesn't mean I don't know what they are. Can we circle back to this at another time?"

There's a beat of silence, then she laughs out loud. It's a

beautiful laugh, and it goes on and on, then fades. She tips her head to the side. "Circle back?"

I shrug.

That makes her laugh again.

"Your face," she breathes between giggles. "You're *so* drunk, aren't you?"

I give her a shameless grin. "Yeah."

"Circle back to this at another time." She wipes her eyes. "That's good."

I try to latch on to something similar that might make her laugh again. "I'll put you on my calendar."

She nods, her smile growing. Whiskey goggles make it look almost endearing. "Yes, definitely."

I give her another line. "We can do a three-sixty review on where things went wrong between us."

Her shoulders shaking, she steps back and leans against the opposite wall. "Oh my God," she whispers, tipping her head up to the ceiling. "I like you so much more when you're drunk. And not angry."

I wince.

There's a long, silent pause, then she slowly lowers her chin and looks at me, really looks at me. "I think I understand why you got mad, though."

I shrug. It doesn't matter. The season is over.

"You didn't need to hit on me," she finally says. "That's... The rest of it, I understand. But being used like that is a trigger for me. Guys that look like you manipulating girls that look like me to get what they want."

"That's some bullshit," I say. I'm so tired. And horny. Even though my dick likely won't work after all the whiskey, I'm fucking aching, and this bombshell of a woman just said *girls that look like me*, and I don't even know what to say to that.

So I don't say anything, and instead I cross to her and bracket my arm beside her head.

She's almost as tall as me, warm and solid between me and the wall, and she smells like spicy honey tonight.

It makes my head spin.

"I will never manipulate you to get what I want. That's not in my DNA. I don't know what that history is that makes you look at me and see someone else, but I'm not that guy."

"You're a lot like him."

"You don't even know me."

"I don't want to know you," she breathes. "I don't want…"

Her gaze has dropped to my mouth, so I don't believe her. Liquid courage makes me stupid, or stupidly brave, because I reach for her, my hand finding her hip—nice—and then her hand—also nice.

She jerks against my touch, a start of surprise, but she doesn't pull away. Her fingers are fucking soft against mine. I don't tangle our fingers together, just rub mine back and forth against hers. Knuckles bumping, skin getting used to a new touch.

In my chest, my heart thuds hard and heavy.

"Tell me everything you don't want," I whisper.

A shiver rolls through her.

"I bet you don't want me to tell you again how pretty you are." I lick my lips, because she's looking at them, and because she smells good, and because I'm thirsty. Not for something I can find in a glass. I've had enough of that tonight.

I want to drink Kiley up, instead.

"I bet—"

"Stop," she whispers.

I drag in one final, regretful pull of her spicy honey scent, and step back. "Okay, pretty girl."

She glares at me, which makes me grin.

"You know, Kiley Forge, most people like me."

"I'm not most people."

"Oh, I'm aware. You're very special."

A little laugh of disbelief slides out of her. "Why are you doing this?"

"I can't stop myself."

"Glutton for punishment?"

"Not a glutton at all, anymore. Not sure what happened." Except I do. It's her, it's this city, it's this team. It's my growing friendship with TheatreGirl, who at one point was the only person in Hamilton who liked me, and that meant more than she'd ever know.

I left the man I used to be in Miami, and I might not find him again until I head there at the end of the week.

Maybe in Hamilton, Ontario, I'm the kind of guy to moon over tall bombshells with serious disdain for me.

I try to make a mental note to ask TheatreGirl if she ever feels disdain for me, but I fear I might not remember when I'm sober.

I shake my head. "Ignore me. I'm drunk."

"That explains why you led with the pretty line."

That makes me frown. "You're always pretty."

She rolls her eyes. "Okay."

"Hey." I catch her arm, my hand going to her elbow, my thumb fitting perfectly over the curve there. She's warm and responsive, her pulse jumping against my touch, and that just makes me want to tell her she's pretty all over again, so fucking pretty. I lean in so we're eye to eye, so Wednesday Fucking Addams knows I'm fucking serious. "You're a bombshell."

She rocks back on her heels, her tits bouncing. "What's your game, here?"

"Why the fuck would I have a game here?"

She tips her head forward, so our foreheads are almost touching. "Because you're a player who always has something going on."

"Not lately. It was nothing but hockey and now it's just nothing." I try to focus on her face, but I can't. We're too close. And the wall is right behind her.

Laughing under my breath, I drop my head to her shoulder. Fuck, she smells good.

"Do I?" She's laughing at me.

But I'm smiling, so it's like she's laughing with me. "Did I say that out loud?"

"Come on, Ty, let's get you home."

"Did you come to rescue me?" I lift my head again, and she's right there.

Big eyes. Dark hair.

The bossiest mouth I've ever been this close to.

"I don't need rescuing."

"What do you need?" The question whispers out of her.

The air between us takes on a new charge.

I swallow hard and try not to look at her lips.

I fail.

"Oh." She sucks in a surprised breath.

"It's not—"

"Fuck it," she breathes.

She pulls me in, slanting her head, and she presses that bossy, perfect mouth against my lips.

It's soft at first, like she's surprised she's done it and isn't sure what to do next.

My hands fall to her hips, needing to hold on to her but not wanting to take over.

I want to take over so fucking bad.

Then she exhales and the whole feel of the embrace shifts. She turns demanding, a kiss that stakes itself out, that grabs hold and takes and takes and takes.

She licks into my mouth like she's a girl who has secret needs herself.

That's all this is. This is filling a dry well, this is satisfying a physical frustration. I can taste it.

For Kiley, this kiss isn't personal. It's as close to business as one can get with one's tongue in another's mouth.

I am incidental to the kiss, which is more of a punishment than if she tried to make this an actual punishment.

Because for me, this is mind-blowing, life-altering, and shocking on an elemental level. The power of it winds tight, creating a desperate need for more.

My hands curve around her full hips and draw her close. My thigh finds its way between her legs.

Even as I feel her getting her fill, easing back, being done, all I want to do is press her into the wall and stretch this out.

But this kiss could never be enough.

Too soon, her tongue slips away from mine, leaving my mouth hollow and empty.

And because she's sober and I'm not, she has no problem extricating my leg from between her thighs before I get a chance to do anything good with it.

"No more of this push pull," she whispers against my lips. "Tomorrow, we're two new people. Just neighbours, okay?"

"Yeah," I say hoarsely, because what else should I say? *Kiss me again, please. Take me home and kiss me all night. Why isn't your mouth attached to mine right now?*

But I don't beg for kisses from women who don't want to give them.

"Are you okay to get home by yourself?" She asks it quietly. Politely.

Clearly saying that even thought we're going back to the same building, she'd rather not get in an Uber with me and my mouth.

"Yeah," I say hoarsely.

"See you round, neighbour." She ducks past me.

I watch her walk away, stunned at myself that all I could manage was saying *yeah* twice.

At least neighbour sounds better than despicable.

CHAPTER 20
KILEY

By the time I get home, Ty has followed me on Instagram, and commented on my latest photo, a mirror selfie of an outfit I love, ripped jeans and a blazer combo.

The fit is smokin! he wrote.

I give it a heart, because I acknowledge all the comments on my posts, but I don't follow him back. Boundaries, buddy. We are not flirting. You are not going to slide into my DMs so I can be a dirty hookup.

Not that I'm opposed to a dirty hookup, but I'm not into that with someone who I'm going to have to see at my best friend's house for the rest of time.

Then I open Tinder and swipe right on as many reasonably attractive men as I can, my mind racing with surreal thoughts and pointed recriminations.

You did not just kiss Ty Connor.

Why the fuck did you just kiss Ty Connor?

Don't first name, last name him. He doesn't deserve that respect.

How dare he call me pretty? How dare he kiss me back?

How dare he put his tongue in my mouth and make me feel things? That is not the deal I've made with the universe. I am not supposed to know what that feels like.

I should send BeastMode a message, too, because he's actually who I wish I had kissed tonight, and he's the only person I should be swiping right on, too.

Something changed tonight.

And not just because of the kiss.

Something happened while I watched Harper and Kieran text back and forth, while we planned her wedding to the love of her life, and then when we went as a girl gang to rescue him and his teammates.

My heart softened to the idea of dating again. Not hooking up, not adding a few more notches to my belt on this year of being slutty, but having a boyfriend again.

It might be time.

I might be ready.

If my year of being slutty has extended as far as kissing Ty Fucking Connor, I can probably consider it a failed project.

Time for Project 2.0.

A boyfriend project.

THEATREGIRL

Hey, I know we've circled around this a few times, but...do you want to meet up?

———

I try not to take it personally that BeastMode doesn't reply.

A day goes by, and I check the Lusty app more than I'd like to admit.

It's fine.

We don't know each other.

He could be travelling for work again for all I know.

His silence makes it easier for me, a couple of days later, to accept a date with an electrician named Ben. I'm not excited by Ben. Looking at his pictures, I'm not even sure I could ever get excited about kissing him, although he has a nice-looking mouth and strong arms.

Plus, he's funny. And he's a dog guy.

Maybe I just need to meet him in person.

I have to take the bus, so I'm in a rush by the time I get home. I only have half an hour to shower and get changed before I'm supposed to meet Ben at the coffee shop around the corner.

So of course I almost barrel into Ty.

He's coming out of Harper's apartment. *His apartment.* Looking like a shampoo model, effortlessly making a Henley look ridiculously good.

"Forge," he says carefully.

"Connor." I wheeze, because I'm out of breath.

So far, so good. We're both respecting the bounds of neighbourly conduct. Zero mention of The Kiss.

He catches me by the arm, heat singing my skin where his fingers have wrapped around my elbow. "Hey."

That's less neighbourly.

"Can't talk." This is true on more than one level, since my lungs hurt. "Gotta go."

"What's the emergency?" He lets go and looks at my scrubs, then up to what I can only assume is a disaster of a ponytail. Sweaty, frizzy, frazzled. That's me at my finest.

"No emergency." I press my hand to my side and force

myself to take slower breaths. "What are you doing? Leaving the country soon?"

In the next fifteen minutes would be super convenient.

"Heading out for dinner," he says slowly. "Sorry to disappoint, Forge."

"Harper promises me you're going to Miami for the summer."

His eyebrows pop up for a beat, then relax. "Does she? I'm going to her place for dinner. Do you want to come along and we can discuss my travel plans as a group?"

Shit.

"It was more of a casual aside," I say breezily.

He nods. "She wasn't wrong. I'm leaving tomorrow."

"Good." It just comes out, but whatever. It's the truth. It is good that he'll be gone for a while. I shouldn't have to pretend otherwise.

He presses his hand to his chest. "Ouch." But then his expression clears, and his mock pain is replaced with a genuinely cocky grin. "Listen, I want to ask you—"

"Nope, I gotta go." I scoot around him and take the stairs two at a time. Now that I've caught my breath, the escape is easy. And then, just before I duck into my apartment, I remember it was my idea for us to be nice neighbours. I lean back around the stairwell wall and give him a bright smile. "Have a great summer!"

While my shower heats up, I crack the bathroom window because my steam vent has stopped working. By the time I get out of the shower and am wriggling into my cutest casual underwear, there's a text message from my bestie.

HARPER

Please play nice with Ty.

KILEY

Did he tattle on me?

He said you brushed him off. You could
have come with him for dinner, you know.

Get in a vehicle with the ego? I don't
think so.

Kiley!

Harper!

I can't believe you'd pass up dinner just to
avoid spending time with Ty. You're being
childish.

I roll my eyes.

KILEY

As a matter of fact, I have a date. Okay?
Love you. I'll be nicer to Ty when he comes
back.

HARPER

oh! Okay. Love you, too. Where are you
going?

I tell her the name of the bar we're meeting at, then I put my phone in my purse and finish getting dressed. As it's a gorgeous spring evening, I put on a black sundress that makes my tits look amazing, then add a wrap sweater so I won't be cold on the way back.

I see Ben as soon as I walk into the bar on Locke Street. He looks exactly like his profile photo, and he's watching the entrance from a table up against the front window.

Warm hazel eyes crinkle at me as I wave. He smiles,

revealing even white teeth, and his freckled cheeks round in a really nice way. "I'm Ben."

I hold out my hand.

His eyebrows curve up, amused, and he wraps his fingers around mine, his grip firm, his palm nice and warm. Not sweaty at all.

He's an inch or two taller than me, and he has a close-cropped beard.

There is literally nothing wrong with this man, Kiley Jane Forge. He ticks every possible box you might measure him against.

I take a deep breath. "Nice to meet you in person."

He holds out a chair for me, then tells me about the beer they have on tap, and the cocktail he was considering having. "If you're going to have a drink?"

"Absolutely." I skim the menu that I'm already familiar with. They always have a seasonal sangria that's good. But maybe I need something stronger tonight. "I might have an Old Fashioned."

He chuckles under his breath. "Great minds."

"Yeah?" I slide him a sideways glance and smile.

He explains a pretty detailed theory about why he thinks it's the best first date drink of choice, which is both funny and logical.

We place our order, then dig into what else we have in common. Dogs, herbal tea, pizza as the perfect midnight snack, red wine, hiking.

And hockey.

He blushes when he admits he's a huge Highlanders fan, and he cried the night they were eliminated from the playoffs.

I cover his hand with mine. "A lot of people did."

He nods. "Did you get to any of the games this year?"

"Yep." I hesitate. I wouldn't reveal this to a one-night stand, but if we're auditioning people for the role of Potential Boyfriends, there's no point in hiding Grant's job. "Actually, my brother works for the team. He's a doctor."

"Oh!" Ben's eyes flare with a new level of interest.

Great.

Once again, Kiley Forge is not nearly as hot as Kiley Forge, sister of Grant Forge, best friend of Harper Roberts.

Why did I think this would be different?

But then Ben tamps it down. Visibly. He gives me a sheepish smile. "Sorry, that is cool. But it's not as cool as getting to share a drink with you."

"I… Thank you." I lift my glass and cheers him.

"You get that a lot?"

"More than you could ever know."

One eyebrow curves up. "More for me to discover?"

I smile, then hide it by taking a sip.

He chuckles. "I'll take that as a maybe."

Tentative warmth starts to curl and stretch inside me. "It's a maybe."

This time, it's Ben who reaches for my hand. His fingers tangle in mine, and there's a lot to like about the way that feels.

Give this guy a shot, Kiley Jane Forge.

"Let's do this again," he says. "Sooner than later, if I get to pick."

Oh, that's nice.

"I'd like—" I cut myself off.

Ty is outside, walking up to the door.

No.

But yes. He pulls the door open and steps inside, his gaze sweeping the place and quickly landing on me. And Ben.

And Ben's hand on mine.

For a second, I imagine his gaze narrowing, and there's this wild *what the fuck* reaction that starts to brew in my heart.

But then whatever I thought I saw is gone, and he's just grinning.

He calls out my name, as if he's just accidentally run across me in this bar. As if we're friends.

Ben follows the line of my attention. His fingers tighten down on mine as he recognizes the person walking towards us. "That's…"

"Yep," I say, popping the p.

Ben stands.

I don't.

Ty grabs a chair. "Do you guys mind if I join you?"

"Yes," I say.

"Not at all," says Ben. Then he glances at me guiltily. "Or maybe…"

I wave my hand. "I bet Ty isn't going to stay long, right?"

"How do you… Oh, your brother?" Ben nods, answering his own question.

I'm not about to explain the rest of it. "It's a small city."

"This is really cool," my date says, looking like he wants to kiss the man who I kissed just a few nights ago.

If this were fan fic, we'd all end up together in bed.

As this is real life, I'm going home alone to investigate hockey player-shaped voodoo dolls.

"Did I interrupt a date?" Ty asks.

"Yes," I say. Again.

Ben pauses, the drinks menu halfway across the table in Ty's direction. Like he just remembered that yes, this is a date.

And I swear Ty's laughing on the inside as he waves off the menu. "It looks like you guys are almost done, so I won't bother."

"We could have another," Ben offers.

I shake my head. "I should get going soon." I gesture between them. "Would you like a photo together?"

This time, I don't imagine Ty's eyes narrowing at me.

I give him a very genuine smile as Ben hands over his phone. "And I bet Ty would love to hear about where you were for each of the playoff games." I look directly at the interloper. "Ben watched them all."

Ben looks like he's holding his breath, waiting to see if I share the fact that he cried.

I don't. That's a nice secret between us. I wouldn't ever betray someone's trust like that.

Ty pastes on his posing-with-a-fan smile and I take a bunch of photos, making sure Ben gets a really excellent collection to remember this night by.

Then I hand over his phone, drain the last sip of my drink, and stand up. "I'm going to head out now. Maybe we'll do this again, Ben. Somewhere a little less popular next time?"

I don't wait for him to answer.

I leave Ty with him and head straight out the door.

———

Half an hour later, there's a knock at my apartment door.

I know who it is before I even open it.

"What was that stunt at the bar?" I demand when I yank it open.

Ty shrugs and leans against the doorframe. A subtle waft

of sunshine and sea salt drifts towards me. "I think you had a temper tantrum and stormed off."

"You interrupted my date."

He nods. "Yeah. To ask you a favour, which I tried to ask earlier, but you blew me off. And at the bar, you didn't even give me a chance to say anything. Rude, Kiley. So rude."

I gape at him.

"It's okay. I smoothed things over with Bert for you."

"Ben."

"Right. I told him that you're an amazing kisser and—"

"You did not."

He pushes off the doorframe and grins wickedly before stepping into my apartment. "Of course not, neighbour. That's our special secret."

"That was a one-time only event under very extenuating circumstances."

"A pity kiss?"

"Sure, let's call it that." I wave my hand in the air. "What's the favour you want to ask of me?"

"Right. Since I'm going to be out of town, I was wondering if you could move my truck around a bit so it doesn't look abandoned?"

"Excuse me?"

He holds up his hand and a key swings into view, dangling from a keyring hooked over his middle finger. "You can use it if you want, too."

"I—"

"I noticed you take the bus to work. You might as well drive my truck instead. If you want to, that is. I don't know if you're car-free by choice."

I open my mouth and the truth almost spills out. *Definitely not by choice. I had to mooch off my brother and my best friend for the last year, and I always feel like I'm one paycheque away from being a self-sufficient grown up again, but I don't want to pull the trigger and spend my savings on a car again.* Instead of letting all of *that* tumble out, I suck in a calming breath, then reach out and snatch the keys.

Surprise slashes across his face. "You'll do it?"

I squeeze my hand around the cool metal of the keychain and try to ignore the way I think I can still feel the warmth of his fingers trying to hook mine. That's a trick, just like his charming smile, and I know better than to fall for too-handsome, too-charming men who never get told no. "Sure, okay. I'll be your truck bodyguard."

"I was thinking of you more as a truck babysitter, not a bodyguard. There's a key to my place on there, too. In case you need anything."

I pretend to consider it for a second. "Do you have anything good in your freezer?"

"Hoping you'll find some dismembered body parts to report to the police?" He doesn't look fazed in the slightest.

"Exactly," I say breezily. "And then I'll write a tell-all book about my harrowing experience."

"Smart." He nods sagely. "I like a girl with a plan. But seriously, the TV and couch are going to be pretty nice."

"You're getting a new TV?"

"That's why I went to Harper and Kieran's for dinner tonight. To coordinate moving and furniture delivery dates while I'm gone."

I try not to physically react to the way all of that sounds not-at-all-temporary. "So if I have a TV watching emergency, I'll know exactly where to go. Got it. Thanks, neighbour."

"You're a hard nut to crack, Kiley Forge." He straightens up. "But we *are* going to be great neighbours."

"Especially when you're in Miami," I say sweetly.

He shrugs and laughs. "Yeah, I hope so." Then he leans in. "And before you know it, I'll be back for the wedding."

Oh.

Right.

Four days in close proximity in the middle-of-nowhere Manitoba.

The Highlanders billionaire owner, Jack Benton, has gifted Kieran and Harper the use of the team plane to transport guests from Hamilton.

Until this moment, I hadn't realized that meant Ty and I would be travelling to the wedding together. *With forty other people.*

But still.

I'm going to need to gird myself against Ty Connor's remarkable, and remarkably annoying, charm.

Instead of replying, I wiggle the truck keys as a non-verbal confirmation that I will take care of his vehicle, then I yank open the apartment door.

Chuckling, he sees himself out.

I flop on the couch and grab my phone.

KILEY

Did you tell Ty where to find me?

HARPER

What? No.

Why? Did he show up at the bar?

Yes.

Interesting.

Nope. Not interesting.

What aren't you telling me?

So, so much.

But she didn't tell me about her first hook-up with Kieran for two long years. And it's not like I've had sex with Ty. I never will. Keeping a single kiss a secret is hardly the same thing.

KILEY

He wants me to use his truck while he's gone.

HARPER

Nice.

Is it?

Time will tell.

CHAPTER 21
TY

Thirty-six hours later, I wake up in my condo in South Beach and stare at the ceiling. For a moment, it feels like I never left, like I never moved to the land of cold, dark mornings.

I really did have the best fucking life here.

I roll out of bed and get dressed for a run.

It's gloriously hot already, and all the beautiful people are out soaking up the sun.

This I know how to do. Run down Ocean Drive and find someone, anyone, to celebrate being home again. To celebrate a return to my best fucking life, if only for a few weeks.

There are plenty of good candidates, too. Did South Beach get the memo that Ty Connor is back in town, and decide to show off their best assets?

I'm blessed.

I'm about to introduce myself to someone when my phone vibrates in my hand, and a weird déjà vu sensation knocks me off my pursuit.

I was almost in this exact same position, pursuing a

woman for an early morning tumble in the sheets, when I got the call about the trade.

Today, though, that cold slither of *what now* is quickly replaced with a hot, heady sizzle when I glance at my messages. Because it's the off season, and this has nothing to do with hockey. And yes, this woman is now thousands of miles away, but she gets my blood pumping in a good way.

Also, I owe her an apology.

THEATREGIRL

Hey, it's your monthly reminder to update your Tinder bio. Gotta keep it fresh!

I wince. Her last message to me was a proposition that I couldn't take her up on, for my own reasons. And then I didn't hear from her again, and because I was tangled up in my "what if" questions about Kiley, I thought that was for the best.

Now she's back in my inbox, but in a *I'm moving on* kind of way.

My first reply makes it clear that I'm reading her vibe. We're friends.

BEASTMODE

Thanks, buddy.

But then I add a direct apology, because that's the kind of guy I am. I don't hide from my mistakes.

Listen, sorry I didn't reply to you last week about meeting up.

Don't worry about it. Momentary madness.

We all have nights like that. But you're
good now?

I'm great.

I'm glad to hear it. Genuinely.

Thanks. I'm glad we're friends.

Of course. Same.

Have you been busy?

I tell her in the most nonspecific way possible about the busy season at work ending, but now I'm travelling again to prepare.

BEASTMODE
It never ends, basically.

THEATREGIRL

That's so interesting. Sort of like my current
job, but the exact opposite of theatre work.
Everything there is a fixed duration.
Summer stock, a touring show. Everything
is a contract, and then you're tossed in the
air, unsure of where you'll land next.

It must be amazing for you to miss that
uncertainty.

There's nothing like seeing a production
come together just in time for opening
night.

How goes the job search, then?

I'm still looking.

> You gotta do more than look. Do you want me to be an accountability partner?

> Maybe. I'd like to be out of this city by the end of the summer for sure.

> That's a good goal.

> Then I'm going to need you to hold me to it. That's what friends do, right?

I almost type back that I need her to, in exchange, hold me to a promise to get laid while I'm in Miami, but that's not how friendship works. It's not tit for tat.

And for whatever reason, we never worked out, but it wasn't for lack of interest. It would be fucking rude of me to rub it in her face that I'm hooking up with other people.

Or that I'm going to, because right now it's just a hypothetical plan.

I think of Kiley's soft mouth and how her fingers slid between mine, making me feel white-hot with need.

I'm not going to find that here, I know that.

But Kiley wants nothing to do with me. I can't make her see past the false impression she has of me.

She thinks you're a reckless idiot and an indiscriminate fuck. Both of those things are accurate.

They're…somewhat accurate.

I've never been a guy who has a type. I'm pretty indiscriminate in my appreciation of tits and ass. Soft, lush skin and a hot, wet mouth is a wicked combination across the board. That doesn't make me indiscriminate, it makes me a lot of fun to a wide range of people.

As for the reckless idiot part…that was specific to a few bad moments at the end of the season.

But that's all water under the "never going to happen" bridge.

So I need to move on. Find more people like TheatreGirl, who likes those parts of my personality. I'm promiscuous? Great, so is she. I can be a filthy-mouthed jerk? She gets off on that.

But she's back in Hamilton, and we're just friends.

I need to balance out the fun and games online with some in-real-life physical connections.

I turn around and head home. I'm thinking too much, and not fucking around nearly enough.

It's time to get laid.

———

I don't find anyone online.

I go out with some of my former teammates instead, most of whom are married, and we talk about golf and working out, and gossip about people around the league.

And when I get home, and I see that she's online, I say something reckless to the girl who never minds that kind of thing.

BEASTMODE

I wish I was back in Hamilton right now. I need you.

THEATREGIRL

I don't think you do, friend. If we really wanted to hook up, we would have.

Harsh but fair.

That's me.

I failed us, sexy girl.

We were only ever meant to be friends.

Then can I confess something to you, friend to friend?

Of course.

I haven't had sex since January. I'm afraid my dick is going to forget how to do things.

LOL!

No, seriously, I'm in a rut.

Me too.

Really?

Must be something in the water.

Want to compare strategies?

LOL

Oh, you're serious… Yeah, sure. Why not?

She tells me about her brother's strategies, which all sound like things I used to do myself.

And that night, I swipe enough to consider it a really good effort. I even get a couple of matches. But I don't do anything about them, because I can see how it would play out.

Drinks. Standing close enough that the scent of suntan oil winds its way around my brainstem. Touching, teasing, and then back to my place.

I just can't see myself actually getting hard for suntan oil anymore.

I want to hear out-of-control giggles after I make a northern girl explode with pleasure.

My cock twitches, but it's not TheatreGirl I imagine now. It's Kiley, laughing with me in the back hallway at the arcade bar.

I want to be challenged.

I want…

Frizzy dark bangs.

A tall, solid body.

Tits that would overflow my hands.

I want spiced honey and sass.

But I need Kiley to want me back, and that's not on the table.

CHAPTER 22
KILEY

I pour myself into work. I have three twelve-hour shifts in a row, followed by an extra night shift a day later that I pick up at the last minute.

It's definitely easier to leap on a shift when I can drive myself to the hospital in Ty's truck.

For the first time since Harper started seeing Kieran, it truly feels real that we're never going to carpool to the hospital again. And she's stopped taking extra shifts, so we don't work together nearly as often.

Which also makes me question how long I'm going to keep working there myself, because one reason I applied for the ward clerk position in the first place was to work with my bestie.

The other reason was to have some stability. And money.

I now have enough money in the bank to buy myself a car when Ty returns and takes back his truck.

But do I want a car, if I might get on a plane and fly to a walkable city somewhere to work a theatre contract?

It feels like there are some big questions hanging over me.

Right now, though, I'm just adjusting to the quiet life. In a few weeks, the pre-wedding hangouts will ramp up, and I'll see people a lot. For now, I'm focusing on finding my own vibe again.

I've spent a lot of time scrolling on Lusty for anything and everything artsy on my nights off.

I've gone out for drinks a few times with people from the hospital, too, but nothing there has stuck beyond single outings.

So other than my brother and my engaged best friend, the other person who I'm closest to is Harper's mom.

In my defence, she's the coolest mom I've ever met. And like Harper and Grant, she's known me my entire life, which makes opening up easier.

I don't trust easily.

Every time I have let in someone new, really let them in and gotten vulnerable, I've gotten burned. With three exceptions. So yeah, I'll stick to my tight little friend pod, even if one of them is my best friend's mom.

I'm on my way to Angela Roberts' house when Harper calls me from the hospital. "Are you busy?"

"On my way to your mom's to help her with the invitations."

"You guys!" Harper sighs. "That's so sweet. I'm sorry I'm stuck at work."

"It's fine. This way we can gossip about you."

She laughs. "Rude."

"I'm kidding. You know she's just going to grill me on why I stopped writing."

"And now I'm suddenly not sad that I have to work," she

says sympathetically. "Don't let her bully you into starting again if it's not for you right now."

"I won't."

When I first came home from Vancouver, I thought I wanted to write a novel. I picked up an older attempt I'd made, revised that a bit, then started a couple of new projects. None of them got that far, but Angela was a big cheerleader.

"Listen, I was actually calling to pass on a message from Ty."

"Oh?"

"He wants to see how the truck is doing."

I roll my eyes. "Okay. Tell him the truck is fine. Why didn't he just, you know, ask me?"

"Because he doesn't have your number," she says reasonably.

Minor detail.

"But you could give it to him," I point out.

"But you wouldn't want me to."

She has me there. "Well, now I want his number so I can reply directly."

"I don't know if I can give that to you," she says innocently.

"Harper! I'm his truck bodyguard. I should be able to communicate directly with the…"

"Truck Daddy?"

"Never call him that again."

"Truck parent, then." She sounds so proud of the mental mayhem she's causing for me.

I sigh. "I regret this conversation deeply."

"That makes one of us. I'll reach out to the truck parent

and find out if he would like direct contact with the truck babysitter."

"Bodyguard."

"Can I give him your number?"

"No!" I screw up my face. "Yes. Of course you can."

He texts me five minutes later, just as I'm parking in Angela's driveway.

TY

This is the truck parent.

KILEY

Please forget that she ever said that.

Can't do that. How's the truck doing? You haven't driven it that much.

How do you know that? I'm literally driving it right now.

Sounds unsafe, should I be concerned?

Just kidding, I know you're parked.

Excuse me, stalker, how do you know that?

The truck has an app.

Of course it does.

That's how I know how many miles you've put on it, which is not many.

I'm taking it to work! That feels like enough movement to keep it feeling loved.

I saw those trips to the hospital. What about groceries?

It's called walking and taking the bus, stalker. Maybe one day you'll lose your hockey fortune and experience it for yourself.

Bite your tongue, babysitter. I have a very safe, conservative investment portfolio.

I'm sure you do.

Please drive my truck more. And remember that I can track wherever you go on the app, so if you hit any strip joints, know that I'm very proud of you.

This is an inappropriate truck parent/babysitter conversation.

But I think I can grill my truck bodyguard on where she goes with my precious vehicle, right?

I walked right into that.

I have to go put stamps on wedding invitations.

Put something extra in it for me.

Like poison?

He puts a thumbs up on that. How does one top an enthusiastic emoji reply to a poisoning threat?

One does not. One puts the phone away before one goes any further down the path of weirdness.

I hop out of the truck and find Angela coming around from the backyard, carrying gardening stuff.

"What is this?" she exclaims, taking in the shiny monster.

"A loaner. I'm babysitting this for a hockey player who is out of town. The guy who moved into Harper's apartment."

"A hockey player moved into her place? She said they found someone to sublet it, but she didn't say who." She brushes dirt off her hands. "My daughter likes to keep secrets from me."

This is a mother-daughter debate I don't need to be a part of. "So what are we doing today? Gardening first, and then invitations?"

"Nope, I'm all done with weeding. Let's go inside. You can tell me what's new with you while I scrub up, and then we'll get to it."

Inside, the table is covered with stacks of invitations and envelopes, as well as neat piles of stamps and a master list of invitees.

While she scrubs her hands clean in the kitchen, I confess about the job search, leaving out BeastMode specifically. "I have a friend who is encouraging me to dip my toe back in those waters and just apply for something. Maybe a twelve week contract for the fall."

"That's exciting."

"I haven't told Harper yet."

She gives me a careful look. "Okay. I won't either. Do your parents know?"

I roll my eyes. Angela knows I'm not close with them. "No. And they won't care. It's not like they think being a ward clerk is great either. It's only Grant and Harper who will worry."

"They just want you to be taken care of." She smiles. "But I understand that you need to fly far and wide to feel whole. I see myself in you. Don't make the same mistakes I did and wait until you're in your fifties to go on those adventures!"

"I won't."

She puts on music, and we settle into our tasks. Before I know it, we're down to the final few invites, and it's almost teatime.

Angela puts the kettle on and we power through as the water heats up.

I send a picture of the completed task to Harper, who replies with a long line of heart-eyed emojis.

I show her mom.

Her cheeks turn a very pleased shade of pink. "It was the least I could do after the kids told me they wanted to give *me* a wedding gift. Which feels backwards, but I won't argue with them. They're sending me and Darnell to Belize to meet some of my cousins."

I clap my hands together. "Oh, how amazing!"

"I know, I'm so excited."

The tea kettle whistles.

Over some tea and a slice of spice cake, we talk about the next wedding task on our to-do list.

Because the wedding is taking place at Kieran's cabin in the middle of nowhere, and the only hotel options are a small inn at a golf course, and a sketchy motel off the highway that Kieran isn't sure he can recommend.

The solution that we settled on was a caravan of rented RVs will be set up on the edge of Kieran's property, and because those have multiple beds with some dividing curtains and flimsy doors, they're a decent choice for a group of friends, but we don't want to force people to stay together.

I've been putting off the decision of which room I want to

lay claim to as the maid of honour, because nothing feels quite right. The options are a bedroom in Kieran's cabin, which makes sense the night before the wedding, but for the wedding night itself, it feels a bit too…close.

On the other hand, the golf course inn will be overflowing with hockey players. No thank you. Which leaves the third option as sharing an RV with my brother.

I'm underwhelmed by all the options, and I tell Angela that when she reminds me that I need to pick a room before the RSVPs start to roll in.

"I'll probably stay in the main cabin."

"You don't sound excited about that."

"Where are you staying?"

"Darnell and I are staying with Kieran's parents."

"Oh, right. Of course."

She shoots me an inquisitive look. "You seem nervous."

"Nope."

"What's going on?"

"Nothing." I chew on my bottom lip for a second. "I guess I'm feeling very…third-wheel-y about everything."

"Oh, honey." She nods empathetically. "Of course. But a hot single girl is an asset at a wedding, yes?"

"Maybe." I shrug. "I'm trying to detach from the hockey crowd a bit. No drama there. I just want to find myself."

"How's the writing going?"

I wrinkle my nose.

"Well, that's part of your problem. Sweetheart, you are an artist. You will only find yourself on the page. Get back to writing. Write me something magical or ferocious or emotional, and you'll feel better."

"I never finish anything."

"Let's go back to my studio and look at all the half-finished canvases. Starting art is part of the process. We only finish what needs to be finished."

I smile at her positivity. "Well, then, nothing I've written so far needs to be finished."

"Ah, now you're getting it." She winks at me. "So I can pencil you in for staying with the hunky hockey players?"

I shudder. "No. I'll…" I wince. "Grant and I can share an RV."

She makes a tutting sound, but scribbles my name down under *Glamping*. "There's still time to find a date, you know."

Time, yes. I have time.

What I don't have is any interest.

CHAPTER 23
TY

Marsh's wedding invite arrives. I log in to their wedding website and RSVP in the singular. Then I book a room at the golf course and join the group chat.

TY

What's up, wedding chums

RUSTY

You at the golf course?

Of course

GUSTY

Marshie is staying with us the night before
the wedding

How bad are the black flies?

RUSTY

Living in Florida has made you weak,
my man

SMASH

> We'll dip you in citronella

I send them a photo of me flipping them off, then I go online and order the happy couple the most expensive item on their registry—a top of the line espresso maker that I'm surprised the coffee connoisseurs on the team, Gusty and Mitchell, didn't grab first.

Wedding guest duty complete.

Then I send a group chat to the other Florida-based players who are already out of the playoffs, and let them know I'm ready to start training at the player development academy we like to skate at in the off-season.

Time to get back on the ice.

I've been roller-blading every day for a second bit of cardio, but it's not the same. And skating up and down the South Beach strip is associated with hooking up in my head, and that's still not going well. My dick just isn't interested.

So I can only assume he wants to be shoved in a jock and punished with some ice time.

I have my hand on my junk, trying to coax him into being excited at the thought of pussy, when my phone vibrates.

Terrible timing, Petrov, I think to myself.

But it's not a reply from my Russian former teammate.

It's a Lusty message from TheatreGirl.

THEATREGIRL

> What's your strategy for weddings? Do you go stag or do you try to find a date?

BEASTMODE

I always go by myself. Weddings are a
danger zone.

Right.

I love a good wedding hook-up, though.

I don't know how much opportunity there
will be for that at this wedding. The guest
list is a lot of couples, and people who work
with my nemesis.

That's messy. Definitely go for one of the
couples instead.

What???

You haven't been a wedding night third?

You have?

I blame the fact that I'd been stroking myself before we started chatting. Most women don't want to hear about threesomes. They're happy to have them, especially if they're the middle of the post-wedding sandwich, but they want to think it's special.

BEASTMODE

Yeah. Not recently.

THEATREGIRL

Fascinating. You taught me something new!

Time to change the subject.

BEASTMODE

How are the dating trenches treating you?

THEATREGIRL

No threesomes, that's for sure.

Twosomes?

I had a date the other night. It was…fine. It was a redo, actually, and at least this time the date wasn't interrupted by an asshole, but I think the damage was done.

An asshole?

never mind

Hey, friends care about bad dates

I'm sticking out my tongue at you. How's your updated bio serving you?

It's not really. But I have an even more serious problem.

Oh no, what?

It's personal. And crude.

LOL oooooh. Okay. What's the problem, big boy?

I can't jerk off.

She sends a long line of laughing emojis.

BEASTMODE

You're a brat.

THEATREGIRL

I'm sorry. When did this problem start?

Right around when we stopped chatting
about sexy stuff.

Whose fault is that?

Mine. Completely mine.

Silly boy. And to think that once upon a
time, I only had to send you a voice
message and you'd be growling in my ear
for me to come like a good girl.

Fuck. Now I'm getting hard. I glare at my traitorous dick, but he's not wrong. She is hot. My blood churns hot in my veins as I stab out my reply.

Was I that predictable?

I preferred to think of you as reliable

reliable for what?

a good time

I swallow a groan.

But now I'm just your friend...

You're playing a game with me

Am I?

You are. Naughty girl.

Maybe you're just easy.

I'm definitely easy.

Then she sends me a breathy little whisper of a voice message. I play it on a loop, fisting my cock hard and fast until I shoot off like a geyser.

Panting, I slam my thumb on the microphone button and grunt out, "You are a dirty, dirty tease, and you know it. What am I going to do with you, hmm?"

There's a long pause before she writes back.

THEATREGIRL

Anything you want.

———

Anton Petrov texts back some time while I'm having a lazy late afternoon nap.

PETEY

You've been back for days. What took so long to reach out? No shame in being out of the playoffs so soon. More time to party, ya?

Your silence means you're busy with pussy. Good man. Come to the club tonight.

He adds an address, and a devil emoji.

PETEY

In case you've forgotten.

My first instinct was to pass, but the little jab about me moving on can't go unanswered.

TY

> You can take the player out of Miami, but you can't take Miami out of the player. I'll be there.

Then I do a second workout for the day, focusing on some of the functional movement and flexibility exercises the Highlanders team wants me to focus on.

One of my favourite things about being a professional athlete is having a complete team around me that not only supports what I do, but they're deeply invested in how I can do it better.

After fighting for every opportunity to play hockey growing up and not having any fucking support until I hit juniors level, the last thing I'm going to do is risk pissing off the support staff.

So while I'll hit the club tonight, I'll take care of my body first.

I push myself through the workout, then I pull two servings of lasagna out of the freezer. While they heat, I have a shower.

"Missed you," I say to my steam jets for the third day in a row.

I need to get on finding an apartment in Hamilton that I can renovate.

I'd like to have TheatreGirl in the shower.

An image of her on her knees, doing anything I want, shimmers in the steam.

Water droplets all over her skin.

My cock in her mouth, lips stretched wide.

Sounds of pleasure echoing off the tile as I find the limits of her ability to swallow me. A moan turning to a choking sound as my tip lodges in her throat, and still she fights to breathe, to keep taking me, because she is a *very good girl*.

I close my eyes and tip my head back, my throat working. My body goes tight, sore muscles straining again.

Cupping my balls, I ignore my flexing dick.

I'm not going to jerk off to a fantasy. I'd rather go out amped up and find someone to bring home.

But as soon as I think that, Kiley strides up to me. We're in that arcade bar, and she has a knowing look on her face.

"Gonna bring a club girl back to your place? Better be careful the Hamilton message boards don't see photos of you living it up in Miami. Might push on some bruises."

"Fuck," I snarl out loud, my dick flagging.

People do take pictures of me at nightclubs. I never mind. Living here, it helped my reputation as a player who embraced everything South Florida has to offer.

And it's not like it's a secret that I'll be living here in the off-season.

I release my aching balls and rinse off. When I get out, I scowl at myself in the mirror that defogs in an instant—another thing I need in Hamilton.

Although the more I hear the utterly un-fun voice of Bossy Tits in my head, the less I like my reflection staring back.

"You're a fucking stud," I say out loud. "Don't let her get to you."

By the time I pull into the VIP valet line for the nightclub Petrov is part owner of, I've shaken it off. He invested in it a few years ago along with three other Russian hockey players who play on other teams, but who live in the Miami area in the off-season.

The beautiful blonde concierge at the door recognizes me. "Welcome back, Mr. Connor."

"Thank you."

"Would you like your usual bottle service?"

I nod in acknowledgement. "Is Anton here yet?"

"Not yet," she says. "But there are a few players in the lounge."

I make my way to the back, where another bouncer guards a space that is relatively quiet compared to the heavy thump of the main club. I'm greeted like a returning king, which I love.

A hostess brings in a drink cart and I offer a round to everyone in the VIP lounge.

It's not just athletes back here. Business associates, musicians, and beautiful women slide in and out of the oversized curved booths. I watch all of it from a distance, not vibing with anyone for more than a shared beverage.

I've been here for almost two hours when Anton finally arrives. "The baby wouldn't settle," he says gruffly.

I cackle. That's legitimately funny. "Never thought I'd see the day, Petey."

"What? I'm an excellent family man."

"I'm sure you are."

"It's different with three kids. My wife can't do it all."

I nod. "No, that's good. That makes sense."

And then I start laughing again.

He grins. "You're drunk."

I shrug. Probably.

Two young players, a Russian-American and a French-Canadian, come in. I don't know either of them well, but Anton makes the introductions and I wave at the bottle service girl.

"Drinks are on me tonight, boys."

They cheer loudly.

Both of them speak fluent English, which isn't always the case with young foreign players. We're getting on well enough when the francophone pulls out a small vial and taps out two lines of cocaine on the glass table in front of him.

I look at Anton, who shrugs.

They each do a line, and I think that's going to be the end of it. But it doesn't take long for the Russian kid to ask for another hit.

And after the French kid sets it up, he pulls out his phone, giggling like an idiot, and holds it up like he's a fucking Hollywood director, framing the shot.

A shot that has me in the background.

I leap up and knock the phone out of his hands, sending it tumbling onto the couch they're sitting on. "What the fuck, dude?"

"Live a little." He gives me a lopsided grin. "It's the off-season."

I shake my head. "Do what you want, but don't take fucking video of it. And never put another player in the shot, you hear me? That's a disaster in waiting."

"Oh fuck. Yeah. Okay. Sorry, man."

I pick up his phone, make sure it wasn't recording any of that, and tuck it into a pocket on his shirt. "Keep that away for the rest of the night."

I pace over to the drinks cart, but I've lost interest in partying.

Fuck.

Fucking fuck.

I shove my hands through my hair, then scowl at Anton. "I'm going to go."

He lifts one meaty shoulder. "All right. Tomorrow, then. Bright and early."

Apparently sleep is not something Petrov needs or wants in the off-season.

"Tomorrow," I mutter.

The next day, I meet Petrov and Craig Roslin at the ice pad where we've done off-season training for a decade.

Petey razzes me the entire time for turning into a square. I slam him into the boards a few times just for fun.

But most of all, we shoot a lot of pucks, and it feels fucking amazing.

"Missed skating with you fuckers," I say as I strip off my gear after the gruelling practice.

Craig chuckles and heads straight to the shower.

"It's more fun when you aren't scoring against us." The big Russian sprawls naked on the opposite bench. "Maybe we'll put some muscle on you this summer, mmm?"

"I weigh two-ten, Petey. Go fuck yourself."

"Two hundred and ten pounds at the start of the season, maybe. Official weight, yes?" He slides an assessing gaze down my body. "One-ninety right now. At most. Get on the scale."

I scowl. "I lose water weight when I skate."

He grins. "Tomorrow, then. Before we skate."

Fuck. This fucker sees right through me. "I'm putting on weight this summer, don't you worry."

"And keep it on during the season, yeah? That's the real

struggle for you. You get weak by playoffs. That's why you got traded." He shrugs like he hasn't just shredded me straight to my deepest fear.

Is that why I got traded?

I never managed to drag Miami all the way to a Cup win. The ring I have, I won as a rookie, when the team was led by others.

"Fuck off," I say easily.

Roslin stalks back in, rubbing his furry belly that curves above the low-slung towel.

Petrov snaps his fingers. "Yes, hot dog man."

Craig laughs. "What did I do?"

"Tomorrow, we take this one to the ball game. He needs to eat like you."

Roslin and I exchange a look. There's no point telling Petrov that our different body shapes have nothing to do with how many ballpark dogs we consume.

But there's nothing quite like taking in a game on a sunny afternoon.

"Sure," I say. "Sounds like fun."

"Can we get different seats, though?" Roslin makes a face. "My ex-wife started dating a guy who has season tickets right behind mine."

"No shit." I start laughing. "Dude, that's brutal."

"Yeah." He shakes his head. "She left me, you know? I don't know why she'd want to rub my face in it."

I think about interrupting Kiley's date with that ginger fellow. Brad? Brent? Ben.

Nice guy.

Not for her, of course, but nice enough.

"People do stupid shit for weird reasons," I mutter. "But yeah, we can sit wherever."

"Good seats, though," Petrov interjects.

Roslin rolls his eyes. "He likes to get on the TV broadcast."

Vain motherfucker. "Definitely missed you, Petey."

I grab my shaving kit and hit the shower. After the steam has gotten under my skin and I'm scrubbed clean, I shave my face, since I didn't bother this morning.

TheatreGirl had been online when I woke up, and that had felt like a better priority.

I felt a twinge of guilt about how readily I dove back into sexting with her when it's Kiley I'm picturing half the time.

I rinse my face and frown at myself in the mirror.

I didn't like Roslin's story about his ex-wife. It tugs at some weird thread of guilt I have about getting the details of Kiley's date out of her best friend, and then going to crash it.

Fuck.

I crossed a line, probably.

Not that I regret it.

She looked good that night. She always looks good, but she'd put extra effort into her outfit, and I ruined it by interrupting—

My brain skips on something I can't quite place.

I shake it off and get dressed, then take the long way back to South Beach, enjoying the fuck out of my Lambo.

It's not until I'm picking up dinner from the best Italian restaurant in South Beach that night that something Theatre-Girl said comes back to me.

I had a date the other night. It was…fine. It was a redo, actually, and at least this time the date wasn't interrupted by an asshole…

No.

It has to be a coincidence.

But…

She has a wedding to attend this summer, too. She brought that up at the exact same time I was RSVPing to Marshie's wedding. That's some weird-ass timing.

I go to multiple weddings every summer. It's a fact of life when you work with dozens of people in their twenties and thirties.

I don't know how much opportunity there will be for that at this wedding. The guest list is a lot of couples, and people who work with my nemesis.

Her nemesis.

I try to remember what, if anything, she's told me about that guy before.

Nothing comes to mind.

Could I be her fucking *nemesis*? While I'm tangled up over the memory of her fucking mouth going soft against mine?

The possibility of TheatreGirl being Kiley, even the remotest of possibilities, does something very strange to my brain.

There's an angry buzzing in my ears I can't shake. A kaleidoscope of moments spins through my mind. When she's glared at me, snapped at me, squared her shoulders and challenged me.

I once accused her of actively trying to undermine me. I have to consider the possibility that she has been messing with me all along, and this is just another twisted game.

CHAPTER 24
KILEY

TY

Are you working today?

KILEY

No, I'm home.

Do you have Puck?

No, she's with Grant. Why?

Just checking.

You're being weird.

You always think I'm weird.

Not when you're playing hockey.

You like watching me play?

This doesn't feel like official truck bodyguard business. Get to the point.

> I want to have some things delivered to the apartment today. Could you hang out down there and buzz them in?

I'm still staring at the screen when he texts again, saying thanks.

As if it's a done deal.

As if I'm his personal delivery receiving girl.

Huffing a breath, I grab his keys and go downstairs to let myself in. It's strange to see Harper's apartment completely devoid of her stuff.

I don't go into the bedroom—that's out of bounds even for an invited upstairs neighbour. But I prowl to the kitchen. He doesn't have a table, so it's just a clean, empty space. Also empty is his freezer. No body parts, no ice cream.

The fridge is similarly empty, only a couple of bottles of sports recovery drinks on the door.

Maybe some of his deliveries will be snacks. One can only hope.

"The nerve of him," I say to Harper when I have her on speakerphone.

"But you went down to his apartment?" she asks.

"I don't want to inconvenience the delivery drivers. He says there are *multiple* deliveries, Harper. Who does that? Who spontaneously decides to order a bunch of shit to an apartment they aren't even living in?"

"Well, he's going to come back," she says, far too reasonably.

"Mm-hmm." I open his fridge. Completely empty. "If I'm here for hours, I'm going to be forced to order takeout on his tab."

"Your fridge is just upstairs."

"Nope. I'm not allowed to leave his apartment now." I sigh dramatically. "Have you seen the new couch he bought?"

This doesn't even look like Harper's place anymore. The last of her furniture was cleared out last week by movers, and now the living room is dominated by an oversized sofa, a padded ottoman instead of a coffee table, and a huge TV.

Before she can answer that, the apartment buzzer sounds.

"Hang on, the first package is here." I buzz in the delivery driver, who brings up a giant cardboard box like it weighs nothing.

Because, I realize as I take it, it really doesn't weigh much at all.

"Curious," I say to Harper, who now has water running.

"What is?"

"Ty's first delivery is big, but doesn't weigh much. I wonder what it is?"

"Don't open his packages."

I don't acknowledge her warning. Instead, I'm texting Ty.

Harper can hear the clicking, apparently. "What are you doing?"

"Asking His Highness if I need to check the contents on arrival."

TY

Sure, you can go through my personal
belongings. No need for secrets
between us.

"He says I can check." I peel back the tape that is barely holding the box closed, and frown. "Pillows. He had me upend my entire day to receive *pillows*."

"You weren't doing anything else today," Harper points

out. "Listen, I gotta go. Shannon's having a spa afternoon at her place later if you want to come to that."

That could be a good excuse to get out of this shipping/receiving position I've found myself in.

The next delivery is almost an hour later, and it's exercise gear. Strength bands, a yoga mat, and some foam blocks.

I look up a video on how to use them, and I'm in the middle of a nice back stretch when the third delivery arrives.

More pillows.

Followed soon after by even more pillows.

They're all ordinary bed pillows, too, no variation in size.

KILEY

Did you order too many pillows, maybe?

TY

No such thing.

I've counted six so far. How many heads do you have?

Are you sure you want me to answer that?

Don't be disgusting.

Despicable, disgusting…tsk tsk on the name calling, Forge.

How long is this game going to go on for?

There are two more pillow orders arriving, I think. Can't remember. I got attached to the extra pillows in the hotel. Great for getting into the exact right position, if you know what I mean.

TMI

Gotta go. I'm heading out to a baseball
game. You should watch the game on my
TV. I'll wave to you.

I gasp, outraged. Instead of searching for the game, I
open my computer and look for jobs I can apply for that will
take me away from this apartment building by the time Ty
moves back for pre-season training.

I find a few that look really good, and tweak my resume
to be exactly what they're looking for.

I'm thinking of going upstairs to grab some food for
lunch and change into workout clothes when I get another
message, this one from someone I like a lot more than the
truck parent.

BEASTMODE

What are you doing today?

THEATREGIRL

Job hunting.

BEASTMODE

Still planning to find a new adventure?

Today more than ever.

THEATREGIRL

At this point, I'd go almost anywhere and do
almost anything. How about you? What are
you doing today?

BEASTMODE

Watching baseball with some friends. Miami
vs. Atlanta.

I drop my phone.

And then the apartment buzzer sounds again.

"Let me guess," I mutter to myself. "More pillows?"

This box is heavier than the others. It does have pillows in it—extra large ones, larger than the others—and some bedding with stupidly high thread counts.

I add it all to the growing pile and text a photo to Ty.

KILEY

Is this everything? I need to go run errands of my own soon.

He replies with a thumbs up.

That's it.

KILEY

Did you wake up on the wrong side of the bed and decide to test the limits of our neighbourly kindness? Because I feel like I'm being punked.

TY

No. Shit, no. I'm sorry. I'm… I guess I got carried away with bantering. Go run your errands. It's fine. If there are any more deliveries, they can sit outside.

Someone might steal them.

Then someone will have nice pillows.

More pillows???

I don't know. I told you, fever dream.

I shake my head and put down my phone. That is going to be one very well propped up puck bunny.

An unexpected stab of jealousy sears through me.

I try my best not to picture him tossing some petite little hockey fan, or his high maintenance friend from Miami, around on his bed. Wedging pillows under her ass because she's so small he can't just have sex with her normally.

I fail miserably.

I can practically hear the moans and groans.

"Uhhh, Ty!"

"Fuck, you're so sexy."

Another searing stab of pain steals my breath.

It's not jealousy I'm feeling, I realize.

It's a flashback.

I scramble away from the sofa and force myself out the door of Ty's apartment.

I text Harper to find out what time the afternoon of spa treatments at Shannon's place starts, then I go upstairs.

Time for lunch, and a long, sweaty walk. Then I'll spoil myself with some pampering from the *Kiley New Car* fund, because I don't need a new car.

I need a new life, and it might as well start with a fresh bikini wax.

———

By the time I get home that night I feel so much better. I don't even care that I trip over what looks suspiciously like a build-your-own-sex swing package for Ty. I lug that up the stairs and throw it in his door, then carry on up to my apartment without another thought in my weird neighbour's direction.

An afternoon with the WAGs is good for the soul, because they are funny and wry.

And generous. Shannon refused to let me pay the aestheticians she hired for the afternoon. I've been plucked and polished and painted, and now I'm ready for the upcoming May long weekend.

I've fallen off my pledge to myself to go on a date every single week, and be open to hooking up to everyone with good vibes.

That pledge was made specifically because I'd been neglected in past relationships, but especially in how Crys gaslighted me to think that *I* was the reason we didn't have a better sex life.

I know now that wasn't the case.

But one morning spent in Ty Connors' apartment undid all of my confidence, letting old self-doubts worm their way to the surface. I never want to be jealous of another woman's successful hookup. Even with a hockey player I kissed once. So what? If he's not for me, he might as well be for someone else. Anyone else, even Little Miss High Maintenance who needs all the pillows.

Besides, I have options galore. There's Ben, who made it clear he'd be up for another date, and an invitation back to my place.

And there's BeastMode, too.

Maybe it's time to test the horny limits of our friend zone.

I do a quick internet search for the score of the baseball game he went to, so I can lead with that.

Miami won. I wonder who BeastMode was cheering for, or if he was neutral on the game.

I click in to some tweets about the game, looking for a bit

of context, and then I pause.

Because one of the top tweets is about the hockey players who were the loudest cheerleaders at the game.

There's video.

I click on it, because I'm curious.

The camera zooms in on the stands as the announcers say they have some local celebrities watching the game today. "Local hockey legends Anton Petrov and Ty Connor, who was recently traded to the Hamilton Highlanders, but it looks like he's back in the Miami area to train for the summer. Petrov and Connor…"

I don't hear the rest of what the announcer says because Ty tucks his phone away and gives a wave. His gaze manages to find the camera, and it's as if he's looking directly at me.

His grin broadens, and I feel myself squirm, even though he can't actually see me.

"You cannot ruin my day," I snap at him.

Then I close my computer and grab my phone.

THEATREGIRL

> Would now be a good time to tell you I'm wearing that penguin onesie you wanted to see me in?

BEASTMODE

God. Yes. Fuck, yes.

I pump my fist in the air. He tells me that he's still with his friends, but he's going to ditch them as soon as humanly possible.

It takes him seven minutes.

You hot tease. I'm going to have a lot of fun working that zipper down in one-inch increments. Bet you're all warm and toasty inside. Soft skin, maybe nothing else.

I'm definitely wearing underwear under a penguin onesie.

But no bra?

I squirm.

THEATREGIRL

No bra.

BEASTMODE

Good girl. There's nothing sexier than getting that first glimpse of breasts being happy and free. God, I'm getting hard just thinking about it.

I look down at my outfit.

THEATREGIRL

And what if I were wearing jogging pants and a tank top?

BEASTMODE

Still no bra?

No, I'm wearing a bra.

Fuck, that's hot, too. Do you like to have your nipples sucked through the bra fabric?

Nobody's ever tried.

Their loss. I bet you'd make the prettiest sounds when I did that.

You're so hot. Why aren't you taken? Why
aren't you doing this to someone IRL?

I'd rather chat with you.

That's sad.

Only because I haven't painted a vivid
enough picture of us cuddling on a couch
watching baseball, my hand in your jogging
pants, edging you slowly through the entire
game. You can't cum until our team comes.

That's less sad. I squirm again. I like the way he says *our team*. But I don't want to think about the baseball game earlier.

THEATREGIRL

Can it be a hockey game instead of
baseball?

Dots appear. Disappear. Appear again.

BEASTMODE

Yeah. It can be a hockey game.

CHAPTER 25
TY

Over the next few days, I go back and forth on whether TheatreGirl and Kiley are the same person. My boneheaded attempt to trap her in my apartment and then trick her into revealing something about me at the baseball game, or the delivery babysitting—anything—backfired, and I just pissed Kiley off.

It doesn't help that I accidentally delivered some patio furniture to the apartment in Hamilton two days after the pillow incident, that I genuinely meant to ship to Miami instead.

I texted Rusty and Jenson to get them to help Kiley get the stuff into my apartment, but I still got an earful from her in my text messages.

If she *is* TheatreGirl, there's no way she knows I'm Beast-Mode, though. That's one weird silver lining of pissing her off. When she came back to me that night all horny and needy, that was pure.

And fucking hot.

Our DMs have kept up in the same way ever since.

With each passing day, it becomes clearer and clearer that I'm in the wrong city.

I need to go back to Hamilton and I need to deal with this out-of-control need to pin Kiley down and have a serious conversation.

I have some charity obligations that take up most of the week, and I've just about convinced myself that I'll head back after Memorial Day—a week away—when the group chat for the guys going to Kieran's wedding lights up about a party for the Canadian long weekend. I'd forgotten that the Victoria Day holiday is a week earlier.

> **RUSTY**
>
> Who's in town this weekend? May 2-4 BBQ at Kieran's on Sunday. Doubling as an engagement party, so if anyone wants to go in on a group gift, let me know.
>
> **GUSTY**
>
> I'm down.
>
> **HOONER**
>
> Becca and I will be there. She says the girls have been working on the wedding playlist requests for the DJ, so we gotta bring some recs for that.
>
> **TY**
>
> What time is the party?
>
> **RUSTY**
>
> You gonna be back in town, man? That's great.

I'm already looking up flights. There's one Sunday morning that looks good, and I can finish up my obligations here before I leave town. I fire off a text message to Nina, cancelling a lunch we had booked for the following week, then go back to the group chat.

TY

Yeah, I'll try to be there.

Kiley can't dash away from me at an engagement party.

———

I don't tell anyone I'm coming for sure. I definitely don't say anything to Kiley.

When I land in Toronto on Sunday, I arrange for an airport town car to drive me straight to Kieran's house, because I know she's already there thanks to the app on my phone that tracks my truck everywhere.

Marshie lives on a quiet street in a nice neighbourhood, just a few houses down from Haler. Hooner bought a place just around the corner, and the captain lives not far away, too.

Even though a good percentage of the team is walking distance away, there are cars lining the street, so the guest list is more than just players and their families. My own truck is in the driveway, with two vehicles behind it.

A wicked, heated thought crosses my mind. *Kiley can't escape easily.*

I immediately follow that with a warning to myself to settle the fuck down.

There's a sign on the front door pointing to the side gate, and I can hear that the backyard is full of people, but I also see movement inside, and I'm carrying a duffle bag I'd like to stash somewhere, so I try the door.

It's unlocked, and I let myself in. Immediately, I hear raucous laughter from the living room.

The front half of Kieran's house is dominated by a wide staircase, and then the foyer narrows into a hallway off of which are doors that lead to the garage and his den before spilling into a large open kitchen and family room space.

Kiley is holding court in the living room half of this space.

Her long dark hair is twisted up in two buns today. She's wearing a black off-the-shoulder cropped t-shirt that reveals a hot pink strappy tank top beneath it, but that's the only pop of colour anywhere on her body. Her hips and lush thighs are wrapped in faded black jeans that taper down to bare feet. Even her toenails are painted in a dark colour that pop off the light carpet.

She's arguing with her brother and Hiro, gesturing at a flip chart.

I have pretty quick visual processing skills, but not quick enough to figure out what she's giving a God damned presentation on—at a holiday weekend get together!—before her eyes flash in my direction and she goes still.

Hi, neighbour, I mouth.

I lift an eyebrow, waiting for her reaction. Gauging my reception.

Her mouth does this careful thing, her lips tugging to one side. Like she's considering what to do next.

The whole time, she holds my gaze, and it's hot and searing and unwavering.

Then she gives a little shrug, as if she's barely affected by my arrival, but I'll do.

"Ty probably wants to play," she says, lifting her voice.

The people congregated on the couches turn and say, as one, "Ty's here!"

Then they all burst out laughing. I'm guessing that has something to do with the half-empty jug of sangria on the coffee table.

"I want to play what?" I ask, moving in closer.

Is it my imagination, or does Kiley flush as I circle around the nearest sofa?

She tosses her shoulders back. "We're building the wedding playlist."

"Isn't that the job of the DJ? And the band?" I look around for the bride and groom to be, but they both must be outside. "They are going to have a band or a DJ, right?"

Kiley plants her hand on her hip and hits me squarely with a stern Wednesday Addams look of absolute judgement. "What, are you too good for a wedding reception run off my iPhone?"

I think about the top of the line espresso maker I bought the happy couple. The luxury home they live in here. "Is that a serious question?"

"It was more of a pointed suggestion for you not to be a snob," she says.

"Kiley, stop teasing him." That's her brother. "This is just research for the DJ. And because my sister is a control freak—"

"Says the doctor."

"Which one of us belongs to the professional union of stage moms?"

"You're such a dick," she snaps.

"You love me."

"Respect. My. Profession." She grabs the nearest throw pillow and wings it at him as he laughs.

"I do, I do, I'm sorry." He drags in a deep breath. "For the stage mom joke only, though. Not the song suggestions. Can we get back on track?"

I snap my attention back to Kiley. Doesn't she work at the hospital? That was the one piece that didn't really fit for TheatreGirl, but if her training is actually in the arts…

She uncaps the marker in her hand and scrawls *The Chicken Dance - Grant Forge top request* on the pad of paper on the easel.

I laugh out loud.

At that moment, Kieran and Harper come inside.

"Bud!" Kieran exclaims, holding out his hand to me as I cross to greet them. "I didn't know you were coming!"

"Kept it on the down low," I say, grabbing him into a bro hug.

"Welcome back, Ty." Harper gives me a hug next. "How long are you here?"

Over her shoulder, I find Kiley's gaze. "That depends."

My upstairs neighbour arches a brow. *On what?*

I jerk my chin at the flip chart. "Do you know they're planning your wedding reception?"

Harper giggles. "Yeah. What do we have so far?"

Shannon Tilman calls out a few of the songs that aren't "The Chicken Dance."

"'Uptown Funk', 'Cupid Shuffle', 'Low' by Flo Rida, 'Best I Ever Had'…"

Ani Hale jumps up. "We forgot 'About Damn Time'!"

Her husband groans. "Not my vibe."

"It's not your wedding!"

Kiley clearly agrees with Ani, because the Lizzo song is added to the list, and Kieran gives his nod of approval, too. Then he chuckles. "My mom literally warned me we'd have

'The Chicken Dance' this morning. So that's a good call, Grant."

"You're welcome," the doctor cheerily said, raising a thumbs up in the air.

That got him another throw pillow tossed his way, but it bounces off him and ricochets in my direction.

I snatch it, an excellent excuse to close the gap between me and Kiley.

"Hello, stranger," I murmur as I set the pillow back in its rightful spot.

Then I peruse the chart. "Where are the slow dance songs?" I snag the marker from her hand. "You don't mind, do you?"

Beside me, she goes rigid. Kiley's posture is always spectacular, I've noticed. Makes me think she'd be a very good girl, eventually, when she gave up trying to be a brat.

But now her back is extra straight, and she's holding herself extra still.

"I thought you worked at a hospital," I say.

"Pardon?"

"We can talk about that later." I find a blank spot on the page and hover the marker over it. "What's the vibe? Are we playing Michael Bublé?"

"Our first dance is 'I Don't Remember Me (Before You)' by Brothers Osborne," Kieran offers. "What's your favourite country ballad, Ty?"

Clearly, he's read Kiley's mood and decided he's Team Kiley.

Joke is on him. I'm also on Team Kiley. Team Secret Stage Manager. How did I talk to her for months online and she never told me she also worked at a hospital? All those night shifts?

You never told her you were a hockey player.

That's different.

That's…a basic safety concern.

I frown.

Kiley snatches the marker from me and hip checks me out of the way. "'God Gave Me You' by Blake Shelton."

"No. Absolutely not." I yank the marker back. "If that's the vibe, at least go with Kane Brown and 'Thank God'."

"Never heard of it," someone calls out.

"Google is free," Kiley hollers back, making me chuckle. She rolls her eyes, then grudgingly admits, "I like that song."

Excellent. I scratch that on the paper as people start to yell out other songs.

"The Bones" by Maren Morris.

A cover of "Drops of Jupiter" by Jess Moskaluke.

"Beautiful, You Are" by Ruby Amanfu.

"A Thousand Years" by Christina Perri, which I write with capital letters and Kiley corrects me on for each word in the title.

"It doesn't matter," I tell her.

"It does." She looks at me like I'm an idiot.

Well, this idiot likes to push her buttons. I lean in. "What about 'Every Breath You Take' by The Police?"

She gapes at me. "He's a stalker."

"I hear some people like dark romance," I say blandly.

Her eyes narrow. "Not for a wedding."

"'Wicked Game'?"

"The song about *not* wanting to fall in love?"

Her brother pushes himself off the couch and crosses to us, taking the marker. "I'm tagging in, because it seems we've derailed."

Kiley leans over and grabs the sangria pitcher. "I'll refill."

Her phone is tucked in her back pocket, and my eyes go straight to it.

"And I'll...head outside and say hi to everyone else," I mutter, trying not to look at Grant's sister's ass right in front of him.

Although it really is a spectacular ass, and watching her stalk away is more fun than I've had in weeks.

But fingers crossed, it's barely just scratching the surface of the fun Kiley and I are going to have today.

CHAPTER 26
KILEY

I'm watching Ty through the kitchen window as I slice fruit for the sangria jug when Shannon slides up next to me and leans against the counter.

"That was fun," she says slyly.

"What was?"

"The marker fight. The antagonism. The way Ty Connor only has eyes for you."

I shrug. It was the Forges and a bunch of married people. "In that particular group, it was me or my brother. Unless you think Max would want Ty to be checking you out? The man is an unrepentant flirt. He had to point it somewhere."

Shannon ignores that. "Go talk to him."

"Ty?" I laugh. "I talk to him plenty. I'm his truck babysitter, don't you know?"

She shrugs. "I'll finish this."

At that moment, Ty slides onto the outdoor couch next to Mo Ahmadi and his date. I remember what BeastMode said about threesomes at weddings, and my cheeks burn.

Guaranteed, Ty Connor has threesomes more often than anyone else at this party.

"I think I'm going to get the dips out," I say.

But Harper has already done that.

And then Ani wanders into the kitchen. Before Shannon can recruit her into the *Ask Kiley About Ty* campaign, I slip away, muttering something about finding more ice.

There's a laundry room on the way to the garage, and that's where Kieran and Harper have a deep freeze.

I flop on top of it and tug my phone out.

THEATREGIRL

What are your thoughts on bickering as flirting?

BEASTMODE

It really only matters what your thoughts are on it. Why?

No reason.

Are you on a bad date?

lol no, definitely not a date

Is he not your type?

Why do you assume there's a he involved?

Just a hunch

He's definitely not my type

But I am?

You would be more my type if you were here, that's for sure

And where is "here", exactly?

My best friend's laundry room

Why haven't we met in person?

I don't know

Did you want to?

So fucking much

Did we miss the window?

I don't think so

I gotta go. I'm supposed to be getting ice.

Do you need a rescue?

No, it's okay. I can't leave this party.

But I want to, suddenly, so damn much.

Hot, frustrated tears spring to my eyes, which makes no sense. So I put my phone away and wipe them away, then check my makeup in a little mirror above the washer.

The tears were mostly on the inside, a momentary bittersweet indulgence, and now I'm *fine*.

Taking a deep breath, I open the door, then freeze.

Ty is leaning against the wall on the other side, his gaze hot, hooded and locked on me. His phone is in his hand, and he slowly twirls it in his fingers. "You forgot the ice."

CHAPTER 27
TY

Until she told me she was in the laundry room, I wasn't completely sure that this infuriating, beautiful, off-limits neighbour of mine was also my sexy, giving, secret-sharing friend online.

In hindsight, I should have known from that first kiss at the arcade bar.

Just neighbours.

Fuck that.

"Kiley—"

She spins around and yanks open the freezer, muttering about ice options.

I can practically hear the thoughts screaming through her head right now, all variations on *this isn't happening* and *what the actual fuck?* and *I'm going to kill him.*

She can take all the thinking time she needs.

I need a minute, too. To look at her, really look at her, and to see all of her. To drink her in.

I've liked looking at Kiley Forge since the first second I

laid eyes on her, but from the moment she looked back at me, there's been a wary hostility that I've had to navigate.

But on the other hand, I now have months of knowing her from the inside out.

All this time, my sexy girl has been right in front of me. Everything crashes together now. The memory of her breathy sounds and all of her vulnerable confessions— including the fact that some asshole hurt her a year ago.

She had good reason to be wary of me.

I remind her of that guy.

I am her nemesis, who I encouraged her to steer clear of. I cockblocked myself repeatedly.

I'd laugh about it if it weren't so damn painful.

Two minutes ago, she was *this close* to begging me to come and rescue her.

Not you, Ty. BeastMode.

I lean against the doorframe and tap out another message to her. It'll be my last message to her as BeastMode. From here on out, she's getting the real deal, and we'll find a way to reconcile whatever misunderstandings have stood between us.

Her phone, returned to her back pocket, audibly vibrates. She ignores it.

I clear my throat. "That message says, *we should have had this conversation a while ago.*"

She sighs, still staring intently at the freezer contents. "There's nothing to discuss."

That couldn't be further from the truth if she tried.

I step inside, the door swinging shut behind me.

She shoots me a wary look as I close the gap between us, reach past her, and firmly close the freezer.

Scooting to the side, she holds up her hands. "This is

not… this isn't happening. Mistakes were made, granted. Let's just move on. Big mistake, now in the past."

"No can do."

She gives me an exasperated look as I advance on her.

"I'm not sure we agree on what the mistakes were, for one thing. And for another, we need to talk about how we share some very hot secrets."

"Nope. No. You and I don't share anything except for an apartment building." Her voice loses its confident, steady note. "Which you should move out of, by the way. Because you can afford to live somewhere nice."

I have to fight not to smile. That's quite the bossy over-reaction.

"I like where I live just fine." I stop in front of her, turning her so her back is against the counter that separates the pantry and laundry parts of the room.

"This is *not* happening," she denies again.

Except it is. It can't be helped.

I nudge my thigh between her legs, loving how she shifts against me. Underneath her bossy exterior is a hot-blooded woman who has been telling me for months that deep down, she just wants to be a good girl, a sexy girl. My girl.

I'm whatever kind of girl you want.

That was a TheatreGirl confession that lived rent-free in my head.

Kiley Forge is not about to just say something like that out loud to me now. She still thinks she can boss her way out of this. "I'm serious."

That makes two of us. "Not only is this happening, but it's been happening for months."

"Exactly. Months of lying."

"All right." I drop my hands to her hips, pulling her

tighter against my thigh. The warm, soft apex of her thighs, even in jeans, feels forbidden and perfect. There are too many layers between us. I need to feel her pussy on my bare skin. "No more lies."

I lift her up, setting her on the counter beside the washing machine.

She gasps as I lean in and grab her wrists, holding her hands flat to the counter, trapping her with my body weight. "Ty…"

"You wanted to meet me in person," I say softly. "Here I am."

Her breath catches, then she whispers my name. I see the fight in her eyes, the denial, but I hear the little crack in her voice, too.

We have a lot to talk about. There's going to be some complicated feelings in both directions.

But right now, all I want is to be the guy she needed a few minutes ago. I *am* that guy.

I release one of her wrists so I can catch the back of her neck before she can pull away from me. I lean all the way in, breathing in her honey-scented hair. "I'm here," I repeat, my voice rough. "What do you need, Kiley?"

She pulls back, little curly wisps of hair that escaped from her buns brushing against my cheek like silk. Now we're staring at each other—and it's not fight I see in her gaze now.

There's a spark of raw, glittering desire there, and as the silence stretches between us, it flares brighter and brighter.

She's a breath away from me, and that's still too much distance between us.

I crush my mouth against hers, making the first move,

but she responds immediately. Her tongue pushes back, and this is nothing like our first kiss.

This is fire. This is deeply personal, raw and potent, and beautifully confused. *You? Why you?*

It's the kind of intoxicating kiss I vaguely remember from my teen years, when every opportunity with a girl felt life-changing.

And I want more with every fibre of my being. I pull her closer, moving my mouth against hers, getting deeper. Tasting, licking, swallowing. God, she tastes good.

It's making me hard, dangerously hard, given that we are at a party full of my teammates and her best friend is ten feet away.

Her hands sink into my hair, holding on as our tongues lash back and forth. I yank her hips forward, thrusting my cock against the seam of her jeans, needing her to feel as crazed as I do.

She moans, and it's husky perfection. I think of the sounds she's made for me before, and my balls churn in anticipation.

"Do you—" I manage to get out as she pushes up my t-shirt, putting her hands on the flexing panes of my abs. "We could go—"

Tap tap.

I shove away from the counter and pull Kiley off, too, putting her between me and the washing machine as the door opens.

"Did you get lost in the freezer?" Harper asks, laughing before she fully steps inside and sees me.

Her head tips to the side, and her gaze cools. Then there's silence for a beat before she says in a much quieter voice, "Kiley, you okay?"

"Yep," the woman I was just kissing says brightly. She pushes past me, avoiding eye contact as she yanks open the freezer. "We were just debating the pros and cons of the hollow ice from the ice maker, you know? It melts so fast. Which do you prefer? This will be fine, I guess. Tell Kieran to buy more big block ice next time, though."

Then they're gone, and I'm left standing alone in the laundry room with a rock hard dick so fucking obvious I can't follow them.

Great.

Just fucking great.

By the time I make my way back to the party, everyone is outside. The backyard is strung with white lights and decorated with ribbons of twisted crepe paper. A pile of gifts sit on a table, and I grimace that I forgot to even bring them a card.

I'm not here for the party, though. I'm here for Kiley.

Harper's gaze snaps to me across the outdoor space, and I give her a tight smile before I snag a beer from the cooler on the deck.

She doesn't smile back.

Fuck.

Yeah, I moved into your apartment and now I'm kissing your best friend, but I swear I have the best of intentions because I fell for her online, first…

It doesn't help that Kiley is steadfastly ignoring me.

She makes eye contact with a lot of people. Players, neighbours. She has a big, excited embrace for Harper's mom when the older woman arrives. But by the time I manage to introduce myself to Angela Roberts, Kiley is on the opposite side of the yard, suddenly busy with a game of *Pin the Glove on the Hockey Player*. It's one of three "Pin

The…" games set up around the yard. There's also *Pin the Veil on the Bride* and *Pin the Stethoscope on the Nurse.*

"She's glowing today," Mrs. Roberts says to me.

I jerk my attention away from Kiley, but not before Angela gives me an arched brow over a knowing look.

How the fuck could she know?

"She's always got that vibrant energy," I say, because it's true, and because I don't want to confirm that anything is different about today.

Even though everything is different now.

But I also think it would be a very naïve reading of the situation to think that I made Kiley *glow.* Burn, maybe.

It's gonna take a lot to get her to trust me. Until then, I need to assume the worst about how she feels, because to *me,* it looks like Kiley has been eyeing exit routes out of this party since she fled the laundry room.

Mrs. Roberts moves on, and I pull out my phone.

TY

I need to talk to you

It's a lot of fun to watch Kiley quietly go through an internal struggle to check the message or not. I love the little huff she makes as she yanks out her phone—and the cool, masking expression that falls onto her face when she reads my text.

I'm onto her. She can't hide her real thoughts and feelings and frustrations anymore.

KILEY

I'm sure we'll talk at some point

TY

just for a second

why?

       because I think you're thinking of bolting

Her head jerks up, and she looks in my direction.

I smirk. *Come here*, I mouth.

She rolls her eyes. But she also gets up and sways those curvy hips my way—and then right past me, heading to the cooler.

I tip my beer back, taking a long sip as I watch her lean over, presenting that generous heart-shaped ass I was so close to getting my hands on.

I'm not the only one who is checking her out, too. Roan "Smash" Dodaj's eyes are trained on her, and an unfamiliar possessiveness starts to burn in my chest.

"Smash," I snap.

He jumps. "Yeah, bud?"

"Let's play *Pin the Veil on the Bride*." I jerk my chin. And then, because I need to know if this feeling is in fact about Kiley, I add, "And grab me another beer."

As he ambles over to the cooler, his attention eagerly pointed in Kiley's direction, the strange heat crawls up my throat.

I am not a jealous man. On that damn kink test she had me take, there were multiple questions about sharing partners. And my honest answers based on all my previous experiences put me squarely in the ethical nonmonogamous camp.

As long as nobody is getting hurt, I do not care. Or at least I didn't.

But this young buck, who is taller and heavier than me, is

looking at the girl I was just kissing, and I want to tear him limb from limb.

That's…not great.

I'm not a good boyfriend. I know it. Kiley knows it. I'm not under any illusion about what she's looking for, and what she'll accept from me.

I cannot go all caveman on her.

But fuck if I don't want to.

I really, really want to.

As Kiley makes her own drink selection, Dodaj copies her, taking the same can of what looks like seltzer water, and grabbing a beer for me.

They exchange a laugh, and I have to swallow back another bark. I settle for a glower as Smash reluctantly leaves her side.

"What's wrong with you?" he asks, still laughing, when he sees my face.

Three months of sexual frustration is what is wrong with me.

Before I can answer him, I hear a familiar bark, and Puck arrives at the party. She's leashed, and the person holding her lead is clearly Kiley's mother, with her father right behind.

The senior Forges have that vibe about them, where they are a couple who spends all their time together, and they dress similar, and somehow over time have morphed to even look like each other more than they probably did when they met. They're both tall and dark-haired, with strong, athletic builds like their adult children.

Mrs. Forge doesn't have Kiley's curvy shape, exactly, or maybe that's just her khaki shorts and pastel polo shirt talking.

Because despite the physical similarities—thick, dark wavy hair, long limbs, stern expressions—Kiley definitely has a fashion flair that pulls away from her family.

I watch, intrigued, as they greet Harper with friendliness. She introduces them to Kieran, and then they find Grant in the crowd.

"Are we playing, or what?"

"Yeah, yeah," I say to Smash, although my heart is not in it. And I still need to talk to Kiley.

I let him blindfold me, then quickly stick my veil on the fence—nowhere near the bride cutout. "Your turn."

A few other people join us, which is good. Gives me more time to keep an eye on the Forges. After a few minutes, I realize they aren't going to continue on to find Kiley—and she isn't going to seek them out, either. She heads for the patio door, going inside.

I frown. "Actually, I gotta go see someone," I say, abruptly abandoning the game.

I find Kiley standing in front of the flip chart covered in wedding song suggestions. There's nobody else in the living room right now, but this space is open to the rest of the house, so I resist the urge to grab her and kiss her again.

"Hey," I say quietly, stopping beside her.

She gives me a tight smile. For once, the sharp look doesn't feel like it's about me.

I could ask her about her parents. I could mention that I saw Puck.

Or I could try to make her laugh.

And the last option feels safest right now.

I jerk my chin to the easel. "How do we rank these? Because you know the order you give them to the DJ in will matter. The lower down on the list, the less likely they'll get played."

Her lips twitch and her eyes spark. "So the Chicken Dance should be at the top, right?"

"Are you going to make me flap my arms around on the dance floor, Forge?"

"You know it, Connor. It's a classic."

"Okay, so that's the one spot for sure." I wiggle my fingers. "Where's the marker?"

She reluctantly hands it over, and I flip back to the page with the livelier dance music on it. I write a big number one next to the polka song.

"And that way, the kids and old people can get a dance in before they leave the reception," I say.

Her eyebrows raise. "I like the logic."

"It meets with the stage manager's approval?"

Heat visibly slashes across her cheeks. "Yes."

But she looks pleased that I guessed her occupation by training. *Stage mom.* I don't have any siblings—that I know of—but I can see how that would have gotten under her skin.

"One day, when we aren't busy with this very important task, I'd like to hear the story about how a stage manager came to work at a hospital."

Even though I say it gently, she stiffens and grabs the marker.

"No story there," she snaps. "This song second, yeah?"

"Sure." I think about how she's looking for a new job. No story, my ass. I point to another song on the list. "And this one third?"

She scribbles a number three next to it so aggressively, she gets some black ink on my fingertip.

"Watch it," I warn, then snatch the marker back. The tip slides across her palm, streaking ink over her skin, too.

"Hey!"

She tries to snatch it back, but I'm not just a few inches taller than her, my arms are also longer.

Holding the marker high over her head, I grin down at her. "Say please."

"Never."

I tsk at her, and her eyes flare wide.

Her pink mouth has never looked more kissable than in this moment.

"You are a brat," I whisper. "And listen: don't even think about ducking out quietly."

The spots in her cheeks darken, but she still boldly lifts her chin. "Why not?"

I lean in, inhaling one last lungful of spicy honey to last me until tonight. "Because, neighbour. You're my ride home."

CHAPTER 28
KILEY

Instead of jumping for a marker Ty is holding just out of reach, or acknowledging the fact I drove his truck here—and so ergo, I will need to drive him home—I turn on my heel and head back outside, his chuckle following me the whole way.

As I step onto the deck, I make eye contact with my mother.

Great.

"Hey Mom," I say brightly.

I get a polite smile and nod back.

The breakdown of my relationship with my parents started when I was twelve, not that they would know that. By the time I left home to go to journalism school at eighteen, I felt their disappointment so keenly, it was the final straw in me feeling like their "kid".

Now I'm just another adult they are related to, who they don't have a lot in common with, that they see a few times a year at social events and holidays.

"This is your mom?" Ty asks from behind me.

Of course, he followed me out.

His hand glances over the small of my back, then my hip, as he strides forward and holds out his hand. "I'm Ty Connor. I live downstairs from your daughter. She's a fantastic neighbour."

"He also plays for the hockey team," I add, providing a bit more context. "So he works with Grant."

"That's true, too," he says easily. "Although I know Kiley better. Hey, Puckster." He drops to a knee and greets my dog like they are long-lost friends. "I missed you while I was gone."

Puck, the little traitor, licks him happily, fully on board with Ty being our buddy now.

It's sweet, the little show he's putting on for my parents. I'm not sure what vibe he picked up on that made him think this was necessary, but it's wasted energy.

My parents don't care about anyone other than themselves—and Grant, who is the representation of everything they've ever wanted for themselves.

I am irrelevant in their lives.

They don't dislike me. They just don't understand me or value anything I do.

"How's the pickleball going?" I ask.

My dad answers, going on at some length.

To be fair, I don't care about their interests, either. It's a mutual disregard.

When my dad stops talking, Ty asks a couple of questions that show he knows something about pickleball. Since he inserted himself into this, I leave him to it and slide away.

"Did you abandon Ty to your parents?" Harper asks when I join her.

"Maybe."

"Is that punishment for him trapping you in the laundry room?"

I don't answer.

She waits a beat, then nods. "Okay. That's fair. I kept my secrets from you, so turnabout is fair play. But babe, at some point, you owe me the tea."

My cheeks feel hot, and I nod.

She leans against me. "Are you okay?"

"I don't know."

"Do I need to beat him up?"

I choke on a laugh. "I don't think so."

"I'd feel better if you didn't sound unsure." Someone calls her name, and she reluctantly stands up, her gaze lingering on me.

Yeah, me too, I think. I give her a bright smile and a thumbs up.

———

We leave at the same time as the Calhouns, who want to put their son Charlie to bed at a reasonable hour.

Ty makes an excuse about being tired from the flight, and I don't make any excuse at all. I'm just his driver, since I was babysitting his truck.

As I drive us downtown, Ty watches me, and I watch the road.

"Stop looking at me," I finally say as I take the exit off the highway.

"I like looking at you."

I can't believe that. I change the subject to a question that has been pinging around in my brain all afternoon. "How long have you known?"

To his credit, he doesn't hedge. "I didn't know for sure until today. When you said you were in the laundry room…that was when I knew for sure. But something clicked into place a week ago that made me wonder."

What the hell did I reveal?

He clears his throat. "You told me about your second date with Ben being better since I didn't crash it like I did the first one."

"Oh." A strange guilty feeling comes over me. "I…it wasn't…"

"It's okay," he says quietly, although his voice is tight, and it doesn't *feel* okay. "Ben's a nice guy."

"He is." I swallow around a lump in my throat. We're only a block from home now, thank God. This is too hard, suddenly. "I'm not going to have any more dates with him, though."

"Good."

When I glance sideways, Ty has stopped looking at me, and he's staring out the window.

I turn onto our street. It's packed tonight, so I need to go past our apartment building to the very end of the block before I find a spot.

After I park, I hand the keys back to Ty. "There you go. Your truck is still in one piece."

"Kiley, you can keep driving—" He tries to catch my wrist, but I pull away just in time.

I hop out of the truck and head toward the apartment.

Behind me, the passenger door opens, then closes.

Ty's footsteps follow me into the building and up the stairs. Past his apartment, all the way to the top floor.

I don't look back. That lump in my throat is so big it

hurts now, and I don't want to think about why I feel like this.

I shove my key in the lock, but Ty covers my hand with his before I can turn the handle. "Stop running away from me."

I go still, and into that stillness floods a deep awareness of his body behind mine. Big, hard, hot.

He murmurs my name, then slowly turns me around, his hands on my arms, then one to my shoulder and the other to my hip.

"You've known that I'm…me…for a week," I manage to get out as he pins me with his electric green gaze. "I've known you're…you…for a few hours. We aren't coming to this conversation from the same place."

He exhales roughly. "Does it help or hurt if I admit that I spent a lot of that week wondering if you were fucking with me, and knew all this time?"

"What?" I straighten my shoulders, outraged. I push up to my full height, bringing us closer to standing eye to eye, and I glare at him. Something about the brightness in how he stares back at me tells me that if he has to choose between me running away from him and me yelling at him, he'll take the latter. "Why would you think that about me?"

His hand on my hip tightens, his thumb stroking a distracting arc up and down on the padding over my hipbone. "You've made it clear that you think it's funny when I'm fucked with."

My mouth drops open.

He shrugs, not breaking eye contact. "And you like to wind me up."

"Uh, you do the same thing? Both sides of your personality. Or do you not remember texting me things like, *what are you wearing?*"

"And you were always there with an answer that would drive me fucking crazy, weren't you, Little Miss No Panties?"

"Yeah, well you have a little miss in every port."

He laughs. "Good one."

I push at his chest. "Now who's the liar? You couldn't wait to get back to Miami and see Little Miss High Maintenance."

"What are you talking about?" He bats my hands off his chest, catching one wrist and stretching it up above my head, pinning me to the door.

My breath hitches. "The woman at the bar, in the bikini."

"Sounds like a figment of your imagination." His grip tightens and he leans in, his lips close enough to mine that I can feel the sensation of them on my mouth, a distracting tingle I don't need right now.

I twist my head to the side and glare at the doorframe. "Weird. Because I distinctly remember seeing your hands all over her."

"When the fuck was that? There hasn't been anyone other than you in so fucking long, I think I might go crazy with need."

"At the bar I took my friends to at your recommendation!"

He stares at me.

I stare back.

"No, seriously, what are you talking about?" His eyes are wild, his expression genuinely bewildered.

"You. The hotel bar. A woman in a trench coat, teasing you…"

He frowns, his gaze shifting up and away as he thinks. "Do you mean *Nina*?" His attention snaps back to my face. "Were you with the WAGs that night? I didn't see you there."

"I was..." I swallow hard. "I might have been hiding from you."

"Oh, Kiley." He laughs. "You sexy little brat. That wasn't a hook-up. What did you call her?"

"Little Miss High Maintenance," I mutter.

"Well, that's accurate." He leans in again, his lips once again close to mine, and I hate how my heart leaps at the return of that sizzling, almost-kiss sensation. "She's my *agent*. I have never, and will never, fuck her."

"Your agent?" I shake my head. "But the bikini top...and she said something..."

"Yeah, she's a brat, too. You two would get on like a house on fire, I'm sure. I don't remember what she said. I do remember telling her to put her jacket back on and stop teasing me." He smiles, and it's one of those whole face smiles where his eyes crinkle and his mouth is wide and soft.. "Were you jealous?"

"No," I lie, my heart flip flopping in an out-of-control manner.

"Liar," he says.

And then he kisses me. It takes me by surprise and steals my breath, making me lightheaded as his tongue demands entrance to my mouth. Oh. *Oh.*

My arms curl around his neck, pulling him in close. He presses his whole body against mine, every inch of him, and there's his cock, right up against my mound.

Oh. Fuck.

He's rock hard and long, and that buzzing sensation that

had started when his lips were just close to mine has expanded to a full-on rage of bees throughout my entire body.

I need him closer. I need him inside me. I need more of this kiss, so much more it will stop being a kiss and turn into something we can't turn back from.

Which is exactly why it needs to stop.

Every cell in my body screams as I put my hands on his cheeks and break our kiss, ducking my face.

The silence is deafening.

His chest heaves against mine, making my nipples tighten. "You okay?"

No. "We really shouldn't be doing this. It's too messy."

"Shouldn't?" He puts his finger under my chin, and against my better instincts, I let him lift my face and take my mouth again. Not just let him. I push into the kiss, craving every delicious second of it with a desperate hunger I barely recognize.

I've kissed so many people in my year of being slutty, and not a single one has made me this ravenous for a second kiss.

This time, he's the one who pulls back, and his gaze is victorious. "Shouldn't do that, huh?"

I suck in a ragged breath. "Definitely not."

He nods. "Why not?"

"Because…" I trail off. "It's hard to explain."

"Try me. Is this about your year of hook-ups?"

The accuracy of his question steals my breath as easily as his kiss did.

He drops his gaze to my mouth. "Did you kiss Ben like that?"

The buzzing is back, loud and distracting. "No," I confess.

"Then tell me why we can't do this." He pushes in against me, his cock making the rest of the point.

I've never wanted to be naked with anyone more.

I understand how, from his point of view, that makes perfect sense. We clearly have intense chemistry, and in a perfect world, I would get to know what it is like to ride Ty Connor into the sunset.

But after Crys, I had to put myself first. I looked at the mistakes I made in the past and made two commitments to myself. No more falling for handsome flirts. And no repeats. Two very simple rules that I can't break just because of two amazing kisses.

Four amazing kisses, if you count the one earlier today and the one in the arcade bar.

Which makes me squirm, because I don't need to have the thought in my head that every kiss with Ty might be incredible.

There can't be any more kisses! No matter how incredible they might be!

But when I open my mouth to tell him that, nothing comes out.

"Let me guess." He brushes his thumb over my bottom lip, his gaze hot and hooded. "You need whatever we do to be locked down. No expectations, no strings attached. Just sex."

My belly quivers at the promise of a hot night of Ty in my bed.

Sex.

Just sex.

"I can be what you want," he says, his voice low and confident. "But I need something, too."

"What?" My voice sounds breathy and far away.

"I bet you want this to be a one-time only thing."

I nod weakly. That is one of my two rules.

He tips his head back, and my gaze gets lost in the lines of his corded throat. I want to press my mouth there, and there, and there…

Then he swallows hard and drops his attention back to my face, locking his eyes on mine. "But we've already broken that rule."

CHAPTER 29
TY

"What do you mean, we've already broken that rule?" Kiley searches my face, curiosity lighting up her gaze.

Arousal churns hard, hungry in my veins.

It doesn't help that I ache in *painfully celibate for far too fucking long,* and now the girl I want is in my arms.

And I know her stubbornness on this point comes from a place of hurt. I want to be a balm to that injury. I know our chemistry has been something she's turned to when she's scared before.

Triumph roars inside me. *Yes.*

I've hooked her. Now I just need to reel her in. I lower my voice to the growl I've used when sending her voice messages. "I don't count as one of your one-time-only hookups, sexy girl. Not when we've made each other come. We're past our first time, you and me. If you invite me in tonight, it's going to be our *next* time."

And I won't want it to be our last time, but that's a truth better kept to myself.

One thing at a time.

"A loophole," she whispers. A slow smile curves over her mouth, pulling my final thread of self-control dangerously thin. "I like it."

That breathy admission snaps that thread in two.

With a growl, I take her mouth again, this kiss the hardest and most demanding of all, and I blindly turn the key in her door handle at the same time.

The door behind her back swings open and we stumble into her apartment together, our mouths fused.

"My key," she gasps.

Right. Bad neighbourhood.

How soon can I move her to a nice safe condo in the sky?

Tamp that shit down, Connor. She doesn't want you to be all possessive over her.

I spin around and grab the key, then deadbolt the door.

When I turn back, she's kicking off her shoes. I do the same, then prowl after her as she leads me to her bedroom.

"Nice place," I say, not taking my eyes off her.

"It's the exact same as yours," she says breathlessly.

"Good. Then you'll know where to find my bed the next time you need this."

She rolls her eyes.

I cage her against the doorframe. "Take my shirt off."

"Why can't you do it?"

"I want your hands on me." I cup her face. "And mine are busy."

Her fingers slide under my t-shirt, making my abs contract at the fiery touch. *Yes. God yes. More more more of that.*

I taste her lips again, then trail my mouth to her neck. Up to the sensitive spot behind her ear, then down the soft length of her throat to where her pulse is fluttering frantically at the hollow between her collarbones.

My shirt coming up between us interrupts my exploration of her skin for a moment, then I dive right back in.

"You smell incredible," I groan. "And you taste even better. I'm going to devour every inch of your bossy body. Do you know that? Do you know you're going to be consumed right now?"

She laughs, a throaty, sexy sound that I can feel through my lips.

Then she pushes me back, flicking her gaze over my bare chest and abs with heated interest, and I flex for her. With a wicked smile, she leans in and sinks her teeth lightly into my chest.

"Jesus Fuck," I gasp. "Did you just bite me?" I grip her jaw and lift her face up. "Bad girl."

"Are you sure?" She's breathless.

No, I'm not fucking sure. My cock is straining the limits of my jeans. "There will be consequences for permanently maiming me," I grind out.

She laughs and pulls my mouth to meet hers. "No biting, got it."

As she kisses me, her fingers push under the waistband of my jeans. Clever, flexing fingers curving over the top of my ass. She lets out a little sigh, a very satisfied sound that goes straight to my soul with a sizzling brand.

I need to regain some control here. "If you're going to maul my ass, the very least you could do is show me the tits that have haunted me for months."

"For months?"

"Do you know how fucking much you jiggle?"

"Yes, I am painfully aware of how much I jiggle. What does that have to do with—"

"I jack off to your tits on a daily fucking basis. So if you don't mind, I would like to see them. Now."

"You are such a gentleman."

"I'm a gentleman who needs to suck on your nipples."

She blinks at me in disbelief, then pulls up her t-shirt as if challenging me to make good on that promise.

I catch her hands and take over, stripping the soft black cotton away. Her arms float down, framing two creamy mounds spilling out of a skimpy, strappy hot pink yoga bra. The vision makes my mouth water.

These were right upstairs from me all this time. *She* was right here, with her breathy anonymous whimpers and her tight, perfect little nipples…

Reverently, I ghost my fingertips over her trembling skin before I hook my finger into the scooped neckline and ease her pillowy soft flesh out into the air.

And there they are, two pale, delicate discs with tender peaks that tighten under my inspection.

Circling one beautiful tip with my thumb, I murmur, "I should have been doing this every fucking minute of every fucking day."

She tips her head back and lets out an earthy moan that makes my cock leak.

I pinch the other nipple. "This is the one you sent me."

"What?"

"I'd recognize it anywhere. I've had a photo of this nipple on my phone for months. You sent me this."

"I didn't send it to *you*," she protests. Because she wouldn't have if she'd known. I know that. But I also need her to know that *was* me. That BeastMode *is* me.

"Yes you fucking did. And you moaned in my ear." I reposition my fingers, pinching more of her flesh, enough to tug. To bring her closer and show her who is boss. "It was my words that made you hot. It was me who made you come. You remember that?"

"Yes," she breathes.

"Good. I don't want you to think it was a mistake. It doesn't fucking feel like a mistake. Don't get me wrong, luscious. We've made wrong steps here, but not in letting each other be wild and free."

She trembles on those last words.

I release her nipple, relishing the way she physically shudders at the sensation of blood flowing back into the tip. Then I catch her in my arms, pulling her right up against me again. Letting her feel my arousal for a moment before I put her back against the doorframe.

"Arms up. Hold on to the frame and arch your back."

She rolls her shoulders, lifting her arms above her head, stretching her torso. I cup the heavy weight of her breasts in my hands, savouring the softness that makes my fingers ache to feel her everywhere. "That's it. Present your pretty tits for me. Can you hold still if I have a taste?"

She sucks in a breath and holds it.

I lean in, my lips brushing the curve of her ear. "You gotta keep breathing, Forge. Can't have you passing out until I've tasted every secret spot you've been hiding from me."

Her exhale is shaky but beautiful, trusting and compliant.

Never in a million years would I have guessed Kiley to be this obedient. And I'd bet anything that she won't be this well behaved again for a while, so I'm going to take full advantage while I can.

I kiss and lick another trail down her neck, pausing everywhere I find her fluttering pulse. Knowing how affected she is adds an incredible layer onto what I'd already fantasized about. All my future jerk-off sessions starring Kiley will feature this wild, needy pulse jumping against my mouth.

It's only topped by the first taste of her breasts. Her nipple is hard, a tight bead against my tongue, but the rest of her is velvety soft and so fucking sweet. I suck more of her tit into my mouth, pulling with abandon now.

Her body shakes as I pop off and glance up at her face.

She's gazing down at me in wonder.

"Don't let go of the door," I say huskily before repeating the attention on her other breast. It's so fucking easy to love on her tits. Her nipples seem to be connected by a live wire to the rest of her, and flicking and sucking it gets the most amazing responses.

Trembling.

Shaking.

Moans.

But I'm not in a rush to make her come just yet. I just want to get her worked up. Then I'll stretch her out on her bed and start wringing orgasms out of her.

So I let go of her breasts, letting them bounce. I drag my hands down to her waistband. Holding her gaze, I flick the button on her jeans free, then peel the zipper open.

Her panties match the pink bralette.

Under her moody goth girl exterior, Kiley Forge is electric and sexy as fuck.

She shudders as my knuckles graze her belly, but even as that tremor wracks her body, she holds the position I put her in.

That kind of obedience has to be hard for her, and she deserves a kiss.

"I knew you were a good girl deep down," I murmur against her lips.

She huffs a surprised laugh. "I didn't know that."

I'm smiling as I take her mouth. Slow this time, making sure she's fully with me in this moment, that she wants my fingers to keep exploring.

She kisses me back like she's made of liquid need.

Hot relief pulses through my veins, and I slide my fingers into her panties.

Here she's lush and soft, too, a perfect puffy pussy that was made for my fingers to sink into. And when I find her clit, it's like coming home.

The way she moans into my mouth can only be compared to the soul-deep satisfaction I once felt at waking up to a sunrise over the ocean, knowing I'm going to get to play an NHL hockey game that night.

Getting Kiley's slick arousal on my fingers is actually better than the perfect life I once had, because it's not going to get yanked away from me at the whims of others. Staying knuckle deep in heaven, on the other hand, is up to me and my skill alone. Keeping this girl happy just skyrocketed to my top priority in life.

I pull my hand out of her panties—just to get us moved to the bed—and lick my fingertips as she watches, her lips parted and her eyes wide.

Nostrils flaring, feeling like a beast, I swallow her essence. "Delicious."

"Who are you?" she breathes.

I grin. "Your online friend, in the flesh."

"Ty..." She shakes her head.

"We're just getting started." I crowd up against her. "You turn me on like nobody else. You are singular and perfect and I even like the way you bite me. Now take off your pants."

She squirms away, pushing those jeans over hips that haunt my dreams.

I get a show as she bends over, sliding them down her long, thick thighs.

She flicks a *what next, boss?* glance my way.

"Sit on the bed."

She does as she's told, a very good girl indeed.

Triumphant, I pull a strip of condoms out of my pocket.

She smirks when I toss them on the bed. "You're always prepared, aren't you?"

Is she thinking about the fucking condom she found in my parka? That is old news.

I wrap my hand around her throat, my thumb pushing her chin up, and fuck, I love the way her breath catches when I make her look at me. "I bought these on my way to the airport. To use with you, and only with you. I haven't needed condoms at all since the day I met you, and I knew if there was a chance to be the next notch on your bedpost, I was going to take it with both fucking hands. Got it?"

"Got it," she whispers, her breath hitching.

I rub my thumb along her jaw, then release her and trail my fingers down to her chest to cup a breast again before pushing her backwards with my fingertips.

She flops onto the bed, her breasts bouncing, her belly jiggling, and my cock presses so hard against my fly it hurts.

I cup my erection. "Look what you do to me."

Her eyes flash. "I want to see more than just your jeans."

I shake my head and sink to my knees. "I have plans

before I free my cock. The second he gets close to your bare skin, it'll be game over and I'll need to be buried inside you."

"Sounds terrible," she drawls sarcastically.

I hitch one of her thighs over my shoulder and trace a finger down the warm middle of her panties. "Patience, luscious."

"I'm not known for that." Her voice quivers as my wandering fingers catch the elastic edge of her panties and draw them to the side, giving me my first glimpse at her pussy.

I exhale reverently. She's fucking gorgeous. Dark pink folds glisten invitingly. I stroke my thumb up one pussy lip, grazing around her clit, then down the other side.

"Hello, beautiful," I murmur.

"Luscious, beautiful…you've got a way with words." She squirms and spreads her legs wider.

"It's easy when I'm inspired," I whisper, leaning in to give her a kiss. Her hips snap at the contact of my mouth against her sex, and I plant my hand low on her belly, pinning her down.

A headiness fills me as she squirms under my possessive, claiming touch.

Mine.

Mine to taste, mine to pleasure.

I kiss her again, open mouthed this time. Licking between her pussy lips, licking up her delicious taste. Raw, sexy sweetness, a potent nectar that works its way inside me like nothing else ever has.

Mine mine mine.

I cover her whole cunt with my mouth, sucking now.

"Oh, Ty," she breathes. "That's so good."

Of course she likes this. She's my sexy girl.

Yanking her panties off so hard I hear them tear, I spread her legs wider and take a wide, long lick from between her cheeks up to her clit and then back to her core for another, deeper swipe. Thrusting my tongue all the way into her tight hole. Tasting where I will fill her up until there is nothing left between us.

Fuck, she's ripe.

With each pass of my tongue, her body goes softer, softer, softer. Blooming, nectar dripping out of her. I circle my attention to her clit, kissing and sucking it the way I did her tight nipples, and it has the same responsiveness, but ten times bigger.

Kiley's moans are music to my ears as I pull her hard little bud into my mouth, sucking her clit until she sinks her fingers into my hair.

And then she gasps that she's coming, and that's an electric shock to my system. Need spirals down my spine, pulling my balls tight.

I lick her through her climax, a roar of need in my ears. I shove my hand into my pants, squeezing the tip of my cock so I don't jizz in my pants.

As soon as her legs fall wide, languid and temporarily sated, I shove to my feet and strip. My cock is so hard it aches. She watches me get naked, her gaze hooded, her mouth swollen, her lips red with lust.

We're both silent as I sheath myself, but that stops as soon as I'm between her thighs, my cock hanging heavy, desperate to get inside her.

I palm a tit, squeezing her flesh between my fingers before I scoop my hand up to circle her long, soft throat. "It's about time we did this in person," I say huskily.

She laughs, breathlessly, then lifts her mouth to kiss me.

As her tongue pushes into my mouth, I fit my cock against the entrance to her pussy and sink my tip into her tight, hot cunt.

That alone could be enough to make me blow. Fuck. I pause and snarl down at her, "How the fuck do you feel this good?"

"Practice," she gasps.

I growl and snap my hips, claiming another inch of her. "I'm going to ruin you for all others."

"Bold claim. Show your work." She giggles, but then screams as I roll my hips and press again, surging into her all the way. "Oh, Ty!"

"Damn straight." I savour the deep squeeze of her body around me, her pulsing heat stroking every inch of my cock, then I anchor us to the bed, her hands in mine, and start moving.

She winds her legs around me, taking every thrust as good as I give it. Our bodies are fucking magic together, and my jealousy fades as pleasure takes over.

Months, I've thought about this in the abstract. Days, I've plotted how to make it happen for real. Hours, I've hoped it would come to this tonight.

But it's only been in these magical minutes since we stumbled through her door that I've really come to understand what this wild connection we have means.

Kiley Forge is mine.

And she has been mine since the moment we met.

"I'm going to need to feel you come on my cock," I say.

She writhes beneath me. "Then I'm going to need you to release my hands so I can rub my clit."

I tighten my grip on her wrists. "Can I do it?"

She shrugs.

Shrugs!

Rearing up to kneel on the bed, I hitch her legs over my thighs, lifting her hips up and presenting that pretty little clit I've already kissed to one orgasm.

I'm pretty fucking sure I can rub it to another one.

I trace my thumb around where my cock is planted in her body, gathering up her slick and drawing it to the top of her sex.

"You tell me if I'm not hitting the spot just right," I say confidently.

She rolls her eyes, which is just as bad as a shrug.

My other hand tightens on her hip, pulling her deeper onto my cock.

"I don't know what kind of mediocre sex you've been having with guys like Ben." I roll my thumb over her clit, watching her face. "But I want to make you come. A lot. Repeatedly. I want to watch you make yourself come, too, but that's not going to be the standard with us."

Her eyes lose focus somewhere around *not going to be,* which makes it hard for her to argue on *the standard with us.*

I snap my hips, thrusting into her tightness again, timing the roll of my thumb on her clit to the deep glide of my cock against it on the inside.

I slide my other hand from her hip to the hot pink yoga bra pushed down to a band just below her breasts. A convenient handle. I wrap my fist around it, my cock thickening at the new leverage. Her tits bounce against my knuckles as I pound in and out of her body.

"God damn, you have a pretty pussy." She's so slick and pink and snug. I could watch myself fuck her all night long. "And your clit is perfect, too. Do you always get this hard?

You're straining for my thumb, aren't you? Eager little clit. Eager girl. Sexy girl."

She's panting for me now, squirming on my cock. "Please, Ty."

"Please what? Tell me."

She sobs. "I'm so close."

"Yeah?" I give her more of the same pressure against her clit, and it throbs back at me.

God. Damn.

I've never been more invested in making a girl come before.

Every sense is dialled in, focused on the way she's tightening around me, the way the flush on her neck is drifting to her tits, and the tension ratcheting up in her body.

Her sexy, unfocused gaze.

Her parted lips.

That pulsing, needy bundle of nerves beneath my thumb.

I drive into her again, bucking hard now, and she arches her back, her hips slamming into my own.

Fuck.

Yes.

She screams and her clit starts fluttering like mad. I feel the same spasm deep inside her, and it's too good, it's too much.

I thunder my cock deep inside her and fall forward, yanking her into my arms as my hips snap.

"Oh my God I can feel you," she breathes into my ear.

And then she starts laughing. It's a soft, wild, out of control giggle that rolls over us, her body shaking with the after effects. She twists her head into her pillow, pressing her lips together.

No. Fuck no. None of that.

I catch her chin and pull her back, kissing her. I want to taste that fucking laughter. It's mine now.

She's mine now.

There's a little hitch in her breath, then she kisses me back.

I don't roll off her until my heart stops pounding, and my legs are threatening to cramp up.

I excuse myself to the bathroom to deal with the condom. There's a bird hopping around on the windowsill, and I give him a stupid-assed grin. "She liked that a lot, bud."

The bird bobs his head in approval.

Back in her bedroom, Kiley is sitting up and has covered herself, the white bedsheet pulled over her breasts. She gives me a smile that says we're done for the night. "I need to work in the morning, so…"

I sit on the side of the bed and circle her ankle with my hand. "You sure I can't talk you into taking a bedtime shower together?"

"I—" She swallows hard, something bright flaring in her gaze.

Good, I want her to like that idea, even if it's not tonight.

But she still shakes her head. "It would be faster if I clean up alone."

Sure, faster. But not nearly as much fun. "All right." I flick the sheet off her leg and kiss her knee. "But we're going to do this again soon."

"Confident in yourself?"

"Confident in us." I climb on top of her.

She stops me with her hand pressed flat to my chest.

I glance down at the hand, then back to her.

She takes a deep breath. "Give me the eight days you had, okay?"

Her gaze is steady and calm. Sure of herself, and as hard as it is to hold back, I see her. At the door, she was conflicted, but desire won out. Now that we've sated our baser instincts, physical need won't win any arguments.

I sit back, catching her hand so I can kiss her palm before releasing her. "I know you need to protect yourself. That's all right. I'm going to show you that I'm a guy you can trust."

Pain flashes in her eyes, then her expression shutters.

And I realize my mistake.

She doesn't want me to know that about her. She doesn't want me to see her as vulnerable.

"It's cool." I roll out of her bed, naked as the day I was born. I make a slow show of pulling on my clothes, giving her a good eyeful.

She makes no effort to hide that she's watching.

This part, she likes.

"You'll see me soon, Forge."

"I'm sure I will." Indecision flares on her face for a moment, then she crooks her finger at me.

My heart leaps at the promise of one more kiss, and I lean in with pleasure.

She smiles against my mouth, which feels so fucking good. I'm never going to stop delighting in how good that feels. "No more talking about other people when we fuck, okay?"

I want to punch my fist in the air at the confirmation that we will be doing this again. "Okay."

"Yeah? That easy?"

"Well…"

She tips her head to the side, eyebrows cocked.

I try to look chagrined. "You gotta know I wanted to find

you for so long. We were so hot together online. But there was this other woman who I wanted just as much—"

She shoves at my chest.

I wrap my arms around her, grinning into her hair. "She lives upstairs from me and she's the bossiest brat I've ever met, but there's something magical about her."

"Oh." Her fingers curl, a possessive grip that takes hold of more than just my t-shirt.

"There isn't anyone else for me." I find her gaze and hold it. "So I'm not sorry for getting possessive when I'm inside you. Because you're really special to me. You have been for longer than I should admit."

A stunning smile spreads across her face.

"Get out of here," she whispers.

I nod. I'm going. But I'm not going far, and not for too long.

CHAPTER 30
KILEY

The next day, I wake up to a good morning text from Ty. And it's early, too, because I'm working today.

TY

I hope you slept well last night. I woke up thinking about you. (This is a no pressure text, I know you need seven more days to come to terms with the fact that I'm awesome both online and in person)

Grinning, I roll out of bed and tap out a quick reply as I'm brushing my teeth.

KILEY

You're up early. I'm going to work, so if I ignore you for the next four days, it's just because I'm run off my feet.

TY

Want a ride?

My heart leaps. I shake my head, but I don't type out *no*. I don't answer at all. I get dressed, throw a lunch in my backpack, and leave my apartment—only to find Ty waiting on the landing between our floors.

"You really need to stop lurking outside of doors," I mutter through a smile I try really hard not to make.

"Why?" His eyes twinkle. "The best things happen when I lurk, waiting for you."

There's another inconvenient flutter in my chest. "Where are you going this early in the morning on a holiday?"

"The hospital, to drop you off. Then probably the arena to get a workout in."

My mouth falls open.

"Relax," he murmurs, gesturing for me to take the stairs ahead of him. "I heard you moving around above me, and I was awake. I need coffee. Let's go."

I snap my lips together and nod. I don't want to run for the bus stop anyway, and I can buy him a coffee as a thank you.

Once we're in his truck, I direct him to my favourite coffee spot. And then I say, "listen, this is very nice, but you can't drive me to work every day."

"Why not?"

"Because I need some space!"

"To process us."

"Yes."

He nods. "So just if it's raining, maybe..."

I laugh.

"Or you could keep the keys to my truck and drive yourself."

"No."

"Do you want me to buy you a car?"

"Ty!"

"What kind of car do you like, anyway?"

I shake my head. "I'm not having this conversation with you. Don't be ridiculous. The more over the top you are, the more time I will need."

"Nope. We agreed on eight days." He parks the truck. "But I promise you I'm not going to pressure you into doing anything more than accepting a ride. Let me be your friend, okay?"

"I don't need a ride home. I like to read and decompress on the bus after work."

He looks like he wants to argue, but I need some boundaries, and the bus home is genuinely nice after work.

"And every day that you drive me to work, I'm going to insist on buying you coffee," I add. As far as compromises go, it's pretty weak.

He looks like I've given him the moon. "Deal."

———

Confused bees are still rioting under my skin as I sign in for work.

On the one hand, I asked for eight days and he barely gave me eight hours.

On the other hand, he didn't try to kiss me—although he did look at my mouth in a hungry way—and friends give each other rides places.

He wanted to see you this morning. He heard you moving around and wanted to see you.

"What happened yesterday in my laundry room?"

I jump in the air, spinning around and clutching my iced coffee to my chest. Thank goodness it's already half empty, or it would be all over my scrubs. "Harper!"

My best friend raises her eyebrows. "Yep. Your bestie, remember?"

"I'm familiar."

"Are you also familiar with the bestie code about sharing hot guy secrets?"

I wince. "Okay, but do you have any grace and understanding about how hard it is to actually share those secrets when the hot guy in question is on the next level?"

She rolls her eyes. "You didn't like that answer when it was Kieran."

"Fair point." That doesn't make it any easier now that the shoe is on the other foot.

"So…what's going on?"

I play dumb. "You're here. At work."

"Yep. This place where we both work," she says with a smile. "What a surprise."

"I didn't know you were on the schedule today."

"Last minute fill in."

"I thought you weren't doing those this summer." I glance at the clock. There's still fifteen minutes before our shifts begin. "Do you have to go take report from the night nurse?"

"Already done. I'm just going to make myself a cup of coffee. I'd ask you if you want one, but I see you're good." She glances at the cup in my hand. "That's not on your bus route."

"I got a drive."

"Oh? Is Grant here?"

I clench my jaw. I'm pretty sure she knows he's off this week. "Nope."

"Interesting."

I glance around, but nobody comes to interrupt us.

She already knows that Ty and I were alone in the laundry room yesterday. And I'm guessing she's deduced that we kissed.

So why don't I want her to know the rest?

I chew on the inside of my cheek.

"Did Ty drive you to work this morning?" She asks it so gently, like I'm made of glass.

Fuck, I hate that feeling. I haven't been made of glass for a year. That's the Old Kiley.

"Yep." I pop the p, just to prove I'm cool with it.

She looks delighted. "It's okay to like Ty."

"Is it, though?" I shrug. "We've barely figured out how to be friends."

"Some people make better lovers than they do friends."

Heat blazes through me, and it must be obvious, because her lips pull into a tight, surprise O. "Did you…?"

I close my eyes and nod. "Last night."

"Oh my God. And it was…?"

I nod again. "It was *oh my God*."

She squeals.

My eyes snap open. "No. You can't get excited about this. I'm not sure *I'm* excited about this yet."

"Why not?"

"Because it turns out we'd been flirting online for months and didn't know it." I take a deep breath. "Anonymously. As other people."

Her eyes go really, really wide. "Did you catfish Ty Connor?"

"He catfished me! Not once did he let on he was a hockey player!"

"So how did you figure it out?"

"I didn't. He did. A *week* ago. I found out yesterday, right before you walked in on us in your laundry room."

"Oh my God." She presses her hand to her mouth and laughs silently. "I'm so sorry."

"I'm not. If you hadn't interrupted us, who knows what might have happened in there."

She winces.

I stick out my tongue. She deserves that for grilling me so early in the morning.

"So did he sleep over last night?"

"No, I kicked him out because I had to get up early for work."

"Then how did he come to give you a drive to work?"

"He heard me moving around above him. Which, by the way, you never told me you could hear that much."

She grins, wickedly. "You can't. He must have really been listening for you."

I make a face.

"Hey, you know what they say. If he wanted to, he would. And he did, so…he wanted to. Don't discount that."

"Don't make this all uber-romantic. One upside to the whole online-anonymous-identities thing is that I know him, and vice versa. We're both clear that we're just looking for hook-ups right now. It's just sex." I pause. "Really good sex."

She doesn't look convinced. "Mr. Just Sex got out of bed at quarter to six in the morning to bring you to work?"

"Yes." I take a swig of cold brew and try not to think about how he let me buy him a coffee, the whole time trying to get me to tell him what kind of car I want to drive. "We're neighbours, and sometimes friends, and now, apparently, maybe something else."

Fuck buddies? Exclusive fuck buddies?

I shiver as I remember his possessive dirty talk.

It doesn't all fit together like a neat, complete puzzle, but that's asking too much when the hot guy online turns out to be the cocky hockey player living downstairs.

But there's no way Ty is anything more than a very good time for me this summer.

And once it's over, I'd rather not be known as Ty Connor's ex-fling.

I follow Harper to the coffee maker in the staff lounge. Other people come in and out while I think exactly how to say this.

"Listen, about me and Ty—"

She glances at me. "You want to keep it a secret for now?"

I nod, relieved. "Yes. Exactly."

"Of course. I get it. The early days of a relationship are really precious and fragile. Don't worry, your secret is safe with me."

"It's not a relationship…" I start to say.

But then we aren't alone, and we both have to go to work.

It's probably better if she thinks that, anyway. It's kind of sweet that she believes in that fairytale for me.

———

TY

Good morning. It's so early. Need coffee.

KILEY

You don't need to drive me in if you want to go back to sleep!

I'm good. Let's go. Tell me you've got
another fun coffee place to try today.

You know I've got a whole list of them.

———

"Good morning," Ty says on the third morning, yawning as I join him in the apartment hallway.

"Have you considered going to bed earlier if you're going to moonlight as a chauffeur?" I tease.

"I'll catch a nap this afternoon." He shoots me a quick glance. "You're still good taking the bus home?"

"Yeah." I pause. "Thank you for this, though. I like our coffee…"

He grins. "Our coffee dates?"

"They aren't dates."

"Of course not. Where are we going this morning?"

"The nearest drive-thru," I snap.

Which is a lie. I've picked a hipster place he's going to love.

———

By the end of my fourth shift in a row, I'm dragging, and I consider texting Ty for a ride home. But it's a really nice evening, I have a hot dragon rider science fiction romance novella loaded on my ereader, and I could use the bus ride time to disassociate.

I told Ty I needed as much time as he had to think about what it means that he's BeastMode, but we're halfway through the eight days and I haven't thought about it almost at all.

It's hard to, because Ty—my hot neighbour—is being really, really nice. Flirty, but respecting boundaries.

I have a couple of days off in a row now, and I'm very tempted to suggest we spend some of that time together.

Is that smart? I don't know.

But when he dropped me off at work this morning, there was a moment when I'd opened the passenger side door, but I hadn't hopped out, and he was just looking at me across the truck cab and I could have so easily crossed the console in the middle and given him a long, hot goodbye kiss.

I wanted to, with everything in me.

The only thing holding me back was that I asked him for some time.

I don't even remember why I needed that time, and yet here I am, clinging to it.

You're afraid, you dummy. You've caught feelings, and feelings are scary and risky and bad.

The thing about feelings is that you can't just nope out of them. So if we're going to keep hooking up (and more, because he sure seems to like driving me to work in the morning), then I need totally different boundaries than I was originally thinking.

There's no keeping Ty at arm's length. He'll just keep showing up on the other side of every door I open.

I flip to the next page in my story and then realize I hadn't absorbed anything I'd just read, so I turn back. I read the same few paragraphs over and over again until the bus reaches my stop, and then I hurry off.

I don't see Ty's truck on the street, so I head all the way upstairs to my apartment. I switch to listening to an audiobook while I make dinner, and once I've fed myself, I continue the self-care by dragging myself into the bathroom for a shower. I'm going to sleep like the dead tonight, I swear.

I open the window to let the steam out, then wander back into the kitchen to grab my phone so I can keep listening to the audiobook in the shower.

My scrubs get tossed in the laundry basket, and then I step into the hot spray.

What a long set of shifts.

Was it only four nights ago that Ty came up with me? My head spins as I soap myself up and rinse off. I'm reaching for the shampoo when I hear a flutter, followed by a chirpy kind of coo.

I peer around the shower curtain and see a bird sitting on the open window sill.

I wave at it. "Shoo."

It cocks its head to the side.

"Shoo," I repeat, then rattle the shower curtain.

It flies straight at me.

Shrieking, I yank the shower curtain in front of my face, as if a flimsy piece of vinyl is going to protect me from a prehistoric flying assassin, and then I duck just as it makes glancing contact where my face was.

"What the fuck?" I scream.

The bird doesn't answer. Not really. It lands somewhere on my vanity and chirps at me, which is sort of a response. A *fuck you, lady* kind of response.

"Get out!"

It doesn't do that.

I peer around the curtain again. It's sitting on the faucet, admiring itself in the mirror. Slowly, carefully, I slide my hand to the door and I snatch the towel hanging there. Heart pounding, I consider my options.

I can make a break for the door and abandon the bathroom. It's the bird's territory now, until it gets tired of hanging out in it. But I'll want to brush my teeth before bed, and my phone is right beside the bird, the audiobook racing on at 1.5x speed. I'll want that, too—and I need to pause the book.

Reader priorities.

Damn it.

Maybe I can use the towel to herd it back out the window.

I turn off the shower and step out of the tub.

The bird ruffles its feathers at me. I don't speak bird, but that feels aggressive. I square my shoulders, ignoring the fact that I'm naked and don't have shiny, glorious feathers. I know how to make a dog know that I'm the alpha. I can do that with a bird.

"I said, *get out*," I snap firmly. And I swing the towel at the vanity to make my point very clear. The bird flies for the ceiling and the towel hooks around the faucet. I yank it back, adrenaline coursing, and there's a moment of unexpected resistance, then it gives way and my whole body slams into the door behind me. A high pitched, watery hiss joins the surreal late-night soundtrack of feather ruffling and chirping coos.

In disbelief, I stare as a narrow stream of water starts to spray out the side of the faucet.

"You fucking jackass," I snarl at the bird, although I'm the one who just made this situation worse.

In the distance, there's a hard knock at the door of my

apartment. I drop to my knees, ignoring the bird now as I look for the water shut-off valve under the sink.

It's not there. Well, it is, but the handle is broken.

"Fuck," I groan.

"Kiley, you okay in there?"

"Oh my God." I lift my voice. "I'm fine."

"Kiley!"

I scramble to my feet and wrench the bathroom door open, towel held loosely in front of me, just in time to see Ty kick his way past the mediocre lock and lurch into my living room, fists raised.

So I scream and put my hands up.

His eyes go wide.

"What the fuck, Ty?"

He snaps his attention past me. "Are you okay?" His gaze is firmly locked on the top of the bathroom door.

"No! A bird interrupted my shower and then I broke—"

"You're naked," he said sharply, interrupting me. "And I don't think I'm supposed to be enjoying that again for four more days."

I squeak and double over, grabbing the towel off the floor as he turns around. "Stay turned around."

"I won't move an inch. A *bird* interrupted your shower?"

"I need clothes for this," I mutter before dashing to my bedroom. I grab a pair of lounge pants, a sports bra, and a t-shirt, yanking them on before I run back into the kitchen and drop to my knees, looking for a tool or something under the sink cabinet there to turn off the water supply in the bathroom.

"What are you doing?"

"Looking for a wrench."

"To kill a bird with?"

"What?" I find a hammer. That's not going to work. I toss it over my shoulder, and Ty swears as it lands with a clatter. A glance over my shoulder tells me he's come to stand right behind me. "I'm not going to kill the bird. What's wrong with you? I need to turn off the water supply in there. I broke the faucet."

"Oh shit." He spins on his heel and opens the bathroom door, then ducks to the side as the bird flies past him. "Hey, buddy. You don't belong in here. Wow, that's a lot of water."

"Thanks for point that out, Captain Obvious." I turn back to rummaging.

"Where is the master water shut off for the apartment?" he calls out.

"No clue."

Wings beat against the inside air of my apartment, and I look up just long enough to see the bird fly across to my living room.

God.

A second after I shove a box of latex gloves out of my way, Ty's hands are on my shoulders.

I jump out of my skin.

"Whoa there. I'm not the bird. No need to kill me. Let me see what I can do."

"The leak is—"

"In the bathroom. I know. I wrapped a towel around it to stop the spraying, and I turned off your phone. It's wrapped in another towel, but I don't think it got too wet. Hey, let me look for the tools." He moves me to the side, turning me so my back is against the kitchen counter. He glances sideways. "Are there any tools in here?"

"I don't know. I inherited this apartment from my brother." I groan and bury my face in my hands.

"I've got a toolbox downstairs. I'll be right back."

He disappears. I listen to his footsteps as I track the bird, which is now hiding on the top of my bookshelf.

When Ty returns, he pauses at the entry to my apartment to look at the frame for a split second—because he broke it! —and then he strides to my bathroom.

Since the bird is in my living room, I open the balcony door, hoping it will leave that way now. Then I make my way to the bathroom, dread mounting.

Everything is wet. The wall. The mirror. The vanity. The floor.

Ty's jeans, from kneeling in the water. His shirt from… I'm not sure what.

But when he stands up and peels the sopping wet towel away from the faucet…it's not spraying anymore.

"You turned it off." I sag against the bathroom doorway. "Thank you."

"No problem."

"I mean, you also broke my door."

"Yeah. I guess I did."

"I'll call the building super and—"

"Let's take a look." Ty grabs his toolbox and I trail after him again.

"You need a new doorknob for sure." He winces as he looks at the frame. "And I may have cracked this, but I think it can be patched up. If we replace this trim piece and paint it, nobody should be any the wiser." He glances at his watch. "Are there any twenty-four hardware stores in this city?"

"Probably not." My head is spinning for a totally different reason than it was earlier. "How are you this handy?"

"I've lived on my own since I was sixteen."

Oh.

I suddenly remember a conversation we had about growing up poor and eating Mac and cheese with tuna, and I wonder how that sixteen-year-old kid fed himself.

He works his jaw back and forth before changing the subject. "Anyway, I'm sorry about all this."

"It must have sounded wild from your side of the door?"

"I thought you were in trouble." He clears his throat and gives me a look that sends a slither of chill straight through me. "I thought it was a date gone wrong."

He was coming to my rescue? I suck in a shocked breath. "Why would you think I was on a date?"

"I heard voices up here. Murmuring and…then the shower started, and the talking continued. It sounded like a conversation."

"My audiobook." I laugh in disbelief. "Oh my God. Ty— How could you think I'd bring a date home?"

He shrugs, his shoulders bunching up, looking extra big with the damp t-shirt clinging to him. "Why wouldn't you? You've got this plan, and you asked for time."

"To think about—" I swallow the last word.

He goes still, his face softening as he looks at me. "Us?"

"Yes."

He has the good graces to look chagrined. "But what about…"

I raise my eyebrows in disbelief. "The dates I went on? Like the date you ruined?"

"That was one date. There were others." He mutters it.

I step closer to him. "Can I tell you a secret without it going all the way to your head?"

He gives me a small smile, his eyes warm and pleading. "You can tell me anything."

I lift my hand and touch his damp t-shirt. His heart thumps against my palm through it.

Eight days was so ridiculously specific. I can't stay away from him that long. And when he huffs a little growl and pulls me in for a hug, I can't deny the relief I feel at being back in his arms.

I love the smell of his skin and the warmth of his body. I love the way his heartbeat picks up speed when I lean into him.

I curl my fingers into his t-shirt, making a fist, and I thump my hand against him gently. "You ruined every single date whether you were here or not."

He laughs, hoarsely, and his eyes glitter like emeralds. "Not going to say I'm sorry when I'm not."

I lean in, and he does, too, until our foreheads are touching.

"You thought I had a date?" I have to repeat it, because it feels surreal.

"I'm fucking glad you don't, doesn't that count for something?"

"Yeah, it does." I press my lips together. "What if I did have a—"

"I'd have torn him limb from limb." Ty's jaw flexes and his hands skate up my back, touching me as if to make sure I'm fine.

From my bookshelf, the bird decides this is a good time to re-insert itself into the group chat. It coos, then ruffles its feathers.

We turn to look at it, and it flies straight at us.

"Jesus," Ty gasps, pushing me down and bringing his arm up over his face.

"Now's your chance, killer," I say. "That's my bad date.

Tear him wing from wing."

CHAPTER 31
TY

I stare down at Kiley, then back up at the bird, who is flapping around her kitchen looking rather desperate to get outside now.

I grunt and put my hands on my hips, trying to figure out the path this bird will want to take, so I can make it easier for him. "You don't want me to kill the bird."

"No, of course not." She climbs to her feet. "Okay, let's… do something to get it outside."

And then I can fix her door well enough that I can drag her off to a bed to continue our conversation about how I ruin all her dates.

That's the best thing I've heard in weeks. Months, even.

Evicting the bird takes the better part of an hour.

Getting the latch to line up enough to put the door back in the frame—so at least it looks normal from the outside—only takes ten minutes.

Talking Kiley into letting me stay the night takes longer, but I don't like that the door isn't actually secure.

And for other reasons, I want her in my arms all night long.

So I persist, and she gives in, her eyes flashing.

"We could treat it like a proper date," I say. "Sit on the couch and watch some TV first?"

"This is not a date. Improper or proper." But she glances at the couch with enough longing, I don't care what we call it.

I tackle her to the cushions and make her laugh.

"God, you feel good," I mumble into her neck.

She protests something incomprehensible.

I smile and hug her harder. "Shut up and let me just hold you."

"I'm letting you!"

"Seriously, we both need a cuddle right now."

She sinks her teeth into my shoulder, making me yelp.

"You bit me again!"

"No maiming, though. I followed the letter of the law."

She kisses the light imprint her teeth left on my shoulder, then wriggles out from under me, her cheeks pink and round from smiling. "Okay, maybe this counts as an improper date."

I rearrange myself so I'm sitting sideways, looking at her profile. Her hair is damp and loose, dark waves spilling everywhere. I twist a strand around my finger, loving the silky slide of it against my skin. "And what would be a proper date that Kiley Forge might like?"

She presses her lips together.

"Bookstore visit?"

She sits up straighter, trying not to smile.

Nailed it in one.

"We can do that," I murmur. "What else? A really nice foodie restaurant?"

"This doesn't feel fair," she whispers. "You know me already."

I shift closer and trace a line up her neck, to the point of her chin, and then with my fingertip, turn her face so she's looking at me. "You know me, too. What's a proper date for me?"

Her eyes dart left and right, thinking quickly. "Lunch, not dinner. Something outside, like going for a hike and then hitting a food truck spot."

"Love it." I'm curious about the specificity. "Why not dinner?"

"You don't get as many of those to decide for yourself. So I figure in the off-season, you have a long list of dinner wish list places. I wouldn't want to take one of those away from you." Her lips curve. "So I'm in charge of the lunch dates and you're the dinner boss."

"I like the sounds of there being lots of dates."

"Me, too," she admits.

"I'm sorry I ruined your other dates. That was mean of me. I should have taken them over instead. The guys were all wrong, but the premise was good. How many dates do I owe you to make up for that?"

"Ummm…" She swallows hard. I trace my fingers down her throat to the pulse point at the base of her neck that tastes so sweet. Her pulse flutters against my touch.

I raise an eyebrow. "Is it a lot?"

"Well I had a plan to go on at least one date a week for a year. A different place, a different…guy…each week. At least one. If there was opportunity for more than that…"

"I get the idea," I grind out. "When did that go off the rails?"

She doesn't answer.

"Kiley."

"Let's watch TV."

"How about you tell me what I owe you?"

"I definitely don't want you to *owe* me dates!" She glares at me.

I won't be deterred. "Poor choice of words. How many dates can I contractually commit you to?"

She makes a frustrated little growling sound. "You want to know the truth?"

"Always."

"I haven't had a good date since you joined the team. You ruined my entire slutty year, halfway through it, just by moving to this city."

That's the best fucking news, and I cannot grin. I cannot—

"Don't look so pleased with yourself."

"Sorry." Not. Sorry. I'm beaming. I pull her against me, filling my hands with her warm, soft body. I curve a palm over her ass and squeeze. "We can get that year back on track. I'm more than willing to make up for last time. Just use me as much as you want. I like slutty Kiley."

I like slutty Kiley so fucking much, and now that I have her back in my arms, I'm not letting her go again.

CHAPTER 32
KILEY

That night, Ty sleeps over. And all we do is sleep—and talk, and kiss. But he doesn't try to get inside my clothes, and I don't initiate anything either.

When I wake up, he's looking at me, a smile on his face.

"Good morning," I whisper.

"The best morning," He rolls me onto my side and curves around me, his hand sliding immediately under my top to cup my belly, his fingers toying with my waistband. "How are you feeling today?"

I squirm back against his obvious erection. "Is that a leading question?"

"Sure. Yes." His lips brush the curve of my ear. "We still have three days to go—"

"It's fine."

"Fine?"

"I don't need more days. I want you."

His fingers push into my lounge pants like he's been waiting hours for me to say that, and he groans when he finds me bare beneath the soft cotton fabric. "God, I love the feel of you on my fingertips."

And I love the lusty way he says that.

Being wanted by Ty is as special as it gets, I think.

I work my hand in with him, our fingers jockeying for position.

"What are you doing?"

"Helping," I whisper.

He flips me onto my back and grabs my hand. "I don't need your help."

"It's just that we have things to do this morning, and I know my body best…" I trail off as he licks my fingertips.

"I'm not arguing that."

"Then why are you holding me by my wrist?"

"Because *I* want to know your body that well, too. I'm only going to learn by doing, so we don't need to rush this morning."

"It's just that it's hard for me to—"

"Wasn't that hard last week." He arches a brow, looking stern.

I want to argue with him.

But there's something in his clear dominance that also makes me go still, quiet…and I don't hate it.

I don't hate the firmness with which he shuts down the fight in me.

When he seems sure I'm not going to argue again, he continues. "Every man before me who didn't make figuring out your pleasure their number one priority has made it more difficult for you to trust me when I say it would be my fucking honour to spend a few weeks learning all the ways your body likes to get off."

"But—" I cut myself off.

He kisses my fingertips. "But what?"

I soften at the invitation to provide a counter. "There's really only one way I get off." I wriggle my index and middle fingers. "These two fingers on my clit."

"That's strange. I remember you coming pretty fucking hard when those two fingers were pulling my hair, right? And then…clutching your pillow?"

Heat sears through me. "That was…it had been a while…"

He releases my wrist, and my arm falls beside me. Then he grabs my waistband and tugs my pants down.

"Let's test this again, then." He shoulders my thighs apart and smiles at my pussy. "Hello, beautiful. I've missed you."

Well that's not fair. If he's going to directly sweet-talk my sex, she'll probably purr for him pretty fast.

"Now listen," he says confidentially, as if it's just him and my pussy, and Kiley Forge can't hear their conversation. "She wants me to do this real quick, because she has things to do today. But I want to take my time. I thought I was going to have to wait another few days before we got to kiss again, and—"

"Ty!"

He grins and lifts his head. "Yes, luscious?"

"Stop teasing." I bite my lip as I gaze down at him. His hair is golden in the morning light, his features so perfect it's almost hard to look at him. "I believe you. You want to make me come. So…please?"

"Please make you come? It would be my pleasure." He dips his head, maintaining eye contact, and his tongue swirls over my clit in a shockingly good approximation of the slow rolling rub he got me off with the first time. "Is this good?"

I nod feverishly.

He smirks. "I know. It made you drip already."

His tongue slides down to my entrance and I tip my head back, letting out a throaty moan.

He pulls that slickness up to my clit and licks me again, a firm swirl, followed by a sucking pull that shoots me off the bed.

And then he gets serious. He pins me down, folding me in half, knees up towards my chest, and he feasts.

At first my brain tries to fight for control. *It feels so good, but it's not quite the right pace. He's so good at this, but I'm thinking too much.* Overthinking about overthinking has to be a special level of self-sabotage.

As if he can hear my thoughts, he keeps shifting up what he's doing, trying different things.

It's his firm grip on my thighs that actually gets to me. The tighter he holds me down, the less I can think, and the more I start to feel.

Hot, needy, frantic feelings. A desperate ache blooms low in my belly, pulled taut by what he's doing with his mouth.

And then he adds his thumb, the way he used it before, and his tongue licks lower, circling my entrance.

I suddenly feel so empty it hurts.

"Ty, I need you."

"You've got me."

"I need you inside me."

"Come for me and then I'll give you my fingers."

"Your cock."

"No condoms."

My head thrashes back and forth, my pussy clenching around nothing as he rubs at my clit.

His tongue is right there, teasing me with an intrusion, but he won't push into me, not yet. Not until I come.

So needy.

My hips spasm, driving my clit against his thumb, and then I'm exploding, and he's groaning against my pussy.

"That's it," he moans. "Oh, you're a good girl, aren't you?"

He laps at my entrance as I laugh and sob, and then he pushes on top of me, his fingers spearing into me as he kisses me. I taste myself on his mouth as he swallows my giggles.

"Fuck my hand," he growls. "Give me another."

I push at him, my brain only partially working. "Top drawer. Condom."

"Yeah?"

He drags his fingers out of me and hops up.

He only slept in his boxers last night, so I get an unfettered view of the muscles in his bare back, his tight, round ass, and down his legs as he searches for the condom.

My mouth goes dry. His body is a work of art.

He twists around, holding up the condom. "Is this mine?"

"Umm…"

He laughs. "You kept it."

"And look what a good idea that was."

"You. Little. Brat." He lunges back to the bed, flipping me over and bringing his hand down lightly on my ass. "Do you have any other trophies from our arguments?"

I shake my head and press my face into the pillow.

He pushes my shirt up, his hand smoothing over my back before curving around to cup my breast. "You should be groped every morning."

"I agree."

His hands sink into my hips, shifting my position. He grabs the pillow he slept on and pushes it under my belly. "You got any more pillows?"

"Are you serious?"

"Oh right, I forgot, you like to rush in the morning." I get another swat for whatever imagined grievance that is about. "Next sleepover is in my bed."

Before I can guess at what he does with a dozen pillows when a girl is in this position, his cock nudges at my pussy, and the feelings replace the thinking.

The thick invasion splits me in two, filling me up in a way that doesn't feel possible. He's so big in this position it feels like he's permanently creating a Ty-shaped cock space inside me.

"This time you can rub if you want."

I'm still boneless from the first orgasm, my limbs heavy and my nerves buzzing. But as he thrusts, driving waves of pleasure through my body, I feel the coiling tightness of a second potential orgasm.

At first it feels like it might be enough for my clit to just be stretched and tugged by the thrusting, but as I listen to the sounds he's making—intimate, incredible noises, like he's profoundly enjoying being inside my body—I get needy for more.

I push my hand between my legs. And then it all slams into place. Perfect, effortless friction. Pressure like I've never felt before, not exactly, not in this combination, and I'm there, I'm coming, and it's hard and fast and brilliant, so fucking good, I can't even believe it.

I scream into the pillow, wild and laughing again, and Ty's grip tightens on my hips.

"Oh, you fucking brat. Don't you fucking milk me. I'm not done fucking you— *Fuck.*" With a dark-sounding grunt, he shoves into me one more time, his whole body vibrating with need as he releases in long, heavy spurts. "Take it, you brat. Take my come. You wanted it that bad, huh? Needy cunt. I fucking love— Uhhhh. Oh…"

His sounds of release break through my post-orgasm reactions and I fall silent, just listening and feeling as he holds onto me, tight as can be. Twitching. Groaning.

"Are you okay?" He tumbles beside me, searching my face. "You stopped laughing?"

I smile at him. "I was listening to you. You're noisy. In a good way. I like it."

"We're both noisy." He gasps and then yanks me into him, kissing me deeply, and only lets go when he needs to suck in a breath. "Jesus, you are good at that. You were right, you get yourself off better than I do. Fucking clamped down on my cock and didn't let go."

"Is that good?"

He blinks at me, than hoots an unexpected laugh. "Good? Kiley, you're the best fuck of my entire life. Yeah, it's good. Come here, you brat."

"You keep calling me that," I whisper into his neck as he gives me a full body hug.

"Yeah, because you're a brat. My brat. Held out on me for *months*. When we could have been fucking like that? There will be punishments later."

"What kind of punishments?"

"Can't tell you that yet." He kisses my forehead as he levers himself out of bed, suddenly refreshed. "Come on. Our first proper date is going to the hardware store."

CHAPTER 33
TY

"What do you think about building a list of date ideas on Lusty?" Kiley's in the passenger seat of my truck, scrolling through her phone, looking for brunch options near the hardware store.

She looks damn good in my passenger seat, too, especially freshly fucked in the morning. It's damn near perfect.

That odd sense of possessive pride stirs in my chest again, unexpected and unfamiliar, but feeling right all the same.

I have never craved anyone the way I want Kiley. There's something about the way our relationship unfurled, slowly and over time, online as strangers and in person as nemeses with chemistry, that has unleashed more feelings than I ever thought possible.

"Places to go on dates?"

"Yeah, or I think we can sequence..." She taps on her phone, thumbs flying. "Yes, we can combine a restaurant and a movie theatre, for example. So we can build complete dates."

"Look at you." I flash her an impressed smile. "You're a wizard on apps, aren't you?"

She looks surprised and pleased that I noticed that. "I don't know. I'm a deeply online person. It annoys some people."

"Not me." I squeeze her knee. "Okay, what can we bundle together to be dates… I'm thinking."

Since I know she had drinks with Ben for a first date, I want to level up on that to a proper meal.

Of course, since I started the day eating her soft, sexy pussy, I've already won. But still, there's the principle at stake: I want to be the best first date Kiley has ever had.

A meal is a must.

But she's already on that, hunting for brunch options.

And then our activity today is going to the hardware store, which is…niche, to say the least.

I'm already thinking I'm going to find out if she has a tool belt fantasy, and I'll buy whatever we need to make that a reality.

But I'm still missing something to take it over the top… something that's safer to tell our grandkids about.

Isn't that the point of the perfect first date? So that by the end of it, you know you're going to marry this girl, and you've built the first memory she's never going to get tired of reminiscing about?

Kiley has no idea I've raced way ahead of her, though. She's still adorably focused on brunch, and the app. "I could add you as a collaborator to the list, so we can both build out event elements."

"Sure." I turn the corner, then return my hand to her thigh. "I didn't know we could both add to lists."

"Oh yeah." She raves about the new list builder tool, which I don't think I've used yet.

Then she announces her top two picks for brunch, an Italian place near the hardware store, or a drive out past Kieran and Harper's place to a mill that overlooks a waterfall.

Top tier date options for sure.

"Put them both on the list, and we'll hit whichever one we don't go to today on the next date. Are you working tomorrow?"

That gets me the softest, sweetest smile. No sass. No sternness. Just the secret woman behind the bossy exterior. "I have three days off."

I park in front of the hardware store and give her my full attention. "I want them all. Three full-day dates in a row. I'll back off when you go back to work."

Her brows pull together a tiny bit as she worries her face into the most delicate frown.

I brace myself for her to tell me I'm walking, talking red flag, but after a beat, she unbuckles her seatbelt and flies across the console, wrapping herself around me.

I tug on her ponytail. "Hey, do you like tool belts? Because I have an idea..."

After we collect what we need for the doorframe repairs, Kiley makes a command decision and picks the Italian eatery for brunch.

"Because Italian is your favourite, right?"

That gets her a hungry, growly kiss before I correct her. "You're my favourite."

I take her hand as we walk to the restaurant. She smiles as she glances at our intertwined fingers. "How does this compare to your usual first dates?"

"No comment."

"What? Why won't you tell me?"

I tug her close, then loop my arm around her shoulders and kiss her cheek. "Because I'm trying to impress you."

"You don't need to impress me after that wake up this morning, and that is not a BeastMode answer." She pokes my side. "We know each other better than that."

She's got me there. That's true.

"Would it help if I go first?"

No. But I'm guessing she's not going to let this go. "Sure."

"I haven't done a breakfast date all year. That's why I asked. I like drinks in the late afternoon or early evening, either at a coffee shop or a bar. No commitment, you know? The date can be over in an hour if need be."

"Yeah, okay, I like drinks, too. But at a place that serves food, because I'm always hungry."

That makes her laugh. "Fair."

I hold the restaurant door open for her. "And I do like a breakfast date."

"I knew it," she crows.

Usually followed by a pre-nap romp, but I'm not telling her that. I don't want to hear her coolly say that sounds nice, like she's not jealous at all, because she's put present me in a different compartment than than past me, or some very reasonable answer like that.

Once we're seated at a booth, she pulls out her phone and glances at it briefly. Then she giggles. "Okay, so now on a date I'd probably reference something that's in your bio, but it's literally just workouts and Italian food. We've basically covered the food, and it feels silly to say, *so you like to hit the gym* to a professional athlete."

I chuckle. "That's a good opening line. What's your bio?"

She rolls her eyes. "You have to check it stealthily. You can't ask."

"Right right." I clear my throat. "Uh, gotta check my phone for a second."

She hides behind her menu as I refresh her Lusty profile.

Breakfast for dinner. Hot springs. Reylo fan fiction.

"I think we talked about a lot of this online," I say softly, feeling a spike of heat as I remember her telling me about the filthy stories she reads online. "What hot springs have you been to?"

Her eyes light up. "A couple of years ago I was working in Calgary, and I did this loop through the mountains. It was a dozen different hot springs in six days on this circular path that was almost a thousand clicks."

I do the mental math. Six hundred miles. "That's pretty cool. I've been to Banff a couple of times for weddings, did you stay there?"

Her lips twitch. "I slept in my car at campsites."

I don't look away. "That's cool."

"Is it?" For the first time in a week, I get the full Wednesday Addams mask.

I frown. "You don't think I've slept in a car?"

She sucks in a little gasp. "Oh. No, ummm…"

"Hey…" I reach across the booth and take her hand. "I was teasing."

She presses her lips together and nods. There's a flash of something I can't read in her eyes. "Have you? Ever slept in a car?"

"There was one wild weekend in college."

She tips her head to the side. "I didn't know you went to college."

"One year." I flick a glance at the menu, but I don't see anything on it. I lift my eyes, meet her cool but receptive gaze, and the whole story tumbles out. "I had a great coach when I was fourteen. He knew I had talent, and called in a lot of favours to get eyes on me. Thanks to him, I was tapped for the junior development program, and I left home when I was sixteen. From that point forward I was on the draft radar. That coach...all he asked me was to give college a shot. He told me I'd get a scholarship, and I should take it, even if the team that drafted me wanted to sign me right away. That he didn't want me to go to the big show until I was nineteen at least. I think he wanted me to fall in love with school in a new and different way."

"Did you?"

I laugh with a healthy amount of regret. "Nah. But I was drafted by Miami, and their development program agreed with the coach. I was dragged through my only year on campus by a team of tutors."

"Hot tutors, by any chance?" She sticks out her tongue.

"All of them," I admit. "The hockey program knew what worked for me. And it was fun, having that year to party. Because the following year, Miami was super hot, and the game..." I shake my head. "My body wasn't really ready to play against men."

"But you did it."

"I did. I think I was held together by spite and athletic tape by the end of the year, but I also won the Cup in my rookie year, so...it was worth it."

She frowns. "Spite?"

"My family never thought I'd make anything of myself."

"Oh." She makes a face. "I'm sorry."

At first I think she's just sympathetic, but then I notice the barest glitter at the corner of her right eye. A tear. The air between us goes still, but it's interrupted by the arrival of a waitress.

Have we looked at the menu?

No, I'm busy wondering what I don't know about this woman who I thought had told me everything in our online chats.

She buries her face in the menu, so I do the same.

I order eggs Benedict. Kiley gets a tomato stew with eggs, like an Italian twist on shakshuka. And we both get double espresso.

When we're alone again, she gives me another level look.

"You're very good at pulling yourself together," I say.

A smile pulls at the corners of her mouth. "I have a lifetime of experience tamping down my natural instincts to be dramatic."

"Your family...?"

"Very contained."

"They don't like that you work in the theatre, do they?"

Her mask falls away, and she makes a face, pursing her lips and wiping at her eyes for a second before shaking her hands in the air. "So I went to journalism school at a time when the entire news industry was collapsing thanks to the rise of the internet. And that didn't faze me at all—I'm an online girl, I can pivot. Plus I found storytelling fascinating, and that's all that journalism is, right? Well, the worst possible thing happened. I went to college and discovered..." She leans in and lowers her voice dramatically. "Creative writing."

I laugh. "Oh, the horror."

"When I told my parents I'd dropped a business elective and picked up a writing class, my father's email back was a link to the average earnings of a writer. No text to the email, just the link."

"That's cold."

"That's my parents. They only care about one's ability to pay down a mortgage at an accelerated rate."

"So a daughter who sleeps in her car…"

"Oh, they don't know about that. I would *never* tell them that."

"What about your brother?"

"Oh, Grant is great. He loves me exactly as I am. But he's…contained. He's a proper Forge. He has a firm partition between his personal life and what my parents can know about him, and he likes it like that."

"I was actually thinking that you are good at compartmentalizing your feelings. But you don't like that?"

"Ummm…" She thinks about it. A myriad of emotions ripple across her face. "How deep do you want to get with this question?"

Really fucking deep. I take her hand again and squeeze her fingers. "You can tell me anything. And I'll dig up something to share, too."

She takes a deep breath. "When I was twelve, I discovered my dad was having an affair. I thought…" A lost look passes behind her eyes, and for a second, I think she's going to change the subject. But then she swallows and keeps going. "I thought my mom should know. I wrote her an anonymous note, but she knew it was my handwriting. And then my parents split up. They told us about it in a family meeting, in a calm, cool way. They were going to have a trial separation, they called it.

"It lasted three months. And then my dad moved back in, and they've been together ever since. My mom told me, the night before he came back, that marriage was about compromise, and I was too young to really understand, but one day I would be in her shoes and I would get it then."

Her voice takes on a sharp edge as she finishes the memory.

I'm stunned silent.

She leans back in her chair, flicking her napkin over the curve of her belly. "I know we look like a pretty typical family. Boy, girl, mom, and dad. Grew up in a decent neighbourhood, went to good schools. My parents moved to a nicer house a few years ago. Outwardly…"

"It sounds pretty fucking hollow on the inside." I don't care how judgmental that sounds. "That's not right, what she told you."

Kiley gives me a tight smile. "I know that now."

I think about the fact that she's been cheated on, repeatedly. I say her name, low and rough, but then we're interrupted by our food arriving.

She picks up her fork, her hand shaking.

"Kiley."

Slowly, she lifts her head.

"You should never know what that is like. That's not compromise, putting up with that. Compromise is…" I gesture around. I'm not a relationship expert, but this feels pretty fucking basic. "Italian or Food to Table. Watching a game or watching a movie. How much screen time a kid can have. Not *infidelity*."

She smiles, but it doesn't reach her eyes. "I've learned

that the hard way. It's okay. Nobody's ever going to cheat on me again."

This time when she looks down at her meal, it feels final. Like I've pushed enough for a first date.

Grandma, what did Grandpa do on our first date? Well, kids, he made me cry and reminded me that my parents are fucking monsters in matching khaki shorts.

I carefully cut into my eggs. They're delicious, despite the sour taste in my mouth, and I like listening to the savouring sounds Kiley makes as she eats, too.

It doesn't take her long to soften, and start glancing across at me again.

Each time she does, my smile gets bigger.

"Have you done any other road trips like that hot springs loop?"

She looks delighted at the subject change. "Yep. Every time I got a new job, I'd do a winding road trip to move to that new city. I usually had at least a few weeks, sometimes longer." She tips her head to the side. "That's funny that you ask about road trips. That's in my Tinder bio, but nobody ever asks about it. Which is weird, because it's a great first date conversation. What your dream road trip would be, etcetera. That could spill into any number of travel conversations."

"Clever. And my dream road trip would probably be the ring road around Iceland." I point my fork at her. "Speaking of hot springs."

She sighs happily. "Yes. Amazing. I love it."

"Arizona is pretty amazing, too. The California coast..."

"I've done that one!" She tells me about a theatre festival she worked in Napa, and another short term gig in Oregon, and the epic drive between the two jobs.

By the time we exhaust the road trip talk, our plates are empty, and we've nudged them to the edge of the table.

"Anyway..." She looks at me, really looks at me, and then deliberately drops her gaze to the table, looking in the direction of where my cock is thickening just out of view. All it takes is a single, sultry look from her and my inner primate takes over. "How are we going to do these repairs? Am I playing the super cute Handyman's Assistant, or would you rather I be the sexy Lady of the House who forgot cash for a tip?"

I wave for the bill.

It doesn't matter what the role is. I'm going to fix her door, and then she's going to thank me on her knees.

I am a lucky, lucky man.

CHAPTER 34
KILEY

We spend the next three days mostly in bed. My bed, Ty's bed. My shower, my couch, and then his couch. His bed again, because his excessive pillow count is actually genius.

And we build a comprehensive date list on Lusty.

"I should go upstairs and sleep alone tonight," I say the night before I go back to work.

"Should you?" Ty kisses his way down between my boobs, which is a very convincing place to make the argument that no, I shouldn't.

"I need to sleep."

"We'll sleep. I'll be good. Do you want to sleep in my shirt?"

I shake my head. I want to sleep naked, pressed up against him.

I'm tired the next day, but I smile the whole way through my shift, too.

———

Over the next month, we start to tick away at the list of date ideas.

Grant goes on vacation for two weeks, and Puck is delighted to get to spend days with Ty when I go to work. Every so often, I get a notification that another entry has been added to our date list, and it's something dog friendly.

We tick off three of those in quick succession, but as soon as Grant returns, I pick up a few extra shifts to cover my time off around the wedding. And there's a lot of maid of honour responsibilities, too. The bachelorette spa weekend is around the corner, and I spend more time than I'd like sourcing incredible things for swag bags that will blow their WAG-y socks off.

While Ty is technically off for the summer, he's still skating almost every day with his teammates who live here. And he's been working with his agent a lot, too, coming up with strategy to improve his image going into the next season, which makes my heart squeeze.

I had no idea how sensitive he was about his early reception by Highlander fans—and how raw it must have felt for me to rub salt in that wound.

He brushes it off when I bring it up, because he's not the type to dwell, but I think of it every time he takes a call from Nina and tucks me into his side like I'm his good luck charm on this mission. I listen to how earnestly he wants to be liked here, what he's willing to do to endear himself to the people of Hamilton, and I think to myself, *we're going to get this done together.*

In between work and our proper dates, we have a lot of almost dates. Early morning coffees, late night booty calls, and dirty texts in between.

And we write funny reviews for our dates, together, which is more fun than I ever thought possible. We also rate the individual elements, like the food and the vibe. And in a stroke of genius that makes our list quite popular, we also rate each date for how well it leads to sex.

Two weeks before the wedding, in the last week of June, we go to a music festival. He wears a baseball cap, a faded t-shirt, and athletic shorts that make his ass look biteable. I wear a sundress and hightop chucks, and let my hair do its naturally wavy thing. It's our last chance to just be Ty and Kiley, doing our private thing, before the madness descends upon us.

Before everyone finds out we're dating, I guess, because there's no escaping—that is what we are doing. We've formalized it with a list and everything.

Also, every time I look at Ty, and he's looking back, my heart feels like it's going to explode.

"Is it weird that nobody recognizes you yet?" I ask after we buy a beavertail from a food truck and head back to the blanket we've stretched out on a small rise of grass.

"It's different. It's not bad, though." He slings his arm around my waist, his hand curving around my hip, and he tugs me close. "Good timing when I'm trying to prove to a girl that I'm just a regular guy."

"Is that what you're doing?"

"Am I not succeeding?"

There's nothing ordinary about how Ty in the slightest. "I mean… I don't want to get specific, because it will go to your already inflated ego, but I have a lot of experience with regular guys—"

"Don't remind me—"

I carry on innocently. "And you are most definitely… irregular."

He shouts out a laugh, drawing attention. But to the people around us, he's just a guy in a baseball hat, cackling at something his girlfriend said.

Maybe it's the fact that I'm so ordinary looking that masks that he's a literal superstar in their midst.

For a second, I have a flash of what Ty's life in Miami was like. Sexy people. Sexy *women*, dripping off his arm. Being recognized as a god everywhere he went.

And then he moved here, and out of context of the hockey world, next to me, he blends in to the blue collar population attending a folk festival.

"Please be specific about my irregularities," he murmurs when we reach the blanket.

He takes the beavertail from me as I think, and rips off a piece of the cinnamon-sugar dusted fried dough.

I push away the spike of jealousy I feel about his past, and focus on how nice that cinnamon sugar is going to taste on his lips.

This is his present. I am his present, and that's all that matters.

"You…go downtown more than anyone else," I whisper back.

"My favourite place to go on my favourite girl's body." He kisses my shoulder. "Licking your pussy is the highlight of every day."

I blush. He probably has licked it every single day, too. The man has his priorities sorted for sure. "And I love that."

"Good." He nuzzles my cheek. "I love that you appreciate what a foodie I am."

I laugh out loud. "Foodie?"

"Dining connoisseur," he says seriously. "Expert in all feasts downtown—" He cuts himself off, chuckling. "Look at how much you blush at that."

"I'm not blushing," I lie.

"You sure are, and it's making my dick hard." He spins around, sitting up. "Come and sit between my legs."

"I don't think that's going to help your erection."

He tugs me right up against him. "I didn't say I need help getting rid of it."

Giggling, I arrange my skirt so I'm not accidentally flashing anyone, and then lean back against his solid chest.

He lazily feeds me nibbles of the beavertail, and when we're finished, I catch his hand and slowly lick up every speck of cinnamon sugar.

When I'm done, he cups my face and kisses me slowly, savouring the last taste of our treat with me.

There's something really magical about spending a whole afternoon, humming with awareness about just how wanted you are. The little circles Ty draws on my arms feel like foreplay. The soft kisses he presses against my temple as we watch acts change on the main stage make me want to combust.

And then as dusk falls, his touch gets bolder, sliding my skirt up just high enough that his circling fingers can play on my thighs, too.

I arch my back against him.

"Shhh," he whispers. "Don't let anyone know you're a horny brat."

"You're making me like this."

His touch climbs higher, to the edge of the slightly

stretchy anti-chaff shorts I'm wearing under the sundress. "What are these? Spanx?"

"Something like that."

He plucks at the confining fabric. "Take them off."

"I can't…" I squirm as his fingers slide up and under the edge. "They come up over my waist. It's not a subtle thing. It's holding in all the jiggle."

"Mmm, I love your jiggle. It needs to be released." He paws at my waist, trying to figure out where the top of it is. "I'll help."

I glance around. There's a stand of trees not that far. "I'll go over there." I twist around and poke him in the chest. "Don't follow me. I can't get Ty Connor arrested for public sex. Your agent would kill me."

He grins like he doesn't care, but he stays put on the blanket.

The wind picks up as I navigate around blankets and lawn chairs, everyone's attention on the singer on the stage.

It takes a minute to wrestle my way out of the body shaper and carefully step out of it, balancing on one foot at a time. I roll it up tightly and smooth my skirt down, grateful for the cover of darkness and low hanging branches, the leaves rustling faster now.

When I step back into the clearing, a wet plop of rain lands right on my forehead. "What the fuck?"

Some people watching the show have pulled on plastic ponchos, but others are gathering up their blankets and chairs and heading out.

I dodge my way through the crowd, and halfway back to where we were sitting, I find Ty. Or rather, he finds me, unerringly, in the crowd of people, his gaze locking onto mine as he joins me and grabs my hand.

"That came in out of nowhere." I try not to think about the fact that I'm commando as we dash for his truck through the cool, pelting rain.

By the time we get there, we're both soaked to the bone, the street is flooding, and there's a traffic jam as everyone tries to leave all at once.

He wrenches open the passenger door and I jump in.

After he dashes around to the driver's side, he twists over the seat and rummages around in the back for a minute before shoving a clean-smelling t-shirt at me. "Here, use this to dry off."

I press it against my face, my chest and arms, and finally up my legs, squeezing my dress against it and warming up my thighs at the same time.

Once I'm no longer a drowned rat, I look at him—and he's staring at me.

"What?"

"You're beautiful," he says huskily, reaching across the console.

I melt into his kiss, tasting his raw hunger. Outside, rain pelts the window, and further away, cars are honking at each other. But inside the quiet, dark confines of the cab of his truck, there's nothing but the warm demands of his mouth and the racing beat of my heart.

"I didn't even get a chance to tease you before the rain came in out of nowhere." His breath is hot against my lips. "I need you, Kiley. Can you be quiet?"

"Here?" I blink my eyes open. We're not under a street light, but there are people streaming past us. Cars ahead and behind.

His mouth curves in a wicked smile. "I'm just...helping you put your seat belt on."

He reaches across me and grabs the buckle, drawing it slowly across my breasts, then lower, down to my hips.

The click as it snaps into place makes me jump—as much as I can, now belted against the leather seat.

"Shhh," he repeats, his eyes searching my face. "Okay?"

I nod.

He squeezes my breasts through my sundress, then drops his hand to my lap. "Tilt your hips for me. Spread your legs. You can reach up and hold on to the headrest if it helps."

My arms go over my head and back on command.

There's something about the calm, gentle way Ty bosses me around that makes my head swim, chasing away all my usual thoughts of obstinance and protest.

He flips up the damp weight of my skirt and groans in appreciation.

"That's my sexy girl. Look at you, naked under this sundress. Shocking behaviour." He chuckles. "I approve."

I close my eyes and lose myself in the illicit moment, being groped and stroked almost in public.

My hips lift off the seat when his trailing fingers finally touch my pussy, thrashing against the seat belt. I curl my inside leg up and Ty catches it, holding me open for him. Now I'm held down and splayed open by four points. His fingers have full access to every inch of my sex, and I'm so wet for him, I can feel it even before he pushes between my lips there.

"What a silky treasure you have here. Fuck, you're slippery tonight, aren't you? You brought a needy pussy to the park."

"Ty…"

"Tell me what you want."

I want his touch. I want his fingers inside me, and on my clit.

"I want to come on your hand," I gasp.

"Good girl. Let's make that happen." His forearm is a hard, muscled band against my inner thigh, and that long press of his skin against mine amplifies all the pressure he brings to my most sensitive spots.

My clit, my entrance. And then lower, as I writhe against his touch, and my breath goes still.

"Can I touch you here?" The question is a whisper, but it's the loudest thing I've ever heard.

His fingertip traces my asshole. I tighten up, and he groans.

"I felt that, luscious. Felt you quiver inside, even before I've done anything. Does this make you nervous? Do you want me to stop?"

I shake my head.

"Tell me."

"No, don't stop." I rock my hips, needing more.

His palm covers my whole pussy, his thumb sliding into place against my clit, and the tip of his middle finger notches right against my tightest hole. "I'm not stopping. Not until you come on my hand. If someone knocks on that window and asks what's going on, you're going to tell them your tight little ass is riding my finger, you understand? You're going to tell them you're making me leak in my shorts, that's how hot this is."

I twist my head towards him and open my eyes.

His gaze is so bright, his face right there.

My body is pulsing, buzzing, riding a chaotic wave that feels like it's growing beneath me. He's an ocean storm and I'm lost, my fate up to him now.

"I want all of you. Every inch of your body is mine, you understand? I want to bury my cock here and have you shout my name as you milk every drop of my seed."

"I'm yours," I gasp.

His thumb pushes over my clit again, the same steady pressure that has built me up to this point, and his finger pushes into my bum, just the tip, just inside the sphincter but it's oh my *God* more than I expected, and I lose it.

Thighs shaking, I start sobbing. My clit is pulsing and my heart is pounding, but it's not like any orgasm I've ever had before.

"Hey hey hey, it's…" Ty swears under his breath and releases my leg, rearranging my body first before lunging over the console and wrapping himself around me. "Hey, it's okay."

I just keep crying. I don't know why. I'm not even sad. I just can't stop.

He kisses my nose, and my lips, and then both cheeks, over and over again, until the tears stop.

"What was that?" he asks softly. "And where did the giggles go?"

I laugh at that. "I don't know."

"I'm sorry."

I clutch at him. "No! That was…" I kiss him again.

There are no words for what that was.

He exhales roughly and holds me against his chest. "Okay. You're okay."

And in his arms, I believe it. I believe that I've found a man who has broken through my walls and replaced the trauma that hardened my heart with something so much sweeter.

The joy of that night carries me as if I'm lighter than air through the days leading up to the bachelorette weekend .

And then, as I'm waiting for Harper to pick me up to head to the spa, I get an email that changes everything.

From: The Travelling Soul Theatre Company
Subject: Re: Stage Manager Application

CHAPTER 35
TY

The weekend of Harper's bachelorette trip to a spa and Kieran's simultaneous house party, I end up being double booked.

"I'm going to be late for your poker night," I tell Kieran when we leave the rink together on Friday morning after a good skate.

I'm enjoying doing my off-season training with him and the local guys, instead of with my usual Florida crew.

"I'm going to Toronto to film a commercial in the morning."

He laughs and shoves at me. "Nice way to slide that in there, Mr. Casual. *Have to film a commercial, no big deal.*"

"Shut up. You've got more endorsements than anyone else on the team."

"Not more than Jenson," he says.

"What's more than me?" Our alternate captain says, stepping into the hallway.

"Ty's trying to catch us in endorsement deals. What's the commercial for tomorrow?"

"Car insurance."

"Nice." Jenson fist-bumps me. "All right, see you tomorrow."

"You'll see me," Marshie hollers as Jenson jogs ahead, eager to get to his car. "Connor might make it if he can escape the spotlight!"

I roll my eyes.

But it's important. While I've appreciated the chance to lick my wounds in private, and date Kiley in peace, it's time for me to level up my profile in advance of next season.

I tasked Nina with finding me more Canadian brand partnerships this summer, and she's delivered. So I can't be annoyed at a national commercial shoot falling on the weekend.

Because I need to be there at the ass crack of dawn tomorrow, I head into the city early and book myself into a hotel.

The first thing I do after I'm settled is text Kiley.

TY

How's the spa?

KILEY

Just posted some pics to Instagram

I hop over there and nearly swallow my tongue.

Holy fuck.

In the first photo, she's wearing a black one piece bathing suit that dips low between her round, full breasts, and she's rising out of the water, her arms stretched out on either side of her, her fingers just skimming the water's surface.

My cock is already hard as I swipe to the next one. Her laughing with Harper, their cheeks pressed together as they sink lower into the steamy water. The next photo is her on her back, floating away in the hot springs.

I stroke my thumb over the screen, where the long, curving line of her thigh is stretched toward me.

A heart appears on the screen, my touch enough to like the post.

I grin.

I do like it. I like it a lot. It makes me think of holding on to that leg as I finger-fucked her in my truck.

My phone rings. Kiley.

"Hey, luscious," I murmur.

"You sound like you're turned on."

I can fucking hear the smile in her voice. "I am. All alone in a hotel room and no sexy girl in a bathing suit to sit on my face. Where are you?"

"All alone in a hotel room, just about to peel off this bathing suit."

"God damn it. How much time do you have?"

"Half an hour until dinner."

"Put your hand between your thighs. Pull the swim suit to the side, like I couldn't wait to get my mouth on you." I yank my shorts down and fist my cock. "Did you see that I liked your photo?"

"That's why I called." Her breath hitches.

"Your tits looked incredible in that first one. I want them in my mouth. Feed me your breasts when I get back. Sit on my lap and tease me with your nipples until I lose control."

She moans in my ear, which drives me wild. I tell her everything I need to do to her, with her, on her. Under her.

And she takes it all so well. "Did you ever take that kink test you sent me?"

"What?" She's panting. "No."

"Take it this weekend."

She doesn't answer.

"Are you rubbing that clit of mine?"

"Yes."

"Remember how wet you got when I buckled you into your seat?"

"Yes."

"I want to do that with rope. I want to tie you up, and I've never done that with anyone, so you're gonna have to give me time to learn. But I'm going to make it so good for you."

She whimpers on the other end of the line. "I've never done that, either."

"There are so many firsts we can discover together."

There's a long stretch. "Have you…"

My cock throbs. "What?"

"You fingered my ass."

"Yeah."

"Have you ever fucked someone like that?" It's a very quiet question. A brave question.

"Never. I'll learn how to do that, too, if you want."

"I've heard some things about it."

"Oh?"

"Girls talk." Her breath is coming faster now. "You could tie me up…"

"And make you mine. I'm going to, Kiley. I'm going to claim every one of your holes as my own."

The edges of my vision go dark, then bright white, as my orgasm roars in and explodes in my head and down my spine and up my shaft.

On the phone, Kiley laughs gently. "Ah, you're so dirty. I love it. I love—"

She cuts herself off.

"Me, too." Two small words. Very gruff. But meant with my whole heart.

When did that happen?

When did I fall in love with the girl upstairs?

"Kiley, I—"

"I have to go," she says in a rush. "I'll text you after dinner."

"I have a really early call time tomorrow, but I'll try to stay up."

"No, don't," she says, her voice achingly soft. "It's okay. We'll talk tomorrow."

———

5:05 AM

TY

Good morning, luscious. I really hope you have your phone silenced.

9:55 AM
KILEY

I did. Good morning. I had the best sleep. Hot springs and phone sex...pretty nice combination. Heading over to the spa again with the girls. Might leave my phone in the locker to be pure vibes with the space.

6:00 PM

TY

Finally done for the day. Hope the vibes were incredible. Driving back to Hamilton soon, then heading to Kieran's for the night. Might text you from the laundry room later.

7:00 PM
KILEY

We keep missing each other. You're
probably on the highway right now. Heading
out to dinner. Text you later!

1:00 AM

TY

I came back to the apartment. It's a hot one
tonight. Glad I got that portable air
conditioner for my bedroom. How do you
live in a building without central air? Miss
you in my bed tonight. Can't wait to see you
tomorrow.

By the time Harper drops Kiley off late on Sunday afternoon, I'm going out of my skin with need for her.

I meet her at the door downstairs, giving Harper a friendly wave.

Kiley pokes me, moving me inside.

"What's that for?"

"Just ensuring we don't have any PDAs," she says lightly.

I frown. "In front of Harper?"

"Yeah."

My frown deepens. "Why can't we have any PDAs in front of Harper? She was a witness to the OG PDA."

She hands me her backpack and pushes past me. "I know."

I follow. "Does Harper know we're dating?"

"Yes…" she says, but it's in a trailing off, hedging kind of way that makes me see red.

"What does that mean?"

"It doesn't mean anything!" She stops on the landing for my apartment. "Your place or mine?"

Mine is closer, but her stuff goes upstairs. "Whichever."

She pushes open the door to my apartment, which I hadn't bothered to lock just to go down and greet her.

I set her bag down near the door and pull her onto the couch. Me sitting on it, Kiley straddling me.

And then I wrestle her arms behind her back, pinning her wrists against her hips. "What aren't you telling me?"

She makes a face. A classic Kiley masking emotions kind of face. Schooling her expressions into stony stubbornness, which is not her natural state with me. Not once I'm inside her brittle exterior.

"What's going on?"

She takes a deep breath. "I have a job interview tomorrow."

I let go of her wrists and cup her face instead. "Hey! That's amazing."

The mask slips, and I see the worry behind it. "Yeah. It is."

"What's the... what's with the sadness?"

"I'm not sad." She sucks in a quick breath. "I am *not*. I can't be. I want this. You know that."

"I...yeah, I think I do." I frown.

"It's a travelling theatre company. The job wouldn't be here."

CHAPTER 36
KILEY

Ty's expression is so hard to read as he looks up at me.

He's perched me on his lap, and he's cupping my face, but…I feel hollow inside. I have all weekend.

"When did you find out?"

And the hollow feeling can wobble, it turns out, when poked. "Umm… Friday."

"You didn't tell me."

"It was right before I left."

He nods slowly. "And because of this, you didn't tell Harper about us."

"Harper knows. From before. I just didn't talk about us, because I didn't know what *us* would be after I have this interview. If I get the job."

Another slow nod. "Okay."

I slide off his lap and curl up beside him. "We haven't talked about this recently."

"Right." He clears this throat. "You've been looking for an opportunity like this, though. I know that."

"And it's just an interview. I might not get the job."

Before he can reply, we're interrupted by his phone vibrating on the ottoman in front of us.

He doesn't reach for it.

It doesn't stop.

"Get it," I say, suddenly exhausted.

He cranes his neck. "It's Nina. She can wait."

But Nina can't wait. The missed call is followed up by two quick text messages as we sit in stony silence.

He curses under his breath and snatches the phone. His brow wrinkles as he reads the messages. "Huh."

"What?"

"A weird collaboration offer from the casting director who was at the commercial shoot yesterday." He shoves his hand in his hair.

"We haven't even talked about that. How was it?" I'm desperate to shift gears, and I feel badly for not starting with that, or talking to him at all about it last night.

"It was fun." He gives me a careful grin. "I liked it. Canadian hockey commercials are next level over endorsements we get in the States. That was like a whole film set! And I had lines!"

I laugh at his boyish enthusiasm. "That's cool. So it went well, and now there's another opportunity?"

"Yeah, they're going to film a hockey rom-com in Toronto, and they'd like me to read for a small part." He laughs. "Can you imagine? Me, an actor?"

"Yeah, I can," I whisper. A large lump has formed in my throat. "When, uh, would this be filming?"

"I'm not sure exactly." He wiggles his phone. "Would you mind if I called her?"

"No, go ahead." I press myself into his side and close my eyes.

We're not doing this, Kiley Forge. We are not freaking out because of the a-word. This man came really close to telling you he loves you the other night. Do not freak out.

"Hey Neen," he says. His chest rises and then falls again. "Yeah, I guess I just want more information first. It wouldn't be great if it got out that I auditioned and *didn't* get a part, you know? And it can't interfere with the season at all. Would the schedule be pretty set?"

He rubs his hand up and down my arm, squeezing when she says something he clearly likes.

"Oh! Just three filming days? And then maybe some reshoots? All right. Yeah, send me the details, but I think if the audition can be done with an NDA in place, I'm interested. Oh, and if they need a stage manager, let me know, I can pass on a name—*oof.*"

I push against him, trying to sit up. I'd gotten lulled into a relaxed state, hearing his voice reverberate through his chest, but now I'm waving my hands frantically.

He's laughing. "Hang on." He covers the microphone. "What?"

"I don't work in film, A, and B, I don't want nepotism!"

"Didn't your brother get you a job at the hospital?"

"No! He told me about a job posting. What the—"

He holds up his hands, then carefully turns back to the phone. "Never mind, that was an overstep. Yes, Kiley's here. Of course it was for her." He covers the microphone again. "Nina wants to meet you."

I glance around. "Is she going to jump out of a corner somewhere?"

"I think she means FaceTime."

I do a frantic once over of myself. I've been soaking in hot tubs and drying out in saunas for almost forty hours, and I twisted my hair up into two buns for the drive home. I probably look like a ghoul.

"You look perfect," he says. "But we can use animal mask filters if you want."

I roll my eyes and gesture at the phone. "Let's get this over with."

The screen changes from a phone call to a video call, and then there was the woman I saw in the bar with Ty all those months ago.

Perfectly made up, perfectly tanned. And grinning like a fool. "Finally! He's hidden you from me long enough."

"Umm…"

Ty growls her name, but she waves him off. "You are all he can talk about."

Ty starts to make a face, and then shrugs. "Yeah, that's probably true."

"I find that hard to believe," I protest.

She leans in to the camera. "No honey, you should believe it. First of all, it's hard to get him on the phone these days. And sometimes he can talk about business. I'm pretty sure that's when you're with him. But when I get him on the phone and he's in the car or at the arena, it's *Kiley this* and *Kiley that*. And I get it. Look at you."

Look at *me*? She looks like she just walked out of a Ralph Lauren ad.

But beside me, I can feel Ty's gaze on my face, warm and steady, so I won't play that comparison game. I know he only has eyes for me.

She gives Ty the kind of look that I give Grant, and it's so sisterly that any final residue of *did they ever?* doubt fades away. "So, Kiley." She wiggles her eyebrows. "Ty won't tell me how you met."

"Really?" I glance at him. It feels harmless. "Online," I say at the same time as Ty says, "At the arena."

"Which is it?"

"Both," we say in unison.

Ty wraps his arm around me. "We met at the arena first. It was like, *bam, hello* for me."

I blush as I make a face. "And maybe more of an *oh no* for me. But then we met again online, on Lusty—do you know that app?—and that was definitely more mutual from the first text. He was very different than I expected."

"Did he tell you we met online, too," she says, wiggling her finger between her and Ty. "On Tinder, not Lusty."

That doused ember of *did they ever?* suddenly flares back to life. *What?*

I jerk around to glare at Ty. "You met your agent on Tinder?"

"We never did anything," he says blandly. "Put your claws away, luscious."

Nina cackles. "It's true. Zero chemistry from the first moment. But he bought me a drink anyway, and asked me what I wanted to do after law school. When I told him I wanted to be an agent, a friendship was born. You, Kiley Forge, are the first woman to meet our guy here and actually hold on to his heart."

"You're full naming me, that's..." I look at Ty. "She knows my full name."

"There was a time there when I used your full name a lot," he mutters. "Anyway, this has been swell, Nina. You've given us so much to talk about tonight, thanks for that. Can't wait to never do this again."

"Oh we're doing this again very soon, in person." She

beams at me. "Do you guys want to fly to Vancouver after the wedding to visit the set of *Good Morning Kitsilano*?"

That lump that had grown in my throat explodes and turns into a living, breathing monster inside me.

"What?" I hear myself say faintly.

"Do you not know it? It's apparently a big hit up there in Canada. The guy who stars in it—"

"Crys Graham," I supply. I sound like a robot.

"That's it." Nina smiles at Ty so brightly it looks like she might explode into a thousand stars. "He's the executive producer of the hockey rom-com you're auditioning for."

CHAPTER 37
TY

Beside me, Kiley has gone very still.

"Wow," she says, an odd note to her voice. "That's quite the opportunity. I can't go to Vancouver, unfortunately. Some of us have work to return to. But Ty, you should go. That sounds…interesting."

I frown at her. "I don't need to go to a set for a totally different production. I'll come back with you."

"No, you should…" She pushes up. "I have to go."

I look at my phone. "Nina, we'll talk later." I gab the end call button and stand. "What's wrong?"

"Nothing!" Kiley exhales, puffing out her cheek. "Wow. I didn't see that coming."

"The audition?"

"Yeah. Wow."

"That's the third time you've said wow in a row. Kiley, you're not a *wow* person."

"Sure I am," she says sarcastically. "And this is a wow situation."

"Do you have any other reactions other than *wow*?" My voice sharpens, but I can't help it.

She quiets immediately, but she's still not looking at me.

A heavy, weighty silence hangs between us for a long moment as she stares at her backpack by the door.

Then she exhales and carefully meets my gaze. "There's just... This is a lot...of change. And... Like, I want you to know that I only want the best for you. I genuinely... I know that when we met, I had a false impression of you, and I clearly conveyed that to you. I need you to know that I have regrets."

Her voice scratches on the word *regrets*.

"I have regrets about not seeing you for who you are, sooner."

"And who am I?"

"You are a good guy." She lets out a watery laugh. "You are. I see how much you want to be a part of this community, and do the right thing by your fans, and elevate the team. I see how driven you are for success, and I think all of that is really, really wonderful."

For a string of compliments, that all sounds deeply dangerous to me when framed like that in her shaky voice. "What are you saying? What are you getting at?"

"Am I not saying this the right way?" Now she sounds lost.

Fuck.

"I guess I'm trying to say I understand that you and I are in different places."

I grab her shoulders. "We're in exactly the same place. We're both right here, right now."

"I know. But we're not. Not really. You're...you. And I'm...me." She shakes off my hands, and suddenly it feels like there's a gulf between us as wide as the Grand Canyon. "When I got that email about the job interview, I knew I was supposed to be excited about it."

"Of course you are! I'm excited about it for you." My voice is rising. I can't help it. Fuuuck. *Calm down. Listen to her.* But it's fucking hard when I don't think she's hearing a word I'm saying.

"You know what my first reaction was? Dread. Dread that I would have to leave you. I got too attached, Ty. And I told myself I wouldn't. I told myself I needed to give *me* my full attention, and I was right."

It feels like we're hurtling towards disaster here. "What does that mean?"

"In the same way that when the season starts up again, you'll give hockey your full attention," she says, as if from a distance now. Far away from me.

I shake my head. "Because hockey is my job."

"And the theatre is going to be mine again."

"And *I* will understand that you need to give it your full attention for a while." God damn it. Am I not saying the right thing here?

She blinks and refocuses on me. "Not a while."

"What. Are. You. Saying?"

"This is so hard," she says, her voice wavering.

My own voice cracks. "Kiley, don't do this."

"I made a promise to myself, a year ago, that I wouldn't… I like you so much. I like you *so* much, but we met at the wrong time in my life. I swore to myself that I wasn't going to do this again. I wasn't going to do another relationship for at least a year. I am Kiley 'Falls in Love With the Wrong Men' Forge. And I need you to know that I know you are *not* the wrong man. But this is the wrong time. And both of those things are equally important for my plan to succeed."

"What plan? Kiley, tell me, what plan are you talking about? Is this about your year of putting yourself first? I want you to always put yourself first. I want to put you first!"

"You can't if you're going to do that show." She's crying now.

"Then I won't do that show," I yell. "What the fuck?"

"I have to go. I'm sorry." She closes the gap between us and kisses me softly, and it's as desperate as any kiss we've ever shared, but not in the good way. This tastes like tears, and it doesn't matter how tightly I hold on to her, because she's gone even before she slips out of my arms.

I've fucked up.

I don't know how, but I have, and since I'm in the dark, I don't know how to fix it.

I follow her into the hallway. It's hot today, sticky and humid outside the weak air conditioning in my apartment, but I barely notice as I listen to her race up the stairs.

As I follow, and knock on her door. "Kiley, come on. Don't run away from me."

"Please go away. I need to be alone."

"I don't understand why."

She doesn't respond to that.

Which leaves me on the stairs between our apartments, Googling who the fuck Crys Graham is, and why it feels like he might have just broken up the best relationship of my entire life.

Google doesn't have any answers on the second point, but lots of information for the basic who, what, where, when, and why.

He's an actor in his mid-thirties who has had bit parts in TV and film over the last fifteen years. Last summer a pilot he wrote got picked up, set around regulars who walk, bike, jog, and do yoga every morning in Vancouver's Kitsilano neighbourhood. It was the surprise hit of the fall, and in addition to it being renewed, he's also inked deals to make some movies for a streaming service.

Enter the hockey players they want to cast.

I scroll down through his Wikipedia page, but there's no connection to Hamilton.

I go back to the search results and keep looking. I search again, this time adding Kiley's name to the search bar. That delivers no results.

I get it on the third search, though. I'm a dummy, but not an absolutely idiot. "Crys Graham Vancouver Theatre" delivers a ton of results. As someone with a Wikipedia page that gets edited down repeatedly, I understand why most of these roles aren't featured there, but god fucking damn it, I'd have appreciated the theatre connection to have been the first Google result.

I stand up again and return to her door. I knock firmly. "Kiley, open up."

She doesn't answer.

I press my forehead to the door and close my eyes, my chest aching. "Come on, TheatreGirl. Don't shut me out."

When that doesn't get her to open up, I resort to texting.

It's how we started, after all.

But I hate typing out these words.

TY

I'm going to go out on a limb and guess
that asshole is the guy who cheated on you.

She still doesn't open the door.

And I start to burn.

I take a step back. I repaired the door frame once, I can do it again.

Then the latch sounds, and slowly she turns the handle.

I'm pushing through the door as soon as it cracks open, and I pull her into my arms.

"No," she whispers.

I turn her around, pressing her to the inside of the door. My hands skate up her sides, one going to the side of her neck, the other roving until it lands on her waist. "I was going to kick in the door."

"*No.*" Her voice cracks.

"What's going on, Ki? Because I don't get it. Some other fucker broke your heart, and you give me the cold shoulder?"

She shakes her head.

"That's what this is, though."

"It's just too hard," she whispers.

"Okay. So it's hard. We'll figure it out." I sound desperate, because I am.

And she sounds broken. "I can't. That's not who I am."

"Who are you?"

"I'm a good time girl. I'm not—"

"Whatever the rest of that thought was, it's bullshit."

She pushes at my chest. "Says one slutty good time girl to another."

The words snap between us like an electric charge.

The message is loud and clear. Whatever she thinks she's not—a forever person, a lover, a partner—she doesn't think I'm that, either. What we have, in her eyes, is strictly sex.

Fuck.

"I don't see you like that," I say tightly. "I look at you and I see endless potential. For you, for me, for us. You don't feel the same?"

Her eyes are wide and easy to read. She's not lying to me when she shakes her head. "I've never seen a future for us."

My chest hurts. I rock back on my heels.

"You should go," she says, her voice cracking.

"You want me to leave?"

"I need you to."

I hate the sharp edge to her words, like they're hurting her just as much as they pain me to hear them. *Don't do this*, I want to argue. *Don't cut yourself off from me, from* us.

But she needs me to go. She's said that, and I can't argue with it. I have a lifetime of moving my body where it needs to go, even when I don't want to go there. Nobody wants to get slammed into the boards, but I'll put myself in the path of a two-hundred-pound speeding bullet. I can walk away from Kiley.

Humidity slams me in the face as I open her door. Fucking shitty apartment building with its lack of central air.

I don't look back as the door closes behind me.

I stand on the top step for a moment, the silence on the other side of the door deafening. Then I take the stairs as quickly as I can. The sooner I get into my apartment, the sooner it's *done*, and then I can make a next-steps plan.

I have to accept the fact that whoever Crys was to her, he's hurt her in a way that I can't immediately fix.

I think about calling Harper, but if Kiley wanted her friend involved, she'd make that call herself. And it's a week until the wedding—I'm not going to be the asshole who makes this week about me and my problems.

I think about calling Kiley's brother, too, but that's a nonstarter because Grant and I have a professional relationship that probably needs a firm firewall around it.

Also, we've never had a personal encounter outside of work, so *Hey I think I accidentally broke your sister's heart today* isn't a great opener.

But if I don't fix this in the next two days, it's going to be hella awkward when we all get on a plane together and fly to the middle of buttfuck nowhere for Kieran and Harper's wedding.

And if Kiley doesn't want anything to do with me, then I just have to lock down the way my body responds to the smooth soft expanse of her skin, the electric brightness of her smile, and the sharp slice of her quick wit, which will be pointed at my heart with deadly precision.

CHAPTER 38
KILEY

This feels like an awful kind of déjà vu. A nightmare of my own making, but I can't live in a world where my mistakes are thrown in my face over and over again.

No matter how my interview goes tomorrow, I'm giving notice on my job and my apartment, I'm buying a car, and I'm driving into the sunset.

From the floor, my phone vibrates. I don't think it's Ty again—I've hurt him enough that he'll give me my space now—but I'm still disappointed, like a fucking fool, when I pick it up and it's not him.

You made sure it wouldn't be.

It's Harper, instead.

HARPER

Babe, I just tried the pocket latte from the bachelorette swag bag, and OMG

You're the best, you know that?

I shake my head.

No, I'm the worst. The literal, actual worst.

There's no way this fight with Ty doesn't bleed into her wedding week, and I hate that. I hate that I was such a fool I didn't see this coming.

I flew too close to the sun, falling in love with someone so far out of my league.

I have two days to pull myself together and be the smiling, happy maid of honour. Nothing else matters right now.

Fingers shaking, I swipe out of her messages and text my twin.

KILEY

I need to see Puck. Can I come over?

GRANT

Of course. Everything okay?

God, no. But I can't let him know that. I can't let anyone know just how broken I am.

CHAPTER 39
TY

I listen to Kiley's footsteps hurry around above me, and then dart down the stairs past my apartment. Useless, impotent frustration coils all my muscles tight as I move to the window and watch her go down the street, on foot, her head ducked.

If she's going out for a bit, I need to give her space when she gets back.

The desperate need to pounce on her and try to fix this isn't going to make anything better.

I find a pad of paper and write her a careful note, since I'm pretty sure right now she'll throw her phone into traffic if she sees another text message from me.

I'm going to the arena to workout, and then I'm going to check out one of your Lusty recs for dinner maybe. Takeout. Eat it in my truck alone, probably.

I'm going to try and give you space here, but I need you to know I'm really sorry I brought him back into your life in the most unexpected of ways. And I understand if you don't want to talk about it, but I'm right downstairs whenever you need a hug.

You saw me at my worst, Kiley. You know that I know what it's like to be scared and frustrated. Please trust me. I'm not that guy, and I'm not your father, either.

I read it back a few times. It's too much. It's an avalanche of feelings, and then I hate that, so I tear the piece of paper off the pad and rewrite just the middle paragraph again on a fresh sheet.

That's the note I slide under her door before I head to the arena and let myself into the team gym for a punishing, exhausting workout.

Two hours later, that's where Grant Forge finds me. He has Kiley's cool, assessing gaze, and every other time I've seen him, he's been a calm, collected professional.

Right now, his short dark hair is standing on end and his chiselled cheekbones have hot slashes on them, making him look more like his fraternal twin sister than usual.

Fire and ice runs in the family, I see.

"My sister wants me to give you a message."

"Okay."

"It's not. What did you do to her?" His hands ball at his sides, loose fists.

I exhale and move away from the free weights, into the open space where we do stretches.

Do not kick the doctor's ass. We're on the same team here.

In more ways than one.

Also, while I don't doubt my ability to beat him or

anyone else, it's not like Grant Forge won't put up a good fight. He's taller than me, and we probably carry a similar amount of muscle. He just usually hides it under a collared shirt.

"Where is she?" The question tears out of me. No delicacy to it. No subtly.

His gaze narrows. Assessing, assessing. "She's back at her apartment. Puck is with her."

Relief zaps through me. But of course she wanted her dog. I should have thought of that first.

Would this afternoon have gone completely differently if instead of trying anything else, I'd have simply said, *Let's go for a walk and find your favourite four-legged friend.*

But I didn't.

I nod. "That's good. What is the message she wants to pass on?"

"She needs to focus on the wedding this week." The words rasp out of him, like he doesn't want to repeat them.

"We don't leave for two days yet."

His expression tightens even further. "I know."

I can't spend the next week being bitten by black flies and mosquitoes, pretending that all she is to me is the pretty maid of honour at the wedding.

That will actually kill me.

"I know she needs space, but I want to talk to her before we leave."

He shakes his head. "She really doesn't want to talk right now. She, uh, told me about you. And her." He rubs his jaw. "She's scared."

"I know." I hold my hands out wide in that universal symbol for *I'm not armed, buddy.* "She doesn't need to be scared of me. But I understand. I do."

"She told me what she told you, about our parents." He shoves both of his hands through his dark hair. "I didn't know."

I stagger back. She was carrying that all alone? At *twelve*?

"She's always protected me like that." His face twists in regret. "Which is wrong. I should have protected her."

"I know we don't know each other well, on a personal level, Dr. Forge—"

He laughs. "Call me Grant."

I'm not sure he'll want me to after I say this. "Did she tell you that your mother told her, when she was a twelve-year-old girl, that she should expect to be cheated on? That the same thing would happen to her one day, and then she would understand what adult relationships and compromise were all about.

"That moment in time is directly tied to *this* moment in time, and in between those two points, I bet there's a lifetime of her being taken advantage of, of her normalizing being treated like shit because *that's what a marriage was in her eyes.*"

Now it's him who takes a step back, because I've paced towards him, and I'm yelling.

"That's not what a marriage is," he snaps back.

"Who has shown her that? Nobody!" I roar. I slap my hand against my body. "These shoulders are strong enough to carry Kiley forever. But she has to let me pick her up."

He looks at me warily. "What do you want from her?"

I shake my head. "That's for her and me to talk about first."

"It's not temporary, is it?"

"Fuck no."

He looks past me, thinking. Then he mutters something

under his breath before saying, "You know the saying, *always the bridesmaid, never the bride?* It's a hard week to be reminded that you've never been good enough to be someone's forever person. And my sister has never been great at multi-tasking. She's incredible when she throws herself into a project, but she also gets very single-focused about it. Be gentle with her. Let her be the maid of honour, and find a way to give her space so she can do that fully. Once the wedding is over—"

"I can't wait that long."

"You just told me you'll carry my sister on your shoulders forever. But you can't do it for a week?"

Fuck.

I swallow my frustration and nod. "Of course."

"Showing up for her isn't always going to look like the same. It's not always going to be…" He flexes.

I laugh.

He looks surprised.

I laugh harder. "You look like her when you're mocking me. I promise, that's a compliment."

He groans. "I wasn't trying to mock you."

"It comes naturally for a Forge, don't worry about it."

I cross to him, stopping a few feet short of where he stands.

"Look, I don't want to put the cart before the horse. I know there are things your sister needs to figure out in her own time, and there are things I want to say to her but she needs to be willing to hear—and I'm not going to say them to anyone else, first."

I stop and laugh again, because it's that or cry. I should have figured this shit out a week ago.

"Bud, I didn't even know I had a heart until I met your

sister." I jab a finger at my chest. "I thought this was a chunk of ice, and I liked it that way."

He leans in and holds out his hand. "All right."

I take it, give it a good squeeze, and then after a pause, I yank him in for a tight hug.

"She's got Puck for the night?" I ask.

"Yeah. For a few nights. She's going to do the hand-off to my parents right before we head to the airport Wednesday morning."

———

That night, I lie on the couch and listen to her move around the apartment above me. Puck is always by her side, it sounds like.

The next day, I lose myself in a longer-than-I-expected list of errands.

I swing by Kieran and Harper's house to give them their wedding present, the fancy espresso maker, because it doesn't make any sense to take a wedding gift all the way to Manitoba only for it to come home again on the plane with us.

I pick up my suits from the dry cleaner, and hit a golf pro shop because all my gear is in Miami, and while I can rent most clubs, it's nice to have at least one that feels like it's just right for me.

And I spend a lot of the day thinking about what Kiley has told me. Every conversation feels like a puzzle piece, and we've had so many, it feels like I have to have all the pieces, but I can't connect them all in the right way.

While I'm waiting at the dry cleaners and when I'm in like at the golf shop, I scroll through our messages.

Text messages.

DMs.

Our shared Lusty list.

Her reviews on her own account.

Her comments on my posts.

It wasn't Ty Connor who got the girl. It was BeastMode, and then Ty Connor swept in and stole her. Claimed her as his own, but was she ever really *mine*?

Or was she ours the whole time, and I missed what she needed because I wasn't being both sides of myself enough to see her fully.

I get home at dusk.

Inside, the apartment is quiet, and the apartment upstairs sounds quiet, too. I hang my suits by the door, then go into my bedroom to pull out my suitcase.

That's when I hear a scurry almost overhead.

Not quite, though. More to the front of the building.

I cock my ear up and listen.

Kiley and Puck are on the balcony above me.

I stalk to the kitchen and grab a cold drink from the fridge, then quietly let myself out onto my own balcony, right beneath her.

"Puck, shhh," she whispers.

There's a heavy thump above me as Puck sits, which makes me smile because I can be a bastard.

But because I'm not fully a bastard, I try to ignore the little hitch in Kiley's breath as she sucks in an almost inaudible gasp.

Sorry, luscious. I can't stay away from you.

I don't believe Kiley doesn't want me. I don't believe that for a second. We're electric together. And in between those moments of incredible connection, there's nothing but softness.

We are not the problem.

And other than not fucking asking her who the cheating jerk was—because I couldn't anticipate this coming up—I'm pretty sure I'm not the problem.

She likes me. She even said it as she tried to push me away.

She's not the problem, either. She's perfect. Reading back through all of our messages, I fell in love with her all over again. It's all there, going back to the week we met—once we found each other, the ground shifted beneath us, bringing our tectonic plates together.

We are one.

She even gave up dating other people even before she knew who I was.

Ben does not count.

If anything, her drinks with Ben counts as one of our improper dates.

I'm claiming that moment as precious in our private history.

Which means the problem lies outside her, and me, and us.

I stretch out on my never-used-before patio furniture and try to think if I've even looked out at her balcony. Is she in a chair up there? A hammock?

Kiley's a hammock girl. If she doesn't have one, I'm buying her one.

And then a house with trees so she has somewhere to hang the hammock, for reading in when she comes home in between theatre jobs.

What, is my balcony not good enough for you?

I can hear her bratty reply as if she was curled up next to me here, poking me in the chest.

I love that you love your balcony. But I want us to have central air and fewer neighbours so you can scream louder.

I stare up at the underside of her balcony.

Right now, we're a long way away from that kind of conversation.

She whispers again to Puck to be quiet.

I shake my head and pull out my phone.

I look at my messages, then I look at the Lusty app. It's a toss-up, but I choose the place where we started—where she says she fell for me at first text.

BEASTMODE

I can hear you up there.

Dots appear, then disappear.

A long pause, and then more dots.

THEATREGIRL

I'm not doing anything.

BEASTMODE

I can hear you thinking.

I'm trying really hard not to think. My thoughts are the problem.

Wish I could distract you from them.

Please don't.

I'm not. I'm sitting down here, texting a buddy online. I'm not knocking down your door, demanding to hold you, to distract you, to make you feel good.

She doesn't reply to that for a while. I don't blame her. It's way across the line. But it had to be said.

Darkness falls.

She gets up at one point, letting Puck go inside, maybe to eat dinner, but she comes back to the balcony.

It's not the same as holding her, but it's something. That she came back to being right above me, knowing I'm sitting down here, just waiting for her. That means something.

Finally a message pops up.

I'm sorry.

For what?

Many, many things.

This sounds familiar. Maybe we could call it even?

You have nothing to be sorry about anymore. You're...wonderful.

Hey, can I use some of that goodwill to ask how your interview went today?

I hold my breath as she types what must be three or four answers, that's how long the dots appear on the screen.

THEATREGIRL

It went really well.

I exhale in relief.

BEASTMODE

Good. Good. That's really good. I'm glad. I
hope you hear more before the wedding,
and that'll give us something else to
celebrate.

CHAPTER 40
KILEY

Puck wakes me up Wednesday morning, because I've apparently slept through my alarm, but her bladder is a reliable back up.

"Okay, okay, give me a second."

I did not sleep well. Better than Sunday night, but not as well as Monday night after our unexpected DM exchange.

All day yesterday, I was expecting more interaction with Ty, and he wasn't around at all. He texted me a brief good morning message, and then disappeared in his truck and didn't come back until really late.

I tried to distract myself with packing, but it wasn't that successful.

Even now, I grab for my phone.

And my heart leaps when I see four messages from him in a row, sent not that long ago.

TY

Hey, good morning. We might as well drive to the airport together, right? Just...makes sense.

What time are you dropping Puck off at your
parents?

I'm guessing it's pushing my luck to
suggest brunch on the way…

I take that last one back. I'm very busy this
morning, actually. But if you want to
carpool, I'm your guy.

I ignore my racing pulse as I type back a quick response.

Morning. Sure, Puck and I would appreciate
that. I need to take her out for a quick walk,
and then I'll figure out the best timing.

You want me to take her?

I almost say no. But I need to take a shower, and brunch sounds…nice.

It would probably be for the best if I'm not doing the whole awkward *I love you but I'm self-sabotaging our relationship* dance in front of our friends.

KILEY

If you don't mind, that would be really
helpful.

One minute later, there's a polite knock at the door.

"That's for you, Puckster."

When we greet him at the door, he has the world's most polite, distanced emotional mask up, and it tears at my heart.

"Hey there, Puck." He looks at me first, but it's her he addresses himself to. "Ready for a walk?"

Not trusting myself to speak, I give him a grateful smile and hand him her lead.

"Doggie bags?"

I grab those. "Thanks," I manage to get out.

He gives me a quick smile, and then they're gone.

I crumble against the back of the door, sinking down to the floor just for a minute. That's all the time I can allow for melting down.

Then I race through my shower and getting dressed. I triple check the Maid of Honour list I have. Everything is packed and ready to go.

When Ty knocks at my door again, I'm right there and I yank it open.

Surprised, he gives me a more natural smile. "We're back."

"Brunch sounds great," I blurt out. "If you still want—"

"I do." He searches my face for a moment. "All right, let's go. Do you want help with your bags?"

"I've got them."

Excited, Puck follows Ty back down to his place as I wrestle my suitcases down to the street level.

Ty hasn't packed as much stuff as me, but he isn't planning to wear Spanx for the next four days in a row, and he probably doesn't need three different outfits every day either.

After he carefully stows all of that in the bed of his truck, he opens the passenger seat and gestures for Puck to hop into the back.

He stops me from following her in, though.

"One quick ground rule," he says quietly. "I don't want to talk about us."

My heart does a confused face-plant onto the sidewalk, and my expression must match that.

"Not because there isn't an us." He swallows, the corded lines of his throat working hard. "There is. But I don't want this week to be about anything other than you having an awesome job interview and starring in this wedding as the maid of honour."

I frown. "It's not—"

"It is." Two small syllables, but they're firm. "That's how I see it. For me, this week is all about you. And that is more important than us."

My mouth falls open.

He smiles slightly and brushes his knuckle under my chin, pressing my lips together again. "There will be time for us later. Let's just be friends this week."

Friends don't sizzle like they've just been burned from a casual touch on the chin.

We drop Puck off first. Ty looms fiercely right behind me as I politely give a brief update on her to my parents. They don't ask why I'm with the hockey player, and I don't offer any information.

He puts his hand on the small of my back as we walk back to his truck, then opens the passenger door for me.

We don't talk about that when we go to a diner out by the airport.

He asks me about the interview, which I gush about, and then I find the nerve to ask him if he's had any more commercials booked or other casting calls.

He gives me a look that I can't decipher and just laughs shortly. "No. That's not really for me."

I frown. "But you had fun."

"I have fun at amusement parks, too, but I don't want to work at one." He grins as he tucks into his pancakes.

I'll circle back to that next week, maybe.

He gets a text message from someone who has already arrived at the airport. "Player group chat," he explains between bites.

"Anything I should know before getting on the team plane?"

"There are always more drinks than the flight attendants let on."

I giggle. "Okay."

He flicks a glance across the table that is, for a second, absolutely incendiary. "I don't usually like having a seat mate, but I'd make an exception every time for you."

I suck in a breath, and his shoulders roll up, then back.

"Sorry," he mutters. "Forgot myself there for a second."

I shiver. "It's okay. I…umm…I think I'm going to sit with Shannon? She says Max likes to spread out."

"Yeah, that's true. He's another solo seat player." He crumples up his napkin. "We should head out."

This diner has retro looking bills that are part of the whole aesthetic, so after Ty pays, and he leaves the bill on the table, I snap a quick photo of it. I don't put everything on Instagram, but I do like to fully document my life.

It's a short drive to the airport. We're departing from the same private plane area that the team flies out of regularly, so Ty knows exactly where to park and how to get to the tarmac.

Harper and Kieran have just arrived ahead of us, and I squeal when I see the matching *Mr To Be* and *Mrs To Be* t-shirts they are wearing.

Harper throws her arms around me, then we hop up and down.

Kieran and Ty are laughing at us—with us—when we finally stop.

"Shall we, my bride?" Kieran says.

"We shall, my groom." She swoons for him, then races up the metal stairs to get on the plane.

I grin at Ty. "After you…guest."

"Oh no, after you, maid of honour."

I feel his gaze on my back with each step. But once we're on board, he hands me off to Shannon to get the tour, and fades away, drifting to the back of the plane.

Giving me space.

Keeping *us* on an even keel, I realize.

We might not be talking about *us*, but he's making sure I feel *us*—and not in a way that is too much.

"So this is the team plane," Shannon says, ever the captain's wife. "Every seat is big enough to accommodate a seven-foot-tall hockey player."

I blink at her. "Do we have any of those on the team?"

"Not yet, but you never know. And if we did acquire a player like that, we would want him to be comfortable." She introduces me to the flight attendants next, two middle-aged men who immediately recognize me as Grant's sister.

"That's impressive," I whisper to Shannon as she leads me back to where we're sitting, a few rows ahead of Ty.

He catches my eye and smiles for a split a second before returning to whatever he's reading on his phone.

Harper's mom and her boyfriend arrive next, and then suddenly the plane starts to fill up. My brother is one of the last to board, and he looks for me as he comes down the aisle, but he has to keep going to the back to find an empty seat.

"You good?" he asks as he moves past, pausing to look at Shannon.

Maybe he's wondering why I'm not sitting with Ty.

I give him a reassuring smile. "I'm good. Ty drove me to drop off Puck, by the way."

He exhales and grins at the same time. "Okay, good. Great."

Shannon's watching me curiously through that, but then it's time to buckle in, and the pilot comes on over the announcement system.

"Hello to the wedding guests. Welcome aboard Highlanders Air. I'm Captain Fiona, I've got First Officer Matt up here with me, and your flight attendants today are Mario and Steve. We'll be your crew home again, after Kieran and Harper get hitched. Our flight time today should be two hours and thirty-five minutes…" She continues, giving the flight number and an estimated takeoff time. "So at this time, I'll ask you to take your seat and fasten your seatbelts. Steve will give you a quick safety briefing, and then we'll get this party started."

I've only taken a couple of flights in my life. Most of my travelling around North America for work has been done in a car, in part because I am almost six feet tall, and I have long legs, but not an unlimited budget for the good seats.

As I take my seat next to Shannon, my knees easily clear the seat in front of me. With room to spare. And my hips have wiggle room side to side in the plush seat, too.

She notices me kicking my feet, and does the same. "It's pretty nice, huh?"

"Yep." I giggle. "Really nice. Is this how you always travel?"

Shannon's not as tall as me, but she's not short, and she's all leg, so her knees are basically in the same place as mine.

She lowers her voice. "Always. Even before Max. Even when I was living with four other girls in a one bedroom apartment in Manhattan."

"How did you manage that?"

Her eyes sparkle. "That's a story for another time."

"You tease."

She laughs.

We quiet down for the safety briefing and takeoff, but as soon as we're in the air, we start chatting again.

Harper is all the way at the front of the plane, with Kieran, and Ani and Becca are sitting with their husbands. I think this is the first time Shannon and I have had extended one-on-one time, and she's fascinating.

She also loves all my questions, which I apologize for a couple of times, but she brushes that away. "No, don't be sorry, I love it. Do you know how often Max tells me nobody cares about my modelling career?"

I don't know how to respond to that.

She must realize how that just sounded, because she rephrases, and then changes the subject back to more current topics, but it sticks with me.

"You're a great storyteller," I tell her, to be reassuring. "All of them. And I follow the team really closely, but you've told me things I've never heard about."

"I don't think it's me so much as your questions are really good." She pauses. Looks at me. And bites her lip.

"What?"

"It's silly."

"I like silly."

"Do you know anything about podcasts?"

"I listen to them." I shrug. "Why?"

"I had an idea for one. Something like 'WAG the Tale' or 'The View from the WAG Suite.' I'd interview a different hockey spouse or partner in each episode, because there's a misconception that most hockey wives and girlfriends—and significant others, because we're not all women!—are like me." She gestures around the plane. "And in fact, on this team, most of the time I'm the only one just like me. Harper is a nurse, Ani is an artist. Andrew Mitchell is dating a lawyer, for goodness sake!"

"That's a great idea for a podcast. I bet you could pitch it to one of the sports broadcasters if you wanted."

She shakes her head vigorously. "No, that's not how I want to do it. I did some fill-in spots as a weather girl when we lived in New York, and Max hated it. I'd rather it be more of a hobby."

This is not the time or place, but at some point, we're circling back to that point, because I have some questions. And a newly discovered desire to put Max Tilman in his place.

"Would you think about helping me? I can pay you."

"That's not really my area of expertise."

"But it's similar, right? Theatre work, production."

I start to demure, and then I think about how Tilman has made his wife feel like something she has a clear passion for should just be a hobby.

We're not doing that today.

"Yeah, I bet I can figure out how to produce a podcast," I say thoughtfully. "Though I should warn you—"

I cut myself off.

"Warn me about what?"

I glance to the front of the plane. Harper isn't in listening range. Neither is my brother. "I haven't told anyone else yet—" Other than Ty, who doesn't count, because of course he would be the first person I'd tell. He's the only for-sure supporter I can count on. "But I'm actively looking for a job that will take me on the road this fall."

"Oh!" Her brows furrow for a second, but then she smiles. "I'm pretty sure podcasting can be done anywhere, right?"

"Yep, I think so."

"Then that's fine. And..." She mimes zipping her lips. "I won't tell anyone."

"Thanks. I'll share with them after the wedding, if it pans out." I hesitate, but then the truth rushes out. "Ty knows. That's it."

A flare of something lovely and bright jolts through her gaze. "Really? Oh, that's so nice."

"It's— He's—"

She squeezes my hand in hers. "He's supportive of this job search?"

"Very," I whisper back. And then I smile, and it grows and grows, until it feels as bright as the look in her eye. "I wasn't expecting him. And we had a fight... well, I freaked out, more like it. I showed him all my jagged edges, you could say."

"That's the trick, isn't it? Finding the person who fills in all the jagged edges? Because we all have that. And mismatched edges are...hard."

"Do we all have that?" Nobody else in my family does.

Not like me. "You don't look like you have any jagged edges."

Shannon smiles, smooth and perfect. "Literally everyone does. Some of us are just trained to make them look invisible."

CHAPTER 41
TY

I regret saying I would play every game of golf. This far north in Canada, sunrise happens so fucking early it hurts.

"I need more coffee," I protest.

The inn at the golf course is fine, but their brew is weak.

And I didn't sleep a wink last night.

After our plane landed, we were split up into two groups. Those staying at Kieran's cabin got in a fleet of SUVs that will be on standby for ferrying people around all week.

Those of us staying here at the golf course all piled into a school bus, because the chartered coach had apparently broken down.

As I watched Kiley get chauffeured away from me, I realized the error in my decision to not sit next to her on the plane. It might have been our last chance to be in close proximity for days.

The wedding party had a rehearsal last night, with a small dinner at Kieran's summer home, so the rest of us had a family-style meal at the golf course.

It was fine.

I missed Kiley.

And then sleeping a few miles apart was really, really hard.

Even when she wasn't speaking to me, I knew she was just upstairs, and that helped.

I resist the urge to pull out my phone and text her at five-thirty in the morning and ask for a rescue from the insanity that is my teammates wanting to get the first tee time.

"The glampers have coffee," Gusty promises. "Mitchey and his lawyer girlfriend are on it. We'll go there after the game."

After?

Good. God.

The fresh air helps, and the golf course blessedly sprays for black flies and mosquitos, so I'm not bitten alive at least.

Three hours later, I finally get to pile into one of the rented SUVs and we're driven the ten minutes down the road to Kieran's summer house on the edge of a glittering lake. The long gravel drive is decorated for the wedding already, and I have to admit it looks great, like something out of a movie.

Kiley looks even better. She's standing outside one of the RVs, wearing a long sundress, her shoulders bare, the skirt fluttering around her legs, and it takes everything in me not to take her in my arms in front of everyone and lay claim to her mouth the way I want to.

Her gaze finds mine immediately and she smiles.

Good morning, I mouth.

The smile grows.

I'm grabbed by someone, Gusty I think, and dragged toward Mitchey's caravan. "Coffee!" He shouts.

Behind me, Kiley is laughing. Following.

I twist around, wanting to see her, even as I'm carried along by my enthusiastic teammates.

In the morning sunlight, she looks like a soft, earthy goddess, amused by the mortals desperate need for caffeine.

But once we're all sprawled on the picnic tables in the makeshift coffee shop, she joins us. The goddess made mortal, too, but her desire for a taste of the good stuff.

"Sit with me," I say, tugging her down right next to me.

She searches my face. "How'd you sleep?"

"Terribly," I admit.

I hope she can fill in the rest.

She nudges her arm against mine, and that has to be good enough for now. Once we have coffee, there's a massive tent arriving, and then there will be more decorating to do.

"Kiley, what's the agenda for today?" Russ asks.

She starts listing the itinerary hour by hour, and my heart sinks.

Not just decorating.

I'm going to be lucky if I see her again before sunset tonight. And this far north in Canada, that is probably a hundred hours from now.

———

Eleven hours later, I regret my mental moaning about how far apart we had to sleep last night. Because the universe heard me, and decided to do me a big favour—that is deeply inconvenient to literally everyone else.

Ten minutes after we arrive back at the inn, at dusk, there's a loud shout, followed by banging on our hotel room doors. A pipe has burst, and water is rushing down the corridor.

"Jesus Christ," I say, shutting my door again real quick, not that it helps. Water starts burbling in under the door. I grab my suitcase and my hanging suit bag, then make a run for it down the hallway.

The staff at the hotel is very apologetic, but they're booked up solid—and while they can hopefully get our rooms dried out in a day or two, we'll need emergency shelter for the night.

Do we need assistance with that?

It's ten of us who are affected, and we're all attending the wedding.

"Well, fellas," Russ says, pulling out his phone. "I guess we're crashing the glamping party."

CHAPTER 42
KILEY

I'm sitting by the lake, wrapped in a blanket, chatting with Shannon, when the line of cars return a half hour after they leave—which we definitely weren't expecting.

Hockey players spill out, carrying their suitcases.

"Oh no," I say, scrambling to my feet.

I mean that on more than one level.

Obviously, something has gone wrong.

But also, now Ty is going to need somewhere to bunk—and my brother isn't in my RV tonight, because he rented a car and headed into Winnipeg for two days to visit the medical school there.

Earlier, I was teasing him about not knowing how to relax on vacation.

Now?

Now I'm both grateful and terrified that I happen to have a trailer all to my self.

And from the look on his face, he's thinking about that, too.

Will he want to share my bed if I offer?

———

It takes what feels like forever to get everyone a place to stay.

I keep very quiet. Nobody points out that Grant is gone, and suddenly there's just Ty.

"I've got an extra bunk," I say quietly.

Cool, so cool.

Not making eye contact with anyone.

"Great. Thanks." He's better at the cool thing than I am.

Is his heart pounding a mile a minute?

I gesture with my blanket-covered arm towards the glamping area.

"So…" I glance down at his feet. "Are you wet?"

He chuckles, just low enough that the people walking ahead of us probably can't hear it. "Yeah."

My RV is the closest to the cabin. Inside, I left an LED lantern on so it wouldn't be dark when I returned, and I'm glad I did, because I'm feeling big and clumsy as I turn around in the tight space.

"Grant is sleeping there, but he's not here tonight, so you can—"

"Do you want me to sleep there?"

I turn around.

Ty is right in front of me, his gaze fiery and challenging.

"No."

My answer hangs between us for a second, then we're kissing, and I'm pulling him towards my bunk, but also tripping over his suitcase.

He picks me up and lifts me around that, then I yank him onto the small double berth I'm sleeping in.

"This caravan wasn't built for tall people, was it?" He

bangs his head off an overhead storage cubby as he peels up my shirt. "Why did you get—" He cuts himself off with a satisfied groan as his hands cover my tits. "Never mind, I don't care. Is that the pink yoga bra or another one?"

The light really isn't carrying this far in, and everything is very dim. "Different."

"I fucking love how you spill out of these." He ducks his head and pulls at my nipple through the soft fabric.

"Oh *God*."

He laughs against my tit. "Shhh."

"You fucking shhh," I snap.

That makes him lift his head. I can't read the expression on his face. "Does everything need to be a fight with you?"

"Says the man with his mouth on my nipple." I mean it to be teasing, but it comes out pointed.

And he stops. The whole vibe shifts. "What the fuck does that mean?"

Nothing, shut up Kiley. Stop it.

But he waits. There's no getting out of this.

"It means you like it when I'm sharp."

"Is that what you think?"

"Isn't it a little bit true?" I try to push up to sit.

He shoves me back down, bracketing himself on top of me. "Let me make this very clear. I like it even more when you're soft."

"You've never—"

"I have, Kiley. Don't fucking lie to me right now."

That shuts me up. Because I don't know where that denial came from.

Of course he has.

So many times.

Why am I like this?

Why can't I stop being defensive?

"I know you have." I nod. "Yeah, that was...I don't know."

He traces his fingers over my lips.

In the dark, everything is heightened. The sound of him breathing, the weight of his body on top of mine.

"I know what that was." His voice is rough like sandpaper. "That's what keeps you safe so it's fine when it all comes crashing down."

I suck in a gasp.

Because yes, I know it will, one way or another. This is not the kind of explosive chemistry one plays with and then walks away from uninjured.

Even though I've built myself up, there's still a part of me that believes I don't really think I deserve this kind of sex, this kind of love. I don't think I deserve Ty.

And so I fight against him at every turn.

Which is not what I want.

And it's not what he wants.

So I go soft.

"This isn't going to crash down around us," he says, his voice taut. "I'm never going to let that happen. You understand?"

Yes.

I open my mouth, and nothing comes out.

He yanks down my bra, freeing my nipples, and he sucks them savagely.

"Yes," I breathe.

His mouth pulls harder against my tit.

"Yes."

He switches sides.

"Yes!"

He rips my panties in his need to get inside me.

It's raw and rough, both of us still mostly clothed, and from the first thrust, he's nailing a spot inside that feels different.

He pushes my hand between us to my clit, a wordless instruction. *Get there, because I want to fill you up.*

I tighten my fingers on either side of my clit, my nerves already firing hot.

His thrusts are deep and steady. His hand sink into my hair, holding me in a cradle of his arms.

Fucking me.

Taking me.

Showing me what he just told me, that I'm his, and he's never letting me go.

My thighs come up around his waist, climbing his body as my cunt pulls on him tighter and tighter. So close, so close.

And then he's grunting in my ear, a strangled sound of pure release, and I come as he jerks in the circle of my legs, his cock sawing in and out of my pussy.

His breath rushes out of him as my climax pulls him back in.

"It's okay to come in me," I breathe.

He snaps his hips forward and buries himself deep.

―――

"Okay." Ty exhales. "Now that we got that out of our system, can we talk?"

I don't know how long it's been. Minutes?

But my pulse is still careening wildly as I nod.

He slips out of me and swears.

"It's really okay," I say.

He pauses, then kisses my forehead. "We should have talked about it first."

"Yeah."

He rolls over, then reaches back and slides his hand between my thighs. "I like feeling it run out of you, though."

I squeak and twist away from him. "The sheets!"

He shoves something—maybe his shirt—under my ass and rolls me back. "I don't have as much to do tomorrow as you do. I'll find a way to covertly do laundry. And then we don't need to worry about making a mess tonight."

"More of a mess?"

He groans. "Yes, more. Fuck." His voice shifts, takes on a self-lecturing tone. "Ty, get your shit together and talk to this woman."

"Are we speaking to ourselves in the third person now?"

"It can't hurt." He rolls onto his back.

I follow, putting my head on his shoulder.

"What does Ty Connor want?"

"He wants you to fall asleep listening to his heartbeat."

My throat tightens up, and I think he misunderstands my silence as more fear, more arguments.

"You asked. It's the truth. I'm not going to lie to you. I'm not going to tell you I don't miss you, when I miss you more than my next breath."

"I miss you, too."

"Then let me back in." His voice is raw now. "I don't know if I'm doing this right."

"You are."

"I might not get it this right once the season starts again, you know. There might be bumps in the road where you need to be the rock for us."

"What do you mean?"

"You got scared this week, luscious. But I got scared at the end of the season. You saw that. Nobody else did, but you…you were there. That's not my finest hour. I'm not proud of feeling that way. And I can't guarantee I won't lose my shit like that again when everything is on the line."

I run my fingers up his chest and onto his neck. He swallows hard against my touch.

"I've told you things about my path to the NHL that I haven't told anyone else. I've had a single-minded dedication to escaping the poverty of my childhood my entire adult life. I don't have any experience balancing that and…"

I wait, but this time he doesn't continue talking.

"I love your fire and your dedication. I promise that."

"I know."

"What kind of balance do you need?"

"It's new." He twists his head, and my fingers slide up and around his jaw. He kisses my thumb as I trace his lips.

"What is?"

"Loving someone. I love you. And I want to do that right. I want to balance that with my career."

You are so hard to love. It's a startling thought that comes out of nowhere. It knocks the breath out of me.

It doesn't seem hard for Ty, and he's never loved anyone like this. He just told me that.

"You'll balance it just fine," I manage to get out. "And you can help me figure out the same, because I love you, too."

He pulls me on top of him, and our mouths come together.

Kissing the man I love is a lot like kissing the man I think

I hate, it turns out, but with a lot more relief woven through the complicated feelings.

Because now I know that I'm supposed to feel like this, this deep longing, this wild hunger.

"Balance isn't my forte," I admit.

"Fuck balance. Ignore that I said that. Don't you dare give up any part of who you are for me. I love all of your parts, and I want to see you shine. I need you to be happy. Fully happy."

I wrap myself around him. "I am. Oh, I am."

He strips us both down to nothing, and then he enters me again. Making love to me, the way he has for weeks now. Holding me down, making me feel every bit of his love.

And when I come, it's not laughter or tears that follows my orgasm, but a perfect sense of completion.

CHAPTER 43
TY

By Friday night, they've fixed the leak and the carpets in the inn are mostly dry. Kieran comes back with us for a late afternoon game of golf and a sunset steak dinner.

Kiley stays at the cabin with Harper, and I try not to text her all night, but after dinner, I give in.

TY

What are you up to? Pillow fights?

KILEY

Everyone is in a penguin onesie, it's really weird

Bring me your zipper, I need to touch you

Are you drunk?

No, just horny

Aren't you supposed to be paying attention to the groom right now?

I send her a photo of Kieran and Russ playing darts.

Thrilling stuff.

Your turn for a photo. Cleavage is acceptable. So would be just a smile...

You did not just tell a girl to smile

No, that would be wrong

Very. Go away.

I miss you

She sends me a photo of her smiling, that also captures her cleavage.

KILEY

You will survive

Bold of her to assume that, but I'll trust her faith.

The only thing that helps me sleep that night is the looming threat of another five-thirty wake up call—and the goodnight text Kiley sends, with another selfie, this one of her tucked into bed. I think I can see a bit of Harper beside her, but all I focus on is my girl in penguin-print flannel PJs, winking at the camera.

———

Dawn comes too early. I play better, though, which is something. Not as good as the groom, but that's to be expected.

Then we have a feast for kings, a massive breakfast spread that Kieran devours.

When he's done eating, he stands up and lifts his mimosa

in the air. "Guys, I want to thank you all for coming out for this wedding, and making it special for Harper and me. I'm going to head back to the cabin sooner than later, because frankly, I miss my bride-to-be, and I like to be close to her."

The similarity to what I've been thinking about Kiley hits me right in the chest.

He circles the table, shaking everyone's hand. "See you all soon, yep. Thank you, thanks."

I stand when he gets to me. He gives me an up and down. "You all right?"

"Yeah." Hard to believe it was a week ago when I showed up on his doorstep, holding a wedding gift and feeling real fucking sorry for myself. "Looking forward to watching you get married this afternoon. It looks good on you."

"Feels good."

I clap him on the shoulder, then return to my breakfast, because I am not in a rush.

Kiley has forbidden me from bothering her until after the ceremony—a sacrifice I will make for her and her alone.

———

A few hours later, I take my seat next to Armstrong and Gustafsson in the rows of chairs set up behind the cabin. The lake is off to the right, the forest is straight ahead, and the sun is shining. Music provided by a string trio carrying on the breeze finishes the perfect setting for Kieran to pace back and forth, looking every inch a proud but eager groom in a well-tailored midnight blue suit.

At the discreet nod from a woman dressed all in black, wearing a headset, the string trio starts a new song.

Picking up on the cue, we all turn and look toward the cabin.

Kiley comes around the corner first, wearing a pretty-in-pink, one-shouldered dress that wraps around her curves and flutters to the ground in a floating chiffon.

Her hair is *sleek*. Her bangs are smooth and sweeping to one side, her usually fluffy long, loose curls tamed into dark, shiny waves, like something straight out of Old Hollywood.

She smiles as she passes me, and all I can see is that shiny mouth wrapped around my cock as she gazes up at me.

Fuck.

Not the time, cock. Not the time.

But now that we're getting back on track, he's not listening. All the time is the time. Every minute of every day.

The music shifts again.

Okay, maybe not the next thirty minutes.

Everyone rises, and then the bride comes around the corner of the cabin on her mother's arm.

The wind picks up enough to lift the veil trailing behind her as she floats toward her groom.

I follow them with my gaze all the way to the floral arbour, and then when Angela Roberts takes Harper's flowers and stands next to Kiley, my love is all I can see again.

I'm hopeless, and I don't care.

It's a nice wedding, of course. A spectacular setting for me to have an unfettered opportunity to gaze on Kiley's beauty.

It's a little surreal to listen to heartfelt vows as my heart pounds, as she smiles and her cheeks turn pink, and I think that's because she can feel me looking at her.

I really, really like looking at her.

"Do you take this man to be your husband?"

"With everything I have and with everything I am."

"Do you take this woman to be your wife?"

"Forever and ever."

They exchange rings, and then the minister says, "You may kiss—"

Kieran doesn't wait for them to finish. He takes Harper's face in his hands and kisses her. He keeps kissing her, until she sucks in an audible inhale, which he takes as a brief pause before he wraps his arms around her and dips her back, kissing her again.

"Friends and family, it is my great pleasure to introduce Kieran and Harper Marsh for the first time as husband and wife."

Their matching grins are blinding.

They run down the aisle, and everyone spills out after them, the afternoon filling with cheers and laughter.

"You look beautiful," I murmur quietly.

I've found Kiley by the water. The photographers are taking pictures, and she's waiting to be pulled in.

She smiles, still looking ahead. "Were you surprised to see me in pink?"

I trail my fingers over her bare shoulder, then lightly down her spine, to the cleft between her plump ass cheeks. "Not at all. Pink is one of my favourite colours on you."

She stiffens, as if a lightning bolt just zapped up her spine.

I like having that effect on her. "Save me a dance?"

"Oh, Ty." She slides a liquid, lusty gaze over her shoulder at me. "It's you and me and the 'Chicken Dance', for sure."

I laugh out loud, and then she has to go, so I head in search of the bar.

But yes, that is definitely happening.

———

Despite the tease, she does look for me for the first dance of the night, when everyone joins the married couple after they've had the floor to themselves for the Brothers Osborne song, "I Don't Remember Me (Before You)".

She's been watching me all afternoon, and I like her hot gaze on my skin just as much as I like looking right back at her.

As soon as the DJ invites everyone to join the happy couple, she finds me across the dance floor. I cross to her and take her in my arms.

"What song is this?" I ask.

"It's the one from *Four Weddings and a Funeral*."

"I don't remember that from the playlist debate."

It's called "'Love is All Around' by Wet Wet Wet. It might have been a last minute addition."

I tug her closer. "It's perfect."

She's wearing heels today, and we're exactly the same height. Her body fits against mine in a way that makes my head spin. "Tell me the 'Chicken Dance' isn't next."

"Exactly next."

I sigh in mock regret. "We're going to have a hard-on problem."

"Ty!" She laughs and throws her head back, which doesn't help, because that presses her thighs against mine, and makes me think about biting her where her throat meets her shoulder. "God, you're like a teenager."

"I was never this randy then. This is all you." I hold her tighter and breathe in her scent. "And how good you smell."

Right on cue, that's when the song ends, and the polka strains of the Chicken Dance start.

Everyone shifts to the new beat, and Kieran's nieces and nephews push to the centre of a circle, leading us all in the dance.

After that, the DJ plays a mix, featuring some of the songs we requested, and we dance until the jackets come off, and Hayden Calhoun gets hoisted up on Rusty and Gusty's shoulders. "Tarps off, boys!"

I yank my tie off and hand it to Kiley. "That's for later."

She mouths something I miss as I unbutton my shirt.

During the season, a tarp is your sweater, your hockey jersey.

But for hockey players in the off-season, aka wedding season, it means the tuxedo shirt, and there's a point in most wedding receptions where they come *off*.

And then the party really starts.

———

"You want a drink?" Russ asks when we tumble into our chairs for a break.

Kiley has been pulled away by Harper.

"Yeah."

He disappears.

I broodily search the tent for my sexy girl, finding her unerringly fast. She's sitting sideways on a chair, her legs crossed, her chiffon dress flowing over her hips like a cloud.

The music shifts again, easing into a slow song. "To give the tarps-off boys a breather," the DJ says, making the whole tent laugh.

Across the table, Shannon pokes Max. "Let's dance."

He makes a face, then slowly rises and holds his hand out. His wife happily takes it, and they disappear onto the dance floor, sweeping past Russ, who is returning with two drinks in hand. His gaze follows the captain onto the dance floor, then he plunks one of the drinks in front of me.

"Cheers."

He doesn't hear me.

"Hey, Russ."

He jerks back and I hold my glass up to his. "*Cheers.*"

"Right." He downs half his drink.

"Whoa." I'm laughing, but that dies as I follow his gaze and realize he's still staring at the Tilmans. "What's going on?"

"Nothing." He realizes I'm looking where he's looking. "It's not like that."

"I didn't say anything."

"I would never—"

I cut him off. "It's fine. But maybe… do everyone a favour and get on Tinder?"

He looks like he's going to argue, but he doesn't. We finish our drinks in silence, then he pulls out his phone.

I slide a glance sideways. "What are you doing?"

He shrugs. "Getting on Tinder."

"I didn't mean right now." I laugh. "You got premium? Line up some chicks for when we get home."

Home. Since when did Hamilton start to feel like home? A happiness blooms in my chest at that nice surprise.

Because it is now.

He's tapping on the screen. "You pay for premium?"

I used to. I let my account lapse after I met Kiley. "Yeah."

He laughs. "Well, yeah, I guess I'm going to need to, because the only person within fifty miles of me right now is Kiley."

My glass skids out of my hand and halfway across the table. "What?"

He turns his phone in my direction.

There's Kiley. Ki, her profile says. Road trips.

I frown.

"Don't worry, I'm not swiping right on Kiley," Russ says when I shove out of my chair.

"Nobody is," I growl. "Nobody but me."

"You?"

I already did. Months ago. "Don't say a fucking word."

He holds up his hands. "I would never. I'll, uh, change my location and we can pretend this never happened."

I yank my phone out of my pocket, simultaneously looking for the app and tracking where Kiley is. She's left the conversation Harper pulled her into, and now they're circling the room again.

I skirt the edge of the dance floor as the slow song ends and the DJ starts "Cupid Shuffle." People surge back to join in, but Kiley is still making the rounds.

I'm getting closer to her.

My pulse is pounding now, like I'm a hunter, and she's my prey.

Then she's right in front of me, just on the other side of a table.

"Are you having a good time?" she asks one of Kieran's relatives. Gives them a stunning smile. "Amazing. Yeah, get out there, this song is—"

I catch her by the wrist and pull her away from the dance floor and out of the tent.

"What's going on?"

I glance around. Nobody is looking at us. By the end of the night, I'll be kissing her in the middle of the dance floor, but she wants to keep us on the down low so we're not distracting from the wedding.

"Ty!"

"Where's your phone?"

"It's in my purse at the head table."

I take her wrist again and lead her there. "Do you still have Tinder on your phone?"

She narrows her eyes at me. "Yes, probably. I tend not to delete apps. Why? Do you?"

"No. But I'm going to download it again so I can show you something." I go the App Store and tap on the icon. *Yes, use my data for this download.* It's important.

I open it up, then slide it over so it nudges her phone. "Your turn."

"What are we doing?"

"Just open it up. Start scrolling."

Curiosity wars with stubbornness, but curiosity wins out. Her gaze flicks from the guys on her phone to me and back again. "Do you want to see me swipe right on some of these country dudes holding up fish, or..." She sucks in a breath.

She's found my profile.

Less than a mile away.

Right next to her, in fact.

Her finger hovers over the screen, and she flicks that confused but curious gaze back up to my face. "You think this guy might be my type?"

I shrug. "That's up to you."

She swipes right.

It's a match.

Her head jerks up. "When did you…?"

"Right after I was traded. I forgot about it until just now. It's a long story that's probably none of our business, but it ends with Russ finding your profile and then I remembered." I grab my phone and swipe back through my photos, all the way to February. "I took a screenshot of your profile pic."

"You *what?*" She snatches my phone. "That's me. Like, months ago. I've changed it a few times."

"I told you."

"*Months* ago."

"That's what I'm saying! The day I was traded." I lean over and swipe to the next photo, an emo selfie I took on the plane.

"Are you alone on a private plane?"

We've moved on from the fact that we're fucking soulmates, apparently. "Yeah."

"Sweet." She jerks her head up. "Do you usually fly private? Because I've decided I like that."

I grin. "Not that often. This was the team owner's plane."

She turns her attention back to the photo and her brow pulls tight. "You look sad."

"I was just traded away from my—" I cut myself off. *Home.*

But it's not that anymore.

"The only place you'd ever played pro hockey in. No, I get it. But those seats look *nice.* Leather?"

I'm laughing now. "Yeah."

"I can't even imagine." She looks at me again, and this

time, she's not distracted by the deluge of information I just shoved at her. "You swiped right on me?"

Finally. We're processing this realization with the appropriate gravitas.

"From day one, luscious."

She looks at me in disbelief, then laughs and throws her arms around my neck. "You should kiss me again."

"Right here?"

"Right here."

"People will see."

"I hope they do."

"People will know I love you."

Her breath hitches and she nods. "And they'll know I love you, too."

CHAPTER 44
KILEY

It doesn't take long after the kiss for my brother and my bestie to strong-arm me into an emergency *what the fuck* conversation.

Grant appears out of nowhere, gives Ty a big grin, and says, "You don't mind if I steal my sister, right?"

Before Ty can respond, Kieran is basically shoved at him, and Harper waves a bottle of champagne at me. "Let's go have a private toast."

They drag me outside.

What is it with everyone thinking I won't just go willingly somewhere?

"What are we toasting to, Harper?" Grant asks.

"Love," Harper says brightly.

"You guys can let go of me, you know."

"Can we?" My brother sighs dramatically. "If we do, will you tell us everything?"

"Because we think you've left out some pertinent details," Harper adds.

"Some details are private," I protest.

We're leaving the tent area. The white lights strung up around it are now behind us, and the lake is right ahead.

Harper steers us to the boat house, and they finally release my arms when we have to go through it single file to get to the dock on the other side.

Harper hands Grant the bottle of champagne, then kicks off her shoes and sits down, letting her toes trail in the water. She pats the dock next to her. "Join me."

I do the same.

Grant holds the bottle out, pointing the cork at the lake. "To love?"

My whole body is shaking with laughter as I nod. "Yes, to love."

"It's love?" Harper swoons and leans against me. "Babe, you have to tell us *everything*."

A loud pop cracks through the night as my brother sends the cork flying into the water. He hands the bottle back to Harper, who hands it to me.

I take a fortifying sip of bubbles while Grant toes off his shoes and rolls up his pant legs.

"Well," I say, trying to decide where to start. "The day that Ty was traded to Hamilton, he swiped right on me on Tinder."

"Shut. Up." Harper slaps me, and the bottle of wine almost goes sailing after the cork.

"Settle. Down." I shove the wine at her. "Have a drink."

Her eyes are as big as saucers in the moonlight as she tags a swig. "Has it been going on ever since?"

"Oh, no. I didn't swipe back. That happened…tonight."

My brother frowns. "But you were crying about not being good enough for him a week ago. How did you get together before that if not Tinder?"

"Wait, *what?*" Harper glowers at Grant. "You didn't tell me there was crying!"

"She swore me to secrecy because of the wedding." He holds up his hands. "And Ty promised he was going to get them back on track."

"He did. We are," I interject. "Let me tell the story."

They try their best to contain their questions as I take them back to meeting him as BeastMode, which Harper knew but Grant didn't, and then through the last week, which Grant knew but Harper didn't.

"And now you're all caught up."

They look at each other. Then at me. "You've skipped some details."

I blush. "I skipped the private stuff."

"But that's the good stuff," my brother says dryly. "Was it weird, having already told him so much about yourself online, but not knowing it was *Ty?*"

"Very weird." I chew on my bottom lip. "But it was Ty. That was the thing I had to come to realize. That my resistance about this guy in front of me wasn't about him, it was about who I was seeing him as. Which was a projection of all the guys I've dated before, and..." I wave my hand. "You know, shit from watching our parents relationship, etcetera. It wasn't *him*. It wasn't real. So that was a process."

"And he's good to you?" Harper looks concerned. "Like, *really* good? As good as you deserve?"

Warmth blossoms in my chest as I think about just how good he is. "He's so good to me. The absolute best. I..." Tears threaten to spring to my eyes, but I stare out at the dark endlessness of the lake and push through the tiny little bit of disbelief that still threatens to disrupt this magical feeling. "I love him. And he loves me."

"Grant," Harper says solemnly. "You need to find somewhere else to stay tonight."

"Me? Why me? Can't she go back to Ty's hotel room?"

I bury my face in my hands. "Can we not talk about where I'm going to have sex tonight?"

My brother pats me on the back. "As long as we're all in agreement that you are getting lucky tonight, the where doesn't really matter."

I groan. "Shut up."

He wraps his arm fully around me and squeezes. "I'm so proud of you. I'm guessing you won't need any more Tinder advice now?"

"Nope."

"You know, if you think about it, I'm basically responsible for you two getting together." He sounds pleased with himself.

"How do you figure you get any credit for this?"

"Did he not swipe right on you before anything else that followed?"

"Again, I'll say, shut up."

"Does this mean it's Grant's turn to fall in love next?" Harper asks.

"Never going to happen." He grabs the bottle of champagne and takes a long drink.

"Famous last words, my darling brother."

He shakes his head.

And there's nothing particularly revealing in his silence, but my twin intuition says there's a reason he's not open to falling in love any time soon—and he doesn't want to share it yet.

So when Harper opens her mouth to maybe poke at that bruise a little harder, I change the subject.

We talk about the wedding, and how perfect it was.

We drink champagne, shoulder to shoulder, kicking our feet in the water.

And when Kieran and Ty come looking for us, just as we're nearing the bottom of the bottle, Grant gives me a grateful look.

"I love you," I whisper to him as Kieran helps his bride to her feet.

Grant bumps his shoulder against me. "We're going to be okay. We've got each other. And now you have Ty."

I smile up at my boyfriend. He offers his hand, and I let him pull me up and into his arms.

He holds me as the others walk away, heading back to the tent, and then he kisses me under the moonlight.

CHAPTER 45
TY

The day after the wedding, everyone flies home on Highlanders Air—except the bride and the groom. We leave them at the cabin for some well-earned alone time. They're going to go from there to Italy for the second part of their honeymoon.

Which sounds amazing, but I'm happy to spend this summer closer to home.

My home.

Hamilton, Ontario, right around the lake from where I grew up in Buffalo, New York.

Hamilton, Ontario, birthplace of Kiley Forge.

I don't stop grinning for weeks.

It takes an unexpected visitor to the arena to ruin my good mood, but when that happens, it happens hard. Like a thunderclap warning from the gods above.

"Hey, Connor, you've got a VIP visitor!" Haler sticks his head into the treatment room where I'm getting taped up.

"Expecting someone?" our trainer asks.

"Nope." I roll my shoulder, then grab my t-shirt and

head back to the dressing room without putting it on. It could be Nina, it could be someone from one of the companies who I'm doing endorsements with, it could be a former teammate.

It is none of those people, though.

I stop in my tracks when I recognize Crys Graham standing next to my stall.

"Ty Connor," he says. "It's a pleasure."

He doesn't introduce himself.

He expects me to recognize him.

I don't give him the pleasure, even though I immediately clock him as the guy who fucked with Kiley's head probably every single day of their relationship. The asshole who had my girlfriend before me, and treated her like shit. The motherfucker who— I cut off my thoughts before they show on my face. "And you are…?"

He laughs. "Hard to place out of context? I'm Crys. Your agent talked to you about working on my film."

"Oh. That." I step around him and start to get dressed for the ice.

"You're a hard man to track down."

I frown. "Not really. Why did you want to find me?"

"I want you in my movie."

And there's something in how he says it that makes me realize it's true. *He* wanted *me*. Not the casting director. Him.

My already dangerous feelings turn murderous, because there's only one reason why he would target me for anything.

I choose my words carefully. "I'm not an actor."

He flashes an easy, charming smile. His gaze, though, remains piercing. "You don't need to be. You just need to be yourself."

"Oh yeah?" I snatch my jersey from my stall and yank it over my head. "Hey, do you skate? Is that where this movie idea came from?"

"Yeah, sure." Another smile, this time cockier. "I played triple-A."

"Do you still play?"

"Not as much as I'd like to."

"Beer league?" I'm shoving equipment at him now. "Haler, get this guy some skates."

Crys sets the pads aside. "I'm not sure—"

I stop moving and give him my hardest *don't try me, motherfucker* stare. "Bud, if you want to talk me into your movie, you gotta do it on the ice. Show me your stuff." I step into his personal space. He smells like patchouli, I swear to God. "Show me the type of man you are, and I'll give you my answer."

He laughs. "All right. You might be surprised."

Oh, I'm fucking surprised all right. Surprised he walked into my barn and thought he could impress me.

"Tell you what," I say, smooth as can be. "We'll play an easy three-on-three. You can pick your wingers."

If my teammates thought they were done practicing before, they've all quickly gotten on board.

He picks Gusty and Jenson—fame being the most important element for him, of course—which leaves me with Calhoun and Watanabe.

They're young and lesser known, but they're also hungry tiger cubs who like nothing better than to beat their older teammates.

This is going to be fun.

I stalk out to the ice first, and the others join me one at a time.

"What's going on, bud?" Gusty asks.

"Just follow my lead."

"That doesn't answer my question."

I swoop around him, warming up. "You don't want my answer."

It's not like skating circles around the actor is going to be hard. I could do this in my sleep.

But it's choosing the right moment to tell him that I want nothing to do with him or his project…that's the tricky part.

I'm at a full burn when he joins us.

Good, he looks nervous.

I glance at the clock above us, then to the upper deck.

Nobody's watching yet, but that might change.

I'll let him dangle for bit. I need a practice anyway.

Gusty takes over explaining the rules of three-on-three, since I'm not about to help this guy at all.

Then it's on. And it's fun, playing an NHL game around him. Making him sweat. Making him feel abso-fucking-lutely incompetent.

I tip the first goal into their net.

Then Haler scores on my team, which Crys crows about, even though he didn't have fuck all to do with it except he didn't actively spoil it like he did the first two plays they tried.

And then I see we've caught an audience.

Good.

Time to turn the pressure on.

I chase him down and win a puck battle against the boards. I'm a fucking pussycat with him by any reasonable standard, but it makes him mad.

It sucks him in, and then he's chasing me down.

Bring it, Mr. Fancy Pants. Mr. TV Deal. Mr. Movie Maker.

He launches himself at me, thinking he's going to forecheck me into the boards and steal the puck, but I saw this coming from the blue line.

I baited him into this, and I'm not going to miss my opportunity to turn it into an attack.

I twist, then pivot back, lightning quick, and I smash him at my full strength into the plexiglass.

It's a legal hit, in the numbers. But it had to hurt, having me at my full summer weight slam into him and hold him there.

I hope seeing Kiley sitting halfway up in the stands hurts even more.

"Why'd you come here, you fucking prick? Was it to make her feel bad, somehow? Never going to happen on my watch," I snarl. "I don't know how I got on your radar in the first place. Do you perv on her on Instagram? Do you wish you'd treated her better? You could never treat her well enough to hold on to her, even if you did keep your weasely dick in your pants. But that woman? That woman? I fucking love her. I'm going to marry that girl, and I'm going to protect her from jackasses like you for the rest of her life. Do you fucking understand me? Do you???"

I hear my name called in the distance, my teammates warning me.

I lean in harder. "I'm sorry. I didn't hear that."

"You're insane," he gasps. "I don't care about her."

"I don't believe you for a second. There are hundreds of hockey players who you could approach."

"Get off me."

"Look at her." I thump him in the head, smashing his helmet against the glass again. "She came home and found you fucking someone else in the shower."

"And then she stole my fucking notebook." He sounds more wounded over that than the bruises I've hopefully given him. "She's a bitch, man. Don't let her—"

My gloves go flying and I kick his feet out from under him, taking him down to the ice.

I manage to land three really good hits before Hiro drags me off the guy. "All right, Connor, that's enough."

I shake off my teammate. "Yeah. We're done here."

I power over to the tunnel, then leap off the ice, flying down the rubber mats now.

I need these skates off. I need to get to Kiley. I need her to know what that was about.

But when I get to the dressing room, she's already there, on the other side of the swinging doors.

"Come here, sexy girl," I say softly, and she races in to me.

I catch her in my arms.

"That was foolish," she whispers.

I'm not sorry. "Had to be done."

"Not you. Him. Why would he think he could walk into your barn and clown you?"

God, she's perfect. "Because he's a wounded narcissist?"

She shudders. "He sure is. And it looked like you broke every bone in his body." She stops. "Wait, you didn't, right?"

"Probably not." I kiss the tip of her nose. "That's enough about him. I've reasserted my dominance. Reclaimed my woman, and my barn."

"Your woman?" She sounds delighted.

"Mmhmm." I pick her up and spin her around. "I'm so much taller than you when I'm in skates."

"It's nice for a change of pace."

I slowly set her down, then cup her face in my hands, my

favourite way to hold her. "I love you, Kiley. I didn't really hurt him. I told him to leave you the fuck alone. That's all. And maybe I gave him some bruised ribs. But that was his choice. Now let me get out of this stuff and we can—"

There's a ruckus in the hallway.

I make a face at my love. "We do not need to stick around for that. Come on."

I grab her hand and we head through the treatment room to the hallway on the other side that leads to the equipment area—and the storage room where I first got close enough to breathe in her spiced honey scent.

"We can hide in here," I tell her.

She giggles as I press her up against the shelves. "How long do you think we have to hide?"

"Hours," I murmur, pressing my face into her neck. "Hours and hours."

EPILOGUE
KILEY

Miami Beach

November

"How's my girl?"

"I'm good," I murmur into the phone. "I miss you."

"Tell me how much." Ty exhales, like he's just stretched out on his hotel bed.

"I miss the taste of you in my mouth." My pulse pounds as I say that. But he loves it when I talk dirty, and it's true.

I do miss giving him blow jobs. We did that a lot over the summer, and now…well, it's going to be weeks before I get to hear the sounds he makes when I swallow his cock.

And my empty mouth is my own doing, so I can't pout.

The appreciative growl in my ear is almost as good as hearing it in person, though.

"When you say things like that, it's very hard not to stroke myself, you know." And then he makes a little sound that tells me he didn't even try not to.

I grin and roll onto my back. "Are you hard?"

"Very."

"Big?"

"Always for you."

"I want to lick you," I whisper. My eyes drift shut. "Wish I'd given you one more blow job before I left…"

"I'll be there in three weeks. And after I eat my fill of you, you can get on your knees for me." Ty takes over the conversation, talking me through us both having orgasms.

As I twitch through the afterglow of a very nice release, I lazily tell him that another packaged arrived for him today.

One of his most endearing traits is his inability to pick the right address for his online shopping. If he's set up an address on a website, that's where that package is going forever.

Not that either of us are home in Hamilton to get anything there right now. And I shouldn't poke him to send things to an address we won't be using for much longer— because we just bought a big loft close to the arena, and we're moving in together after Christmas.

"You should open those," Ty says, his voice full of sleep.

"Oh, are they for me? That's sneaky."

"Mmm, not exactly. They're definitely for me. But I like you getting worked up about them…"

"Should I do it while you're on the phone?" Because the packages are on the console table at the entrance to the condo, and I'm a boneless mess in Ty's bed.

"Nah, open them tomorrow night."

"Okay, I will." I smile. "Love you, mister."

"Love you more, luscious."

And then we say goodbye and go to sleep in separate

beds. Him in a hotel room in Atlanta, and me in his bed—in Miami.

The job offer that I got came with an unexpected interesting twist. The rehearsals are taking place here, so I wouldn't have to rent a place or be put up by the theatre company.

I already have access to an incredible condo, right on South Beach.

I've been here for a week, and it's still a bit surreal.

Ty really did have the perfect life here. And now, for six weeks, it's my life, too—and it's me who is rollerblading down the strip.

My boyfriend is being a very good sport about how I co-opted the lux life while he is in the rough early season trying to figure out how to bring out the best in himself and the other Highlanders.

His team is going through a rough patch right now. Really rough. Some of them aren't speaking to each other on the current road trip they are on, and it's so intense, Ty doesn't even want to talk about it. And he loves to talk about everything with me. The man is an external processor who will keep me up late debriefing games.

So I worry about him.

But I'm loving my new job. It's incredibly fun to be back in the theatre space, herding a cast through rehearsals. And there's something magical about being able to do this contract without worrying about what I do next, because my boyfriend is taking care of the bills at home. If all I do in the new year is produce Shannon's podcast (which I'm going to push her to do, even though her life has changed a lot since the summer), Ty will be thrilled for me.

How can I not worry about a man who makes my life that easy, and celebrates everything I do?

My phone vibrates with a new message.

TY

I can't sleep.

KILEY

You want to talk again?

Always, but you need your sleep, too.

Let's talk until we drift off. Do you think the line will stay live until the morning?

Only one way to find out.

———

The next morning, I put on my new pair of oversized, mirrored sunglasses and stumble to the nearest coffee shop for an extra-large, extra-espresso anything.

But it was worth missing sleep last night.

I'm smiling when I arrive at rehearsals. I'm still smiling ten hours later when we call it a day and I head back to the apartment, making it just in time to catch Ty's game.

There are a few new players on the team who I don't know that well yet, so every game this early in the season feels uncertain.

Tonight, though, they dominate, controlling the play through all three periods. The Highlanders spend way more time in their offensive zone than Atlanta does. A year of experience in the league, as a team, makes all the difference, and they win 4-2.

Alone, I cheer like I'm in a sports bar.

And then I look at the contents of the three packages Ty had delivered over the last week.

The first is a sex toy that is designed to suck at my clit.

The second is a two-pack of dyed bondage rope, one black and one pale pink, almost the same colour as the bridesmaid dress I wore for Harper's wedding.

And the third is a web cam.

None of these are "accidental" deliveries after all.

And all of them can be used tonight to celebrate the win, just as soon as Ty gets back to his hotel room.

I take my time, knowing he has to do press availability and then travel to the hotel with the team. I light some candles, then run a bath.

Ty has the world's nicest bathroom here in Miami. A giant walk-in shower with jets coming from all angles. A separate tub built for people who are over six feet tall. And a view of the ocean during the day.

Once the tub is full, I turn off the lights and open the window. The ocean is black now, but there are cruise ships and container ships off the shore, and I can hear waves, and music from further south down the strip.

I send some music of my own to the speakers that are wired into the bathroom and bedroom, then sink into the water and close my eyes, letting my imagination run away with the setting—more cosmopolitan and sexy than Hamilton by far.

I see Ty binding me in the rope, then taking me out for dinner to one of the restaurants he likes here.

At the end of the summer, we came down to Miami for a week, using my vacation time before I left my job at the hospital. It was a delicious blur of good food, incredible sex, and perfect napping, but the weather was generally horrible. Rain storms and insanely muggy heat, so we didn't go for the long walks on the beach and around the city that I'd been hoping for.

"It's better in the winter," he told me then.

I got the job offer on our last day here. "I'll hold you to that," I told him as I broke the news that I was going to be joining this touring production. "Because I'm going to need to use your apartment for six weeks in the fall."

"Our apartment," he said, then promptly put the dates they play his former team in my calendar, along with six appointments for "in-person sex" around that game.

He also scattered "online sex" and "phone sex" appointments across the other eleven weeks.

Tonight is one of those calendar reminders, at midnight.

Good thing tomorrow I don't need to be at the theatre until early afternoon.

After my bath, I rinse off in the steam shower and wash my hair. I braid my hair and twist those plaits into buns. Tomorrow my hair will be a riot of chaotic curls.

Even after all the pampering, it's only eleven.

Still, I check my phone.

Sure enough, there's a message from Ty. I light up inside, all warm and tingly.

TY

How's my sexy girl? Not too tired?

KILEY

Even if I was, I'm all excited now. You won! And I opened your packages.

Naughty girl. Did you like what you found?

Mmhmm

It'll take me a bit of time to get alone, but
you should get started with them.

You don't mind me getting a head start?

Mind? I'm halfway hard just thinking about
it, even with an audience.

I set up the web cam on my laptop. It clips to the top, and has a much better picture than the built-in one. Crisper image and a wider field of vision.

Then I unwrap the bundles of rope.

Ty loves to pin me down with his hands, and he regularly buckles me in now, tugging my seatbelt tight—remembering the first time he used that to restrain me when we were caught in the rainstorm.

He also used his tie to bind my wrists together the night of Kieran and Harper's wedding, something we both loved.

But proper bondage rope…this takes it to the next level.

I squirm as I wrap the black rope around my wrist. Heat pulses through me, and I stretch out on the bed, my still slightly damp skin warming up from the inside out.

I take a picture of the rope against my skin and send it to Ty.

It takes him far too long to reply, but when he does, it's a long string of groaning letters.

TY

unnngggggggg

I'm going to tie you up and make you be a
good girl for me

you better like that, because I love it already

KILEY

I like it

I like it a lot

I'm squirming

Fuck

Good

I press my thighs together until my muscles tremble and my core throbs, then let them fall apart. My clit feels like it wants that sucker toy already, but I'm going to make myself wait the way Ty would if he was here.

I want you slick for me tonight

Are you touching?

Waiting for you

That's not what I was expecting you to say…don't you want to rub your soft pussy? I would.

I'd rather wait until you can watch

So I shouldn't tease you

I laugh in *oh, I should have seen this coming.*

KILEY

You can tease me

TY

Good answer, I was going to anyway

I don't need the toy, then, because the words fly back and forth between us. Almost an hour has gone by when he tells me he has to go for a little bit, but he'll see me soon.

TY

Use the toy. That's why I sent it. I love you.

I bring the toy to my clit and it pulls at me with surprising suction.

"Oh my *God*," I yell, dropping my hand so it pulls off.

Then I immediately put it back there and let it take me to a fast, surprisingly satisfying orgasm.

Well.

Hello toy.

Panting, I text Ty the update.

KILEY

That thing made me come in like thirty seconds. You may have created a monster, because I'm still horny.

TY

Give me the next one with your fingers only. Make it last.

My hips jump as I touch my pussy lips. Even before I get to my clit, I'm thrashing my head back and forth, because *nooo*, it's too sensitive, but I can hear Ty urging me to do it anyway, to push through and find more pleasure.

My pulse pounds in my ears as I touch myself more carefully. I don't take myself over the cliff, only edging closer and closer, and with my free hand—the one I wrapped rope around—I grab onto the pillow beside me. The rope slithers over my wrist, tightening as I twist my hand, pushing and pulling at the pillow. Anchoring myself there as my legs spread wider, wider…opening myself up so I can touch but not push myself into coming again too soon.

"This is fucking gorgeous."

I scream and my eyes fly open.

Ty is grinning at me from the doorway.

"What the fuck," I gasp.

"Don't stop, luscious." His gaze rakes over me, drinking me in.

"You're in Atlanta."

"I was." He pulls off his team t-shirt, giving me a good look at his ripped torso. He's always more jacked after a game, and I love it so much it makes my head spin.

He gestures at the hand that was just buried between my legs. "I left immediately after the game and flew here. Looks like I got here just in time."

"Atlanta is—"

"An hour and forty-five minutes away by air," he said softly, kneeling on the bed at my feet. "You've stopped, so I should maybe take over?"

"What time is it?"

"Just about midnight." He drops a kiss on my knee. "You smell good. Like the ocean but sweet."

"You have expensive bath products," I whisper, then reach for him, finally convinced he's really here. "Oh my God, I've missed you."

He climbs on top of me and kisses my mouth. He tastes so good I could cry, but I won't because we have precious little time together and I want every second of it to be happy.

When my tongue meets his, he groans in delight and deepens the embrace, sweeping me up against his hard chest.

One hand scoops down to squeeze my ass, then trails

over my hip and goes straight to where I am swollen and sticky and *primed* for release. "You've been edging since I got off the plane."

"You were on a plane when I was doing that?"

"Yeah, how do you think I got here?"

"I don't know!" I kiss him again, arching my back, pressing my breasts into his chest.

He pushes two fingers into my tight cunt and starts rubbing my clit. "Come for me again, and then I'm going to tie you up."

"Oh God."

"Not God. Just your boyfriend." His kiss this time is more commanding, pushing back against my tongue.

Showing me with his mouth that he means business, that he's in charge. And the whirlwind that is my mind goes quiet. Blissfully blank, and there's only pleasure. There's only the pulse of my clit against his thumb, the squeeze of my pussy on his fingers, and then a building intensity that feels just as good as with a toy, but *better* because it's with Ty.

"Fuck, yes, come on my hand," he growls. "I can feel your clit pulsing. That's it, little clit. Come like the champion that you are."

I laugh breathlessly.

He pulls his hand up and sucks on his fingers. "I gotta keep winning games."

"Why? I mean, yes. But—"

"I worked something out with the coach. Important personal time. Not every week, but there was this day off tomorrow, and then around the Florida games, and if we play a game anywhere near your shows..." He kisses me hungrily. "Phone is good. Online is good. This is better."

My heart sings.

He stands and rearranges me so my head is at the edge of the bed, carefully on a pillow, but tipping back. I watch, upside down, as he strips out of the rest of his clothes.

His cock hangs heavy, the tip glistening, as he strides back to me. My eyes lock onto him. His tight sac behind his hard length. His strong, thick thighs.

My hands reach for him, but he catches my wrists as he stops at my head. "Uh uh."

Oh. Right.

While he holds my wrists in one hand, he tips my head back a little more, then spanks my lips with the underside of his cock.

My lips curve as I breathe in the clean, masculine scent of his sex.

"Hold still for me," he growls.

"Is smiling out, then?"

"You think sass is the best thing you could be doing with your mouth right now?" He pushes the head of his cock more firmly to my lips. "Can't smile if you're choking, can you?"

Good point. I open for him and swallow him in, pulling the length of his cock against my tongue. He fills me up and floods my senses, thrusting in and out with a shallow little pulse that never gives me a full break from sucking him.

Not that I want one.

I love making him feel good like this. And this position, specifically, is a favourite. It stretches my body out, and I know Ty likes to look at my tits and belly and the wet evidence between my legs of how much I like this.

I know, because he tells me.

"Fuck, you're sexy," he groans. "Every time you swallow, your tits jiggle. And your hot pussy likes this, doesn't she?

Beautiful, slutty pussy." He makes an appreciative sound, like a rumbling in his chest, and his thighs widen on either side of my head. "Now I had a plan here, before your mouth distracted me."

I squeak, but it's muffled by his cock.

He pays me no heed, lashing my wrists. Once they're bound, holds them just with a single crooked finger, his thumb tracing loose circles over the rope instead of gripping me firmly. Up onto my fingers, then down my forearms. Up and down, he has amazing reach, and it's disorienting and oh so good. The kind of lazy, hedonistic Ty energy that drives me crazy and needy and eager to please.

"I had such plans to tie you up in some complicated pattern tonight," he says, exhaling like he's disappointed, although the way his cock is getting bigger in my mouth suggests otherwise. "And then you were just so fucking sexy when I got here…so caught up in getting yourself off that you didn't even hear me come in…and I lost my head. I needed to kiss you and touch you and get inside you. And here we are."

He thrusts deeper into my throat, making me choke.

He gets bigger again. Harder.

"I think you'll need to make me come in your mouth, so I can concentrate on my plan." Another thrust. "Can you feel me pulsing my seed into your mouth already? It's spilling out of me, that's how fucking hot you are. All I want to do is come for you. In you. On you." He yanks out and jerks himself against my gasping, open mouth. Drops of precome splatter my lips before he shoves into my mouth again. "Fuck. Yes, Kiley, swallow me. Swallow all of me. Take it…"

I gulp his release as he groans and fucks his hips against my face wildly.

His thighs go rock hard as his climax spurts down my throat, and then he sags over me, his whole body twitching in tandem with his softening, pulsing cock.

Once he's finished, he slides beside me. He uses my bound wrists to tug me up, and he checks on my swallowing —"Good? Okay? Fuck, that was hot"—before he turns us around, then stretches my arms up over my head, using the tail end of the rope to tie off on something above me.

"Do you have a tether bolt up there?"

"Yep."

"Is it new?"

"I installed in when we were here in August."

I twist my head, trying to see where he's making a knot. "You did?"

"The rope was on back order, and I didn't want to use just anything on you. I figured we might use it at Christmas." He glances down at me and grins. "Do I need to put something in your mouth again?"

I glance at his cock.

He laughs. "In a few minutes. Where are your panties?"

I make a gagging sound.

"Okay, no panties." He grabs the other rope, then leans over me and kisses me.

Oh, that's a good use for my mouth. Absolutely.

He licks the taste of himself away, kissing me until all that's left is panting arousal. Then he kisses a trail down my body, starting with my neck, before cupping my breasts, licking and sucking at me there for a while, and moving down to my belly, and lower, much lower. To my thighs, and my knees, and my calves. Well beyond my pussy to my ankle, which he catches in his fingers and lifts to his mouth for a kiss before he bends it in.

And then he starts to bind me. First that leg, and then the other, until I'm in a folded open position that probably has some classy, beautiful name, but all I can think is, *I'm a sex frog. He hired a private plane to fly here for the night and turn me into a sex frog.*

This must be love.

There's no other word for it.

He looks pleased with himself, too, to see me trussed up like this, legs folded wide open, arms yanked over my head. He drags his fingers through my dripping centre, then pushes into me.

Slowly, he starts to fuck me with his fingers, his gaze dragging up and down my body.

"You're beautiful," he murmurs.

"Are you talking to my pussy, or—?"

He moves, lightning fast, and catches my chin in his hand. His fingers smell like me, and his gaze is glittering. "It's always you. If it's your pussy, it's you, too. But right now, I mean all of you. Every soft inch on display for me. *You.* You are beautiful."

I nod.

He kisses the tip of my nose. "I like it when we're in agreement. And you know what else I like?"

All of my guesses would be sarcastic and probably unnecessarily self-deprecating, so I hold my tongue and say nothing.

"I like you—no, I *love* you bound like this for me." His fingers reach up to my wrists, then race, featherlight, down my arm and my side to wear my leg is folded up. "Because as much as I love being your safe person to fight against— shh, don't argue, we both know it's true, luscious—I want even more to be the person who makes you fully let go."

I gasp.

He holds my gaze, waiting for my protest.

I shake my head. It's not coming. I'm too overwhelmed with raw feelings to fight. All I have left is exactly what he's asked for—letting go. Being free.

"I've got you," he murmurs as he walks his fingers back to my core and spears into me again. "And you...oh, my beautiful, sexy girl, you have me, too. Inside and out, you are everything I've ever wanted. Nobody has ever given me as much as you. As much sass, as much fierce devotion. Nobody ever made me care enough to take a god damn test and figure out the key to my happiness was mail order rope. You did that."

I let out a watery laugh, which he captures with his mouth, and we kiss in an endless kind way. Kissing kissing kissing...and then just breathing, our mouths hovering right next to each other, panting as he works me closer and closer to another release.

"This is uniquely ours, Ki, and it's the most precious thing in the world to me. You are the most precious person in my whole world. I love you."

I break, climaxing on his hand, and this time it's tears. Good, happy tears.

He kisses me through the end of the shivering, teary climax. Then he unties me and rubs his hands over the rope marks, making sure I'm okay before he presses me into the mattress and thrusts his cock into my pussy.

"Fuck, I can still feel you squeezing me." He groans as he starts to move, riding the aftershocks.

I wrap my limbs around him, pulling him onto me. Into me.

It's hard and fast. He doesn't try to make me come again, he just loses himself in my pussy.

It's raw, rough desire in physical form. My heart is pounding so hard I'm sure he has to feel it as he presses down on me, and I imagine I can hear his heartbeat, too.

He grunts, going still, then jerking hard. Low, groaning noises spill from him as he slams his hips home.

My love, bare inside me. Being fluid bonded like this, with Ty, is wonderful. Not stressful like it was when other partners brought it up. It just feels right, and intimate.

He collapses on top of me, just for a second, then rolls off, and pulls me over so my thigh is curved over his.

I trace my fingers over his brow. "Hi."

"Hi." He palms the back of my head. "Some of your hair is falling out."

"I don't care."

"Good." He closes his eyes and smiles.

"How long can you stay?"

"I need to meet the team for dinner tomorrow night in St. Louis."

"Okay." I kiss his bare chest. It's slick with sweat now. "Shower?"

"Yes, please."

I roll away and swing my hips as I head into the bathroom. After turning on the shower, I quickly pee, then open the door and wave for him to join me.

In the shower, he carefully washes my body, paying extra attention to the rope marks on my wrist and legs.

After, he wraps me in an oversized towel and we fall into bed. He traces lazy circles on my back as I close my eyes and wriggle into my pillow.

When he asks the question, I think I'm asleep. I think I must be dreaming.

"Do you want to get married?"

I'm so warm and relaxed. It's such a nice idea, marrying Ty. I smile.

"Is that a yes?"

My eyes fly open.

He's looking at me, his head on the pillow next to me.

"I'm awake," I say, my voice thick with sleep.

"We can talk about it tomorrow."

"No, now is good." My pulse is skipping now, racing to catch up. "Why did you ask it like that?"

"Because if you don't want to get married, then I'll ask a different kind of question when I give you the ring I bought." His mouth quirks, his eyes steady but not un-nervous.

"Do you want to get married?" I turn the question around on him.

We haven't talked about it.

We've talked about a lot.

Where we want to live, both while he plays hockey, and after. I know he might get traded again, and I'm happy to follow him wherever he wants to go. He wants to live here in Miami during the winters after he retires. I want to keep a home in Hamilton, but like the idea of coming and going.

We've talked about kids. I like them in theory, but don't want to raise them myself, at least not now. He's never thought about being a parent, either.

We've talked about pets. Taking care of Puck when Grant needs help is our happy place right now, but in the future, we might want dogs of our own. But like with kids, maybe we'll always just be happy being aunt and uncle to every furry creature in our orbit.

We have talked about a lot, but it all circles back to, we're filled with wanderlust and the standard relationship milestones that others care about really don't matter to us.

So why bother talking about marriage? Marriage doesn't have any bearing on travel or sex or love, not for us.

But now he's looking at me with the softest, most tentative look on his face.

"Did I give you the impression that I don't want to get married?"

He smiles softly. "Not exactly."

I wait.

His smile grows. "You want me to answer first."

"Yep."

Now he's grinning. "Yeah, Kiley. I want to get married. To you."

"Oh." I exhale. "I also want to get married. To you."

"That's excellent, excellent news." He hops out of bed, naked as anything, and grabs a ring box from his discarded pants.

He doesn't open it right away.

He crawls back into bed, the black velvet rolling around in his loose grasp, and he takes my hand.

"I've been thinking about this conversation ever since you turned the corner at Kieran's cabin and I saw you in that pink dress for the first time. Your hair was…" He touches my face. "So smooth. You were all done up, and it was surprising, because you're usually so earthy and sexy, and that was different. You were stunning, of course. Gorgeous. But it was also not what I expected, you know?"

I nod.

"And as I listened to them exchange vows, I had a really clear thought of, *this isn't what our wedding will be like.* Not *would* be like, but *will.* It felt wild to think about that when our relationship was so new, but it felt right to me. You have always felt right to me."

He takes my hand in his, the velvet box between our fingers now.

"Lately, I've been wanting to talk to you about that. Out of the blue, I want to ask you things like, *hey remember the wedding? Wasn't that great but also not at all how our wedding will be?* And I've had to stifle that because we haven't agreed to have a wedding yet. That feels like a conversation we should have before I start saying *will* out loud."

I'm nodding now. Yes. So much yes.

"So this is me saying, I want to ask you an important question, because it will lead to other questions that I already have in my head. This is me saying, I want to marry you, because I want to be married to you, and I want to celebrate being married to you with our friends and family, and I have some ideas of what that can look like, but before I get carried away with that, I need to know… do you want to marry me, too? Will you marry me, Kiley?"

"I will," I say, quickly, before he can launch into another circular, lovely twist of words that says the same thing.

Ty Connor has been fantasizing about our wedding. His wedding, *to me.*

"I will marry you," I repeat when he just grins at me. "And I really, really want to know what you want our wedding to look like."

He's crushing his mouth to mine now, so he can't answer. He's kissing me, and it's sweet and hot and perfect.

When we break apart, he's got the ring box open.

It's a gorgeous double band that splits open, surrounding a blinding diamond in the middle.

"To start," he whispers, sliding it onto my ring finger. "I want everyone to circle around us when we exchange vows. Just like these little diamonds wrap around this centre stone, I want everyone to surround us as I promise myself to you."

It's already the perfect wedding.

I nod, overcome.

We kiss again, and then we burrow under the blanket, giggling as he tells me about his wedding vision, which isn't really more than that circle. The details will be up to us to decide on, in time. For now, it's enough that we're going to do it.

And it feels special that he asked me here in Miami. "We'll have to go out for a nice brunch tomorrow to celebrate. One of your favourite places, maybe?"

"This is my favourite place. Wherever you are."

"Yeah, but—"

He stops me. "Yes. We'll celebrate in the morning. But we're celebrating right now. I want to go to sleep with you in my arms, because that is a celebration. And I want to wake up to your smile, because *that* is the best fucking life I could ever imagine, wherever we happen to be." He kisses me in a slow, drugging way that makes my heart race. "Waking up with you is better than a lifetime of South Florida mornings."

"But waking up with me here?"

He gives me the slowest, sexiest, most perfect smile ever. "The best of all worlds."

———

Do you want more of Ty and Kiley? (Ainsley says: "Me too, endlessly." Visit this website to get a joyous "them in the future" epilogue and other multimedia content related to this book:

https://ainsleybooth.com/more-ty-and-kiley/

And if you want to be on Ainsley's VIP reader list to get a heads up when new spicy hockey romance releases, sign up here:

http://ainsleybooth.com/newsletter/

www.ingramcontent.com/pod-product-compliance
Lightning Source LLC
Chambersburg PA
CBHW011510010826
48973CB00015B/2910